g

DMB
very Good

Y0-DKO-802

BAYOU LADY

NANCY BACON

PINNACLE BOOKS   LOS ANGELES

This is a work of fiction. All the characters and events portrayed in this book are fictional, and any resemblance to real people or incidents is purely coincidental.

BAYOU LADY

An original Pinnacle Books edition, published for the first time anywhere.

First printing, September 1980.

ISBN: 0-523-40614-2

Cover illustration by John Solie

Printed in the United States of America

PINNACLE BOOKS, INC.
2029 Century Park East
Los Angeles, California 90067

TEMPTATION . . .

Bret felt the heat rise in his groin and a pulse set up a steady pounding, flooding him with desire. He knew he should pull away. Mandy was clearly intoxicated, and he certainly wasn't the type of heel to take advantage of the situation. But she kissed him with such passion, such obvious desire that he could not stop himself. Not just yet. He had waited too long to have her like this, soft and pliant in his arms, the sassy sneer wiped off her lovely face, replaced with raw, pure lust. It shone from her eyes like a beacon and he followed it, like a drowning man giving himself up to the lure of the sea.

I must stop this, Bret thought, even as his hands caressed her bare breasts, unable to release them. He kissed her throat, the tops of her breasts, then took the nipple in his mouth again, powerless to resist. He heard her soft whispers and felt her hands in his hair, urging him closer. With a groan, he drew away and rolled as far as he could to his side of the wide chaise. *Like a bed,* he thought cursing himself for thinking it.

Mandy's long hair had come undone. Her pale silk gown was crumpled down around her waist and tumbled up about her thighs, and he couldn't stop himself from staring at her legs, silvery white in the moonlight. She had lost one high-heeled slipper, and the Bradshaw diamonds and rubies rode high around her neck like a fabulous noose, holding her captive for his caresses. She looked like a wanton gypsy wench, her full lips crushed and red from his wild kisses, her eyes stormy as a turquoise sea, her arms reaching for him. . . .

For my daughter, Stacey,
with love

New Orleans 1875

CHAPTER ONE

The January afternoon was brisk and cold as Mandy
Bradshaw hurried down the sidewalk. Dark rain clouds
had been gathering all afternoon and she gave them a
worried glance, hoping she would reach home before
the downpour that was sure to come. It was not yet five
o'clock but already the street lamps were blazing, each
one haloed in a dull yellow glow, and Rampart Street
was alive with foot and horse traffic. Open carriages
careened down the cobbled street and Mandy stared
contemptuously at the tipsy prostitutes who laughed
boisterously from within. Men in elegant evening
clothes, their diamond stickpins visible even from the
sidewalk, drank from ornate flasks and openly pawed
the women, who shrieked with delight. Mandy turned
away in disgust. *Would things never be the same again?*
she thought miserably.

Even though the hated Civil War had been over for
years, New Orleans was still fighting its own battle, and
apparently losing, for it was obvious even to the
seventeen-year-old Mandy that her beloved city was almost in a state of siege. The Republican Party had become a mass of factions, and even more federal troops
(the city was already crawling with victorious Yankees)
had been moved into New Orleans to help keep the
peace. It did little good. It was more dangerous than
ever to be out on the streets alone after dark. Mandy
remembered *Tante* Caleen's countless warnings as she
turned down a side street that led to Grandmother Bertonneau's townhouse. She would be scolded, she knew,

3

for staying so long at the Arceneaux home, but she had been enjoying herself so much she had forgotten the time. Her best friend, Suzette Arceneaux, was engaged to be married and had invited Mandy over to see her trousseau. And for that one afternoon the girls had managed to forget the ugly aftermath of war that was corrupting their home town. It had been almost like old times as they had sipped hot cocoa, giggling together and speculating about Suzette's wedding night.

Mandy stepped over a pile of garbage that had been tossed from a café's upstairs window, wrinkling her nose at the pungent odor and lifting her skirts high to avoid the mess. Grandmother Bertonneau's house was just ahead, set back from the street and sheltered by four huge oaks, their gnarled branches forming a protective umbrella over the peaked roof. Smoke curled from the chimney and there was a welcoming lantern burning on the gate post. She quickened her pace and was just reaching for the gate latch when she heard a coarse chuckle behind her and something hard was pressed into her back.

"What's yer hurry, honey?" a voice said and Mandy spun around to stare into the heavily bearded face of a Yankee trooper, his thin lips pulled back to expose chipped, tobacco-stained teeth. He was prodding her in the back with the tip of his cane and she saw a dirty, bloodied bandage wrapped carelessly about his left knee. Wildly she looked toward the house and then back at the trooper who had staggered forward to clutch at her arm.

"Hey, Jim-boy, come 'mere and get a load of this sweet lil' Southern belle!" he called over his shoulder and Mandy's heart thudded with fear as another trooper stepped out of the shadows and walked toward them. He was equally unkempt and he held a whiskey bottle to his lips as he squinted at her.

"Please remove your hand, sir. My family is waiting for me," Mandy said quietly, keeping her eyes cast down and forcing herself to breathe slowly and calmly.

4

She had learned, as had other Creole families in New Orleans, to show no emotion whatsoever when accosted by Yankee troopers or the dreaded White Leaguers—and most certainly not to show the contempt she felt. In these turbulent times it was unwise to offend anyone, black *or* white.

"Aw, come on, honey, where's that good ole Southern hospitality we've heard so much about?" The trooper who held her arm stepped closer still and she gasped at the odor of his sour breath and unwashed body. "How about havin' a little drink with me 'n my buddy here?" He took the bottle from his friend and took a long pull, wiping his filthy hand across his mouth and burping loudly. "We been lookin' fer some sweet young thing to show off at André's—ain't that right, Jim-boy?"

"That's right, Warren," the one called Jim drawled as he moved to stand between Mandy and the gate. His eyes raked her body, lingering on the swell of her breast, and he reached out and flicked her cape open. Her young breasts were all but tumbling out of the low-cut, too-tight gown and she silently cursed the war and the poverty it had brought, which meant that she was obliged to wear her old gowns even though she had outgrown them.

She pulled her cape from the trooper's hand and closed it there as she groped behind her for the gate latch. "Please let me pass," she said with more authority than she felt.

"My, my, yer're kinda uppity fer a whore's spawn, ain't 'cha, girlie?" the one with the bandaged knee said. "She-et, sweetie, you don't have to put on airs fer me 'n ole Jim-boy. We know all about you gals what live on Rampart Street."

Mandy's temper flared and she wanted to strike out at the ugly, leering face but she fought for control and kept her eyes lowered. *Don't anger them, Tante* Caleen had warned her. *No matter what, don't anger them.*

"Yeah, tha's right, we was told you little Creole gals

5

are taught right from the cradle how to please a man," the other trooper said. He took a long pull from the whiskey bottle and thrust it at her. "Here, take a slug of this and loosen up a little bit. We ain't gonna eat 'cha."

"Well now, I don't know about that, Jim-boy. She shore looks good enough to eat," Warren chuckled suggestively and both men broke into lewd laughter, passing the bottle between them as they watched her. Mandy jerked free and grabbed the gate latch, practically falling into the yard as she tripped on her long skirts.

"Hey, now, girlie, not so fast." A heavy hand fell upon her shoulder, whirling her around and almost lifting her off the ground. The gate crashed into her knees as the trooper kicked it open and stepped quickly into the yard. She stumbled back and he caught her in both arms, drawing her close to his soiled blue coat. "Now you ain't bein' too friendly, little gal. We don't mean you no harm. We jes' want you to stop by André's with us fer a little drink—"

"Oh, please, I beg of you—let me go!" Mandy cried. She pushed hard against his chest, trying to free herself from his suffocating hold. "My family will be worried—" She blinked away the tears that threatened, straightened her shoulders, and tried to still the wild pounding of her heart. She forced a tiny smile, hoping they were decent men at heart (*damn Yankees!* her mind screamed), and said shyly, "There are many young ladies over on Bourbon Street who I am sure would be delighted to sup with you—"

"She-et, we done had all them whores on Bourbon Street," Warren grunted. He spat a stream of slimy tobacco juice into the rose bush. "We're lookin' fer something' a little—fresher."

"Aw, fer Chrsit's sake, Warren, quit yer yappin' and jest grab 'er and take 'er along," the other trooper growled impatiently. "Our bottle's empty and I got me a terrible thirst. Hungry, too. We can get us a room over at André's and share 'er. She'll loosen up after we

6

get some whiskey in 'er. Never knew me a bitch that didn't like it once ya git started. An' these little ole Creole gals are supposed to be the hottest things in the South." He scratched his belly and adjusted his pistol in its holster, giving Mandy a hard look. "Now you jest come along right nice like, honey, and me 'n Warren'll show you a damn good time. Might even buy ya a pretty—if ya service us real good."

"No!" Mandy jerked her arm free of the trooper's hold, swinging her reticule with all the strenth she could muster. It hit him in the face and he staggered against the gate, cursing. "*Tante* Caleen! Elmo!" she screamed at the top of her lungs. "Help! Oh, please, somebody help me!" She ran toward the house but the trooper's large hand shot out and clamped around her wrist, jerking her off balance. She fell heavily against him and the other trooper jerked the reticule from her and tossed it away. Grabbing a fistful of her cape he ripped it off and flung her against the gate.

"Now you ain't bein' nice at all, little gal," the one with the bandaged knee gritted at her. He had a small cut on his cheek where she had hit him and he rubbed it, glowering at her. "Guess ya be needin' a lesson in manners, girlie." He spat a glob of tobacco juice at her feet, splattering the hem of her gown. "Hold 'er, Jim-boy, and let's see what we got here."

"Oh, please—please!" Mandy cried and struggled against the trooper's hands as they pinned her arms behind her back.

"Hear that, Warren? She's beggin' fer it already." He tangled his hand in her long hair and she sobbed with pain as he jerked her head back cruelly.

She squeezed her eyes shut tight when she felt the calloused hand at her bodice and then the entire front of her gown was ripped open to the waist. She heard their quick intake of breath as they stared at her nakedness.

"Sweet Jesus, Jim-boy, will ya lookit that. Ain't them jest about the prettiest little titties ya ever did see?" He

7

cupped one breast in his hand, pinching the nipple. "She-et, I don't think I've ever seen me a prettier pair."

"Jest as sweet and pink as a fresh cherry off'n a tree," the other trooper said in a hushed voice. He ran his fingers over her silken skin, squeezing her nipples, and she sobbed aloud.

"*Tante* Caleen!" she screamed, then a hand was clamped over her mouth, cutting off further words. She sank her teeth into the smelly flesh and heard him yelp in surprise.

"Why, you little hellcat!" His hand smashed into her face, knocking her back into the other trooper's arms. She tasted blood and her head throbbed with the hard blow. A vivid picture of her mother flashed before her eyes, her lovely young mother, bruised and bloody, her broken body made obscene by the white-robed men who had killed her with their rough handling. White-hot rage filled her and her brain pounded with intense hatred. If she could just get her hands on one of their pistols she would blast them clear into Georgia. She jabbed her arm back as hard as she could, ramming her elbow into the soft belly of the one who held her, her fingers clawing for his pistol.

Kicking, biting, punching, she sobbed wildly and struck out at the hands that returned her blows. She felt her fists sink into flesh and hit bone, scraping her knuckles and sending a jarring pain shooting up her arms, but still she fought. A bony fist slammed into her face and she reeled back, stunned. When the hands came for her again she rushed in to meet them, her long nails raking viciously, her tiny fists doing as much damage as they could. A loud explosion sounded and she flung herself to the ground, fully expecting to see a bullet hole torn in her breast. She heard them cursing and then the sound of another gunshot thudding into the soft earth near where she lay. "*Maman,*" she whimpered. "Papa—help me!" Her head spun and throbbed and she couldn't focus her eyes. She was vaguely aware

8

of other voices, other hands on her, lifting her. It was so dark.

"No!" she screamed, then whimpered pathetically, "No, no—Papa's dead!"

"Hush, *bébé*, hush, *ché—tante* Caleen here." Mandy moaned and flung away the hands that tried to comfort her.

"Papa!" she cried. "I want Papa—please—" She struggled weakly as strong arms lifted her and pressed her face gently against something warm and familiar smelling.

"Carry her inside, Elmo, they is gone. Won't be back no mo' this night." Caleen tenderly covered Mandy's naked breasts with the torn cape, wincing when she saw the cuts and bruises on the girl's face. One eye was already swelling shut and there was blood on her lips where the trooper's fist had split them open.

"*Tante* Caleen!" Mandy cried suddenly. She tried to raise her head but the terrible throbbing sent waves of nausea through her body and she moaned and sank into the safety of darkness.

It was warm and quiet when Mandy next opened her eyes. She snuggled into the deep feather mattress of her bed and glanced toward the light. A huge fire blazed in the fireplace across from her bed and *Tante* Caleen sat next to it in Mandy's rocker. Mandy started to raise herself and call a greeting when a wave of pain coursed through her head, knocking her back to the pillows. She cried out and Caleen was by her side in an instant.

"I be here, *bébé*," the old woman said softly. She stroked the tangled sable hair back from Mandy's damp forehead, her touch as light as a summer breeze. "Hush, now, *ché*, hush."

"*Tante* Caleen, I—" Mandy tried again to raise her head but fell back with a little whimper of pain. "Oh, my head," she murmured. "What happened to my head, *Tante* Caleen?"

9

"Hush, chile, you be fine now. *Tante* Caleen, she fix you up good, yes." She went to the fireplace and poured a cup of tea from the pot keeping warm on the hearth. The clean aroma of peppermint and chamomile mingled together as she carried the steaming brew to Mandy. She lifted the girl's head, gently drawing the pillows behind her back and helping her to sit up.

"Oh, *Tante* Caleen, my head hurts so bad. What happened? I can't remember, except—except that I was at Suzette's and—and—"

"Hush, *bébé*. No need to think on it now. Plenty o' time tomorrow." Caleen held the cup to Mandy's lips, one hand behind her head to steady her. "Drink, now, yes." She tipped the cup, nodding with satisfaction when Mandy swallowed a little of the tea. Rage, black and strong, filled Caleen's body as she saw the puffy split lips, the swollen bruised face and closed eye. She would wait until the child was asleep again, then she would go to her room and mix the strongest *voudou magnian* she could prepare. She would fix those filthy white bastards. Give them some powerful *guignon* for their attack on her baby Mandy.

"I remember now," Mandy whispered. "Those Yankee troopers, they—they—" She tried to focus her good eye on Caleen but the effort caused a fresh wave of pain to wrack her head. Her breast ached with each breath she took and she remembered with horror the Yankee's filthy hands on her, squeezing. "Oh, *Tante* Caleen," she sobbed. "Those troopers, they tried—"

"Hush, *bébé*, do you no good thinkin' on it. You sleep now, yes." The skinny black woman fussed about the huge four-poster bed like a nervous monkey, smoothing the blankets, fluffing the pillows, all the while mumbling to herself in French. She gently placed Mandy's head on the pillows and pulled the quilt up under her chin. "*Tante* Caleen stay with you, *ché*, yes."

"Grandmother?" Mandy mumbled sleepily.

"She be fine, Miz Belle, yes. She sleepin' now." Caleen dropped a light kiss on Mandy's forehead. "Sleep, chile, sleep now, *bébé*. *Tante* Caleen be here, yes." She began humming an old Creole lullaby and Mandy smiled drowsily, watching the wizened little woman hobble to the fireplace, lift a log almost as big as she was, and toss it onto the fire as if it weighed nothing at all. Rain began to fall, playing a hollow tattoo upon the shingles of the roof, and Mandy snuggled deeper into the soft down of her mattress, falling almost instantly asleep.

Belle Bertonneau was not asleep. She sat propped up in bed, sipping sherry and staring at the blank piece of writing paper that lay on her lap tray. Caleen had stuffed the fireplace with extra logs to combat the chill of the rain and now the large bedroom was almost as bright as day. Belle took another, longer sip of sherry before picking up her pen and dipping it into the ink-well. In a small, dainty hand she wrote, "My dear Mr. Bradshaw," then stuck the pen into her mouth and chewed on it thoughtfully. Good gracious, what was she going to say to the man? She took another sip of sherry and leaned back with a sigh. Just the name Bradshaw brought back a flood of memories and she pressed her fingertips to her eyelids to stop the sudden wetness there. "One would think there would be no more tears left to shed," she murmured aloud. She gazed into the flames of the crackling fire for a moment, then raised her eyes and smiled softly at the handsome couple in the painting above the mantle. Johnny Bradshaw Jr., tall and fair, Désirée Bertonneau Bradshaw, petite and dark, holding a chubby child on her silken knee. Amanda Belle, they had named her, for both her grandmothers. The artist had dated it 1860.

If Belle had to pick a year when her world began falling apart, she supposed 1860 would be as good as any. It was early in that year that the South had seceded from the Union and not much longer before the Civil War was on. The Creoles had found themselves in the awkward position of being right in the

11

middle. If the South won, they would maintain their position of a separate class, set apart from both whites and blacks. For as long as Belle could remember, the Creoles had held an exalted and respected position in New Orleans. The *true* Creoles were the descendants of the first French and Spanish settlers with perhaps a little West Indian blood thrown in. They were the aristocrats and refused to mix with the new breed of Creoles which definitely showed a strain of African blood. These people were called *gens de couleur* and were no better than common slaves to families like the Bertonneaux.

On the other hand, if the North won the war and freed the slaves, the Creoles were in danger of losing their status, of being treated like all free people of color. And to the ignorant Yankees, anyone with dark skin looked like a "nigger."

Belle had been thankful that her only daughter had been far away from the bloodbath of the war years. She had not wanted Désirée to journey west with her new young husband, but she knew she could not have stood in her way. Just seeing the two of them together was proof enough that they belonged together. The courtship had been a whirlwind, the wedding almost indecently swift; then they had gone west, their bright young faces eager for whatever adventure lay ahead. That had been in 1858 and when the painting had arrived, Belle's heart had ached to hold her first grandchild.

In 1862, New Orleans fell to the Union troops and everything Belle Bertonneau had held dear began slowly slipping away. The city itself changed drastically as thousands of Americans flocked to Louisiana looking for a way to take advantage of the war-torn South. Carpetbaggers, Germans, Irishmen, freed Negros by the hundreds, adventurers of every sort, brawling boatsmen, ignorant backwoodsmen, they all swarmed into the South. And the genteel French culture was in danger of becoming extinct.

Belle remembered reading somewhere that when the United States took charge of Louisiana it had been like

12

occupying a foreign country, as the state was almost entirely made up of French-speaking Catholics who deeply resented any sort of change or Americanization. These peaceful and artistic people strongly resented the new Protestant leaders and they viewed with shocked distaste the thousands of "foreigners" who ran roughshod over their beloved city. Crude, foreign-sounding American words were making their way into French speech, music, and literature and, once again, Belle was thankful that Désirée was not in New Orleans to see it. The sleepy little city had become a boom town overnight and its citizens found themselves at the mercy of the military authorities. Yankee troops had complete power over the civilian population, even the power of life and death, and they were quick to use it. If a white man refused to step into the street to allow a black man to pass on the sidewalk, the black could have him arrested for being "uppity"—and quite often did.

While all this furor was going on in New Orleans, Belle Bertonneau and her husband, Armand, lived quietly at their country plantation. They had freed their three hundred slaves but most of them had refused to go, preferring to remain and work for Armand Bertonneau as they always had. At least they were assured of three meals a day and a place to sleep, was the way her husband's houseman, Elmo, had put it, while other freed slaves were discovering how difficult it was to be free men. But soon the long-reaching tentacles of greed, hate, and prejudice moved outside the city to touch neighboring plantation owners. There was looting and burning. Families were driven off their land, thrown bodily out of the homes their ancestors had built over a hundred years before. When they came to the Bertonneau plantation, Armand and a handful of faithful field hands made a stand, managing to take at least a dozen or more of the white-robed men with them before it was all over.

Belle, bereft with grief, stood in stunned silence at the edge of the shallow grave, hastily dug by Elmo, and bid her Armand a final *adieu*. For want of a coffin, he had simply been wrapped in a quilt from his bed and placed into the dark cavity in the rich earth he had loved so much. Then Caleen had taken complete control, ordering Elmo about as they prepared to move into the townhouse on Rampart Street, and Belle had let her do it all, too heartsick to leave her bed.

She had remained in that dazed, numb state for the next two months until Caleen again took matters into her own efficient hands and had summoned Johnny and Désirée from California.

The child, Amanda, had been the perfect tonic and Belle had doted on her from the first moment she had taken her into her arms. Little Amanda Belle Bradshaw already showed the great beauty she would one day be. She had her parents' best features: her father's deep blue eyes and the thick black lashes of her mother, a creamy, tawny complexion, thick, dark, waist-length hair shot through with russet and gold. She already spoke both French and English. Belle filled her days playing with her granddaughter while Johnny tried to discover why and how the Bertonneau plantation had been seized. Even though Johnny Bradshaw could never be accused of being anything but a white American, he was fighting for the cause of *gens de couleur* and this made him most unpopular in the new New Orleans. "Nigger lover" had been scrawled across the front of their house so many times, Elmo now kept several extra cans of whitewash on hand to paint over the ugly graffiti.

Just when the citizens of New Orleans thought that things couldn't possibly get any worse, the White Leaguers, the Knights of the White Camellia, and other secret groups began to form. Armed with guns and torches, they marched through the city and new terror reigned in the streets. Not many years before, just one drop of white blood was enough to guarantee special privileges, but now just one drop of black blood was enough to guarantee no privileges at all. And when five thousand Knights of the White Camellia staged a rebellion in 1874, the streets were littered with the bodies of hundreds of Louisianans. Violence reached an all-time high as hundreds of blacks and Creoles were massacred in their homes. Many others fled to distant places like the Bahamas or out West to escape injury and death and even some dark-skinned whites were having a difficult time proving their blood lines.

Belle poured herself another glass of sherry and drank deep, hoping to quell the tightness that gripped her heart whenever she thought about that long-ago day when she had lost both her beloved daughter and her son-in-law. She and Désirée had gone shopping and had stopped at a small café for a bite of lunch. They had just finished a cup of steaming gumbo and were being served a light, delicate *la médiatrice*, when the door was suddenly flung open and five White Leaguers strode inside. One went to the front of the café and read names from a list he held, names of non-whites, which now included Creoles, forcing them to stand when their name was called. Belle's heart had thudded with dread and she had reached across the table to clutch Désirée's hand.

"Belle Monnette Bertonneau and Désirée Bertonneau Bradshaw," the voice rasped and Belle looked wildly about the room at her friends and neighbors, men and women she had known all her life, standing with bowed heads; the ones still sitting had kept their eyes averted in shame. The raspy voice droned on, reading the rest of the names, and then they were forced to leave, after a stern warning to never again darken the door of a white establishment.

Belle had allowed herself to be led outside and helped into her carriage. *Non*-whites. *Gens de couleur*. *Niggers*. The obscene words pounded in her brain. She wondered why Désirée was covering her with a lap robe on such a warm and sunny day until she realized that she was shivering violently and her knuckles had turned white where she grasped her reticule. In her

15

shock and humiliation, her mind refused to recognize what had happened, and she was only vaguely aware of Désirée kissing her and whispering, "Don't worry, *Maman.* I'm going to get Johnny. Everything will be all right, I promise. Go home and stay with Mandy until we get there." Then Elmo had clicked to the matched bays and that was the last time she had seen her daughter alive.

Belle had paced the parlor as the long afternoon dragged by, glancing at the clock on the mantel every few minutes, her heart lurching in her breast each time a carriage rattled by in front of the house. She forced herself to sit at the table with Amanda, swallowing food she didn't taste, avoiding as best she could the girl's questions. But as night fell and Caleen went silently about lighting the lamps, Belle could no longer deny her worst fears.

When the loud shouting came from outside, Belle was expecting it; had, in fact, prepared herself for it. Through the sheer curtains she saw a dozen or so white-robed men gathered on the front lawn, their torches casting tall shadows that danced eerily up the walls and spilled into the parlor. They had flung several bricks through the windows, but one would have done just as well. The one with the message wrapped around it and held in place with Désirée's dainty lace garter. The one that stated in bold, black ink: *This is a warning to all niggers and all nigger lovers. Get out of New Orleans!*

They had gone by the time Elmo had grabbed Johnny's rifle and Caleen had flung open the door. Belle stared down at the broken remains of her lovely Désirée, naked save for a torn and bloody chemise. Her body was covered with cuts and bruises, her swollen thighs smeared with blood and the spent waste of her rapists. Johnny had fared better. There was a black hole between his eyes. His hands were tied behind his back and his blue eyes were wide open. Caleen knelt

16

and closed them, crossing herself, before motioning to Elmo to carry them inside.

"*Tante* Caleen, what is it? I heard noises." Amanda walked sleepily into the parlor, rubbing her eyes and looking curiously at the group at the door.

"No!" The word was torn from Belle's paralyzed throat as she whirled away from the grisly scene on the front step and hurried to her granddaughter. "No, *chérie*, don't look!" She tried to take the girl into her arms but Mandy jerked free and ran toward the door, her face turning whiter with each step. Caleen reached out to pull her away but the girl shook her off. Elmo stood holding Désirée, her white nakedness contrasting sharply with his big black arms, her face oddly serene compared to the tortured anguish in his own.

"*Maman!*" Mandy had screamed and rushed forward, only to halt a foot away and stare with horror at her mother's battered and abused body. "Papa?" the girl whispered and followed Elmo's gaze to where her father still lay on the porch. "Oh, God, no," she whimpered, and sank to the floor in a faint.

Now the same horrible fate had very nearly befallen Amanda. Belle took a sip of her sherry and looked down at the writing paper on her lap tray. Even though she had never met the senior Bradshaw, Belle had heard a great deal about him from Johnny and thought him to be a fair, decent man. Surely he would do all in his power to help his granddaughter escape the decadence in New Orleans. She would need a wardrobe for travelling, hats and boots, proper luggage—Belle giggled suddenly. If her Armand were alive he would tease her about planning the girl's wardrobe before even writing the letter. He used to say that if the Mississippi River flooded, Belle would most assuredly have the proper outfit for a disaster.

With a soft smile curving her lips, Belle bent over the paper, explaining in full why it was imperative for

17

Amanda to leave the South and travel to California until the unrest was over. She requested a return telegram, stressing that time was of the essence, and signed her name with a flourish that was perhaps more sherry than confidence. She would set her seal to it in the morning and have Elmo post it before Amanda awoke.

She set aside her lap tray, turned off the lamp and settled into the warm blankets, listening to the rain against the windows. She didn't want to think about her little Amanda going away, but she knew it was the only way. She couldn't bear a repeat of tonight—so very like that other horrifying night. If she had to give up her granddaughter to save her life, then she would do it gladly.

CHAPTER TWO

It was three days before Caleen would let Mandy out of bed and then she only allowed her to stay downstairs for a few hours before firmly leading her back to her room. The girl's wounds had healed by the week's end and all that remained was her still-blackened eye. She glimpsed it now as she paced before one of her grandmother's many-gilt-framed mirrors. "But I don't want to go!" Mandy wailed for the third time since entering Belle's bedroom. She sank down upon a chaise longue of rich burgundy brocade and turned pleading eyes upon her grandmother. "Please don't send me right away. Let's wait a few weeks and see what happens. Things might get better—"

"Oh, *chérie*, don't make it any more difficult for me," Belle sighed. She was propped up in bed (one of her favorite places to be on these cold, dark winter days), her lap tray, holding a bottle of sherry and two glasses, balanced on her knees. "Come now, *bébé*, and drink a little sherry with your old *grand-mère*. You must know how sorely I shall miss you but I cannot— no, I *will not*—take the slightest chance that something like last week's incident will occur again." Her soft brown eyes were more serious than Mandy had ever seen them and she knew further argument would be futile, but she made one last attempt.

"But I'll be so—so terrified of meeting all of them again. I'll be out of place! I'll be in the way! They won't like me because I'm a Southerner and they're— they're—why, Grandmother, they're *Yankees*!" Mandy's large blue eyes turned deep violet with the realization. "You can't mean to send me to live with a bunch of dirty Yankees! Oh, Grandmother, please!"

"That will be quite enough, young lady," Belle snapped. "I will not have the Bradshaws spoken of in that manner. They are good, decent people and your own dear father's family. You will leave for San Francisco at the end of April as planned. Your grandfather has been kind enough to send you a bank draft for expenses as well as a generous allowance for a proper wardrobe. Now." Belle held out her glass in a toast, her face softening. "Let us drink to the adventure and think only of what exciting days lie ahead. You will have a marvelous trip across country by train and your grandfather has been thoughtful enough to send his own private car so you will not have to mingle with the other passengers unless you so desire. We will begin planning your wardrobe first thing tomorrow morning. Most of your gowns will be made by Madame LaFevre, of course. I will send Elmo to her salon requesting a consultation." She touched the rim of her glass to Mandy's and said gaily, "Come, come, *chérie*, it will be a grand adventure and when New Orleans is once again safe, you will return and enchant me with tales of the Wild West, *oui*?"

"Yes, Grandmother," Mandy sighed. She took a sip of sherry and leaned back on the chaise. Maybe it wouldn't be too bad, and, after all, it wasn't as if she were going away forever. Surely New Orleans would soon be restored to peace and sanity.

"Just think, *chérie*, you shall have such a sumptuous wardrobe! Everything from silk underwear to fur capes! No more cotton stockings or altered gowns for my *bébé*! Oh, how I envy you, Amanda!" Belle clapped her soft, white hands together and Mandy laughed in spite of herself. Her pampered little grandmother had lost none of her love for riches and fashion that once had proclaimed her undisputed belle of the Quadroon Balls of the old New Orleans. Mandy never

20

tired of listening to her grandmother's stories of those glamorous affairs.

The next few weeks were spent in a flurry of shopping and fittings. Madame LaFevre had been delighted to be called upon, and the house on Rampart Street was fairly bursting at the seams with bolts of fine silks and taffetas, lush velvets and furs, rich ostrich plumes and elegant jewels. Mandy's head spun with it all and she finally gave up protesting and let Madame LaFevre and Grandmother Bertonneau have their way with her. Hoops were out and skirts were now pulled back to fall in a soft drape over bustles, showing off much more of the figure than had the bell-like skirts of the '60s. Mandy stood for hours, while Madame LaFevre wrapped her in yards of fine fabrics and cascades of lace, whisking them about her body with the flamboyant deftness of a magician. There were petticoats of silk with dainty embroidery and tucks. Exquisite gowns in every fabric and shade for every season. Flat, smart little hats that tipped flirtatiously over one eye, trimmed with fluttering ribbons, bowing plumes, wreaths of flowers. Dainty chemises in pale silk, trimmed with satin bows. Light woolen cloaks lined in lush mink, beaver, or sable. Satin slippers with three-inch heels in colors that matched her numerous gowns. Silk stockings. And when the more than generous allowance from Grandfather Bradshaw had run out, Grandmother Bertonneau had gleefully pawned what was left of the silver, saying, "Really, *chérie*, we can't let them think that our temporary financial condition has made us negligent of our appearance!"

The cold bleakness of March gave way to a wet and wild April that exploded with bright bursts of sunshine just often enough to keep Mandy's spirits up. She had resigned herself to the trip to San Francisco but could not completely drive away the pangs of sadness at leaving everything familiar. Of course, *Tante* Caleen would be travelling with her. Belle wouldn't hear of Mandy making the trip alone even though she was to have her

21

own private car. On the night before Mandy would leave, she walked aimlessly about her bedroom, checking bureau drawers and trunks, stalling going downstairs for the evening meal that would be the last she would share with her grandmother and the adoring, loyal Elmo. She rather wished that he would be accompanying her to California as well. On one of the numerous shopping trips, Mandy had purchased a copy of Alfred Robinson's *Life in California* and her heart had thudded with fear as she read about that wild and still untamed land. She was more convinced than ever that half-naked savages lurked behind every cactus and uncouth, sex-starved miners leapt on every female they encountered. It would be comforting to have a man as large and formidable as Elmo to travel with but she supposed Grandfather Bradshaw had thought to provide some sort of protection for her. He had certainly thought to provide everything else.

It was odd, but she knew surprisingly little about her relatives on her father's side even though she had spent the first eight years of her life with them. She sank into the rocker by the fireplace and tried to recall those early years. It had been a happy time and her mother and father had kept her wrapped in a blanket of love so safe and snug that she remembered little else. She did recall racing across vast stretches of grassy fields, climbing trees with her cousins, and picnicking by the softly murmuring sea where her mother had constantly warned her not to venture too far into the surf. She also remembered her large and somewhat frightening grandfather with his piercing blue eyes and shock of red hair that had always seemed to be standing on end about something. Her grandmother had died before Mandy was born so she had never known her, although she had been told quite often that she resembled her a great deal. She knew there were aunts and uncles by the dozens and at least two cousins near her own age as well as many friends and neighbors who had dropped in so frequently the young Mandy wasn't sure if they were related or not. She couldn't remember much about the house itself except that it had been enormous, with towering ceilings that almost made her tip over backward when she had gazed up at the elaborately carved beams.

She remembered the garden most of all, as it had been the only place she had been allowed to play alone without adult supervision. There were several fountains where she had splashed for hours, giggling with delight when the cool water cascaded down her back. There were several curved brick paths twisting this way and that and clumps of flowers and bushes in which to play an excellent game of hide and seek. There had been a pony, too, Mandy remembered now, a short, chunky little mare given to her on her sixth birthday by her grandfather. How she had wept when her parents had gently informed her that they must return to Louisiana and she would not be able to take Gingerbread.

She smiled, remembering the name. Upon presenting the young filly to Mandy, Grandfather Bradshaw had told her that she must give it a name and train it herself so it would know no other master. Mandy had stared thoughtfully at the fat, dappled-tan pony with its fluffy mound of flaxen mane and forelock and had been reminded of a chunk of gingerbread with a dollop of whipped cream on top. "She looks just like a big piece of Tokie's gingerbread," the child had declared, and everyone had laughed and agreed.

"Tokie," Mandy whispered. She had forgotten all about the tall, majestic Indian woman, Atoka, who had run the Bradshaw household as effortlessly as if it had been a one-room wigwam. There had always been something good-smelling baking in the big woodburning stove in Tokie's kitchen and Mandy had spent many pleasurable hours there, munching some hot delicacy while Atoka regaled her with Indian tales.

"Amanda! What on earth is keeping you, *chérie*?

23

Caleen has supper on the table!" Mandy jumped slightly at the sound of her grandmother's voice and got hastily to her feet, smoothing her gown as she hurried toward the stairs. Perhaps this "Wild West adventure" wouldn't be *too* awful. The memories were pleasant enough.

Feeling quite the lady of fashion in her burnt orange travelling suit and brown woolen cape with its beaver collar and hem, Mandy followed her grandmother up the narrow steps and into the private car that would be her home for the next several days. They had been met at the depot by a Mr. Stokes, who had informed them that he had been sent by her grandfather to insure that Mandy's trip west was as comfortable as possible.

"Of course, I'll be travelling in another car," Mr. Stokes said as he opened the door and held it for them to enter ahead of him. "But this here bell is connected to my berth." He indicated a velvet cord on the wall near the door. "If Miss Bradshaw needs anything she just has to give this a pull." He demonstrated for them.

"Why, how thoughtful of dear Monsieur Bradshaw," Belle murmured; then her eyes widened in surprise as she surveyed the elegance before her. The car was huge and luxurious beyond belief. Dark panelled walls were hung with rich tapestries and ornately framed paintings. There were wine-colored velvet drapes at the windows, a tufted sofa in the same shade, brocade chairs and an Oriental rug. A teakwood desk stood against one wall and a dining table large enough to accommodate a small party was near the windows at the rear. A glass-fronted armoire held an unbelievable display of exotic liqueurs and next to it was a porcelain sink and serving counter. A door opened off the other end of the car and Mr. Stokes informed them that it led to a private bath and bedroom.

"*Ma foi!*" Belle exclaimed and one tiny hand fluttered to her breast. "I have never seen anything to com-

24

pare with this!" Her gaze lingered on the cut-crystal glasses and gold-edged cups and saucers in the armoire. "Does Monsieur Bradshaw do everything in such flamboyant style, Monsieur Stokes?"

"He sure does, Ma'am," Mr. Stokes laughed. "Why, this is downright tacky compared to J.B.'s own *personal* car." His voice had a rather pleasant twang to it and Mandy found herself liking the sound.

"You mean this is not his own car? But I thought—" Belle broke off in confusion and glanced again around the lushly decorated car.

"No, Ma'am," Mr. Stokes said. "This is just the car he sends for business associates or members of the family." He chuckled at some private thought and his faded blue eyes twinkled with mischief. "J.B.'s car—now that's something to see!" He rocked back on his heels and Mandy glanced at his expensive calfskin shoes, thinking he would probably be more comfortable in a pair of scuffed cowboy boots. He seemed a little too large and rawboned for the exquisitely tailored suit he wore and the deep tan of his skin was that of an outdoorsman.

"*Mon Dieu*," Belle murmured as she walked about the large room, her gloved fingers touching this object and that, her eyes wide with awe. She had been used to wealth and luxury all her life, but she had never seen anything compared to the obvious wealth of Monsieur John Bradshaw of San Francisco.

Mandy looked through the window and saw that the platform was rapidly becoming empty as people hurried to board the train. Two short, shrill blasts sounded and she jumped, clutching Caleen's arm.

"That'll be ole Bill letting us know it's time to be going," Mr. Stokes said. He gave Belle an apologetic smile. "Well, I'll just mosey on down to my car while you folks say your goodbyes." He turned to Mandy and motioned toward the velvet bell cord. "Remember now, Miss Bradshaw, anything at all you need, you just give a good yank on this here bell and I'll be here quicker'n a hound after a hare!" Flashing his shy smile once more he turned and bowed his way out the door.

"Oh, Grandmother, it's too soon!" Mandy wailed. "I thought we'd have more time to—to—"

"Now, now, *chérie*, none of that. What did we agree?" Belle took Mandy into her arms and hugged her close. "You are to be a brave girl and enjoy yourself, *oui*? We will write to one another as often as possible and before you know it, we will be together again." Belle smiled brightly and blinked back the tears in her eyes. "Now a kiss, *bébé*, and off you go on your grand adventure! Remember to record *everything* in the diary I gave you, *oui*?"

"*Oui,* Grandmother," Mandy whispered, then flung her arms around Belle's neck and sobbed, "Oh, I don't want to go, Grandmother! I shall miss you so!"

Belle held the girl close, stroking her back and murmuring, "Hush, *bébé*, hush," then led her to the sofa and gently sat her down. "Come, *chérie*, let me help you with your wrap and then you must lie down and rest a bit before lunch. Caleen will order you some nice jambalaya, *oui, bébé*?" She slipped the cloak off Mandy's shoulders and pressed her back against the cushions.

"All aboard!" a voice bawled just outside the window and they fell into one another's arms, both sobbing, "Oh, I shall miss you!" Then Belle pulled away and hurried to the door. Mandy flung herself after her for one last hug, then threw her arms around Elmo and kissed his tear-stained cheek.

"Goodbye, dear Elmo, take care of Grandmother for me." She bit her lower lip to stop the trembling as they moved quickly down the narrow steps. The whistle sounded again and Mandy was thrown off balance as the train began to move. Black smoke billowed around the car and Mandy rushed to the window for one last glimpse. "Goodbye! Goodbye!" she shouted, waving frantically through the glass. "I'll write the moment I arrive! I love you! *Au revoir!*"

"*Adieu, chérie, au revoir!*" Belle called. She held her lace handkerchief to her nose as the thick smoke engulfed the platform, almost obscuring the train as it chugged slowly away. "May God bless you and keep you safe, *ma petite chérie*," she whispered.

Elmo took her arm and gently tugged her away from the edge of the platform, which was now completely choked with black smoke. "Come away now, Miz Belle," he said. "She be fine, yes."

"Yes, she will be fine, won't she, Elmo?" Belle whispered. She walked slowly beside him, as though she were suddenly an old woman, her step faltering. "*Mon Dieu*, how I pray for her safety! If anything should happen to her, Elmo, I would never forgive myself." She allowed him to help her into the carriage and tuck the lap robe about her knees.

"That big Yankee mon, that Massa Stokes, he look after her, him." Elmo climbed aboard and picked up the reins, slapping them across the rumps of the matched grays, and they set out at a brisk trot. An old black woman, bent nearly double with age, stumbled down the cobbled street alongside them pushing a cart laden with steaming rice cakes. "*Belle cala!* *Tout chaud!*" she called in a thin, whiny voice. "*Belle cala!* *Tout chaud!*"

Ordinarily, Belle would have had Elmo stop and purchase a dozen or so of the piping hot little cakes, but this morning she seemed not to notice the old woman and her fragrant cart. She sat slumped against the cushions, a handkerchief pressed against her mouth until Elmo brought the carriage to a halt in front of the wrought-iron gate on Rampart Street. He helped her down, shaking his gray woolly head when she sobbed aloud and rushed quickly into the house. She would seek the sanctuary of her bedchamber, he knew, and what solace she could find in her sherry bottle.

27

As she hurried up the stairs, Belle called to one of the kitchen girls to come and assist her in removing her gown. The house seemed abnormally quiet and she, too, was silent as the girl undressed her and helped her into a robe. She crawled into bed like some wounded animal, her eyes dark with sadness. Clasping her hands together, she prayed, "Oh, Holy Mother, please keep her safe! Please see that no harm or accident ever befalls my little Amanda. Let her be happy and well in her new home . . ." She crossed herself, murmuring a further prayer in soft, fervent French, gave a sigh and squared her shoulders. Belle did not approve of dwelling on one's problems. A born optimist, she awoke each morning looking forward to the next day.

A soft knock sounded and Gaby, the golden-skinned mulatto kitchen girl, slipped inside with Belle's tray. She smiled shyly as she placed it over Belle's lap and arranged the sherry and stationery her mistress had requested. "Build a nice warm fire for me, will you, Gaby dear?" Belle poured a glass of wine and took a long sip, closing her eyes and letting her head fall back against the piled-up pillows. "These old bones are feeling the cold more and more each year, I vow!" She watched as Gaby expertly stacked the kindling, then placed three crossed logs on top, blowing gently until the flames caught. Perhaps she would train her as her personal maid, Belle mused. With Caleen gone she would need someone to look after her affairs.

She sipped the sherry again before picking up her pen and a sheet of creamy white stationery. Monsieur Bradshaw, or J.B. as he apparently preferred, had asked Belle to write and let him know that everything was proceeding according to schedule. His request had sounded more like a curt command and Belle knew that here was a man used to having his own way. That he was a powerful and self-made man, she already knew, but now she had discovered that he was wealthy beyond her wildest expectations. If that gorgeous plush rail car was used simply for business associates and poor relatives, she could well imagine how J.B. himself must travel and live. So her little Amanda would be surrounded by luxury at last! The child certainly deserved some happiness and ease after the depressing war years and all the hardships they had wrought. Perhaps she would meet and fall in love with some dashing young silver king, land baron, or railroad magnate. Belle's lively imagination took flight and she envisioned Amanda being swept off her feet at some grand ball given in her honor. She knew that San Francisco was fast becoming quite fashionable, that the women were as smart and chic as those in New York or Paris, and she saw Amanda as the smartest, most beautiful of them all. Belle sighed. If she were twenty years younger she would be tempted to journey west herself!

Replenishing her glass, she found herself wondering about the flamboyant Monsieur Bradshaw. She had never seen a likeness of him but, judging from Johnny's Irish good looks, she could well imagine his sire.

Belle couldn't remember much of the times spent talking with Désirée and Johnny about their Western family, even though they had passed many pleasant hours in just such a way. Désirée, her lovely face alight with happy memories of San Francisco, had recounted exciting shopping trips and elegant evenings at the theater, while Johnny had solemnly assured Belle that his family was indeed civilized even if the land was not. "But we're working on it," he had grinned. "J.B. has about a hundred and fifty thousand acres fenced in. Then there's a big chunk of downtown San Francisco carrying his brand, so I reckon we're on our way to becoming respectable."

That California was raw and wild, Belle had no doubt, but it seemed merely the exuberance of the young men and women who would tame it, the strong ones who would build homes and cities and make their fortunes by conquering that rich, savage land. John Banyon Bradshaw had been just such a man. Orphaned at fourteen, he had built his vast empire from

29

scratch, becoming the first millionaire in California by the time he was twenty-five. Johnny had repeated colorful anecdotes about his father so often, Belle knew the story by heart.

In the year 1816, Jonathan Francis Bradshaw walked down the gangplank from the steerage section of the ship that had brought him from Ireland to Boston, Massachusetts, carrying his pregnant wife, Mavis, in his arms. A few hours later, in a small lean-to next to a stable, Mavis gave birth to a son. They called him John Banyon Bradshaw and Jonathan spent his last fifty cents for a bit of Irish whiskey to celebrate his firstborn's arrival. The next day he and Mavis had gone through their pitiful belongings, searching for anything they could sell or trade for food and shelter. Jonathan had gone door to door with his small pack of notions, a jaunty peddler who charmed the housewives with his smiling Irish blarney. He seemed to have a knack for sales and before his son was a year old he had bought the lean-to and converted it into a trading post.

There had been four more sons in quick succession and Jonathan had been forced to find larger accommodations. He built a three-bedroom log cabin just at the edge of Fall River, where game and fish were plentiful and Mavis had ample space for a vegetable garden. Jon's Trading Post had now taken over the stable and had become a familiar hangout for other traders, fur trappers, Indians and the like. Jon had knocked out all the walls, turning it into one huge room that was dominated by an enormous double-faced fireplace in the very center. Here the men would sit with their feet upon the stone hearth, passing a jug between them and spitting comradely into the flames, while on the other side the women would browse and gossip as they did their shopping. Young J.B. had been put in charge of the female side while Jon Sr. played genial host to his potpourri clientele.

It was in this cozy atmosphere of congeniality that J.B. had grown up. Therefore, he had been totally unprepared for the massacre of his family that had taken place when he was just fourteen years old. He had stayed later than usual at the trading post one evening as a new shipment of farming tools had come in. With so many immigrants pouring into Boston these days, he wanted to be sure he had the tools on the display shelves when the doors opened the next morning. If he left it to his father they would remain in their crates indefinitely, and the growing Bradshaw family always seemed to need more money. He rode slowly home, marvelling that the sunken sun still cast a red glow along the horizon. As he rode nearer, however, he saw that it was growing brighter and the night warmer.

He topped the ridge and looked down at the winding Fall River and saw the crimson flames reflected in its shiny surface. With a cry he spurred his horse down the hill toward the burning cabin, flinging himself out of the saddle just as the roof caved in. He made a dash for what had once been the front door but the intense heat drove him back.

There was nothing he could do, of course. Everyone had told him that. He was just lucky, they had said, that he hadn't been at home when it had happened. He was alive and young. He had his whole life ahead of him. But the torment and guilt had ripped him apart. If only he hadn't been so greedy, wanting to take advantage of the new shipment, make more money. He should have been with his father when the small party of marauding Indians had attacked. He was by far the better shot. Maybe he could have saved them.

There had been no funeral. When the townspeople came out the next day to sift through the rubble they had found no remains. J.B. had called on the family priest to read a few words over the heap of smoldering ashes; then he had turned his back and walked away. The next day he sold the trading post to the first man willing to buy, took what supplies he needed and signed on with a trading ship that was setting sail for the California coast. He knew that the treacherous voyage

31

around Cape Horn would take at least nine months and that was fine with him. He wanted to put as much distance as possible between himself and Boston, Massachusetts.

"Beggin' yo pardon, Miz Belle," Gaby said from the doorway, startling Belle out of her reminiscence.

"*Oui,* Gaby, what is it, dear?" Belle glanced at the clock on the mantle and saw with surprise that it was early afternoon. She had languished away the morning with remembered tales of the Bradshaws while the train carrying Amanda had chugged farther and farther west.

"Will mistress be wantin' her dinner up here or will her be comin' downstairs Cook wants to know." Gaby said it all in a rush, her large dark eyes fixed on a spot just above Belle's head.

Sensing the girl's shyness, Belle said gently, "Come, come, *chérie,* I promise you that I do not bite!" Gaby grinned, ducking her head, and Belle thought what fun it would be to take this awkward child under her wing and teach her the graces required of a personal maid. It would help fill the hours and perhaps take her mind off Amanda. "Tell Cook I would much prefer dining in my room for the time being, dear. It would be too— painful—sitting all alone in the dining room . . ." Her voice trailed off and she reached for the sherry bottle, a little surprised to find it almost empty. She poured what was left into her glass and held the bottle out to Gaby. "Take this for me, will you, dear? And you may bring me another when you come up with the gumbo. Tell Cook I only want a little something." She sipped her wine. "I haven't much of an appetite, I'm afraid."

"Yez'm, Miz Belle, I tell her." Gaby backed out of the room and Belle turned to gaze at the painting of Johnny and Désirée that hung above the fireplace. "I think I did what you both would have wanted," she whispered. "I think I made the right decision for your daughter." J.B. would most certainly provide a good home for the girl and Belle hoped Amanda would adapt herself graciously to her new surroundings. Perhaps in time she would come to love California as much as her mother and father had. Belle took a long swallow of wine, anxious for the warmth that would ease the tightness in her breast. She doubted that she would live to see her granddaughter again.

Belle's health had begun to fail with the death of her beloved Armand and the senseless, brutal murders of Désirée and Johnny had almost driven her over the brink. She had hung on for Amanda's sake, living in constant fear, but now the child was on her way to a new life and Belle could let go. The war had brought too much pain, too many ugly changes and Belle could no longer cope. Nor did she have any desire to. She was simply too tired and too ill.

Just how ill, only Caleen knew and Belle had sworn her to secrecy. She had made a bargain with the wise old woman who had been with her for as long as she could remember, first as her personal maid, then as Désirée's nanny and finally Amanda's. If Caleen would travel to California with Amanda, Belle promised she would close the house on Rampart Street and go to the Order of the Holy Family where she would be assured of the best medical attention as well as the protection of the Church. Even though Caleen had not wanted to leave her mistress, she had seen the wisdom in the plan and had helped to carry it out. She would see that no harm came to the girl, Belle knew. Just let anyone look cross-eyed at Caleen's precious *ché* and she would devastate him with one of her lethal *guignon* spells.

Belle chuckled, trying to picture Caleen out in the Wild West conjuring up her dark African spells. She was sure to cause a stir in the Bradshaw household! She was still smiling when Gaby entered with a bowl of steaming gumbo and a fresh bottle of sherry.

"Trout be right up, Miz Belle, and Cook say you eat it all. Keep up yore strength," Gaby said as she placed the soup on Belle's tray and filled her wine glass. She scurried to the fireplace and added a few more logs, then made her familiar awkward exit from the room.

33

Belle shook her head in amusement. Perhaps she wouldn't have enough time to train Gaby as she would have liked, but she would give the girl enough polish to enable her to find another position when Belle let the house go. She raised her glass in a toast, her eyes on the portrait above the mantle, whispered, "To you, Amanda, *bébé*, may you find happiness," and drank deep, draining the goblet.

San Franciso 1875

CHAPTER THREE

The cool night air blew gently through the open window, bringing the smell of spring into the room. The odor of sage, sharp and pungent, was tempered by the sweet-smelling wild roses that grew abundantly up the trellis and filled the night with fragrance. A soft, sibilant breeze swept through the window, rustling the drapes and mingling with the low moans from the bed, its cooling caress drying the perspiration on the writhing bodies that twisted upon the damp, crushed sheets.

"Oh, darling, yes, yes!" The woman clung tightly, arms and legs wrapped in a vise-like grip about the man above her, head thrown back in a paroxysm of ecstasy. "Now!" she cried, "oh, now, my love!" She seemed to explode in his arms, long pale hair a frenzied mass about her face, long, sleek legs scissored about his lean hips to keep him firmly in place as she bucked and thrashed beneath him. Her teeth sank into his shoulder at the last moment, biting back the scream of passion and fulfillment; then she went limp beneath him.

J.B. rolled to one side and lay on his back in the wide canopied bed, staring through the open windows that seemed to frame the night as if it were some massive painting. A full moon lit the softly rolling hills and spilled liquid silver upon the lake at the edge of the forest. Massive mountains loomed dark and shadowy, their snow-capped peaks startling white in the moonlight. He rested his hand on the woman's hip, stroking absently as if petting a favorite kitten, his mind elsewhere now that she was satisfied.

"I love you, darling," she murmured and snuggled in closer, arms and legs wrapping about his body.

"Hmm." J.B. patted her arm affectionately before removing it and pushing himself into a sitting position. He reached to the nightstand and took a cheroot from a leather-tooled box.

"Oh, let me—please!" She leaned across him, her naked breasts brushing abainst his chest as she picked up the candle and held it to the end of the dark brown tobacco. She replaced the candle but did not immediately remove her pendulous breasts. Instead, she moved them teasingly back and forth, the erect nipples parting his thick chest hair and tickling him.

"My God, woman, don't you ever get enough?" J.B. gave a short bark of laughter meant to pass as a lover's chuckle. His thick russet eyebrows drew together in a fierce frown as he caught her wrists in one huge hand and forced her back to her own side of the bed. "Now behave yourself, LissaMarie, and quit pestering an ole man."

"Hah! Old man indeed!" She tossed her head and the pale blonde hair danced on her shoulders. "Why, you put every man to shame for miles around."

"Oh, is that so? And how would you know, Miss? Been comparing, have you?"

"Johnny! That's not nice!" LissaMarie pouted. "You know you're the only one."

"J.B., honey. Nobody calls me Johnny," His voice was suddenly quite hard and the dangerous glint in his vivid blue eyes stilled her tongue. He smiled, rather wolfishly, he imagined, and gave her rounded bottom a smart slap. "Enough of this bull. Make yourself useful and get me a glass of bourbon." She flounced off the bed and he watched appreciatively as her buttocks twitched through the door leading to the bar. She was a handsome woman, built like a thoroughbred mare and just as spirited. Perhaps a little too spirited, he thought.

He sucked in on the cheroot, taking the smoke deep into his lungs, then letting it trickle out in its own time as he turned to gaze through the windows. Lately she had been sneaking into his bedroom three or four times a week, and during the day, when she should have been avoiding him as he had requested, she seemed instead to find ways of being alone with him. Or in the same room with the rest of the family, which was worse, for then she would gaze at him adoringly, her passion naked for all to see. Why, just the other day, Jeramy had made some remark about wishing that he had had a governess like Miss Rosenkilde when he had been a boy. No, it simply wouldn't do to keep her on any longer. Particularly now that his granddaughter, Amanda, was coming to live with them. J.B. sighed. It wouldn't be pleasant, letting LissaMarie go. She was a generous and imaginative lover and, in his way, he was quite fond of her.

She came swaying back into the room and handed him a glass of bourbon. "For you, master," she grinned impudently, striking a provocative pose. The moonlight bathed her in silver, highlighting her pale hair and white body.

J.B. felt a stirring in his loins and said gruffly, "You look just like an angel standing there."

"No one's ever accused me of *that* before," she said with a husky laugh as she crawled into bed. Her hand caressed his chest, slipping down the flat plane of his stomach, teasing, seeking. "But I'll gladly be your angel, darling, or anything else you want me to be." Her hand found what it was searching for and gripped possessively.

"What I want you to be, *Miss* Rosenkilde—" he firmly removed her hand "—is governess to my grandchildren." He took a swallow of bourbon, sighing when her hand found him again.

"But I'm a very good governess, darling." She manipulated him expertly. "Ask the children. They adore me." She let her head fall against his shoulder, marvell-

39

ing as always at how strong and broad it was. Comforting, too, when he was in a tender mood and held her close.

"Yes, that's true enough," J.B. agreed. "Those young hellions do seem to have a fondness for you that was missing with the last governess." He settled back against the tufted-velvet headboard, spreading his legs slightly to give her groping hand more room. Damn, but she was the most insatiable woman he'd ever known. And she had a way of arousing him again and again when he thought he was more than sated. The strong bourbon fired his blood and sent a surge of response through him as she continued her erotic massage. Maybe he wouldn't let her go after all. He could just *order* her to behave herself when the family was present. "I imagine you might have your hands full with my granddaughter Amanda, however. She's bound to be more genteel than these ruffians you're used to."

"I'll have her eating out of my hand within a week," LissaMarie declared smugly. She took the glass from him and raised it to her lips, her eyes meeting his over the rim as she drank. "She's due tomorrow, isn't she?"

"Yes tomorrow morning about ten or eleven. Jeramy's meeting the train in Sacramento." He took the glass she offered and drained the remainder of the bourbon before placing it on the nightstand.

LissaMarie sighed and slipped her arms around him, drawing him down on top of her as she murmured huskily, "Good—then we have plenty of time."

J.B. was dressed and downstairs at his customary time of six sharp. He took his place at the head of the table in the sun-drenched breakfast room, grunting his thanks when Atoka set a cup of coffee before him. The *Californian* was folded neatly by his plate next to the snowy linen napkin and he picked it up and scanned the headlines.

40

"Good morning, Father, anything worthwhile in the paper?" Jonathan strode into the breakfast room and took his place at the other end of the table. His red hair was slicked down and still wet from his morning toilette, the bristly moustache already springing loose from the carefully waxed ends. He rang for coffee and Wilma, the serving girl, came scurrying in and placed it before him.

"About the same," J.B. said, not glancing up from his paper. He found it difficult to carry on a conversation with his eldest son. Jonathan always seemed to be reaching for joviality, pressing J.B. into a closeness he did not feel. J.B. knew it was jealousy of the deceased Johnny and that his big, bumbling son was trying desperately to take the place of his older brother, but no one could do that. J.B. had hoped that one of his grandsons would have some of Johnny's traits, but Jonathan's two sons were, unfortunately, much like their father. J.B.'s youngest son, Jeramy, was more to his liking, but he too fell short when compared with Johnny's memory. Jeramy was as lovable as a cocker spaniel pup and just as irresponsible. He had inherited his mother's lazy charm and his father's virile good looks and according to countless ladies, the combination was dynamite. J.B. had to smile when he thought about his youngest son. There was a warmth between them that was comforting now that Johnny was gone.

"Top of the morning, Pa! Glorious day, isn't it?" Jeramy sailed into the room, dropped a kiss on the top of J.B.'s head and took the chair on his right, swinging one long leg over the back and dropping into it with a plop.

"Goddamn it, Jeramy, how many times do I have to tell you that you're too goddamn old to be kissing your Pa good morning!" He swatted his son with the newspaper and scowled fiercely into his impudent face. "If I didn't know better I'd think you were one of those queer young fops that hang out at Sadies's!" He shook

41

the newspaper into order and a smile tugged at his lips. "But I've paid off too many weeping women who were carrying your bastards to ever—"

"Father Bradshaw!" interrupted a shocked voice and Agnes, Jonathan's wife, swept into the room. She sat down at her husband's right and rang for the serving girl. "Is that any way to talk at the breakfast table? Tsk tsk!" She smiled down the table at him, letting him know she was joking, and added, "And at your age, too!"

J.B. thought of LissaMarie and hid his grin behind the *Californian*, saying only, "Good morning, Agnes, I trust you slept well."

Agnes leaned to one side as Wilma served her coffee. "No, as a matter of fact, I didn't, Father Bradshaw," she said. "I lay awake for hours thinking of poor, dear little Amanda. What that poor child must have gone through—I shudder to think of it." She sipped her coffee daintily, her long, handsome face set in lines of distress. "I do hope she hasn't been too badly affected by the decadence of the South."

"We shall know soon enough," Jeramy said cheerfully. He flicked his napkin open and flourished it to his lap. "If the roads aren't too muddy we should be back by noon." Wilma bent over him with a large platter of crisp bacon and he slid several slices onto his plate. "With the heavy rains we've had these past two weeks, I'm a little afraid of Otter River. It might be flooded down by the bridge." Colleen followed on Wilma's heels with a platter piled high with scrambled eggs and Jeramy raked a large portion onto his plate. "Please pass the biscuits, Jonathan," he said around a mouthful of bacon.

"Otter River's all right," J.B. said. "I talked to Bret Dunlap yesterday and he had just come in that way. Said all the roads are clear from here to Sacramento." He took the wicker basket of steaming biscuits from Jeramy, helped himself to a couple, then passed them on to Agnes.

"Well, I just hope she fits in all right," Agnes said to no one in particular.

"Who's driving with you?" J.B. asked Jeramy. "Lefty or George?" He buttered his biscuit and topped it with a spoonful of Atoka's huckleberry preserves.

"I thought I'd better take George. Amanda's bound to have several trunks and I'll probably need a man with two strong arms."

The ate in silence, each thinking about Amanda's arrival. J.B. was more nervous and excited than he would have admitted at the prospect of seeing his beloved favorite son's only daughter and found himself hoping (foolishly) that she would somehow be just like her father. Jeramy felt only the curiosity of a good-natured uncle and Jonathan and Agnes were plagued with jealousy at the prospect that Amanda might be prettier and smarter than their own children.

J.B. topped his breakfast off with another biscuit smothered in huckleberry preserves and disappeared into his study, closing the door firmly behind him. He sat down at his desk and took a cheroot from the box there. Lighting up, he leaned back in the deep cowhide chair and put his feet up on the desk. The chair sagged with his weight, closing about him familiarly, the thick red and white hair warming him instantly. He had let the women have their say in decorating the rest of the house, but his study was completely his own. The two long sofas were covered in the same cowhide as his chair with the lush hair still attached, broad arms and legs as sturdy as the redwood they had been carved from. Books lined three walls from ceiling to floor and an enormous slate fireplace dominated the fourth. Scattered about the room were mementos of J.B.'s early years and three lush bearskin rugs rested on the highly varnished hardwood floor.

He puffed thoughtfully on his cheroot, impatient for his granddaughter's arrival. He had wanted to meet her train himself but after some deliberation had decided that Jeramy's easy graciousness might do better to soothe any fears the child might have. No one could resist Jeramy's good humor. J.B. knew the trip had been pleasant and comfortable. He had ridden in that same rail car often enough in the past before buying his current car.

He leaned forward and knocked the ash off his cheroot, glancing at the letter from Belle Bertonneau. He had been slightly annoyed at reading that Amanda would be travelling with her nanny. He had sent Ted Stokes to escort her across country and the fact that Belle Bertonneau had seen fit to send her own protection had made him think that he wasn't trusted. And what the devil kind of name was Caleen? He hoped she wouldn't be one of those frog-speaking Frenchies who mistrusted anyone who spoke English without an accent.

On the other hand, she could be a delightful French dish to take the place of LissaMarie when he let her go. He conjured up a picture of a saucy, sloe-eyed maid dressed in a stiff black taffeta skirt that stopped just at the top of her rosy thighs and showed a sassy ruffle of white panties. He chuckled aloud. The French nanny just might prove to be an added asset.

Caleen clutched her shawl to her shrunken bosom with one bony black hand and her tiny brown eyes, as shiny as new buttons, swept the landscape through the carriage window. A field of golden poppies swayed gently in the breeze and a herd of antelope grazed serenely, barely glancing up as the horses trotted by. Caleen sat rigidly in one corner of the lushly upholstered carriage, her attention on the strange terrain and unfamiliar plant life. Huge sycamore trees dotted the land, their branches supporting a choir of meadowlarks and linnets. Sky-blue lupine mixed with the orange poppies in the field and white, black, and purple sage added to the potpourri of color. The most dominant vegetation was the woody chaparral, intricate and inpenetrable shrubbery that spread in all directions. A woodpecker clung to the side of a tree, crying, "Jacob! Jacob!" when a sparrow hawk swooped too close but the meadowlarks and linnets continued their cheery song, unmindful of the danger.

"Oh, look! What are those?" Amanda asked, pointing. "I've never seen deer that look like that."

"Those are American antelope," Jeramy said. "Pretty little creatures, aren't they?" He too leaned over and looked through the window. "Unfortunatly, they're on the verge of becoming extinct. Too many hunters and trappers looking to make a fortune from hides and pelts, I'm afraid. J.B. has warnings posted all over his property to keep poachers away, but it does little good."

He glanced admiringly at Amanda's profile as she gazed through the window. He hadn't been prepared for such a dazzling beauty and had had to remind himself that he was her uncle when she had gone innocently into his arms for a welcoming embrace. Her hair was the color of rich sable and her eyes were as changeable as the sea, turquoise, smoky blue, deep violet, depending on her mood. Her soft lilac gown curved in and out in all the proper places and when her cloak fell open he was treated to the sight of high, youthful breasts. Twin dimples flashed in her cheeks when she laughed and her teeth were as perfect as pearls.

"Are we travelling on Bradshaw property now?" Amanda asked, turning to face him. "Grandmother Bertonneau said the estate was quite large."

"Yep, for the last five miles or so." Jeramy took a cheroot from his vest pocket and lit it, squinting his eyes against the smoke that curled around his face. "See that river over there?" He pointed to a twisting, rushing blue snake that cut savagely through the peaceful terrain. "That's Otter River. It borders our land on this side, coming down from Los Gatos, that big mountain ridge way up there in the distance." He pointed and Amanda leaned forward to gaze up at the craggy, snow-capped range. "Los Gatos means cats and there's just about

45

every kind of feline you can think of up in those hills. Cougar, lynx, wildcat, bobcat—and they're awfully fond of those pretty little antelope we saw a ways back."

"Then we're almost there?" Mandy said faintly. She had been greatly relieved to find that her Uncle Jeramy was actually quite the gentleman, polite and dapper, not at all as she had imagined. His dove-gray suit was in the very latest fashion, shadowed with tiny pinstripes, and he sported a fresh rose in his lapel. His gray kid gloves were as elegant as her own and his smiling, sunny face had put her immediately at ease. He reminded her of her father and she felt herself drawn to him at once.

"Uh-huh, when we top this hill you'll be able to look down over the valley and see our spread." He drew in on the cheroot and turned to exhale the smoke through the open window. "It's quite an impressive sight the first time you see it. I don't know much about the South but I'll wager those plantations can't hold a candle to J.B.'s estate!" He made a sweeping arc with his hand, taking in all that could be seen through the carriage window. "He started buying up every piece of property he could lay his hands on right after the rush in forty-nine, determined to own California, some said. He had a partner back then, Andrew Dunlap, and they both struck it rich in the gold fields. Then they started trying to outdo each other on cornering the land market. The Dunlap spread is almost as big as ours but old Andy died before he could top J.B.'s holdings. J.B. has a hundred and fifty thousand acres and says he won't be satisfied until he makes it an even two hundred thousand." He chuckled at some private thought. "Only thing stopping him is a wildcat meaner than any in Los Gatos—Juanita Arteaga. She owns the land next to that mountain ridge I pointed out and J.B. is determined to get it. So far he hasn't had much luck with the fiery señora."

The carriage bumped over a deep rut in the road and

46

Mandy heard the driver snap the whip over the backs of the straining team, urging them on. They rattled upward, topping the small hill with difficulty due to the deep mud, and Jeramy leaned his head out of the window, calling, "Hey, George, pull up here a minute." The carriage came to a halt and Jeramy leaped to the ground, offering Mandy his hand. "Let's get out and stretch our legs a bit," he said. "You can get a bird's-eye view of your new home from up here." She gave him her hand, picking her way carefully through the thistle sage as they walked toward the edge of the hill. Then she stopped short, gasping with astonishment at the sight before her.

The entire valley spread out below her like some crazy patchwork quilt. An enormous mansion stood in the very center of vivid green lawns. A red brick courtyard curved out from the tall pillars of the porch and was surrounded by a hedge of ruby roses. Several streams slashed blue and turquoise across the land, dividing it into pie slices and tumbling over small waterfalls to spill into Otter River. A sturdy redwood fence rambled for miles along the gently rolling land and more horses than Mandy had ever seen at one time grazed in belly-deep pasture.

A redwood arch curved high above wide double gates, the initials J.B. carved completely through the two-foot thickness. The drive that led to the courtyard must have been a good mile long and was bordered on both sides by stately eucalyptus trees, their thin marmoreal columns and bluish-gray foliage glinting like gunmetal against the sky. Several smaller buildings fanned out to either side and behind the main house, sheltered by a wild profusion of redwoods, pepper trees, elderberry, and majestic oaks.

The mansion, for it certainly couldn't be called a mere house, stood three stories tall with numerous turrets jutting toward the sky, its diamond-shaped windows sparkling like a myriad of mirrors. There were two more brick courtyards to the right of the mansion,

47

the larger one fronting a stable where carriages were parked in regimental order. Mandy walked closer to the edge of the hill, reaching back to take Jeramy's hand. The wind lifted her skirts and tugged playfully.

"I can't believe it. It's—it's magnificent!" Mandy murmured and her fingers squeezed Jeramy's gloved hand. She looked to the left of the mansion and saw part of a lake disappearing into a dense forest and next to its shore a large building that she supposed was a hunting lodge. A wide stream bubbled from the lake's tip, winding gently down the slope in front of the mansion to spill into Otter River at the base of the hill where they stood. A water wheel revolved lazily a little further down and there were several boats tied to a pier connected to yet another building.

"Yes, it really is something, isn't it?" Jeramy said. "Even though I've lived here all my life I'm still sometimes struck with the enormity of it all." He laughed shortly. "I'm afraid J.B. wouldn't approve of that word—he believes that outrageousness is next to Godliness. If you've got it, flaunt it—that seems to be the creed of the West." His voice had a rather bitter edge to it that Mandy had not heard before and she glanced at him from beneath lowered lashes. He stood staring at the vast estate, his handsome profile to her, and she saw a muscle working in his temple as he clenched his teeth. "Perhaps I'm too sensitive, but I sometimes feel embarrassed at the Bradshaw wealth and the way it was accumulated."

"What do you mean, Uncle Jeramy?" Amanda asked shyly. "I thought Grandfather made his fortune in the gold fields. Surely that's nothing to be ashamed of."

"Ah, that's but a small drop in a bucket that runneth over with gold, my dear!" Jeramy laughed and the dark look was replaced with a bright, merry smile. "And *please* don't call me Uncle—you make me feel like a doddering old fool!"

"*Pardonnez-moi* Jeramy," Mandy laughed, squeezing his hand. "You must instruct me in the proper terms of address for my new relatives. I would not wish to commit a *faux pas*!"

"Whatever that is," Jeramy said with raised eyebrows. "Well, shall we go forward into the lion's den, my dear?" He took her elbow and guided her back through the thistle sage to the carriage. Caleen was leaning out the window, her inscrutable gaze sweeping the magnificence below, but she quickly withdrew as they approached. Jeramy handed Mandy inside, slapped the door with his open palm, called, "Let's go, George!" and they were off at a reckless pace down the hill.

Mandy lay on her back on the huge four-poster canopied bed, idly watching Caleen as she puttered around the huge bedroom. It was fabulous, from the high beamed ceilings to the ankle-deep carpeted floors. An enormous fireplace dominated one wall and double French doors opened into a private dressing room and bath. Across from the bed were vast stretches of windows that looked out onto rolling green hills, the roof of the stables and several other buildings that Mandy guessed to be the groom's and gardener's cottages. She had looked down earlier to see a large square of freshly tilled dark soil just planted in long neat rows, some greenery already poking through here and there. Directly below her windows was a lovely rose garden and the brick kitchen courtyard.

She sighed and closed her eyes, her head aching a little from the long journey and all the strange people she had met, the foreign-sounding names still ringing in her ears. She had been properly awed by the overpowering figure of her grandfather as well as his castle, for it certainly could not be called a mere house.

"What do you think of all this, *Tante* Caleen?" she asked, eyes still closed. "And *him*. Do you like him?"

Caleen adjusted her *tignon* to cover her grizzled, sparse hair as she faced her young mistress. "Him one big mon, Massa Bradshaw, him." She nodded her head

49

sagely. "Rich man, like a king, him." She shook out a gown of pale green silk and went to hang it in the large mahogany wardrobe.

"But did you *like* him?" Mandy persisted. "Did you think he was a little, well, coarse, perhaps?" She pushed herself into a sitting position, watching Caleen briskly reshape a hat that had gotten bent out of shape in the trunk.

"Him honest mon, yes. He look at Caleen's eyes when he speak to her, him." Again she nodded in approval. "Him no cheatin' mon, afraid to look straight." She gave a final pat to the brim of the hat, put it into its box and set the box on the top shelf of the closet. She stooped down for another gown, shaking it out and brushing its velvet trim with a small whisk broom. "He like your Daddy, him. Honest eyes, honest mon."

Mandy sighed. That was not what she wanted to hear. Of course her grandfather was an honest man like her father, but was he to be her friend? That was what she needed to know. She had been a little intimidated when he had grabbed her up in a bear hug and swung her around the room as if she were still the little girl he remembered. It had shocked her. Young ladies of seventeen were not treated so intimately in the South. And no one had even bowed or kissed her hand when introduced.

Upon arriving at the estate, Jeramy had swept her inside and called out, "Pa! We're home," sailing his hat in a perfect pitch that settled it on the top rung of the hat rack. Mandy had been shocked that he had referred to his father in so casual a manner. In the South young men called their fathers "Sir" and certainly did not sail their hats through the air with such happy abandon. She had stood clutching Caleen's hand and the next thing she knew she was surrounded by a whirlwind.

"Amanda, little Amanda!" The big, booming voice, sounding strangely accented to Mandy's ears, had vibrated through the huge room, and then she was set upon by a giant. He stood well over six feet, his shoulders seemingly as massive as the mountains she had just travelled through, his thick, once red hair now snow-white. He had grabbed her around the waist and hugged her to his broad chest, kissed her soundly upon the mouth, then whirled her around until her head spun. Setting her back on her feet he had gazed down into her face and said, softly for one so large, "So my little Amanda has come home." His piercing blue eyes went over every feature as if seeking something. "Yes," he had murmured. His hands, as big as whole Virginia hams, held her shoulders as he looked down at her. "Yes, yes, I see Johnny in you. And your dear mother, too. You are a beauty, Amanda, a real thoroughbred."

She had tried to say "Thank you" but the words had stayed in her throat. She reached back for Caleen's hand.

"Come in, child, come in and meet the family." J.B. took her free hand and pulled both her and Caleen into the parlor, a room as lovely and graceful as any Mandy had seen in the South. It seemed filled with people of all ages and Mandy still had not gotten all the faces and names properly matched.

"Your Uncle Jonathan and Aunt Agnes," J.B. said, leading her to a rather portly, red-headed man with a bristling russet moustache, and a long-boned, handsome woman. They both stood, their eyes going over Mandy as if she were a bug under a microscope.

"Amanda, my dear, how good to see you again." Agnes smiled, exposing large square teeth, and Mandy quickly dropped a curtsy.

"Well, well, Amanda dear! Welcome!" Jonathan stood with his hands clasped behind his back, rocking back on his heels as he looked down at her. Neither offered their hand.

"And here's your Aunt Jane, Amanda." J.B. led her to a skinny young woman with huge pale eyes and the strangest color hair that she had ever seen. It was bright orange and as frizzy as a pickaninny's. She stood and curtsied to Mandy, her shy, pale eyes meeting hers

51

briefly, then sliding away. She was as tall as Mandy but as slim as a boy, bosom, waist and hips seemingly all the same size under her dainty dress of sprigged lawn.

"And these young ruffians are your cousins," J.B. said, motioning the three youngsters to rise. "June, she's the eldest." A rather pretty but petulant girl who would be the replica of her mother in a few years bobbed a curtsy, then sat back down. "And this is Jon." He looked Mandy over boldly even though she guessed him to be a couple of years younger than she. "And young James, the hellcat of the bunch," J.B. finished, pushing a freckle-faced little red-headed boy forward. He gave Mandy an impudent grin, showing missing front teeth. None of them had spoken.

"How do you do?" Mandy said formally, her shy smile taking them all in. "I'm very pleased to meet you." And the three of them chorused together, "Hello, cousin Amanda, welcome to San Francisco" as if they had been schooled in the greeting.

J.B. took Mandy's hand, said, "Come along, girl," and led her into another room almost as large as the parlor. A dining table, fifteen yards long, ran the length of the room and there were several men and women lined up in regimental order next to it. Mandy recognized Atoka at once and threw herself into the Indian woman's arms with relief at seeing a familiar face.

"Tokie!" she cried. "I was so hoping that you would still be here!" She hugged her, then stepped back, blushing, not knowing if such intimacy with a servant was allowed in her grandfather's house.

"Miz 'Manda, chile, my, my!" Atoka's dark face lighted up with a smile of genuine pleasure and she hugged the girl to her. "Yes, I's still here, can't get rid of ole Atoka that easy!" She held her at arm's length. "Land sakes, has you ever growed, Miz 'Manda."

The other servants looked on impassively as J.B. led her down the line, introducing each one and explaining their duties.

There was Martha, who was head housekeeper and

52

cook, a plump, buxom woman with an open Irish face and twinkling periwinkle eyes. LissaMarie Rosenkilde, the governess, who looked Mandy over coolly, then dropped her eyes at a sharp glance from J.B. Four maids, young Mexican women, Marta, Carla, Rosa and Quina whom Mandy thought all looked exactly alike. Manuel, the young kitchen boy, and two stableboys, Tim and Pete. Tim had a shock of red hair but large dark Latin eyes and swarthy skin and Mandy correctly guessed that he was one of the Bradshaw bastards. The head groom, a bent and gnarled man with startling violet eyes in a sun-weathered face, called simply Doc, and the two drivers, George, whom she had already met, and a one-armed man introduced as Lefty. There was Benito, the gardener, to Mandy's surprise Martha's husband even though he was obviously Mexican, and J.B.'s valet, Luis, who seemed as if he should be lord of his own manor, so elegant and aristocratic was he.

"And of course you know Ted Stokes, my foreman," J.B. said, taking Mandy's arm and leading her from the dining room. "He's in town, be back tomorrow some time."

Caleen had stood stiff and rather formidable in her bright *tignon* and black bombazine dress, the stiff folds not the least bit wilted from their long trip in Jeramy's carriage. She had nodded curtly to each one, her tiny shoebutton black eyes seeming to reach into their very souls. Later the servants would shudder and say to one another that it had felt that a spider had crawled over their flesh when the strange, monkey-like creature had scrutinized them so solemnly.

"There're so many servants," Mandy said now, swinging her legs over the side of the bed and going to gaze out of the window. "I don't think I'll ever remember all their names, will you?"

"They all look alike, them," Caleen mumbled. She was lining up Mandy's many slippers on the bottom shelf of the wardrobe, her *tignon* knocked askance, showing wiry wisps of white hair. "Mexes, them, yes."

She straightened and went to another trunk to unpack it.

"I suppose we'll have to get used to them, *Tante* Caleen. California's full of Mexicans and Indians, Mr. Stokes said." She lifted a light sheer curtain beneath the heavy brocade drapes and let it slip through her fingers. Everything in the room was so beautiful, so obviously expensive that Mandy couldn't help but be impressed. "*Grandmaman* would certainly approve of the house, wouldn't she? Have you ever seen anything so—so rich?" Not waiting for an answer, she went on, "And the grounds are so vast—even larger than Grandfather Bertonneau's plantation, Jeramy said."

"He your uncle, him. Not proper for young lady to call her uncle by his Christian name." She shook out a beaver-lined cape of beige wool striped with narrow gold threads and went to hang it in the wardrobe.

"Oh, don't be so stuffy, *Tante* Caleen," Mandy laughed. "He asked me to call him Jeramy. Besides, he's much too young and handsome to call 'uncle'." She went to look through the wardrobe. "I wonder what I should wear to supper? I do so want to make a good impression." She took out a high-necked rose gown and held it against her, wrinkled her tiny nose and put it back. Taking out a white and green sprigged chiffon afternoon dress she held it against her and danced about the room, watching the yards of fabric swirling about her figure.

Caleen shoved a royal blue velvet gown into her hands, taking the chiffon dress and returning it to the closet. "This one you wear. Nice, modest supper gown, yes."

Mandy eyed the gown critically, turning this way and that as she looked at herself in the full-length mirror. "Yes, I think you're right. It's perfect." She tossed the gown casually on the bed and went to peek into the bathroom again. The first time she had seen it she had squealed with pleasure. Gold knobs on the bathtub and sink were sculptured in the shape of swans and the

54

heavy marble slabs of sink and floor were veined in wide slices of gold through the milky white marble. Thick, snow-white sheepskin rugs covered the floor.

"Oh, I do wish *Grandmaman* could see this," she cried, wriggling her bare feet into the soft fur. She wore only a chemise and pantaloons, the new narrow style that were worn under the new slim dresses. She had removed her corset but her slender waist was still ridged in red where the tight laces had been. She rubbed them, dying to scratch the welts but knowing that Caleen would scold her. Well-brought-up young ladies did not scratch themselves. She wondered if she could possibly get away without being harnessed into the uncomfortable corset tonight. How she hated it!

"I wonder what time they serve supper in California," she said, going again to gaze out of the window at the rough, hilly land and wild tangle of trees and scrubs. "I'm simply ravenous!"

"Somebody come to tell you," Caleen said. "You wash now, *ché*." She went into the bathroom and began filling the deep marble tub. It would be heavenly to sink into a scented bath and wash away the dust and fatigue of the road, Mandy thought as she stepped out of her underwear. It seemed forever since she had had a real bath.

She stepped into the hot bubble bath and Caleen set to work scrubbing her back, paying close attention to her ears as she always had since Mandy had been a baby.

"Oh, *Tante* Caleen, I can bathe myself," she said rather crossly, snatching the washcloth from the old woman's hands. "Besides, I want to just lie here a moment and soak and think. You go on and finish unpacking."

Caleen mumbled something under her breath as she left the room and Mandy closed her eyes and leaned her head back against the wide rim of the tub. It had been a little unnerving to meet all her relatives at once, and to have them look her over, their faces not really

55

showing what they thought. Only Atoka had greeted her warmly, and Grandfather Bradshaw, of course. The others had looked at her as if she were something quite odd. Well, perhaps she was. She supposed she looked as strange to them as they did to her. Their voices were so different from those in the South. They were loud and rather boisterous with a slight nasal twang that was neither pleasant nor unpleasant—just different. She hadn't thought about her relatives speaking any differently than anyone else she had ever known, but they most certainly did. And, goodness, they ran their words together so fast that she had a hard time keeping up with them. She remembered how young James had poked his brother, Jon, in the ribs when Mandy had spoken to them, sniggering, "Listen to her Southern accent, Jon," and J.B. had silenced him with a withering glance. "Well, she *does* talk funny," the lad had muttered under his breath, stepping behind his mother's wide skirts.

She had also been surprised to see that Aunt Agnes and Aunt Jane still wore hoop skirts, long out of fashion in the South. They had eyed her narrow, chic gown openly and a bit enviously, Mandy thought. She sighed. Her head spun with all she had seen and heard that day. She wondered if she would ever get used to this strange land of strange people. The Mexicans with their broad, flat dark faces and jet hair in long braids seemed like something out of her history books. The men all were giants, or so it seemed to her. They were as massive and rawboned as the savage-looking terrain she had ridden through. The men in the South were more delicately built, with waists almost as small as a woman's and well-shaped heads that spoke of their aristocratic blood lines. The men she had seen from the train window were hard-eyed, heavy-limbed as timber wolves. She shivered a little, slipping deeper into the hot water, wondering if they were as dangerous as they looked. Every one of them had worn a six-shooter strapped low on his hip like the Western badmen she

56

had seen in picture books. Even her grandfather's groom and drivers had had low-slung pistols strapped to their levi-clad legs and she wondered if Jeramy and J.B. also carried a gun beneath the hem of their fashionable coats.

When the bath water began to turn cool she stepped out and allowed Caleen to towel her dry. She slipped into a burgundy satin robe and sat while Caleen dressed her hair, pulling the long auburn tresses back from her face and tying them at the nape of her neck with a wide ribbon to fall in a cascade of curls halfway down her back.

She was dressed and waiting when the summons came to join the family for supper. The dark blue gown had been a perfect choice. The neckline was just low enough to show off the youthful swell of her breasts and the bodice was snug from shoulder to hip where the gown flared out in soft folds to the floor. Tiny buttons, covered in the same fabric as the gown, ran from neckline to hem down the back and a slim strip of black velvet ribbon edged the neck, sleeves and waist. Her slippers were the same shade of royal blue, tied with black velvet bows and sporting three-inch heels.

She followed the maid (was it Marta or Quina?) down the wide curved stairs and into the parlor where the family was gathered.

"Ah, how lovely you look, my dear," J.B. boomed, rising from a chair to take her hands and draw her into the room. "Well, here she is, Jenny, what did I tell you? Isn't she a beauty?" He led her to a graceful young woman with the Bradshaw red hair and Irish blue eyes who was sitting on a striped satin sofa with a very handsome, dark young man. The woman rose at once, taking Mandy's hands in hers and leaning over to kiss her cheek.

"Amanda, dear, how very good to see you again. My, but you resemble Johnny so much." She smiled at her with such love that Mandy blushed and looked

57

down at the floor. "I'd like you to meet my husband, dear, your Uncle Andy." She gestured to the dark, handsome man and he rose and took Mandy's hand.

"Hello, Amanda, welcome to San Francisco. I hope your stay will be a happy one." He was as handsome as any Frenchman she had seen in New Orleans, with his crisp, curly black hair and eyes the color of spring violets. His eyelashes were as long as a girl's, his teeth very white beneath a trim dark moustache. He bowed over her hand, bringing it to his lips.

"Oh, my dear Amanda, you look so much like your father it's almost like seeing a ghost." Tears sparkled in Jenny's soft blue eyes for a moment as she gazed at Mandy, then she blinked them away and hugged her niece to her. "And like your dear, lovely mother, too, of course," she murmured. She smiled. "And aren't you the grown-up young lady now? I simply adore that gown. I saw a similar style in *Hesperian's* magazine just this past month. I must ask my dressmaker to have a look at it if you don't mind."

"Oh, not at all, Aunt Jenny. I shall be delighted to show you all my gowns, if you'd like." She blushed again, sneaking a peek at Andrew Dunlap. He was as handsome as a stage actor—although she wasn't supposed to know about such men. She and Suzette had slipped away from Caleen one afternoon and gone into one of the threaters on Bourbon Street to sit captivated as they watched a forbidden play, in which glorious men and women dressed like kings and queens from the courts of Europe.

"Do you really think those new fashions are going to catch on in San Francisco, Jenny dear?" Agnes asked, her pale eyes raking Mandy from neck to toes. "I'm not sure I approve of young ladies wearing such figure-revealing gowns."

"I think the new fashions are just marvelous," shy Jane spoke up from her corner of the room.

"You look like a million dollars, Amanda," J.B. said, taking her hand and leading her to a chair next to the fireplace. "Marta," he barked to the Mexican girl standing quietly by the door. "Bring my granddaughter a sherry." Turning to Mandy, he asked, "You are accustomed to sherry before dinner, aren't you?"

"Oh, yes, of course, *Grandpapa*," she said, giving it the French pronunciation, and he raised his bushy eyebrows.

"*Grandpapa?*" he laughed. "Well, that's just about the prettiest thing I've ever been called!" He laughed again and took a sip of his drink. It was not sherry, that Mandy knew. It was a dark amber color and smelled strong, like the whiskey she had sometimes smelled on her father's breath.

She was introduced to Aunt Jenny's two children, a lovely girl of ten, Paula, and her equally handsome little brother, Robert, who was a few years younger. They both had the dark good looks of their father although she could see the strong Bradshaw chin and jawline and Robert had J.B.'s piercing blue eyes.

They sat and chatted, the family talking easily among themselves while Mandy looked from one to the other, too shy yet to speak up. She answered politely when asked about her trip and her relatives in the South, then fell silent when the conversation turned to other topics. Marta announced dinner and they filed into the huge dining room, J.B. personally seating Mandy on his right as he took his place at the head of the table. She wondered where Caleen was, then supposed that she was having her supper in the kitchen with the rest of the servants. There was wine served with each course and by the time they had reached the end of the meal, Mandy's head spun a little and she was suddenly so tired she could hardly keep her eyes open.

J.B. stood, bringing the others to their feet, and called for brandy and coffee to be served in the parlor. He looked down at Mandy and his eyes softened. "Why, our little gal is asleep on her feet," he said gently. Putting his arm about her shoulders he led her to the foot of the wide stairway and said to Jenny, "Take her up to bed, honey, she's plumb tuckered out." Dropping a kiss on her forehead he handed her over to Jenny. "We'll have plenty of time to get acquainted tomorrow, little Amanda. You go along with your Aunt Jenny and get some sleep."

"Thank you, *Grandpapa*," Mandy murmured sleepily, returning his kiss.

"Come along, honey," Jenny said, helping her up the stairs and into her bedroom. She undid the numerous tiny buttons down the back of Mandy's gown and helped her out of it. When she saw the corset she laughed and said, "Oh dear, you'll have to get rid of that awful thing at once. It's much too hot in California for so heavy an undergarment. You'll get heat rash."

"Really?" Mandy said, coming a little awake. "Oh, thank goodness, I hate it but *Tante* Caleen insists that I wear it."

"What does that word mean? We were all trying to guess before you came down for supper." She found Mandy's nightgown already laid out on the bed and helped her into it.

"It means 'dear auntie', or 'dear family friend'—it's an old Creole term of affection." Mandy slipped between the cool sheets and Jenny bent to kiss her goodnight.

"I can't wait for you to tell me all the different customs of the South, of New Orleans," Jenny said, tucking the blankets under her chin. "Father says it's almost like a foreign country because it's mostly made up of French-speaking people. Is that true?"

"Yes, I always spoke French—before the Yankees came." A frown crossed her smooth brow and Jenny kissed her again.

"Well, I simply can't wait to hear everything about it. It must have been fascinating. Perhaps I'll ride over tomorrow, if you feel up to company."

"I'd like that, Aunt Jenny," she answered drowsily, her eyes almost closing.

"Wonderful. We'll have Atoka fix us a picnic lunch and take it to the beach. Would you like that? You used to love the ocean when you were a little girl." Mandy nodded and Jenny stood and went to the door. "Goodnight, dear Amanda, I'm so very glad you've come back to us. And, please, call me Jenny—I feel quite ancient with the 'auntie' label."

Mandy laughed. "That's what Jeramy said, too."

"Yes, you'll find that we Bradshaws are quite the vain peacocks. Well, sleep well, darling, see you tomorrow." The door closed softly behind her and Mandy was asleep before her aunt had reached the top of the stairs.

CHAPTER FOUR

Mandy sat on the window seat in her bedroom, her chin resting in her hands as she gazed moodily down on the red-tiled roofs of the buildings below. She saw Benito working in the garden, his back stooped as he hoed between long neat rows of vegetables. In the two weeks that she had been here, she had seen the seedlings push their green noses out of the dark earth more each day, until now some of them stood almost a foot tall. She raised her eyes and gazed out past the stables to the mountain range beyond and the potpourri of trees, the likes of which she had never seen before.

In the early morning sun the sycamore was beaded with leaf buds that shone like glass, as was the tall cottonwood with leaves so shiny they looked wet. The mighty oak was pale green, a gentle pastel with little golden tassels that looked as if the tree wore a halo when the sun shone through. The elderberry was the brightest green of all, lush against the rugged background. In its branches were meadowlarks and linnets, which sang all day long. The hummingbirds, Mandy had discovered, not only sang all day long but all night as well. Directly below her window was a bright profusion of lilacs and roses, their scent as sweet as honey drifting up to her, and under the eaves she had discovered a swallow's nest. In the far distance pussywillows edged Otter River and now and then she could see the splash of water as playful otters performed a graceful ballet in the early morning sunshine.

She turned away and went to flop on her stomach on

the bed. A wave of homesickness washed over her like a black cloud and she wished Caleen were there to talk to. But Caleen was off in the woods somewhere, picking wild mustard and mushrooms and other herbs that she needed for her beloved Creole food. Mandy smiled a little, remembering the confrontation Caleen had had with Atoka the second day they had been there. She had insisted that she be allowed to cook for Mandy (as well as for herself), as decent folks couldn't live on the foreign food served in the Bradshaw household. She considered the huge slabs of roast beef and venison, wild pheasant and quail barbaric and would softly chant a few words of *gris-gris* over the meat before it was served. Atoka was not accustomed to having anyone in her kitchen, especially not this diminutive foreigner with wild eyes and strange tongue, and the battle was on.

Mandy saw them squaring off, Caleen, just five feet tall, wizened and dusky, her bright *tignon* bobbing with indignation as she confronted the almost-six-foot-tall Yuma Indian, her flat expressionless face so still it might have been carved from stone. J.B. had heard the commotion and had settled it quickly. "Now, Atoka, you're head of the kitchen, but I think you ought to let Caleen here cook a little something once in a while. Do us all good to try something different. Them Frogs can be damn good cooks, I hear tell." Turning on his remarkable charm, he smiled down at Caleen. "And you, Miz Caleen, why you're as much a guest in this house as our Amanda is. You just relax and let somebody do the waiting on you, how about it?"

Thereafter, Atoka handled the morning and evening meals and Caleen, in her glory, prepared light, delectable luncheons which the family, surprisingly, had liked very much. It was almost like being back in the house on Rampart Street when Mandy sat down to a lunch of gumbo or jambalaya, although Caleen insisted the ingredients were not quite the same as those found in the South.

Mandy had been sightseeing almost every day, either with Jeramy or Jenny (whom she adored) and still she was not used to the strange architecture of the buildings. The long, low adobes and stately two- and three-story ranch houses still filled her with wonder, and made her long for New Orleans all the more—for the bright green wrought-iron balconies, that lined the twisting cobbled streets. She missed the balconies, the tall stairways that seemed to leap from building to building, the curious covered bridges and little alleyways piercing from one street to another. She loved the bright window shutters which Caleen would fling open every morning and fold back against the walls to let the lazy sun pour in.

But most of all she missed the sounds and smells of the streets that were always so alive in the early morning. The street vendors peddling their wares, the sound of horses' hooves clip-clopping along the cobblestones as they pulled the ironwheeled wagons that had their own distinctive sound. The grits man tooting his long tin horn, and the cream and cheese woman, laden with baskets of cheeses and cans of fresh cream, crying, "*Bele fromage!*" The smiling sausage man pushing his cart and sing-songing, "*Belles saucisses! Belle chaurice!*" Her favorite had been the *cala* woman who had stopped each morning beneath Mandy's window to gesture toward her laden cart of piping hot rice cakes and sing up to her, "*Belle cala! Tout chaud!*" Then Caleen would hurry outside to stand gossiping in the bright morning sun with the other servant women on Rampart Street who were also purchasing breakfast goodies for the families they served.

Later in the day young ladies would dress in their most becoming gowns and stroll slowly down the tree-shaded paths, flirting behind their parasols if a handsome young man should happen to ride by. How beautiful they had been in their fine silk dresses and ostrich plumes with jewels in their dark hair. The young men stared boldly from their handsome carriages or from the backs of their prancing blooded horses. Of course, Mandy had been too young to join this parade of Creole ladies, but she had seen it all from her window and she and Suzette had often practiced before the mirror for the day when they would be allowed to stroll the cobblestone streets in this age-old ritual, or stop at a tea shop to sip and gossip.

She remembered the elegant broughams, phaetons and barouches that had rattled sedately past her house in the early evening, carrying richly attired young men and women to some exciting ball or theater and how she had waited for the day when she, too, would be escorted in such style. Now she would never be courted in such a manner, she thought sadly. She would be stuck in this heathen land until she dried up and turned as wrinkled and ugly as the women she had seen on her trips with Jeramy and Jenny, the tall, rawboned women in their hopelessly outdated gowns and hairstyles, their faces red and freckled from the relentless California sun, their hands as large as a man's even if they did sport diamonds as big as peacock eggs. (They were *nouveau riche*, Caleen had muttered darkly, their excessive jewels made vulgar by size alone.)

"Is everyone so rich?" Mandy had asked Jeramy one day when they had driven into Sacramento for lunch.

"Most folks around these parts are," Jeramy had laughed. "These people got in on the gold rush before the Easterners picked the hills and rivers dry. And those who didn't are either in lumber or cattle. Very profitable in these times."

Mandy sighed and rolled over on her back, staring up at the ceiling. She was restless and wondered what she could do to amuse herself. Jenny had just discovered that she was pregnant with her third child and the ever-solitious Andy had insisted that she stay in bed until a doctor could get out to the Dunlap ranch to have a look at her. Jeramy was in town with J.B. and Jonathan, and Aunt Agnes was busy in the sewing room. Mandy had to chuckle when she remembered how

65

Aunt Agnes had suddenly approached her one morning, with her dressmaker in tow, and demanded to be shown her entire wardrobe, from chemises to cloaks, then had promptly ordered bolts of fabric, piles of fur, ropes of feathers and lace and set to work planning a complete new wardrobe for herself and her daughter June.

She supposed she could go into the music room and listen to Aunt Jane play the piano (it had been shipped in at great expense from New York, she had said, and was one of only four in all of San Francisco) but as much as Mandy liked Jane, she was a bit boring. Shy, timid Jane could sit all day without uttering a single word.

Mandy got to her feet and went to look out of the window again. Benito still bent over his hoe in the garden and she saw Leftly polishing Jeramy's new rig in the stableyard. The two stableboys, Tim and Pete, were raking manure from the stalls and Doc was putting J.B.'s new palomino stallion through his paces in the holding corral. The great creamy-gold creature was utterly gorgeous with his flaxen mane and tail flowing out as he stepped smartly at the end of Doc's lunging rope. The day was as crisp as a newly printed paper dollar and the sun shone down on the stallion's back, turning him an even deeper shade of gold. J.B. had told her the horse was one of the Cordova strain but had been sired and raised on the Dunlap ranch. The famous Cordova palominos fetched a very high price among the ranchers who could afford them and J.B. now had two studs and ten mares in his herd. He hoped to double the size with this new stallion, whom he had named El Sol.

She saw El Sol fling up his beautiful head and whinny long and loud when a little golden-blonde mare ventured too close to the holding corral. Doc threw a dirt clod at her and she snorted and trotted back to the herd of brood mares near the outer barn. Many of the mares were big with foals, ready to drop at any time,

66

Jeramy had told her, now that spring was here. And she was looking forward to seeing it.

"That's Goldie," Mandy said aloud, watching the little mare trot toward El Sol again. "That's it—I'll take Goldie out for a ride."

She dressed quickly in a riding habit of pale mint green trimmed in a darker green velvet, struggled into tight-fitting knee-high riding boots and pulled her flat hat rakishly over one eye.

Running toward the stable, she waved to Benito and Lefty, then slowed and quietly approached Doc lest she frighten the high-spirited stallion. "Good morning, Doc, lovely day, isn't it?" She leaned her arms on the top rail of the corral and smiled at him.

"Morning, Miz Bradshaw. Yep, mighty fine morning. Spring comin' this late means it'll be a cool summer, not so hot as to burn off the grazin' lands." He dropped the lunging rope and let El Sol canter over to whinny at the brood mares.

"I'd like to take Goldie out for a ride. Would you saddle her for me, please?"

"Sure thing, Miz Bradshaw." His beautiful violet eyes, unusal for a man so gnarled and weatherbeaten, smiled kindly into hers, then he turned and gave an ear-splitting whistle, bellowing, "Tim! Get yourself out there and catch Goldie fer Miz Bradshaw!" He was such a small man, hands and feet as tiny and dainty as a woman's, but she had seen him lift a yearling in his arms and carry it into the barn for doctoring. Jeramy had told her that he was the best veterinarian for miles around and did not limit his practice to livestock. If someone from the neighboring villages or ranches took sick and the doctor could not be reached, he had seen ole Doc stitch up a nasty wire cut or deliver a baby with the same tender care and expertise.

"You stay on the property now, Miz Bradshaw, ma'am, ya hear?" He spat a stream of brown tobacco juice into the dust at his feet. "J.B.'s orders, ya understand."

67

"Oh, I will, Doc," she said with a tiny laugh. "Goodness, it would take me a week just to ride to the border of *Grandpapa's* property, wouldn't it?"

Doc guffawed and spat again. "Yep, reckon it'd be about that long ta ride up ta the mountain range and then some. Pretty big spread, ya know." He caught the lead rope from Tim's hand as the boy came to a running halt near the holding corral. "Take 're around back and brush 're down, boy, then get out Miz Bradshaw's saddle and see that it don't need no repairs. Can't have our gal gettin' unseated."

When J.B. had learned that Mandy rode sidesaddle he had had quite a time finding a saddle for her until he remembered that his late wife had also ridden in such a manner. The saddle had been found in the tack room and completely refurbished for Mandy's use. "Now this is just temporarily, honey," J.B. had said. "Just until you learn to ride astride."

Mandy had been appalled. Ride straddling the hourse like a man? It was unthinkable. But she had humored him, saying she would learn as soon as she was accustomed to the western terrain and strange gait of the horses.

Doc gave her a leg up and doffed his wide-brimmed western hat. "Watch out fer rattlers, now, ya hear? They comes out this time o' year."

"What are they?" Mandy took the reins and adjusted her skirt over her legs.

"Rattlers, ma'am—snakes, ya know?" Doc tested the cinch, grunting in satisfaction that Tim had gotten it tight enough, and patted Goldie's blonde rump. "Don't tell me you ain't never seed a rattler afore?"

"No," Mandy laughed. "I haven't. What do they look like?" The tiny tree snakes, water and garter snakes in the South had posed no problem; only the dangerous water moccasins were to be feared.

"They's deadly critters," Doc said, checking Goldie's bit and pulling her long flaxen forelock free from the headstall. "Big ugly bastards—beggin' yore pardon, ma'am. Sometimes they's gray, sometimes black or brown, but they always got big square-like diamonds down their ornery backs. You see one, you hightail it t'other way, ya hear?"

"I certainly will, Doc, thank you for the warning." She was impatient to be off on her ride but Doc had more to say.

"Well, 'I won't worry none. Goldie here'll smell'em afore you can see 'em. Horses always know when they's a snake around." He checked her saddle again, and made sure her boot was in the stirrup properly. "You should oughta take a canteen with ya, ma'am. It can get mighty thirsty out on a hot day like this 'un."

"Oh, no thank you, Doc. I'll stop at a brook if I want a drink of water. Thank you so much for your concern." She turned Goldie and began trotting toward the gate, Doc walking fast beside her, his short bandy legs almost on a stride with the mare's. He unlatched the gate and slapped Goldie's rump, causing the little mare to crow-hop through and almost unseat Mandy. She steadied her with a practiced hand on the reins and turned to wave. "Goodbye, thank you, and please don't worry. I'll be careful."

"See that ya are. Wouldn't like to have J.B. on my ass—beggin' yore pardon—fer losin' his favorite granddaughter, ya understand." He grinned, then called after her. "Watch out fer them rattlers now, ya hear? And thar could be a coyote or two around this time o' year, so ya be careful now . . ."

Good heavens, Mandy thought as she kicked Goldie into a lope to get away from the little man's warnings. She rode between two rows of towering eucalyptus trees that led away from the barn and beyond the horse pasture where the brood mares were kept. It was crisp and fresh in the shade of the trees and when occasionally the sun fell upon her face it felt as welcoming as a kiss.

She turned at the end of the path toward the rolling hills where the terrain was dotted with clumps of woody chaparral, Joshua trees, and bright golden poppies as yellow as spilled butter in the sun. She jumped Goldie over a fallen log, then slowed her to wade carefully through a quickly moving stream, swollen with the melting snows from the mountains. The mare snorted and put her head down and Mandy lossened her grip on the reins to allow her to drink. She buried her nose in the cold water and snorted playfully, one hoof pawing at the pebbles in the bottom of the creek.

"That's enough, Goldie" Mandy laughed. "You just want to play." She pulled her head up and the mare pranced out of the stream and broke into a canter up the little embankment, wanting to run. "Let's go!" Mandy cried, digging her heels in and letting the palomino have her head. She galloped across the rough land, jumping over patches of chaparral that were too impenetrable to run through, her flaxen mane blowing back against Mandy's hands. The sun beat down, warming her face and she reached up to tilt the hat further down over her eyes. *I refuse to turn into an old piece of leather like these Western women*, she thought grimly, tugging the hat firmly into place.

She let the mare run until they were both exhausted, then turned her toward a clump of trees that circled a small pond. Pulling Goldie to a halt, she saw that the pond was actually just a widened part of the same stream she had followed most of the way from the ranch. Beavers had dammed it off on a small rise and a pretty, small waterfall fell a few feet to splash into the pond. She dismounted, took off her hat, and shook out her long hair. She lifted it off her neck, welcoming the cooling breeze that dried the fine mist of perspiration, then secured it on top of her head with a pin. She shrugged off the short jacket of her riding habit and unbuttoned the top two buttons of her sheer white blouse. Her feet felt hot and sweaty in the hightopped riding boots and she pulled them off as well, wiggling her toes in the cool grass. She leaned back, felt something wet and looked about her. She was sitting beneath a plum tree and some of the overripe fruit had fallen to

70

the ground where it had squashed beneath her hands.

"Fa!" she said aloud and went to wash her hands in the pond. The water was cool and she splashed some on her face before lying back on the grass. The plum trees formed a perfect umbrella and she gazed up through the leaves and boughs and saw blue patches of sky and bright sunlight. The sun was white-hot, glaring into her eyes, and she rolled over until she was completely in the shade, then closed her eyes briefly. It was so quiet, so peaceful, she was afraid she might fall asleep. She opened her eyes to stare into the eyes of a sharp-beaked linnet who immediately flew away, squawking. A fat red squirrel ran swiftly down the tree trunk, chattering excitedly at her, then stopped and stood on its hind legs, cocking its head.

"Hello, little fellow," she said softly. "How beautiful you are." The squirrel turned and darted up the tree, disappearing among the branches, then just as quickly reappeared to stare down at her once more. Beyond the plum trees vast acres of white, black and purple sage spread ball-like flowers over the ground, sending a strong, pungent odor to her nostrils. It was so beautiful and peaceful that she lay still for many moments, listening to the quiet, to the soft sibilant rustling of a breeze in the trees, the far-off cry of a sparrow hawk and somewhere the sound of dogs barking. She remembered Jeramy telling her that the Basque sheepherders used dogs to tend their flocks but surely there were no sheep on Bradshaw property.

She thought she heard the angry squall of a wild cat and remembered Jeramy saying that the mountain range dividing J.B.'s property from the Cordovas' was called Los Gatos—Mountain of the Cats. She raised herself on her elbows and looked out across the land at the high bulks of rocky mountains that he had pointed out to her on the day of her arrival. Los Gatos, what a wonderfully romantic-sounding name, she thought, almost hating to admit that she found the Spanish language pretty. She must have ridden farther than she had

71

intended for she was close enough to see the mountains clearly and the faint outline of a fence in the distance.

She saw a plum lying near her on the grass, picked it up and polished it on her skirt, looking for bruises. Finding none, she bit into the juicy fruit and found it delicious. She should have asked Caleen to pack her a light lunch. Next time she would. She ate another plum, then walked to the water's edge and sat down, dangling her feet in the ripples from the waterfall. A few droplets splashed on her pale green skirt, and she quickly jerked her feet out. Caleen would scold her if she spotted her new riding habit. She wished she could just take it off for a few minutes and wade in the clear, shallow pool, just to cool her burning feet and refresh herself for the long ride back. The skirt was heavy and cumbersome, fashioned to protect her legs as she rode. "Oh, fa, why not? Who will know?" she said aloud, then laughed up at the curious squirrel who had jumped at the sound of her voice. She stepped out of the skirt and laid it carefully over her saddle. Goldie was contentedly grazing in the knee-high grass and she loosened her cinch and slipped the bit out of her mouth.

She shivered as the cooling breeze swept over her half-nude body. She wore only thigh-length, snug-fitting britches, lace-trimmed, and a chemise beneath her white blouse. She stepped into the pond and gasped at the biting cold as the water circled her ankles and calves. "It's cold," she said aloud, needing to hear the sound of her voice in this quiet little wooded cove. Wading out into the center of the pond, she splashed water on her face and the back of her neck, not caring if she got her underwear wet. Made of light cotton, it would dry quickly and not show a spot.

She splashed and played in the pool like a child, and like a child she had thought only that she would be punished if she soiled her new clothes. It did not occur to her how she must look in her scanty underwear, her figure as lush and bewitching as a full-grown woman's.

72

Her every curve was clearly outlined by the wet garment so that she might as well have been naked.

So engrossed was she in trying to catch the elusive minnows that streaked by her ankles she didn't see the rider approach until he was almost upon her. Hearing Goldie whinny, she glanced up to see a huge black stallion prancing toward her, his answering whinny piercing the quiet. A rider dressed in the black velvet pants and short bolero jacket of the Spanish don, lavishly trimmed in silver and turquoise, sat easily upon the dancing stallion's back. His flat black hat was cocked at a rakish angle over one eye, the sweatband trimmed in silver dollars and turquoise nuggets the size of robin's eggs. He was so handsome she could not take her eyes off his face.

He drew the horse to a halt near the edge of the pool and sat staring down at her with a lazy grin upon his full-lipped mouth. Still she could not move, but stood, her wet underwear clinging seductively to her body, staring back at him.

"Well, well, what have we here?" he said softly, his dark eyes travelling slowly over every inch of her body. "A water nymph, is it?" He chuckled softly as he threw his leg over the saddle horn and slid gracefully to the ground. "What's the matter, Aphrodite, cat got your tongue?"

Mandy's lips trembled so she could not utter a sound. She lifted her hands to her breasts, shivering as the waterfall splashed behind her, sending a fine spray over her already soaking body.

"Ah, a little Mex gal, eh?" The man pushed the brim of his hat back with one long, tanned finger. A huge diamond flashed on his hand. "*Habla Ud. español, señorita? Como se llama?*"

Mandy still could not find her voice and backed quickly away, her eyes wide with fright.

The man in black swept his hat off with a courtly bow. "*Mucho gusto en conocerla. Me llamo Bret Dunlap. Vive Ud. aqui?*" His brown eyes grew darker, almost as black as his outfit, as he stared at her as no man ever had before. His look made her legs tremble and her heart pound even faster.

Finding her voice at last, she cried, "Oh, go away, please! Leave me alone!" She made a wild dash for the bank, slipped and fell, and was fished out by the stranger, spluttering and gasping. Twisting free from his grasp, she lunged toward Goldie, snatching at her skirt, but the man had her again, holding her easily as he laughed down at her.

"Ah, so you do speak English." He looked at her face, at her huge blue eyes now wide with fear. "Half-breed—must be with those big blue eyes. And some beauty, too, aren't you, señorita?" Without warning his lips came down on hers and his strong arms drew her close to his chest, so close she could feel the hard lumps of turquoise on his jacket. She tried to twist out of his grip but he held her easily, almost casually, and continued to kiss her.

Mandy gagged when he forced his tongue between her teeth, then bit down on it as hard as she could and tasted blood. With a yelp of pain he released her and she flung herself at Goldie, clawing for the saddle horn, but the loosened cinch let the saddle slip with her weight, pulling it under the frightened mare's belly.

"Why, you little hellcat!" the man gritted between clenched teeth and she had the satisfaction of seeing blood on his mouth.

He slapped her full in the face, knocking her to the ground. Then he was upon her, tearing the wet blouse and chemise from her body with one violent yank. Her breasts sprang free and she screamed aloud when he lowered his head and began kissing them.

"That's it, honey," he panted softly. "Fight me—go on. Nothing I like better than taming a wild filly." His hands slipped down to probe between her thighs. She raised her knee and tried to kick him, but he slapped her leg away as if it were a pesky fly, then trapped both her legs beneath his weight.

"No, damn you, stop it! I will kill you if you touch me! I will kill you!" Biting, clawing, punching with every vestige of her strength, she managed to wiggle out from under him and was on her feet and racing toward the black stallion and the rifle she had seen in the saddle holster. The big horse shied away, rolling his eyes and snorting a warning, but she clawed the rifle from the holster and whirled about just as the man reached for her again.

"My, you do play rough, don't you, honey?" he said in the same lazy voice. To her further chagrin he actually chuckled as he wrenched the rifle from her hands.

She wheeled around and started toward Goldie once more but he reached out a hand and captured her again, pulling her back into his arms as if he were reeling in a fish. Staying away from her sharp teeth, he kissed her throat and the tops of her breasts, his hands sliding knowledgeably down her back and buttocks, urging her closer. This time when she brought up her knee, it found its mark. Gasping, he sank to his knees, both hands going protectively to his groin, and she made a dive for the rifle, scooping it up before he could rise.

"Don't move," she cried, her voice trembling with fear and rage. "If you so much as blink, I'll blow your head off!" Tears ran down her cheeks and she wiped them away with the back of her hand, as a child would.

"Hey now, honey, easy with that peashooter," he said softly, but she could see the fear in his eyes. "I didn't mean no harm. Hell, I thought you'd be willing, what with being half-naked out here in the middle of nowhere, trespassing and all—"

"This is my grandfather's range!" Keeping the rifle levelled on him she groped behind her for her skirt and jacket. She stooped and picked them up, holding them in front of her as best she could while she still held the rifle. "You are the trespasser, you—you blackguard!

75

And—and *Grandpapa* will kill you when I tell him what you tried to do!"

"Grandfather?" He sat back on the ground, staring up at her with his mouth open. "You don't mean J.B. Bradshaw, do you?" He shook his head and actually laughed out loud. "No, it couldn't be—you can't be—no, no—"

"I am J.B. Bradshaw's granddaughter from New Orleans, sir." She wished her lips would stop trembling and that the rifle wasn't so heavy. It sagged in her hands and she jerked it back up to her shoulder, aiming directly for his head. She brought her chin up defiantly and said with as much authority as she could muster. "I'm taking you back to the ranch with me and when *Grandpapa* hears what you have done to me, he will see that you are hanged. He will kill you happily!" In her anger her French accent became more pronounced and the man on the ground groaned and fell over on his side, rolling over as he doubled up with laughter.

"Oh, Christ," he gasped between spluttering laughter. "I've done it this time. Jesus, J.B.'s French granddaughter. The old man will kill me, all right." Sobering, he sat up and looked at her, making his expression as innocent as possible. "Miss Bradshaw, I'm terribly sorry. God, you'll never know how sorry. I had no idea—I mean, who would have thought I'd run into old man Bradshaw's granddaughter taking a nude dip under a waterfall miles from anywhere."

"I was not nude, you cad!" She stamped her bare feet, glaring at him furiously. "How dare you speak such words to me, you—you vulgar person!"

"This has gone on long enough." Leaping nimbly to his feet he was upon her before she knew what had happened, wrenching the rifle from her hands. "Now just stand there and listen like a good little girl, okay?" he said with great patience. "My name is Bret Dunlap. I've known J.B. since the day I was born. Your Aunt Jenny is married to my brother, Andrew. I am sincerely sorry that I mistook you for a Mexican girl looking for

76

a little, shall we say, adventure. But you must admit you look more like a peasant girl in your present state of undress than you do a member of the elegant Bradshaw family." He shrugged, grinning, his white teeth flashing beneath the dark moustache. "It was an honest mistake and one I freely admit. But I do apologize ever so profusely, Miss Bradshaw." He made a courtly bow but she saw the laughter in his dark eyes and felt her cheeks flush crimson. The lout was laughing at her! "Now, if you will allow me to escort you back to the ranch—"

"Don't you dare touch me!" she cried, moving quickly backward. "I'll—I'll scream!"

"That would just frighten the horses, Miss Bradshaw. You wouldn't want to do that, now would you?" He started toward her and she screamed and ran wildly the other way, tripping and falling into the pond. This time he didn't even try to control his amusement but stood on the bank looking down at her, laughing as he watched her struggle to her feet, only to slip on the smooth slippery pebbles and fall flat again.

Choking, crying, her long hair wet and dripping into her face, she stumbled up the embankment, grabbing his hand and allowing him to pull her out. "I hate you!" she sobbed, flinging herself face down on the grassy shore and pounding her fists on the ground. "I hate you! I hate you! I wish I were a man so I could beat you up!"

Bret chuckled as he watched her throwing what could only be described as a temper tantrum. "How old are you, honey?" he asked.

"I am seventeen and when *Grandpapa* hears what you have done to me he will kill you for me!" She saw her skirt and jacket crumpled on the ground next to her and grabbed them, covering herself. Seeing dark water stains on the pale green fabric she broke into a fresh torrent of tears. "Oh, *Tante* Caleen will scold me for ruining my new habit. You—you cad! You are a terrible man and I wish I could kill you!"

"You're certainly bloodthirsty for such a pretty young thing," Bret grinned. He went to his horse and removed a silver-edged serape from behind the saddle, shook it out and gently covered her trembling form. He shook out her skirt and jacket, smoothing the expensive fabric as he hung them over a branch. "No damage done that I can see. A little damp here and there, but it'll dry fast in this sun." He spoke easily, friendly, as if this were an everyday occurrence. "Now, why don't you sit up and dry your eyes? I said I was sorry. It was an honest mistake and I promise I won't come within a country yard of you, okay?"

Mandy drew the serape around her, making sure it covered every inch of flesh from ankles to neck, then faced him sullenly. "You'd better not or my *Grandpapa* will—"

Holding up one slim elegant hand, the diamond flashing, Bret sighed. "I know—he will kill me. Damn, are you always so hard-nosed?" He went again to his horse and removed his saddlebags, then sat down across from her, leaning comfortably back against the tree trunk. "I don't know about you, but a good fight always puts an edge on my appetite. Care to join me for a little bit of roast beef and biscuits?"

"How can you think of eating at a time like this?" She was outraged by his blasé attitude.

"I am not the one who was almost ravished, my dear," he chuckled, unwrapping the roast beef from a linen napkin. "And I am hungry. I've been riding since early this morning, and planned on stopping for a little picnic by my favorite water hole—never dreaming that I would find it occupied—before going on home. Our spread is just the other side of Otter River, about ten miles that way." He motioned out across the vast acres of chaparral and sagebrush toward a forest looming in the far distance. "Just beyond those woods. But surely you've been to the ranch, if I know Mother. She would have seen to it that J.B. brought you over."

She stared at him, her lips pursed tightly together. He

shrugged and reached into his saddlebags for a bottle of wine and a tin cup. He poured some, took a sip, and grimaced in pain.

"Jesus, that hurts." Gingerly fingering his tongue where she had bitten him, he took another swallow of wine, swished it around in his mouth, then spit it out. "You're the goddamndest bloodthirsty little gal I've *ever* seen. J.B. won't have to worry about you being able to take care of yourself, that's for sure!"

"I am glad it hurts! I wish I could kill you!" She shivered under the serape, wishing she could move into the warming rays of the sun, but still a little frightened of this strange man.

Bret smiled and shook his head in amusement. Taking a tin cup from his saddlebags, he poured it half full of wine and held it out to her. "Here, drink this. It'll keep the chill away."

She stared at him until he set the cup on the ground and went back to his spot beneath the tree, then she crawled forward and snatched it up. Taking a big swallow she coughed and tears sprang to her eyes. It was the strongest wine she had ever tasted but it warmed her and eased the tight knot of panic in her stomach. The second swallow went down easier and she drank again, almost losing her serape as she held the cup with both hands.

"Sure you won't have some roast beef? It's really quite good. A specialty of the Lacey Palace." He chuckled, his dark eyes flashing with secret amusement. "I hasten to add, just *one* of the many varied specialties of the Lacey Palace." He took a bite of biscuit and roast beef, leaning back against the trunk as if he were having a pleasant picnic with a willing companion. He sipped his wine, then patted his mouth with the elegant white linen napkin the roast beef had been wrapped in. Mandy saw an intricate monogram in raised gold silk thread, L.P. and made a mental note to ask Jenny or Jeramy what that place was.

She sipped her wine, watching Bret Dunlap eat and

drink. He was incredibly handsome, she grudgingly admitted, even more so than his brother, Andy. But Andy was a gentleman and this blackguard, Bret, was a true cad. Still, he did possess a certain charm when he wasn't teasing her. She let her gaze travel over his long lanky legs, up his flat stomach and broad chest to his well-shaped head, seeing thick glossy black hair with shaggy sideburns and a perfectly enchanting, debonair moustache above full sensual lips. He had dimples high up in his cheeks, and his eyes were the softest velvet brown she had ever seen. Jenny had told her the four Dunlap boys were all dark and handsome because of their mother's French-Indian blood.

"Would you like a little more wine?" He refilled her cup before she could protest.

"Thank you," she mumbled sullenly, then thought, *Good heavens, what am I doing sitting here so casually sipping wine with my would-be rapist?* It was too ludicrous for words. And yet she was still a little frightened of him, a little afraid that he might finish what he had started. All men were animals and blackguards. She drank her wine, watching him as he finished the roast beef and biscuit sandwich, then poured himself more wine.

"You still going to tell J.B. I tried to rape you?" he asked matter-of-factly, as if inquiring about the weather.

"I most certainly am! You are a despicable man and you must be punished!" Her eyes blazed hatred and her lips trembled. Her hair was drying in the sun, curling softly against her serape-covered shoulders, and Bret thought that he had never seen a more lovely creature. "If a Southern gentleman did what you have done, he would be called out for a duel! Oh, how I wish I were a man so that I might have the pleasure of killing you myself!"

"If you were a man, my dear, there would be no cause for a duel, now would there?" He smiled lazily, a suggestive expression in his dark eyes. "Are all French

80

ladies so violently protective of their honor? I've run into my share of coy ladies but never have I been threatened with death so often in so short a time. Hell, all I did was steal a little kiss. Nothing wrong with that. Most ladies out here would consider it a compliment."

"I do not consider it so, monsieur! I consider it an insult and one that shall be avenged!"

Bret chuckled at her anger. "It must be that French blood that makes you so damn bloodthirsty. I've heard Creoles have a violent temper when aroused." He let his gaze travel over her. "Are you aroused, my dear?"

"How dare you speak to me so!" Leaping to her feet, she gazed imperiously down at him. "Please leave now. I do not wish to speak further with you!"

"Let me tell you something before you go off half-cocked. J.B. isn't likely to find your tale of horror amusing. In fact, I'd wager that it'd make him down-right unhappy. Young ladies out here do not run screaming for a duel, unless, of course, they have been compromised quite seriously. Then it's not a duel but a matter of justice. We drag the culprit to the nearest tree and string him up." He lit a cheroot and leaned back, sipping his wine. "You, my dear, were not compro-mised."

"I was so! You touched me! You put your filthy hands on my body!"

Bret shrugged. "Like the mountain climber said, it was there. Like ripe fruit, already peeled and ready to eat." He grinned at her, his dark eyes mischievous. "A young lady of good breeding does not go around taking nude baths under waterfalls."

"You—you are beneath contempt, sir! I was not nude!" She stamped her bare foot and Bret laughed out loud.

"Well, perhaps not technically, but your wet togs cer-tainly left nothing to the imagination, my dear. You may as well have been as naked as a jaybird." He tilted his head to look up into her face. "And, I'm afraid that's what I'll have to tell J.B. if he 'calls me out' as you so gallantly put it in the South."

Mandy gasped, her hand going to her mouth and the serape dipped dangerously low over one breast before she jerked it back together. "You would not!"

He shrugged, spreading his hands helplessly before him. "Man has the right to defend himself, tell his side."

"Oh, you—you are worse than a cad! You are a bastard! How dare you imply that I led you on!"

"Now, Miss Bradshaw, ma'am, I'd appreciate it if you didn't bring my parentage into this. My, such a vocabulary for one so young and genteelly bred." He was plainly laughing at her and she stamped her foot again, her cheeks burning.

"Get out of here!" she cried, rushing to snatch her clothes off the branch. "Get out of my sight! I hate you! I never wish to see you again!"

"By your leave, madam," he murmured, stood and bowed. "I trust you can find your way home without further, ah—adventure?" He tidied up his saddlebags and slung them over the stallion's back, then mounted gracefully. He tipped his hat, sweeping it before him with a flourish. "A real pleasure meeting you, mademoiselle. Au revoir." He put his heels to the stallion's sides and was off in a streak of black and silver.

Mandy stood staring after him, tembling with rage. How dare he threaten her! The vulgar Yankee bastard! How she hated him. She would see him dead if it was the last thing she did. No man would ever again put his hands on her without paying dearly. She dressed with shaking hands, buttoning her jacket all the way to her chin to hide her torn blouse. She pulled on her boots and went to tighten Goldie's cinch. Just wait until she told J.B. what this Bret Dunlap person had done to her. She swung into the saddle and headed toward the ranch at a hard gallop.

* * *

Mandy rushed into the house, calling for her grandfather. Marta appeared silently and told her that he was in San Francisco with Jonathan and Jeramy, then just as silently disappeared. Mandy dashed through the quiet orderly rooms, looking for someone to whom to tell her tale of terror. Aunt Agnes was still upstairs in the sewing room and she could hear Aunt Jane practicing her piano. Caleen was still out in the woods gathering herbs and the house was so still and peaceful that Mandy felt betrayed. Someone should be waiting to hear what had happened to her. But everything was exactly as it had been when she had left that morning. Nothing had changed while she had fought for her life—well, her honor, anyway.

Her shoulders slumped as she walked sullenly upstairs to her bedroom and closed the door. Her anger subsided and she began to feel a little foolish. Obviously, ladies in the West were not held in such high regard as they were in the South. She remembered Jeramy telling her on the day she had arrived that she would have to get used to a tougher kind of life than she had known in New Orleans. Well, she would get tough all right. She would get a gun and keep it with her at all times. If men insisted on putting their hands on her she would be ready for them.

Grimly she stripped off her clothes, stuffing her torn blouse and underwear into the bottom of her closet for fear Caleen would question her. Perhaps men in the West did not defend women, but *Tante* Caleen certainly would. She would mix up a strong batch of *voudou magnian* and turn the insufferable Bret Dunlap into a toad. She smiled suddenly. Perhaps she should tell Caleen instead of her grandfather.

She stooped over to fill the tub with water and saw a tiny bruise on her left breast. With a small cry she fingered the bruise, then rubbed it almost furiously as if she could erase it from her skin. Standing before the full-length mirror, she examined every inch of her body, feeling the sore spots where he had held her so savagely. She discovered a couple more small bruises and was swept with unreasonable anger. How dare any man touch her so intimately? It was an outrage. But one that would never be repeated. This she solemnly swore to herself.

Sinking into the tub she scrubbed every inch of her flesh, then lay back and closed her eyes, soaking for several minutes. As much as she hated to admit it, she knew that Bret Dunlap had been telling the truth when he had said that she was in no position to cry rape. She had been in state of undress when he had ridden up. She could well imagine what he must have thought. Her mother had told her the facts of life the day she reached puberty and had explained that she must always be demure in dress and manner or she would give gentlemen the wrong opinion of her. With her scanty undergarments plastered to her wet figure she certainly must have given Bret Dunlap the wrong opinion. However, she stubbornly told herself, he was still a blackguard. He had insisted on teasing her and baiting her in a most ungentlemanly manner even after he had discovered her true identity. For this disrespectful impudence, she would never forgive him.

A light knock sounded on the door and she called out, "Yes? Who is it, please?"

"It's me, Jane. May I come in, please?"

"Yes, of course. I am in the bath but do come in, Jane. She sat up in the tub and arranged the bubbles to hide her breasts, especially the bruised one.

Jane entered shyly, stopping in the dressing room to sit in one of the brocade chairs. "Mandy, dear, I have the most wonderful news! We have been invited to the Dunlaps for supper this evening and you will at last meet Derek." She blushed furiously, her already pink face turning a bright red. She had spoken often of Derek Dunlap, the third son, with whom she had been in love with since they both were ten years old. And that was the problem, she had sighed. Derek still thought of her as a child even though she was almost twenty-three

84

years old. "Almost an old maid," she had laughed with embarrassment. "Why, even young June has more beaux than I do!"

"What did you say?" Mandy gasped, sitting straight up in the tub to peer around the door at her young aunt.

"We have been invited to take supper with the Dunlaps this evening," Jane repeated. "Jenny came over earlier today while you were out riding and said that Bret was due home today from New York where he has just closed some big business deal, and Marie is having a small celebration for him. Oh, Mandy, just wait until you meet Bret. He's almost as handsome as my Derek." She flushed, ducking her head. "I didn't mean that— he's certainly not my Derek. I only wish that he were."

"Tonight?" Mandy repeated faintly.

"Yes, I wanted to let you know before you dressed." She stood and went to Mandy's wardrobe and slid open the doors. "Oh, Mandy, you have so many beautiful gowns, how in the world do you ever decide what to wear?" She ran her fingers through the soft fur of a mink-trimmed cape, sighing, "I wish I could wear something this elegant, but I'm such a beanpole I would just look silly."

"Oh no, Jane, I think you'd look quite grand in the new styles. The slim cut is especially made for slender figures." Her mind was spinning with images of Bret Dunlap, his lips seeking hers, his ringed fingers gripping her bare shoulders, his dark head leaning toward her. . . . She stepped quickly out of the tub and towelled herself dry. "Why don't you try one on?" She slipped into her robe and belted it with trembling fingers. What should she do? If she refused to go she would arouse suspicion at home and hurt Marie's feelings. She wanted very much to scream out what Bret Dunlap had done to her, but was afraid that she would be the one to look foolish. She knew that J.B. was especially fond of the Dunlap family. Obviously, their word would stand for more than hers.

"Oh, I couldn't, really," Jane said, giving Mandy a shy smile as her niece walked into the bedroom.

"But of course you must." Mandy selected a light wool dress of pale blue trimmed in a darker blue at neck and wrists. "Here, try this. See, the waist can be adjusted by this sash. Go on, Jane, try it on."

"Well, all right, but I'm sure it won't fit. I'm so thin in the—in my—uh—bosom area." She flushed furiously and ducked her head again.

Mandy pushed the gown into her hands and grinned saucily. "That can easily be remedied. We simply stuff your chemise with stockings or something."

Jane gasped. "Oh, Mandy, I couldn't!" She turned to let Mandy unbutton her dress and slip the blue gown over her head.

"Maybe you won't have to. It looks wonderful on you, Jane." She hooked the snaps in the back and wrapped the sash about Jane's narrow waist, spreading the folds high under her bust, then tying it in a large bustle-type bow in the back. She turned her and adjusted the soft gathers at the neckline to give her a fuller bosom.

Jane stared at herself in the full-length mirror, not believing what she saw. The gown did indeed look wonderful on her, the wide sash accentuating her waist and adding curves to her lean hips, giving her a softly rounded look. The gathers, as well as the thickness of the fabric, added inches to her bustline and set off to perfection the creamy texture of her milk-white skin. The blue made her otherwise pale eyes seem to grow brighter and the flush in her cheeks was pleasing rather than timid. "Oh, I'm beautiful!" she whispered; then, realizing what she had said, she blushed crimson, turning her freckles to blotches. "Oh, Mandy, I didn't mean—"

"I know what you meant, dear Jane," Mandy laughed, hugging her little aunt to her. "You do look beautiful. Why shouldn't you say it?"

Jane raised her chin and looked at herself again.

"Yes," she said firmly. "Yes, I *do* look beautiful. Oh, I can't wait until Derek sees me!" Then she buried her hands in her frizzy hair and wailed, "Oh, Mandy, what can I do with this dreadful hair?"

"Caleen will dress it for you. Where is she, anyway? Shouldn't she be back by now?" She went to the window and looked out at the late afternoon sun slanting toward the mountains.

"I heard her in the kitchen just before I came up to see you," Jane said, still admiring herself in the mirror.

"Good, then she will have plenty of time to do your hair before I'm ready for mine." She took a blue velvet ribbon from a rack on her dressing table and handed it to Jane. "Tell her to use this in your hair and perhaps a couple of those lovely lilacs in the courtyard." She smiled as she led Jane to the door. "You will be a jewel when *Tante* Caleen finishes with you, *chérie*. And your Derek, he will fall in love with you as if a *mamaloi* had cast a spell of *voudou magnian* over him!"

"Oh, Mandy," Jane laughed. "You and your witches and magic potions. We don't believe in things like that out here in the West."

"*Mon Dieu*! Do not let *Tante* Caleen hear you say you do not believe, *chérie*, or she will cast a spell just to prove her powers!" She giggled and then both girls were laughing. Caleen had set the Bradshaw household on its ear the first week they had been there with her ominous mumblings in African, her mumbo-jumbo in Creole, and her darkly muttered pidgin English. Jane had actually been frightened of her until Mandy had explained that Caleen was harmless and all her *voudou magnian* amounted to was a string of Creole curses offered to some African god thousands of miles away.

They kissed one another's cheeks, then Mandy closed the door and went to sit at her dressing table to brush her hair. Instead of her image in the mirror she saw the darkly handsome face of Bret Dunlap, a cocky smile on his full lips. How could she possibly face him tonight? For go she must. When a dinner invitation was issued, the entire household went or it would be considered a gross insult. She had been to the Dunlap ranch twice before to visit Jenny but both times the sons had been at their jobs in San Francisco. Marie had proudly showed her photographs of her four sons, and Mandy had thought them all quite gorgeous, if men could be called gorgeous. And she would have to say that Marie Dunlap, the matriarch of the enormous ranch, was incredibly handsome.

She was of French-Indian descent and had the high cheekbones, chisled jawline, and dark liquid eyes of her race. A nose that would have been overpowering on a lesser woman gave Marie Dunlap a look of classic beauty. Her mouth was wide and sensual, gently tilted up at the corners even when she was in repose, a mouth that spoke of tasting many pleasures and finding none bitter. She was tall and had the graceful body of a young feline even though she admitted to being in her early fifties. She had had an affair with J.B. when they were both what she had laughingly called "youngsters." "He was mining then," Marie had told Mandy. "And one day he invited me out to his claim to meet his partner, Andy Dunlap." She laughed softly at the memory. "Well, I took one look at that tall, handsome, blue-eyed rascal and it was goodbye, J.B." Their marriage had lasted thirty-two years and yielded four sons, ending in tragedy just five years ago when Andrew Sr. had been gunned down by a drunken cowboy who had mistaken him for someone else.

Andrew Jr., Jenny's husband, was the eldest at thrity-two the "dependable one," Marie always called him. He had taken over the running of the vast holdings with the same efficiency and quiet enthusiasm as his father. Where his brothers had always been wanderlusts, Andy preferred to tend the home fires and Marie credited him with holding the family together with his quiet strength.

Then there was Tod, about thirty, Mandy remembered, as darkly handsome as his brothers but with a slightly devilish expression that Mandy had found perfectly delightful. And Jane's Derek, certainly as handsome as his brothers, and finally Bret.

"Bret's the baby of the bunch," Marie had said. "And I'm afraid we've spoiled him rotten. Can't get that little rascal to settle down for more than a couple of months and then he's off again, across country to New York City or sailing off to Europe." She had shaken her head, smiling ruefully at Mandy. The serene beauty of her face, the proud, almost haughty way she held her head belied the earthy, cowboyish way she spoke and Mandy was still amazed at the contradiction.

He was spoiled all right, Mandy thought grimly as she drew the brush through her long hair. So spoiled he thought he could just take anything, any girl he saw, and—The door opened and she glanced up to see Caleen. "Oh, *Tante* Caleen, hello!" She said it a little too brightly, flushing as if Caleen could read her thoughts about Bret Dunlap. "Did you fix Jane's hair?"

"*Oui,* Caleen fix, yes." She went to Mandy, took the brush from her and began brushing her hair.

"Well, how did it look? What did you do to it?"

"Look plenty better, yes. I tame the frizzes with braid and make the loop de loop around the back."

Mandy giggled at the description but murmured politely, "I'm sure it looks very nice."

"Uh," Caleen grunted. "Hair very nice but that Miz Jane, she very much *machouquer.*"

"Jane?" Mandy asked incredulously. "She hardly opens her mouth. What do you mean, she talked all the time?"

"Talk about lookin' pretty for that young man, yes. Talk talk talk." She gestured with her hands, screwing her face up so comically that Mandy laughed out loud.

"Oh, that's funny, *Tante* Caleen. But I can't imagine Jane talking that much. She must be more excited that I realized. Did you help her with her gown?" Caleen grunted. "How did it look?"

"Look good." She tugged a thick strand of Mandy's

89

hair loose from the rest and brushed it around her finger to form a long curl.

Mandy sighed. She wasn't going to find out anything from Caleen. When the old woman was in one of her moods she clammed up. She was probably offended that Mandy had lent her services to Jane without first asking her permission. She had been in the Bertonneau family for so long she considered that seniority alone qualified her to be consulted on all things. Her title of servant had long been changed to trusted friend. She had always accompanied the family to balls and dinner parties in New Orleans, but here in California she had been relegated to being left behind when the Bradshaws went out. Mandy sighed. They would both have quite a lot of adjusting to do, she feared.

"Welcome! Welcome!" Marie Dunlap boomed, striding forward to take J.B.'s hands in hers. Even in her elegant evening gown, she gave the impression of wearing boots and trousers, her usual daytime attire.

"Ah, Marie, lovely as always," J.B. murmured, leaning forward to kiss her lightly on the lips. They both held the kiss just a heartbeat longer than was necessary.

"Always the charmer, eh, J.B.?" Marie laughed, but her dark eyes were tender when they gazed up into his. He was one of the few men in San Francisco whom she had to look up to. She held out her hand to Mandy. "Come in, honey-bunch, and meet my boys. They've been chomping at the bit all afternoon waiting to get a look at you!"

Mandy blushed and hung back until Jane and Aunt Agnes joined her, then together they followed Marie into the parlor, Jonathan and J.B. bringing up the rear. Mandy saw Bret at once. He was standing by the fireplace, one arm resting languidly on the mantle, a glass of brandy in his hand. The light from the candle caught on the huge diamond ring when he raised the glass to his mouth. He was wearing dove-gray trousers that fit

90

his legs snugly and a shirt of such whiteness as to be blinding, with rows of ruffles down the front and at his wrists. His coat was velvet, dark gray with shadow stripes of black, and he wore it as casually as he had worn the Spanish bolero the first time she had seen him.

"Well, here she is, boys," Marie boomed. "What did I tell you? Isn't she the prettiest little filly you ever did see?"

Mandy would gladly have disappeared through a hole in the floor had one been available. She felt the heat in her cheeks and wanted to turn and flee. She stepped quickly back, taking J.B.'s hand.

"Mother, please," Jenny scolded, stepping quickly forward to Mandy's side. "You're embarrassing the poor child half to death." She laughed softly, shaking her head affectionately at her mother-in-law.

"Oh, honey-bunch, I'm sorry," Marie said to Mandy. "I'm around horses so dang much I sometimes forget how to talk to people!" She laughed and drew Mandy against her high, ample bosom. "Come on in, child, and I'll introduce you proper-like."

Mandy had no choice but to follow her and stand in the circle of her arm while she presented Bret to her. "This is my baby boy, Bret," she said proudly and Mandy had the pleasure of seeing Bret flush in embarrassment. He recovered quickly, however, and bowed over her hand.

"Pleased to meet you, Miss Bradshaw. You're every bit as lovely as Mother said you were." He brought her hand to his lips and kissed it.

Snatching her hand back, she said stiffly, "Thank you." She did not say she was pleased to meet him.

"And this here is Derek." A slightly older version of Bret stood and bowed over her hand, but his eyes were clear blue and innocent, not teasing and knowing as Bret's had been. His face was softer, more gentle, and his hands were as smooth as a woman's. His build was slighter, where his brother's showed hard muscles through his silk shirt. When he smiled it lit up his entire face.

"*Enchanté, mademoiselle. Como tally vous?*" He laughed as openly as a child. "I hope I got that right. I practiced all afternoon."

"*Oui,*" Mandy dimpled, inclining her head graciously. "It was perfect, monsieur."

"You already know Andy," Marie said, leading her past her eldest son, who sat on the sofa with Jenny. He grinned and raised his glass in greeting.

"This is the last one, honey-bunch," Marie laughed as she stopped in front of her fourth son and Mandy almost swooned. Tod Dunlap was by far the most handsome of the four brothers. He had a little more of everything that made the others outstanding. The combination was dynamite. His hair was just a bit darker and thicker, his jawline a touch squarer, his eyes a shade bluer, his mouth a little more perfect, his shoulders a breadth broader, his figure straighter and taller. Even his clothes looked richer and more elegant on his lean, graceful frame. He was electrifying and Mandy could not take her eyes off him.

"Hello, Amanda," he drawled lazily, his gaze travelling over her. He did not kiss her hand as his brothers had done. He stared at her mouth. He had not addressed her as Miss Bradshaw, either, but had murmured "Amanda" as if it were a caress.

"How do you do, Mr. Dunlap?" She inclined her head and lowered her eyes as Caleen had taught her.

"Call me Tod," he said and she nodded her head obediently, hypnotized by the bright blue of his eyes. "Would you like a glass of sherry or perhaps a brandy?"

"Sherry, please," she said faintly, sinking into the first chair she saw. Her knees had begun to tremble so that she feared she might topple over—right into the fathomless depths of Tod Dunlap's blue, blue eyes. Never had she been so aware that she was a female. All vestiges of her childhood seemed to slip swiftly away and she was suddenly acutely aware of her own sexuality. Aware of her breasts moving lightly against the low décolletage of her gown as her breathing quickened when she met his glance. Aware of his bold gaze on her deep cleavage where she had tucked a white satin rose. She watched his lips as he turned and spoke to a serving girl and sat watching him until the girl returned with a glass of sherry.

Tod took the glass from the tray and handed it to Mandy, his fingers brushing hers, his gaze warm on her face. She wished he wouldn't look at her mouth that way, as if he were already kissing her. She forced her eyes away from his and looked toward the fireplace where Jane stood with Derek and Bret. From the flushed, pleased expression on her face Mandy suspected that the men were complimenting her. She did look quite pretty, Mandy thought, in the blue wool gown, her hair in a single thick braid wrapped about her head like a crown and laced through with the blue velvet ribbon. Bret was laughing at something, his head back, his teeth very white against his dark moustache, looking every inch the rogue that he was. But Jane had eyes only for Derek. She stood leaning slightly toward him, her large pale eyes alight with such obvious adoration that Mandy wondered how Derek could not know that she loved him.

Mandy sipped her sherry and glanced about the room, letting her gaze linger a moment on each Dunlap son, marvelling anew at how handsome each of them was. Andy was the strong, silent type, a man you could lean on. Tod was exciting and dashing, perhaps even a little dangerous, where Derek was gentle and sensitive. And Bret was a blackguard, Mandy thought grimly, a teasing ruffian who obviously had no respect for women. She glared at him until he turned his head and caught her eye. He gave her an impudent grin, his dark eyes mocking as he lifted his brandy glass in a small salute.

She gasped slightly, seething inside that he would dare to look at her so, dare to remind her of their earlier encounter, with such an intimate expression. His gaze continued to rake her, until she felt as if she stood before him in her underwear. She turned quickly away, cheeks pink with indignation, and encountered the vivid blue eyes of Tod as he leaned toward her.

"There's a special rendition of Haydn's celebrated oratorio 'The Creation' this coming weekend," he said softly, the expression in his eyes as intimate as Bret's had been. "Perhaps you'd go with me, Amanda. We could drive into San Francisco early enough for a leisurely supper and perhaps a game or two of backgammon before going to the theater."

"Why, Tod, thank you," Mandy said, dimpling prettily and glancing back at Bret to see if he was still watching. "I'd adore going to the theater with you but I'm not sure *Grandpapa* would allow it." She lowered her lashes coquettishly, giggling a little in her embarrassment. This was the first time a gentleman had asked her out and she was confused as to how she should answer him. "You see, in New Orleans young ladies aren't allowed to go out with gentlemen unchaperoned." She blushed when he widened his eyes and stammered, "I— I mean, I'm sure *Grandpapa* would let me go with you if *Tante* Caleen came along, and—"

"Wait just a minute," Tod said. "How old are you, anyway?"

"Seventeen," she mumbled.

"Seventeen—Jesus Christ!" He looked her over carefully.

She blushed and tried to look away but his vivid blue gaze held her captive and she could not break the spell. She was aware of the heavy beating of her heart when his eyes slid caressingly over the swell of her breasts, felt the faint, trembling of her legs and the sudden gooseflesh of her arms as if he had touched her. And she wanted him to touch her, she realized with something close to panic, making her heart pound even faster.

Wanted him to kiss her and hold her close as Bret had done. But Tod would hold her with gentleness and love and—

"Honey-bunch," Marie's booming voice broke into her thoughts and she started guiltily. "Don't let that son of mine monopolize all your time. Come on over here and talk to me." She patted a place next to her on the leather sofa and Mandy got dutifully to her feet and went to her. "My, that's a pretty gown, sweetie," Marie said as Mandy sat down next to her. "Agnes was just telling me you have quite a wardrobe, all Paris originals, didn't you say, Agnes?"

"Well, yes, or so they seem to be." Agnes flushed at being caught with her envy showing. "I've had Madame Bouchard busy most of the day doing some sketches for me—similar to Mandy's gowns." She gave the girl a thin little smile. "Of course they will be Madame Bouchard's own original designs, Amanda dear. I certainly wouldn't dream of copying your gowns."

"Oh, that's quite all right, Aunt Agnes. I'm flattered that you like them." She took a tiny sip of sherry, wondering when this evening would end. Her thoughts were in turmoil. Tod Dunlap had affected her as no other man ever had. She felt weak every time she looked at him and found herself wishing that everyone else in the room would disappear and leave them alone together. She was aware of Bret glancing her way every so often but stubbornly kept her eyes averted. She would not give him the satisfaction of meeting his insolent gaze. It was with relief that she heard the butler announce dinner.

CHAPTER FIVE

Mandy clung to Tod's arm as he hurried her down the sidewalk toward the waiting carriage. A fine mist of rain had begun to fall and she snuggled deeper into the warmth of her fur cape, her gaze trying to take in everything at once. Front Street was alive with foot and horse traffic and music and laughter spilled from theater entrances as they passed. Elegant ladies with raindrops sparkling on their befurred shoulders flirted demurely with gentlemen leaning rakishly on pearl-handled canes. Yellow, mist-wrethed gas lamps lined the sidewalk, casting eerie shadows on wet umbrellas. Streetcars clattered by and newsboys hawked tomorrow's headlines. Shop windows were brightly lit to showcase fabulous art objects, jewels, and gowns.

"Oh, Tod, it's simply fascinating!" Mandy cried as he helped her into the carriage. She settled the lap robe over her knees and craned her neck for one last look. "It's just so exciting! I've never been to such an exciting place in my life!" Her eyes sparkled as she turned and placed a gloved hand on his arm. "Thank you for such a lovely evening, Tod."

"It isn't over yet, my dear," Tod grinned as he settled in next to her and slapped a hand on the side of the carriage to signal the driver.

"Oh, I know, but I just wanted to thank you for taking me to the play. It was wonderful." She sighed happily, squeezing her eyes shut for a moment at the dread thought that she almost hadn't been able to convince

J.B. to let her go. At first he had been adamant, saying she was much too young to go off alone with a scoundrel like Tod Dunlap, but Mandy had cajoled and pouted so prettily that he had finally relented—on the condition that Andy and Jenny accompany them. Mandy had agreed enthusiastically. As smitten as she was with Tod, she was still a little frightened of being alone with him, of being forced to test her new emotions.

The four of them had driven in together, then Andy and Jenny had gone to visit the Dobsons, close friends as well as Andy's business partner. They planned on spending the night in a hotel and driving back to the ranch the following morning. Mandy had never stayed in a hotel before and was looking forward to it with childish glee. Her emotions had been vacillating wildly all evening, from childlike innocence to a stirring awareness of Tod's overwhelming sex appeal. She had been acutely aware of his presence all through the play and when he had taken her hand she had been in an agony of embarrassment and an ecstasy of pleasure. No one had ever held her hand before or gazed at her with such obvious desire. She longed for him to kiss her and hoped she wouldn't faint if he did, or do something utterly stupid, like giggle.

"I'm delighted you enjoyed it, honey," Tod grinned, taking her hand and tucking it into his own. "We'll have to do it again sometime."

"Oh, really, Tod? Do you really mean it?" Mandy cried. "Could we see *The Drunkard* at the Eagle Theater? Oh, Tod, could we?"

He laughed and leaned over to kiss her slightly parted lips lightly, his mouth barely brushing hers. "Sure thing, honey. Any time you'd like."

She gasped, then lowered her eyes, blushing furiously. The kiss had happened so quickly she hadn't really had time to react. She wanted him to do it again. Wanted to fling her arms about his neck and kiss him back passionately, like the heroine had done in the play when her lover had returned from the war. Wanted him to think her a woman full grown, a desirable woman.

"Well, here we are," Tod said, breaking into her fantasies. "We could have walked if the rain hadn't started up. It's only a couple of blocks." He jumped lightly to the ground and reached in to help her out. "Careful of the curb—that's it." He caught her around the waist, swinging her out and away from the carriage, then letting her body slide slowly down his before placing her feet upon the sidewalk.

Her heart thudded so wildly inside her breast that it was painful to take a full breath. She felt her knees trembling and would have toppled over had not Tod taken her arm and pulled her against him. He drew her under the awning and tilted her face up, his fingers strong beneath her chin. "I could get shot for this," he murmured, his dark head leaning in close. "But I'm damned if I can help myself." Then his lips were on hers, his arms holding her tightly against him, so that she could feel his heart beating against her own. He kissed her with a passion totally foreign to anything she had ever experienced in her life and she responded just as passionately. Her body melted against him, every contour fitting perfectly into his, her arms holding him as closely as he was holding her. She felt his tongue probing gently and opened her lips to experience this new sensation.

Abruptly, he released her. "Whoa, honey," he said and she could see that he was as breathless as she. "You'd better behave or you're going to find yourself in a whole lot of trouble." He shook his head ruefully. "Thank God I'm a gentleman," he sighed.

Mandy stood swaying slightly, her heart still pounding wildly, her cheeks flushed, her pulses racing. *What's happening to me?* she thought. *I feel so—so strange.* She looked up at Tod and a warm thrill swept through her, turning her legs to rubber. "Oh, Tod," she whispered, reaching out toward him.

"God, Amanda, I'm only human." Taking her by the shoulders he held her at arm's length. "Believe me, if we were anywhere else in the world, I'd—well, I sure as hell wouldn't be going in to supper!" He ran a shaky hand through his crisp, rain-damp hair, laughing shortly. "But the watchdogs are waiting." He opened the massive oak door and bowed low, waving her in ahead of him. As she passed, he whispered in her ear, "I promise to be good tonight, but just wait until the next time I get you alone, you little minx!"

Before Mandy could respond, Andy and Jenny were coming forward to greet them. "Well, there you are," Jenny said, taking Mandy's hands. "How was the play?"

"It was wonderful," Mandy said, suddenly very glad to see Jenny and very glad to be inside a building filled with people. She glanced quickly at Tod but he was engaged in conversation with the maître d'hotel, looking as nonchalant as ever. She wondered if Jenny could tell by looking at her that Tod had kissed her. Did it show on her face? In her eyes? Surely it must. Something that earthshaking could not go unnoticed. But Jenny was chattering about the nice visit they had had with the Dobsons, totally oblivious to Mandy's emotional state.

"They're joining us for breakfast tomorrow morning before we start home," Jenny said as she helped Mandy off with her cape. "I'm anxious for you to meet them. They're wonderful people and have been dear friends for years. William manages the San Francisco office for Andy and they're partners in the Dunlap-Dobson lumber mill." She tucked Mandy's hand through her arm and began leading her toward the main dining hall, a vast room brilliantly lit by numerous crystal chandeliers. "Grace just told us tonight that she is also expecting another baby, about the same time I am, so it will be fun to compare aches and pains."

They joined Andy and Tod, then followed the

maître d'hotel to an upstairs dining suite that overlooked the crowded room below.

"Oh, it's beautiful," Mandy said, leaning over the balustrade to peer down at the richly gowned and coiffed women and the expanse of dining luxury. Diamonds flashed in the candlelight and cultured voices lilted musically as champagne corks popped at almost every table. Waiters moved unobtrusively through the large room, balancing silver trays high above their heads.

"Come, Mandy, let's sit down," Jenny called, motioning her back inside the suite. Heavy gold velvet drapes completely circled the balcony, giving them privacy while they dined. The walls were dark mahogany and hung with paintings. The high-backed Queen Victoria chairs were upholstered in lush, creamy brocade and the tablecloth was genuine Queen Anne lace, set with Haviland china. An enormous candelabrum stood majestically in the center of the table, a silver serving set gleaming royally in its soft glow.

An elegantly attired waiter, as suave and handsome as any stage actor, appeared with a silver bucket holding a bottle of champagne. He wished them good evening in a charming French accent, swirled the bottle around in the chipped ice for a moment, then set it before them with a flourish, letting them see the date. Moët Chandon—the very finest," he murmured softly.

"Yes, I'm sure it's fine," Tod said, waving away the offered cork. "Just pour, please."

"Very good, monsieur," the waiter mumbled, a little miffed that Tod hadn't sniffed the excellent bouquet of the champagne. He poured all around and settled the bottle gently back into its nest of ice. "I will leave the menus with you, monsieurs, mesdames. Please ring when you wish to order." He gave a curt little bow and exited.

"To Amanda," Tod said, raising his glass. His blue eyes gazed directly into hers and she felt the heat rise in her cheeks.

100

"Yes, to Mandy," Jenny said gaily, clicking the rim of her glass against that of her niece. "We're all so happy that you've come back to California to live."

"Thank you," Mandy said shyly and ducked her head to her glass, taking a big swallow to ease the knot in her throat. But every time she looked at Tod she became so breathless she couldn't seem to swallow. Her mouth was dry and her face was warm and she felt like a complete ninny. If this was love, she wasn't sure she liked it that much.

The mellow champagne soon eased her tension and by the second glass she was able to join in the conversation as if she hadn't just fallen madly in love for the first time in her life. She laughed with Jenny and pretended interest in her stories of Grace Dobson's three-year-old toddler, but all the while her heart sang with the memory of her first kiss. She listened to Tod as he spoke with Andy about the Dunlap enterprises but it wasn't his words she heard, just the sound of his deep, vibrant voice, melodious to her ears. He was sitting so close she could reach out and touch him if she wanted to. She smelled the faint musk of his cologne. And when he occasionally turned his head to smile at her she felt as if a light had been turned on somewhere inside her, somewhere mysterious and beautiful and perhaps a little dangerous.

She passed the entire meal in a state of delicious oblivion, eating, drinking, laughing and talking with the others, but thinking only of Tod's mouth on hers. The meal was lavish beyond description and at any other time she would have paid it the respect it deserved. The oysters Kirkpatrick were divine, as were the frog's legs *la poulette* and the delicate Austrian torte with apricot marmalade and whipped cream. A different variety of wine was served with each course and by the end of the meal she was in a fuzzy, warm state of intoxication. Voices seemed to be coming at her from far away, as if she were in a tunnel, and she had to concentrate very hard to hear them.

"Oh dear me," Jenny giggled, feeling the wine as much as her niece was. "I do believe our little Mandy is inebriated. Father will be horrified." She turned to Andy, laughing. "Some chaperon I turned out to be!"

"You're much too young and beautiful to be a chaperon," Andy teased, taking Jenny's hand. "And if you could read my mind right this minute you would be the one in need of a chaperon!" He drew her to him and kissed her, whispering, "Shall we go up to our room?"

"Andy, you're terrible!" Jenny blushed and slapped away the hand that was reaching for her. "We can't leave Mandy in this state."

"Go on to bed, you two lovebirds," Tod said. "I'll take Amanda for a drive. The fresh air will do her good." He stood and helped Mandy to her feet, holding her when she swayed against him.

"I don't know," Jenny said, looking worriedly at Mandy. "How do you feel, dear? Do you want to get a breath of fresh air or would you prefer to go straight to your room?" She, too, stood and took Mandy's other hand. "I'll take you to your suite and get you settled, if you'd like."

"Don't wanna go to bed. Wanna go for a ride with Tod." She gave him a lopsided grin. "Can we, Tod? Can we go for a ride? I wanna see everything in San Francisco!"

"That's a pretty tall order, honey," Tod laughed. "I can't promise all of San Francisco tonight, but we can take a ride around the park and get you sobered up."

"Now, Tod, you behave yourself with her," Jenny warned, her voice stern. "Remember she's only seventeen—"

"Seventeen and three-fourths," Mandy interrupted, drawing herself up to her full height. "And," she wagged her finger at Jenny, "I am not a child."

"Don't worry, sis, I'll be on my best behavior." Tod dropped a light kiss on his sister-in-law's cheek, then

102

led Mandy to the door. "We'll be back in less than an hour. Don't worry, okay?"

"All right, before midnight, then." But still Jenny frowned. Of all her handsome, dashing brothers-in-law, she trusted Tod the least. He was a devil with women and had left a string of broken hearts and ruined reputations from California to New York City. She raised her voice in a last warning. "Remember, you'll have J.B. to answer to if anything happens to her!" She heard Tod's answering laugh, then turned to Andy and sighed, "Well, he's *your* brother. You know what he's like."

"Oh, Jen, he isn't all that bad. He certainly is enough of a gentleman not to take advantage of a young girl like Mandy." He stood, stretched, then gathered Jenny close, nuzzling her hair. "Come on, stop worrying like a old mother hen and take care of your husband." He kissed her, rubbed his nose against hers, nibbled her lips. "You know what I've been thinking ever since we decided to spend the night here?" She nodded her head, leaning against him. "Something about sleeping in a hotel always makes me randy as a rooster. Reminds me of our honeymoon, know what I mean?"

"I know what you mean well enough," she said saucily, wiggling closer in his embrace. "All you Dunlap men are the same."

He silenced her with a kiss. "Here's the only Dunlap man you have to worry about, sweetheart." Sweeping her into his arms he carried her through the door and down the corridor towards their suite, as she protested weakly, embarrassed lest someone see them—and excited that her handsome husband still loved her with such a burning passion.

Mandy snuggled under the lap robe and watched the rain hissing from the carriage wheels as they rolled slowly down the dark, wet street. Tod sat close, sharing the lap robe, his arm draped casually around her shoulders. The crisp, chilly night air had cleared Mandy's head considerably and she was thoroughly enjoying the still-busy streets. Animated crowds gathered around bar entrances and stood chatting in front of theaters that were just now closing. She watched, a little enviously, as young lovers strolled hand in hand down the sidewalk, unmindful of the falling rain. She wanted to say something to Tod about *the kiss*. It was ever in her mind: her first kiss.

"Let's get away from Front Street and I'll show you come really exciting night life." Tod leaned forward to rap on the partition that seperated them from the driver. "The Barbary Coast, Sam," he called and the driver touched the brim of his cap in acknowledgment.

"The Barbary Coast?" Mandy sobered instantly. "Oh, Tod, do we dare? I mean, I've read about the Barbary Coast. It's supposed to be a truly evil place."

Tod laughed, drawing her against him. "Oh, it's truly evil, all right. Probably the most evil place I've ever seen. But truly fascinating as well. Human life isn't worth a copper penny on the Barbary Coast. There are men there who will slice your heart out for the gold in your teeth." His voice was suddenly excited in a way she had never heard before and she felt a little thrill of fear.

She shivered and moved closer to him. Instantly, his arm tightened around her. He turned to look down at her and she could just barely make out the blue of his eyes in the dim light. They were shiny, bold, dangerous. But they held her as a snake's hypnotic gaze holds its prey. She saw his head bending toward her, down, down, until his lips were mere inches from hers. "Kiss me, Amanda," he whispered huskily. "Kiss me."

With a cry she fell into his arms, her lips parted for his kiss. His arms were like steel vices around her, crushing out her breath, it seemed, and his hard body strained toward her, pressing her back into the corner of the carriage. The kiss grew in intensity and he flattened her upon the carriage seat, his full weight on top of her. She felt a pulse beating in his groin, vibrating

104

against her, sending waves of desire flooding her body. She arched up against him, pressing herself to him, and felt him jerk convulsively. "Jesus Christ, Amanda—!" He kissed her, hard, savage, then tore his mouth away and flung himself back on his own side of the carriage. "Damn, you don't know what you do to me, honey—how damn hard I'm trying to behave like a gentleman." With another groan, he gathered her close again, kissing her hungrily, his mouth bruising her, his fingers digging into her soft flesh.

"Barbary Coast, sir," the driver called, rapping sharply on the partition and Tod jumped as if someone had doused him with cold water. "Consider yourself damn lucky," he murmured to Mandy, then called, "Okay, Sam. Just drive us around the waterfront, then take us on back to the hotel." He straightened his clothes, ran a hand through his hair and lit a cheroot with nervous fingers, all the while watching her. "Honey, didn't your mother ever tell you not to kiss a man like that unless you intend, to, uh—well—hell, you know what I mean."

"No, I don't," she whispered meekly, her eyes filling with tears. "I don't know what I did to make you angry." She twisted her hands together in her lap, looking so utterly miserable that he pulled her back into his arms.

"You didn't make me angry, honey. Far from it!" He shook his head, wondering how he was going to explain to her that she drove him crazy, that she made him more excited than any woman ever had. He supposed it was her innocence, her sweet, wonderfully childlike way of offering herself to him. Not just her lips, but her body. She had responded so naturally to his embrace, so trustingly, that he felt like a heel. Never had he refused such a succulent gift so eagerly offered. She was his for the taking and yet he could not take her. For a variety of reasons, not the least being that she was J.B. Bradshaw's favored granddaughter and only seventeen years old.

"My pretty little Amanda," he said softly, shaking his head at the irony of it. He, Tod Dunlap, womanizer, rake, incorrigible, trying to talk a lady *out* of her passion! "There's nothing in the world I'd rather do than make love to you right here, right now—but you're still a child. A ravishing, bewitching child to be sure, but still far too young for the likes of me." He smiled, encouraging hers, but she merely gazed at him, her lips still parted from his kisses. "Honey, it was nothing you did. On the contrary, I'm afraid it is I who must apologize for not controlling my emotions, for not remembering your tender age."

"I am not a child," she said sulkily, her lower lip trembling most charmingly. "I will be eighteen next month and if I were still living in New Orleans *Grandmaman* would give me a coming-out ball to let it be known that I am of marriageable age. It would be a big fancy ball with all the eligible young men attending and—" Tears welled over in her eyes and ran down her cheeks and she caught them with the tip of her tongue, as a child would. "Oh, how I wish I were back home! It is so different here—so, so difficult to know what is right—what is acceptable!"

"Hey, baby, don't cry, please." He took out his handkerchief and wiped her eyes then pressed it into her hands. "Look, Amanda, I'm going to give it to you straight. You're not safe with me. I'm a grown man with a grown man's appetites. I will not be satisfied with a few stolen kisses in the back of a buggy. I will want more, I promise you—much more than you are willing to give."

"How do you know?" She said it crossly, embarrassment making her irritable.

"I know women, my pretty little Amanda." He sighed eloquently. "Ah, yes, I do know women."

"You just said I was a child."

"But one that is so close to womanhood it's frightening." He puffed on his cheroot, wondering how the hell he was going to get out of this jam. Turning his atten-

106

tion toward the window he pointed. "Look, there's Brandy's Place, the roughest saloon on the Barbary Coast."

She glanced disinterestedly at the garishly lit, noisy little bar with several coarse-looking women leaning against the doorway, smoking and talking among themselves. She suddenly sat straight up in her seat, her eyes wide with shock. "Why, they're smoking cigarettes! I can't believe it!" She leaned out the window to stare at the whores who hooted back at her and made obscene gestures. She jerked her head back inside the carriage, blushing crimson. "Why, they're—they were—those women were—"

"Whores," Tod supplied and Mandy blushed even harder. He laughed. "See what I mean? You're such an innocent, Amanda. You've probably never heard the word spoken aloud before, have you?"

"No, but I've read it in books and I do know what it means." She lifted her chin defiantly and stared back at the loitering prostitutes. "Just because I've never frequented such a lowlife establishment doesn't mean that I'm particularly innocent, Tod Dunlap. Merely that I have a certain respect for myself, a certain class—"

Tod chuckled softly. "Yes, that's the word, all right. You do have class, Amanda, like the rest of the Bradshaws. Just don't let all that pride turn into arrogance." Before she could reply he leaned over to point out of the window. "See that warehouse over there? The one with the boarded-up windows?" She nodded, staring at the big, gray, nondescript building with one bare yellow lantern hanging above a tiny padlocked door. "That's the holding pen for the unfortunates being shanghaied out of the country."

"Shanghaied? I don't believe you." She leaned farther out the window and saw a couple of rough-looking men standing guard at the door, passing a bottle between them.

"It's true enough, I'm afraid. And quite a natural occurrence on the Barbary Coast. Some poor dumb cowboy gets drunk in a place like Brandy's or Beg Red's, the bartender slips him a Mickey and tosses him in the holding pen until there's enough to make a decent shipload. Then—" He snapped his fingers. "Next stop, China."

"But that's horrible," she cried, drawing back inside the carriage lest she be snatched and thrown into the frightful-looking building. "What about the law? Surely they don't condone such a terrible thing."

Tod laughed shortly. "There is no law on the Barbary Coast, honey. Once you step foot on this side of town you're on your own. Didn't you notice that big sign when we turned off Jersey Street?" She shook her head. "It states quite clearly, 'Anyone venturing beyond this point does so at his own risk.' Little girls still in their cradles are warned about the Barbary Coast. These degenerate tars along the waterfront like nothing better than to shanghai some pretty little gal, and have their pleasure with her whenever they want on the long voyage to Hong Kong, pass her among the crew. . . . Hell, by the time they get to their destination they're more than ready for the cribs and whorehouses." He took a last puff of his cheroot and tossed it out the window. "Of course, most of them don't make it. They die or jump overboard before they're halfway there."

"I don't believe a word of it, Tod Dunlap," Mandy said indignantly, but her eyes were wide with fright. "You're just trying to scare me."

"Suit yourself." He shrugged, turning toward the window, smiling in the darkness when he felt her move closer to him. "But I'll bet you one of Ma's palominos that there's at least a couple dozen men and women in there right now waiting for the next ship heading for the Orient."

"You mean they sell men into prostitution as well?" She was incredulous.

"No, sweetheart," he laughed, looking fondly at her. God, she was a cute little thing. "They will be sold into

108

slavery, made to work in the ship's crew until they reach port, and there they're sold as manual laborers to the highest bidder." He pointed to a hazy silhouette gently rocking in the black water next to the wharf. "See that ship yonder, the *Wild Goose*? That's a trader vessel, notorious for its human cargo."

Mandy stared at the huge bulk of wood and canvas, heard the eerie creaking as it rocked in the dark water, the dull slap-slap of waves against its hull sounding hollow and forlorn. Several shadowy figures milled about the deck, readying her for sail, their oaths and curses drifting to her across the fog. The waterfront was stacked with mysterious-looking crates and boxes, lumpy packages wrapped in soiled canvas and tied with huge, bulky ropes. Straw baskets stuffed with unidentifiable objects were being hoisted high above the dock by pulleys while sailors in dark blue wool coats and caps directed from below. She wondered where they were going, all those strange bundles and packages. How many thousands of miles would they travel before reaching their destination?

Crates holding live, squawking chickens were swung aloft and lowered into the bowels of the ship as excited Chinese danced about, jabbering in their own tongue. Oriental as well as white prostitutes strolled the waterfront, stopping to solicit the workers, and an old Chinese woman, bent nearly double with age, hobbled along side of them, a box of apples around her neck, a gray braid three feet long hanging down her stooped back. Buggys, buckboards, and horses milled in the streets and gambling casinos spewed forth rinky-tink music and the strong smell of rum. A small group of men, better dressed than those about them, lounged near the open doorway of Big Red's, their expensive watch fobs gleaming gold in the lantern's light. When they smiled or spoke to one another Mandy could see that they had gold front teeth.

"Who are those men?" she asked.

"Pimps," Tod said shortly. Before she could question him further he rapped on the partition and called out to Sam to take them to the hotel.

Mandy was quiet on the ride back, leaning sleepily against Tod's shoulder as she listened to his deep, warm voice. The dining room was empty when they entered but she saw a large crowd in an adjoining room gathered around gaming tables, laughing and talking. She wanted to ask him about it but she was simply too tired to be curious.

"Well, here we are, honey," Tod said, stopping in front of a hand-carved door with a heavy brass knocker. "How do you feel? Think you can get some sleep now?"

"Oh, yes," She smiled at him drowsily. "I'm so very tired. Goodness, it must be past midnight.'"

"Just," he said, checking his pocket watch. "If we had been another five minutes your Aunt Jenny would have had the law on me, I've no doubt." He took her by the shoulders, turning her towards him, gazing down at her for what seemed the longest time. Then he bent his head and kissed her softly. "Goodnight pretty little Amanda," he whispered. "Sleep tight."

"Oh, Tod, I—" She blushed and looked down at the rich Persian carpet. She wanted to say something clever and witty, to tell him how much she loved him. "I had a marvelous time tonight, Tod. Truly marvelous. Thank you so much." Rising on her tiptoes she kissed him just as softly as he had kissed her. With a low groan he gathered her into his arms, bending her back against the door as his lips devoured hers in a lusty kiss.

"God, Amanda, you'd better grow up damn fast or J.B.'ll be after me with a shotgun!" Pushing her from him he turned and strode quickly down the corridor and down the curved stairway toward the gaming room without once looking back.

She stood for a moment, watching him until he had disappeared from sight, knowing he was going to join the group of laughing, drinking people downstairs, and the lovely, sensual women she had seen there. For one brief moment she thought of running after him, asking him to take her with him. Then she turned back to the door, pushed it open and stepped inside. "I hate being seventeen and three-fourths," she muttered under her breath.

J.B. stood impatiently while Luis adjusted the cummerbund around his master's still narrow waist. J.B. tugged on his black silk bow tie, growling, "Here, Luis, fix this damn thing for me, will you? It cocks up on one side here." Luis expertly shaped the bow tie against the snowy linen of J.B.'s shirt, then helped him on with his jacket.

"*Perfecto,*" the tall Mexican approved, a rare smile lighting up his handsome face. He flicked a tiny bit of lint from J.B.'s shoulder and fussed a moment more with the bow tie.

"God damn it, Luis, leave that damn thing alone before you mess it up again." J.B. strode to the full-length mirror on his closet door and admired himself critically. "Well," he grumbled, not at all displeased with his appearance, "guess I'll do." He turned and sucked in his stomach. "There, that's better." He took a heavy gold watch from his waistcoat and checked the time. "I think I'll have a little snort before I go downstairs, Luis."

"Sure thing, Boss." Luis went to the bar in the corner of J.B.'s suite and poured a tumbler of bourbon.

"Have one with me," J.B. said and Luis poured another for himself. Settling himself into a deep cowhide chair, J.B. took the bourbon and motioned Luis to sit. "Well, Luis, Johnny's little girl is a woman tonight." He took a sip of bourbon, screwing up his face at the pungent taste, then murmuring, "Ahhh." He drank again. "Eighteen years old and ready to be put on the market—according to Agnes." He shook his head. "I don't know, Luis, maybe I'm getting old, but every year eighteen seems younger and younger. Amanda's still a child in so many ways and yet I know she's almost a woman,

111

too. My own Amanda was just sixteen when I walked her down the aisle, but she seemed older, somehow." He chuckled, sipped his drink. "Maybe it's because I wasn't but eighteen myself."

"They grow up very fast, the *niñas*," Luis said. He crossed his long, slim legs and leaned back in his chair. "And the *niña* Amanda is one *hermosa señorita*. She will break many hearts tonight, I think?"

"As long as she's the one doing the breaking I won't mind," J.B. growled. "But just let any of those randy young bucks trifle with her and they'll be looking down the barrel of my forty-five!"

"Ah, the *grandpapa* he is possessive of his little French sparrow, no?" Luis chuckled goodnaturedly, raising one well-shaped eyebrow.

"She's not French," J.B. said, then grinned, adding, "Well, maybe half—but's she's all Bradshaw now, that's for sure. Christ, Luis, did you ever see anybody take to life out here as readily as she has? Why, you'd hardly believe that she's been uprooted and travelled clear across the United States to a bunch of strangers she can't have remembered. But you never hear a whimper out of her, no complaining or whining about being home-sick. She's a real little thoroughbred, that girl."

Luis nodded his dark head but did not comment. He had spoken often with Lupe, the serving girl assigned to Amanda, and she had told him that Amanda spoke wistfully of New Orleans. "She grieves much for her own home," Lupe had said. "She sings in her own tongue when she thinks no one hears and she reads books with words in them that are not English. I have seen this."

"Yes sir, Luis, Amanda's right where she belongs." He took a long pull of his bourbon. "The way she fits right in proves to me I did the right think in bringing her out here." He had conveniently forgotten that it had been Belle Bertonneau who had instigated the plan. "Hell, the South is no place for a young'un to be in times like these. Those damn stupid Rebels are still fighting the war they lost ten years ago." He snorted disgustedly. "Damn fools don't know when to quit. Don't know when they're well off. Hell, they'll probably keep on kicking up a rumpus until every last one of them is dead."

"War between neighbors is not a good thing," Luis agreed, thinking of the long years of fighting between the Mexicans and the Americans that had resulted in him serving instead of being served. But he held no grudges. He could not fault Don Bradshaw in any way, for he was treated only with kindness and respect. And he was paid a great deal of gold to serve the old robber baron, as J.B. was called behind his back by more envious men than Luis.

"No more war talk. My little gal is back home where she belongs and that's all that matters to me." He drained his glass and Luis rose at once to refill it. "Ain't she just about the prettiest little thing you ever did see, Luis? That highstepping walk of hers, the way she turns those big blue eyes on you so damn sassy-like. She's got fire in her, a real passion for life." He frowned and accepted the fresh bourbon with a nod of his head. "A damn sight too much passion, I'm afraid. I've seen the way she looks at that scoundrel Tod Dunlap and I'm afraid she's fallen in love with him. What do you think, Luis? Think I've got any cause to worry?"

Luis chose his words carefully. "She is infatuated with the young Dunlap, this I see, but I think she is a sensible young woman, also. One who can perhaps see through the beauty of the flesh and into the heart." He paused. "I think perhaps if she sees into the heart of Señor Tod Dunlap she will cease to see the beauty of his face."

"Well, I don't know, Luis. Tod's a charming little bastard, no question about it." He took a cheroot from a hand-tooled leather box on the table, bit off one end and spat it into the spitoon at his feet. Luis was at his side at once with a match. "I'd much rather see her falling for Bret," he said as he puffed out a great cloud of

113

smoke. "Now there's a real man for you. Not afraid of getting his hands dirty. All that Tod ever does that I see is hang around the gaming halls and romance half the women in San Francisco."

"When a man is that rich he has no need to feel the dirt on his hands," Luis said lightly, but he, too, felt a certain aversion to Tod Dunlap and hoped that he was right about Amanda: that she would soon see beyond his good looks and into the emptiness of his heart.

"Bullshit," J.B. snorted. "The other Dunlap boys don't mind a little dirt and cow manure on their hands. Why, look at Andy. I've seen him standing hip-deep in mud and shit helping with the birthin' of his cattle come spring." He chuckled. "Why, Jenny's always complaining that he looks more like a stable hand than the head of the Dunlap ranch."

"Yes, Andy is a fine man. A good son-in-law." Luis finished his bourbon and carried the glass to the bar. "I think perhaps it is time to check downstairs and see that all is in order. You do not need me any longer, Boss?"

"Naw, go ahead, Luis. I'll just finish my drink and be right down." He waved him out of the room and sat thinking.

The months had flown since Amanda had arrived last spring. She had brought a new life into the house, a feeling of freshness and youth that J.B. had not been aware was missing until her presence had proved otherwise. She brought a smile to timid little Jane's face and had literally transformed the girl into a beauty. She had wound Agnes around her little finger as effortlessly as she had the rest of the family, much to J.B.'s surprise. He hadn't thought Agnes capable of showing affection for anyone save her own brood of sulky, spoiled children. Jeramy was clearly smitten with Amanda and J.B. knew his youngest son had had to remind himself often that she was his niece. Atoka was devoted to the girl, stuffing her with delicacies from her kitchen and regaling her with hair-raising stories of the old days, then

114

fussing over her when she had nightmares from the horrifying tales or a stomachache from too many sweets.

Old Doc had spent long hours teaching her to ride astride, explaining the ways of the West. He kept her tack polished to a high sheen, fussed with her mare's hooves and made ominous warnings about rattlers and coyotes, frightening the poor child half to death until J.B. had intervened and told Doc to stop his mother-hen cluckings and let the girl be. Tim and Pete, the stable boys, were completely captivated by the Southern belle and tussled fiercely with one another for the privilege of catching her horse whenever she wanted to go for a ride.

And Marie Dunlap was determined to have her as a daughter-in-law. "She's a jewel, J.B.," Marie had boomed on more than one occasion. "A real little jewel of a girl. I love her like she was my own." Unlike most mothers who cannot see their children's faults, Marie saw only too clearly Tod's shortcomings and tried to steer Amanda into Bret's arms. But Bret was strangely cool to her, as she was to him, and Marie was left to wonder what had transpired between them. It was almost as if they had some unspoken agreement to stay clear of one another. J.B. had felt this and wondered about it, also. Not that Bret was disrespectful in any way. The Dunlap boys had been brought up too carefully to be deliberately rude, but there was a coolness in Bret's eyes when he looked at Mandy. And Mandy seemed to go out of her way to avoid any contact at all with Bret at the many suppers and gatherings the two families shared.

J.B. got to his feet and went to pour himself another bourbon. Just one more little one, he told himself, as he carried the drink to the window and stood looking down at the arriving carriages. He should be downstairs to greet his guests but he hesitated still, putting off the moment when he would have to admit to himself that his own Amanda, most precious of all his grandchildren

115

because she was Johnny's child, was no longer a little girl.

"Eighteen years old," he murmured aloud, then shook his head. "Just eighteen." He turned to his mirror and gazed at his reflection. He was an impressive figure in his evening clothes, his full head of thick white hair against the sun-browned skin giving him a sexiness that he took much delight in. He liked it when women complimented him on his looks. He felt a stirring in his groin, thinking briefly of LissaMarie. He had let her go a month after Amanda had arrived, not so much for the fact that she was clearly jealous of the young girl, but because she was getting more and more possessive with him. Her twice weekly visits to his bedroom had become nightly trips and she begged to be allowed to sleep there all night instead of returning to her own quarters. Too often Luis had brought in his boss's morning coffee to find the luscious blonde still curled around J.B., her face angelic in sleep.

J.B. laughed aloud when he remembered the thoughts he had had about the Creole nanny, Caleen, how he had thought she might be a likely replacement for LissaMarie in his bed. A plump, saucy little French dish to spice his life. Nothing could be farther from the truth. Caleen was older than him by ten years. But he grudgingly admitted that she was a smart old cookie, and he recognized her fierce loyalty to Amanda and her age-old wisdom with herbs and healing. When one of the serving girls had broken out in strange rash that no one else could identify or cure, Caleen had briskly packed her with mud and dried herbs, mumbled some African mumbo-jumbo over her, and the girl had been as good as new the very next day. When one the mares' time had come and even old Doc had been at a loss as to why she couldn't throw her foal but instead suffered in agonizing silence, her guts tied in knots and blood gushing from her at an alarming rate, Caleen had brewed a big pot of some evil-smelling potion, packed the mare's flanks and hindquarters, then forced some of the liquid down her throat. Within minutes, or so Doc swore, the mare had heaved herself to her feet and dropped a pair of twin colts on the bloodied straw. "Weren't nothin', no," Caleen muttered darkly as she packed her medicines and prepared to leave the stable. "Just two tryin' to get out at once, yes."

She had even adminstered to J.B. one cold evening when his back was acting up and the rain was settling into his bones and giving him a devil of a time. She had come into his bedroom and propped him up, ignoring his gruff protests as she slipped his nightshirt off his shoulder and began massaging some cool yet burning ointment into his flesh. Within minutes, the pain had all but disappeared and he had been able to get a full night's sleep for the first time since the dang thing had kicked up. And she made one hell of a good mint julep, now that he thought about it.

He went to the door and stood listening to the sounds, the bustle and noise of the house preparing itself for Amanda's eighteenth birthday party. Her coming of age party, she called it. He remembered how she had dimpled prettily and tossed her head, saying, "Now, *Grandpapa,* you will allow me to go unchaperoned to the theater, *oui*?" And he had grumbled fondly, "We'll see, Missy, we'll just see about that."

Smiling, he started down the stairs to greet his guests.

CHAPTER SIX

Mandy stood with the ladies near the musicians' stand. She gripped the stem of her wine glass so hard she feared for a moment she might break it. But she was simply too excited to merely stand still and listen to inane gossip. She wanted to dance and laugh and even flirt a little. Oh, where was Tod? The rest of the Dunlaps had arrived over an hour ago, Derek gasping in surprise when he saw Jane. She did look quite lovely, Mandy thought, glancing over at her aunt. She wore a dress of such dark blue as to appear purple, cut low to contrast sharply with her milk-white shoulders and bosom, and nipped in with tiny tucks to show off her small waist. Her hair was pulled straight back from her face and worn in a low, thick chignon, tiny spit curls at each ear. Her earrings were jet, almost brushing her shoulders when she turned her head, and Mandy had talked her into wearing a light touch of kohl on her eyes and a dab of rouge on her lips. The effort had been worth it, considering Derek's sidelong looks at Jane.

Bret had complimented Jane lavishly before joining the men and as he passed Mandy he had whispered, "You don't look half bad yourself, brat!" She had been on the verge of a sharp retort when Marie had pulled her away to join the ladies. *Damn his insolent hide*, Mandy had muttered to herself, eyes flashing angrily at Bret's back as he lounged easily against the bar. Oh, where was Tod? She wanted to ask Marie but was afraid of looking too forward. When would the dancing start? And where were the rest of the guests? *Grand-papa* had said there would be over two hundred, the elite of San Francisco.

"I know what you must be going through, honey-bunch," Marie said gently patting Mandy's hand. "Your first grown-up ball can be a pretty nervous affair, but don't worry. They'll be here soon. It isn't considered fashionable to be on time, you know." She laughed her loud, open laugh. "I guess you know what that makes the Dunlaps. We were the first ones here!"

"I'm so glad you were," Mandy said sincerely, gripping Marie's hands. "I need you to hold me up when the others arrive. *Mon Dieu*, I do hope I do not faint!"

"Gawd, don't do that, honey-bunch," Marie cried in real horror. "I'm no good at all with fainting females. Give me a real honest-to-God sickness and I can cure it easy as pie, but I'm lost as a newborn calf when it comes to the vapors!"

"Then I promise not to faint," Mandy laughed, hugging Marie close for a moment. She had grown so fond of this big, warm, boisterous woman who somehow seemed more of a mother to her than the lovely, petite Désirée had been. Not that her own mother hadn't loved her with all her heart, but she had treated Mandy as if she were some pretty, pampered doll to dress up and play with, then tuck between silken sheets before going off with her handsome husband. And when Mandy grew older, Désirée had looked on her fondly as if she were a beloved younger sister to cherish and play with. She never spoke a harsh word to her or reprimanded her (this was Caleen's unhappy duty) and would sit for hours talking with the girl about anything and everything, answering all the childish questions without once becoming bored. She was a child herself in so many ways, charmingly spoiled, pampered by her adoring Johnny, doted on by Belle and Caleen, protected fiercely by Elmo. She had been a dainty, porcelain demitasse whereas Marie Dunlap was a solid, hearty coffee mug.

119

"Oh, there are the Dobsons," Jenny said, nudging Marie. "Look, Mother, Grace is showing already." She glanced down at her own still-flat stomach and giggled. "Oh, I'm going to have such fun teasing her. We have a wager who will gain the most weight." She was as youthful as a girl in her pale pink gown sprigged with a tiny green leaf design, a bunch of lilacs in her hair giving off their own natural perfume. No one would ever suspect that she was almost five months gone, Mandy thought. She watched the two women embrace and exchange greetings, seeing the friendship between them, and she felt a tiny pang of loneliness. She missed having a friend her own age to giggle and gossip with and thought of Suzette Arceneaux. How much more fun the ball would be if Suzette were here to share it with her! But Suzette would be married by now, perhaps even pregnant. The thought sobered her and she turned away from the gossiping women, looked again at the door, willing it to open and show Tod Dunlap standing there, his eyes seeking hers in the crowd.

But the next arrivals were all middle-aged, richly dressed and boisterous in their greetings when introduced to her. She smiled and curtsied but did not even try to remember their names. The men drifted off to the billiard room, leaving the women to join the group by the punch bowl, and Mandy wished she could follow them. Why was it the men always seemed to be having more fun? They drank and smoked and laughed, poking one another and tussling with sophomoric abandon. She watched Bret lean over the table and make a difficult shot, sinking two balls at once, and a cheer went up from the men. *Conceited baboon*, Mandy thought sullenly.

The musicians finished tuning their instruments and broke into the first number of the evening, a high-stepping, rollicking polka. Derek moved away from the group in the billiard room and claimed Jane for the first dance, swirling her across the empty, highly-polished floor in a cloud of blue satin and frothy white

120

petticoats. J.B. strode across the room and bowed low before Mandy.

"I believe the first dance is mine," he said, taking her arm and leading her onto the floor. As if on cue the other men claimed their ladies and the party had officially begun.

An hour later the huge ballroom was filled to capacity and still there was no sign of Tod. Mandy had tried not to think about it, tried not to watch the door as numerous partners swung her around the floor and told her how beautiful she was. But she could not respond to their pretty compliments. She wanted to hear those words from Tod and feel his arms about her. *He must come*, she told herself for the hundredth time. *He wouldn't miss my eighteenth birthday party. He just wouldn't.*

"May I have this dance?" Mandy whirled about to see Bret standing there, a half smile on his face as if he wasn't sure what her reaction would be.

"No," she said quickly, then stammered, "I mean, it's taken—I've already promised this dance."

One dark eyebrow shot up and Bret grinned lazily. "Have you now? Then where is he?"

Mandy looked wildly around for a likely candidate and saw that almost every man in the room was already dancing and those who were not were engaged in a game of billiards. She blushed foolishly, hating Bret all the more for catching her in a lie. But she stood her ground and bluffed icily, "He's gone to get me a glass of champagne. I expect he'll return at any moment."

"Oh? Are you going to drink champagne or dance? Or perhaps you can do both at the same time?" His lips twitched in amusement. "Is there no end to your talents then, Miss Bradshaw?"

"Oh—go away, Bret!" She stamped her foot and turned on him furiously. "You're horrid! Why must you always tease me? Why don't you just leave me alone?"

"My, my, still the little hellcat, I see." He stroked his

121

moustache as if to wipe away the grin still lingering on his mouth. "Tell me, have you had anyone shot lately?"

"Bret Dunlap, you get out of here and leave me alone or I'll—I'll—"

"Ah, there's my baby boy," Marie boomed, catching Bret off guard and hugging him to her high bosom. "I see you're finally getting some sense, son." She rolled her eyes in Mandy's direction.

"Hello, Mother, enjoying the party?" Bret kissed her lightly on the cheek, ignoring her pointed glances at Mandy.

"Sure am—it's a swell shindig. Why aren't you kids dancing?" Drawing Mandy to her, she pushed her into Bret's arms. "Go on, you two."

Taking her firmly by the hand, Bret led Mandy onto the dance floor, barely able to keep the triumphant grin off his face. "Sorry—Mother's orders." She glared at him, keeping her body as stiff as a board in his embrace. "You might as well relax and enjoy it, brat," he murmured silkily. "Just close your eyes and pretend it's Tod."

Mandy jerked her hand out of his grasp and would have stalked off the dance floor but he captured it quite easily and drew her back into his arms, keeping his hand firmly on her back. When he spoke again his voice was softly sincere. "I'm sorry, Mandy. That was unfair."

"Oh, I hate you!" But she moved in step with him, her feet following perfectly, her body pressed close. Anyone watching them would think they were merely two young people enjoying a waltz.

"Mandy, there's something I have to tell you. Look at me." She kept her chin stubbornly down, pressed almost to her chest and he put his hand under it and forced it up. "I know how you feel about Tod." *How could I help it*, he thought grimly, *the way your face lights up at the mere mention of his name.* "And I know you've been waiting for him all evening, think-

122

ing—well, assuming that he would be your escort to-night."

"That's none of your business, Bret! What I feel or do not feel for Tod is none of your concern and I do not wish to discuss him with you!" She tripped and felt his strong arm tighten about her waist, helping her re-gain her balance, and she hated him even more. *Mon Dieu*, would this silly waltz never end?

"Look, brat, I'm just trying to save you from making a fool of yourself." He was suddenly angry. Angry at her for being such a little ninny. Angry at himself for even caring. "Tod is bringing someone tonight, a girl—"

"You are lying! How dare you say such a thing! Tod would never insult me so! He loves me!"

"Listen, honey, I'm only telling you for your own good. So you won't be, well, shocked when Tod shows up with a lovely young lady on his arm."

"You are despicable, monsieur," she said icily. "I will not listen further to your lies." Her nails bit pain-fully into his hand, forcing him to release her, and she jerked free and stalked off the dance floor, her head held high, her carriage as haughty as a queen.

Bret squeezed the injured hand briefly, grinning wryly when he saw the four perfect half-moons where her fingernails had dug in. "Little spitfire," he mur-mured. Damn, but she was a proud, arrogant little filly. And getting to an age where she should be taken in hand and broken to the saddle before she developed too many bad habits.

Mandy snatched a glass of champagne from a pass-ing waiter's tray and gulped it down in one swallow. Setting the empty glass on the buffet table she went to find Jenny. She would ask her outright if Tod was in-deed bringing another girl to her party. She refused to believe anything Bret told her.

"Mandy, dear, come sit down a moment and catch your breath," Grace Dobson called and Mandy joined her and Jenny on a striped satin sofa. At once a waiter

123

appeared with a tray of champagne and murmured, "Ladies?"

"Yes, thank you," Grace said, taking one of the long-stemmed tulip glasses. Mandy and Jenny followed suit and the three thouched glass rims.

"Happy birthday, Mandy dear," Jenny said. "My, isn't it a lovely party?" Her blue eyes sparkled and her cheeks glowed from dancing every dance. She fanned herself with a lace-trimmed handkerchief, one foot tapping in time with the music. Grace was equally winded, her round, pretty face as pink as a new plum.

"Jenny," Mandy began, wondering how to ask about Tod without seeming too forward.

"Oh, here are the Arteagas," Jenny cried. "I've been wanting you to meet Ceasare, Mandy, he's such an old darling." She rose, pulling Mandy up with her and leading the way toward the front door.

The most incredible-looking woman Mandy had ever seen stood majestically in the foyer, her jet-black, silver-streaked hair piled high on top of her head and held in place with a turquoise comb at least a foot tall. A pale, shimmery *chalina* floated from the comb, falling to the hem of her gown in the back. She was very tall and her face was as chiselled and perfect as a marble statue, with high cheekbones and ruby red lips, eyes the color of ebony, skin as golden as the dark palomino horses she bred. Her bejewelled hand was lying in the crook of a gentleman's arm, a white-haired, handsome *caballero* dressed in the silver and gold of a Spanish don. His figure was as trim as a young man's and his face was kind and gentle, his eyes warm.

"Ceasare!" Jenny cried, taking the man's hands in hers and stretching up on tiptoe to kiss his cheek. *"Buenas noches! Como está usted?"*

"Ah, Jenny—*muy bien, gracias, Y, usted!*" He put an arm about her shoulders, smiling affectionately down at her from his great height.

"Juanita—*buenas noches, señora.*" Jenny took the woman's hand briefly without the pleasure that had been in her voice when she greeted Ceasare Arteaga. "I'd like to present my niece, Amanda Bradshaw. Mandy, Mr. and Mrs. Ceasare Arteaga, our neighbors."

"Mucho gusto en conocerla, señorita," Ceasare said in a warm, pleasant voice, his accent musically romantic. He clicked his high-heeled boots together, made a courtly bow and kissed her hand.

"Good evening, Miss Bradshaw," Juanita Arteaga said flatly, her inscrutable black eyes sweeping Mandy from head to foot, then moving on to gaze about the crowded room, dismissing her.

"Where's Juan?" Jenny asked. "Didn't he come with you?"

"Si, he is here." Ceasare looked toward the dancing couples on the floor, then chuckled softly. "I think your charming young niece has captured my Juan, eh, *querida*?"

Mandy followed his gaze and saw June dancing with a slim young man dressed in a breathtaking black and silver outfit. She could not see his face but his dark head was as sleek as a wet seal and his body was lean and graceful. June looked quite happy to be in his arms.

"My youngest son, Juan," Ceasare said, gesturing eloquently at the young man. "I will introduce you later, eh?" His soft, dark eyes gazed into hers a moment, as if looking for something, then he said, "But I forget my manners. I wish you a very *feliz cumpleaños*, Miss Bradshaw."

"Thank you," Mandy murmured, adding to herself, "I think." She certainly hoped he wouldn't continue to speak to her in Spanish as if she understood it. She realized that all the Bradshaws and everyone else she had met in San Francisco spoke Spanish as a second language and supposed she would have to learn as well. But for now she found it very confusing.

"Dispénseme, por favor," Juanita said crisply. "I see

125

some friends I wish to speak with." She turned and disappeared into the crowd without a backward glance.

Goodness, she's a cold fish, Mandy thought, not liking the Señora Juanita Arteaga at all. But Ceasare merely shrugged and turned back to Jenny, taking her hand in his. "Ah, my Jenny, and how do you feel, eh? When is the *nene* due?"

"Oh, Ceasare, how did you know?" Jenny flushed and glanced quickly down at her stomach. "I swear, you're a witch, you old darling."

"I know because I see it in your pretty pink cheeks, *querida,* and in the bright lights in your eyes. You are very happy, *si?*"

"*Si—muy, muy feliz.*" She squeezed his hand and leaned against him briefly. "Come, Ceasare, and have a glass of champagne and tell me all the gossip. I haven't seen you in too long a time."

"You have not come to visit my little cottage in too long a time, *querida.*" He tucked Jenny's hand through one arm, Mandy's through the other and led them across the dance floor toward the buffet tables.

"I know, *viejo amigo,* but Andy won't let me ride." She laughed up at him. "You know what an old mother hen he can be."

"*Si,* he takes good care of his *mujer.* This is as it should be." They found seats and sat down together, Ceasare motioning to a waiter to bring them champagne. "Ahh," he sighed after sipping the icy wine. "*Perfecto.* J.B. has most exquisite taste in champagne, does he not?" He sipped again.

"Isn't Lanora coming?" Jenny asked and Mandy thought she heard a slight edge to her voice. "I wouldn't think she could resist a fiesta such as this one."

"*Si,* she is here already." He looked toward the packed dancefloor, shrugged. "But I do not see her in so many people."

"We'll see her soon enough, I'm sure," Jenny mut-

126

tered under her breath, just loud enough for Mandy to hear.

A moment later, Ceasare cried, "Ah, there she is now, *querida*." He raised a hand, motioning, and Mandy glanced toward the dance floor.

The most beautiful woman she had ever seen was walking toward them. Her hair was blue-black, piled high in loose curls that escaped her ivory combs and fell enchantingly upon her bare shoulders. She wore a crimson gown of silk that clung to her body like a second skin from breast to knees, then flared out in hundreds of stiff ruffles. She had the most breathtaking figure that Mandy had ever seen and her face was utterly without flaw. Her skin was the color of old ivory and her eyes were black diamonds beneath thick, silky, sooty lashes. She was holding possessively to Tod Dunlap's arm.

"*Querida—Lanora!*" Ceasare called. "Come and meet your hostess."

Mandy wanted to die. Her stomach did a dull flip-flop and she thought she was going to be sick. Lanora Arteaga was clearly the most beautiful woman in the room. And she was just as clearly with Tod Dunlap. Mandy looked wildly about for some escape, not trusting herself to meet Ceasare's daughter, but there was none. She was trapped. She kept her eyes averted, watching the dancers but not seeing them, knowing she would burst into tears if she looked at Tod's face, wishing she were anyplace else in the world. *Oh, Tod,* she cried silently, *how could you?*

She was aware of Ceasare rising, of voices trilling greetings, smelled the sensual fragrance of Lanora Arteaga's perfume, heard Tod's voice saying her name.

"Amanda! How beautiful you look tonight. Happy birthday." He took her hand and kissed it and still she did not look directly at him. "May I present Señorita Lanora Arteaga? Miss Amanda Bradshaw."

"How do you do?" The voice was only slightly accented, cool, measured. Mandy raised her eyes and looked into Lanora's black appraising ones.

"Good evening, Señorita Arteaga," she said stiffly, then quickly dropped her eyes. She did not trust herself to speak to Tod.

Ceasare called for more champagne and again glasses were raised to her, saluting her birthday. She glanced quickly at Tod, hoping to see something in his face, anything that would tell her he had not wanted to bring this beautiful Mexican girl to her party, that he had somehow been tricked into it. But he was gazing at Lanora, his arm about her waist as they stood close together and sipped their champagne. Didn't he know this was her coming-out party? Hadn't he said to her many times that he couldn't wait until she grew up? Hadn't he kissed her and told her how much he wanted her? Then what was he doing here with that girl? A Mexican girl, no less. She was instantly ashamed of her prejudice and quickly gulped down the remainder of her wine. She wouldn't let him know how much he had hurt her, she vowed, how he had disappointed her on the most important night of her young life. She would be just as cool and sophisticated as he was.

June and Juan joined the group and Mandy saw that Bret was with them. She acknowledged the introduction to Ceasare's youngest son, wondering briefly where the eldest might be, then turned to Bret and dimpled prettily. "Oh, Bret, be a dear and get me another glass of champagne, will you please?" She placed a hand on his arm, fluttering her lashes at him, and both his eyebrows shot up in surprise.

"Yes, of course. Your servant, madam," he murmured, just barely concealing the amusement in his voice. He had only to reach behind him for a fresh glass and this he handed to her with a small bow. The expression on his face was mocking and a little bewildered.

"Thank you," Mandy said sweetly, leaning toward him and again placing her hand on his arm, as Lanora's hand was on Tod's arm. "Isn't it a wonderful party? Everyone has just been so *sweet* to me. And the dancing—*mon Dieu*! I fear I shan't be able to take a step for a week!" She gave a tinkling little laugh, her eyes flirting in Juan's direction, in Ceasare's and Bret's, totally ignoring Tod.

"Well, in that case I'd better claim a dance while you're still able," Bret said easily. Taking her champagne glass he set it on the table and whirled her out onto the dance floor. She laughed up into his face, gaily, as if she hadn't a care in the world. He drew her close, murmuring, "Can I possibly hope that you've had a change of heart? Or are you trying to make Tod jealous?"

"Oh, fa, do not be so suspicious, monsieur," she said playfully, but inside she seethed that he had seen through her little act. "It is a lady's prerogative to change her mind, is it not?" She glanced over his shoulder and saw June flirting with Juan Arteaga, her eyes speaking volumes behind her fluttering fan. Why couldn't she act that way with Tod? Why did he make her feel so tongue-tied and silly? She saw him take Lanora's hand and bring it to his lips, his beautiful blue eyes gazing into her black ones as he spoke to her. Mandy wished she could hear what he was saying, and knew she would die if she did, It was obvious the words were caresses, the way he looked at her.

She tripped and Bret steadied her with a strong hand on her back. "A little too much champagne?" he asked lightly.

"Oh, do not be silly! I am quite accustomed to drinking champagne, thank you." She tossed her head, pulling her gaze away from Tod with difficulty, concentrating on flirting with Bret. "Surely you have heard that the French drink wine instead of water. Why, at home in New Orleans I often had ice-cold champagne with my breakfast!" It was a lie and she wondered why on earth she had said such a thing.

"I see," Bret grinned. "Well, I must say, it agrees

129

with you. Never have I seen you more lovely." Instantly a picture of her under the waterfall came to his mind and he felt a stirring in his groin. With a soft, inaudible moan he pulled her closer until their bodies were touching from breast to knees. He breathed in the perfume of her hair and longed to kiss her. She aroused feelings in him that he had never felt in all his twenty-four years. He had been with countless women, and had known all the ecstasy of lovemaking at its best and at its most casual. But never had he felt such an overwhelming desire as he now felt for Mandy. He wanted to tell her how he felt, take her for moonlight rides, court her, kiss her beneath the silvery branches of the towering lilac bushes, make love to her. . . .

"*Merci, monsieur,*" she giggled and tripped again, almost falling.

"Steady there, honey," he laughed, thinking how charming and cute she was when she was tipsy. Then he saw where she was looking and tightened his lips in anger. She was gazing wistfully at Tod, her big blue eyes naked with love. He wanted to slap her, or shake her until her teeth rattled for being such a little fool. He had to get her alone and try to talk some sense into her before she made a complete ass of herself in front of everyone. "Come on, Mandy, let's take a walk in the garden and get you some much-needed air." He steered her toward the double doors leading outside, gritting his teeth when she glanced back over her shoulder at Tod.

Had he noticed her? Would he be jealous to know she was going into the garden with his brother? She moved closer to Bret, her fingers entwined with his, and threw her head back flirtatiously, smiling up at him. But inside her heart ached, wishing it were Tod's hand she held, Tod taking her into the quiet, dark garden to try to steal a kiss.

The musical sound of water spilling over rocks and splashing into pools filled the night air and mingled with the song of a goldfinch courting its mate. A cool breeze blew wisps of curls across her forehead and playfully lifted the hem of her gown. A full moon hung heavy and golden in the dark sky and bathed the brick path in silver as they walked slowly, hand in hand. Bret yearned to take her into his arms and kiss her; Mandy wished it were Tod with her in this lover's paradise, wishing she would look up and see him striding toward her, pulling her away from Bret and declaring that she was his girl . . .

Another couple, hand in hand, strolled past them and Mandy suddenly felt like crying. All the champagne she had consumed too quickly, plus the shock of seeing Tod with Lanora Arteaga, churned inside her head. Her stomach lurched and she wondered for one wild moment if she was going to throw up. She was suddenly very thankful to Bret for being there when she needed him. And he really wasn't too bad, when he wasn't teasing her or trying to make her mad. She would show Tod that she could interest another man, that she was every bit as desirable as the sultry señorita. She swallowed back the sickness that rose in her throat, gulping in deep breaths of cool air to quell the nausea.

"Let's sit down a moment, shall we?" she murmued so weakly that Bret was instantly alarmed.

"Mandy, honey, are you all right?" Quickly he guided her to a stone bench next to a fountain and sat her down. "Do you feel sick to your stomach?"

"No, no," she murmured, forcing a tiny smile. "I am just so exhausted from all the dancing—the closeness—" She fanned herself with her hand. "*Mon Dieu,* but it was warm inside, no?"

"No, it wasn't all that warm," Bret grinned, the teasing note back in his voice. "I think perhaps you're just the slightest bit drunk, my love."

"Fa!" she scoffed. "I did not drink so much." Tossing her head, she gave him an arch look. "Besides, it is my birthday, no? A time when I leave childhood behind and become a woman."

She had daydreamed of becoming a woman in Tod's arms this night, determined to prove to him that she

131

was grown up enough for a woman's love. The thought pained her and she looked quickly away from Bret's too-knowing eyes. Oh, how could Tod have brought that woman to her party? She had been so sure that he truly loved her and was waiting, as impatiently as she, for this night when she would be considered a young woman in the eyes of the world, and he would no longer have to draw away from her kisses as he had done the night they had gone to the theater. She could feel his mouth upon her still and her cheeks grew warm with the memory.

"You're still a little way from being a woman, short-cake," Bret laughed, unaware of the dark misery in her downcast eyes. "Why, you look like a little girl sitting there, a little girl whose doll has—"

"Oh, you are insufferable, Bret Dunlap!" she interrupted angrily. "Why must you always tease me? Call me a child and—"

"Whoa, what brought this on?" He was plainly bewildered. One moment she was being flirtatious and coy, the next a spitting, hissing kitten. "I'm sorry if I said anything to offend you, Mandy. I assure you I meant no disrespect by saying you look like a little girl. You *do,* you know, whether you like it or not."

"Oh, just leave me alone." Her lower lip stuck out like a petulant child's and she glared up at him. "You always spoil everything! It was such a wonderful party until—" She broke off, biting her lower lip to keep back the tears.

"Hey, sweetheart, it wasn't me who spoiled your party." Anger made his voice sharper than he had intended. "My big brother is the one who brought Lanora Arteaga, not me."

Mandy whirled on him, cheeks flushed, eyes snapping anger. "Why do you mention her? That—that Mexican girl? Who said anything about her?"

You did, honey, he wanted to say. *The worst case of green-eyed jealousy I've ever seen is written all over your pretty little face.* "Well," he drawled, "it seemed to me the party was going fine until Tod showed up with Lanora, so I just assumed?"

"You assume far too much, Bret Dunlap!" she snapped. "I care nothing for your brother. He certainly has the right to bring anyone he chooses to my party!"

"I see," Bret murmured, his heart aching for the pain she was suffering. He was not blind to his brother's charms and he hated like hell to see such an innocent young girl like Mandy falling for him. What had transpired between them that had made her believe that Tod was in love with her? The rogue had no doubt taken advantage of her on one of the nights they had gone into San Francisco together. He was well aware of the times Tod had escorted Mandy to the theater or dinner, chaperoned by Jenny and Andy of course, but he knew his brother well enough to know that he would find a time to be alone with such a lovely young thing as Mandy. A cold chill sliced through him. What if Tod had pushed his advantage, gone beyond a few kisses in the back of a carriage? Would Mandy, in the innocence of first love, have given herself to him? The thought sickened him and he felt all the more protective of her.

"No, you don't see! No one sees anything at all about how I feel! Oh, how I hate California! I wish I'd never been forced to come to this terrible place!" She pounded her fists upon her knees in fury, bright tears sparkling in her eyes. "I want my *grandmaman*! I want to go home! I hate it here!"

"You *are* home, honey, and if you'd quit throwing temper tantrums long enough to look around you'd see that you're very much wanted here. Very much loved." His voice grew husky and he had to grip the edge of the bench to keep from taking her in his arms. "J.B. loves you very much and so does Jenny and Andy and Jane—hell, everyone does. If you weren't such a spoiled brat you'd see just how lucky you are. Not many young ladies are given a home such as the Bradshaws have given you. You have every advantage, every consideration—"

133

"I asked for none of it," she interrupted sullenly. "I wanted none of it. I was packed up like so much baggage and sent clear across the world to this awful, ugly place with awful people! I hate it!" She stuck out her lower lip and crossed her arms firmly across her bosom. "And I won't stay here, either. Nobody can make me stay."

"There's a little matter of J.B. being your legal guardian, not to mention your next of kin," Bret drawled, fighting to keep the amusement out of his voice. Five minutes ago she had been in agony over her unrequited love; now she was pouting like a three-year-old because she hadn't gotten her way. Her people in New Orleans must have spoiled her rotten. What she needed was a good paddling.

Lip still protruding, she gave a Gallic shrug. "Then I shall wait until I am old enough to leave. But nobody can make me live in this awful place if I don't want to!"

"Oh, I'm convinced of that, honey. I don't think anyone could make you do anything you didn't want to do."

"You are right about that, monsieur." She giggled, her good humor restored. "And I do not wish to stay out here any longer. I want to dance and drink champagne and—and have *bamboucher*!" She stood and whirled around, arms flung wide, the champagne now making her feel as if she was floating in air, where a moment ago it had made her feel so very sad. What a strange and heady wine. Fa on Tod Dunlap! She would show him she could be every bit as enchanting as Señorita Lanora Arteaga. She glanced at Bret from beneath her lashes. *Mon Dieu*, but he was an attractive man. Almost as handsome as his brother. But Bret's eyes were brown where Tod's were such an astonishing blue. Well, Bret would just have to do. She would make Tod so very jealous that he would leave that woman and take her away. And dance every dance with no one else but her the rest of the evening. And at midnight he

134

would take her beneath the trellis of roses and kiss her eighteen times—one for every year. . . .

She danced along the path ahead of Bret, laughing back at him, when she saw him suddenly stiffen and hesitate. She followed his gaze and saw Tod and Lanora just ahead. They were standing in the shadows of the rose-covered trellis, arms entwined, bodies pressed close in a passionate embrace. Her heart seemed to have stopped beating altogether. She stared at them, her eyes unable to tear themselves away from the intimate scene. She watched as Tod's hands moved down Lanora's back to cup and caress her buttocks, then watched them move slowly, sensuously up again to hug and press her closer. Watched Lanora's midnight black hair tumbling over Tod's hands as he tangled them in its lushness and bent her head back against the roses. Saw the red lips murmuring and heard Tod's answering murmur before he claimed them again.

"Mandy," Bret whispered huskily. "Let's go inside. Come on, honey."

At the sound of the low voice, Tod and Lanora drew apart and turned to see them standing not twenty feet from them. Mandy thought quickly. Reaching up to pull Bret's head down, she whispered urgently, "Kiss me." Then her ripe young body was pressed the length of him, her lips parting.

Bret kissed her, wishing he had the guts to push her away. He knew full well what she was doing. It was so obvious. Poor, love-struck little brat. But he did object just a little being used like one of Mother's prize palomino studs to make Tod jealous. Then, feeling the ardor and passion in her body, he thought, *what the hell? Why not enjoy it? This is probably the only way she'll ever kiss me.* He moved his hands in slow, caressing circle across her back, wrapping his arms almost twice around her slender frame, and felt his fingers encounter the warm flesh of her breasts. She sighed and wiggled closer, arching her back so her breasts were crushed flat against his chest, her arms strong around him.

135

When the kiss ended she glanced quickly toward the rose trellis, seeking Tod's face. She did not see the swift hurt in Bret's eyes as he followed her glance, nor would she have cared if she had. She cared only what Tod thought. Had he seen her in his brother's arms? Was he jealous? But Tod and Lanora had stepped even further back into the shadows. They were totally oblivious to Bret and Mandy.

Determined to forget what a fool she had made of herself in the garden, Mandy danced every dance with a different partner, flirting outrageously. It was after midnight when Bret finally claimed her for a dance and cautioned, "Take it easy, brat, every female in the room is plotting your murder!"

"How lovely," Mandy laughed. "And is the *Señorita* Lanora Arteaga also planning my demise?"

"I rather doubt it," Bret said dryly. "She seems to be keeping your admirers warm for you between dances." He nodded in the direction of the massive buffet where Lanora stood surrounded by men, each one offering her some tasty tidbit from the laden table. Her long black hair tumbled like a dark cloud upon her bare shoulders, her ruby lips were parted enticingly, and her sultry hot eyes rested briefly upon each man invitingly. But Mandy noticed that she still kept one hand firmly on Tod's arm, and that Tod seemed just as smitten with her as every other man who surrounded her, clamoring for her attention.

"Mon Dieu, mo ganye faim!" Mandy said lightly. "Will you take me to supper, Bret?"

Hungry, my eye, Bret thought sourly. What a transparent little wench she was. "Your servant, madam," he said mockingly, leading her from the dance floor. She clapped her hands together in delight (first checking to see if Tod had noticed her arrival) when she saw the buffet. There were appetizers of oysters, bisque with sour cream and sherry, cold lobster salad, shrimp bisque, tiny grilled frankfurters soaked in brandy and

136

barbeque sauce, Swedish meatballs and gravy, light, delicate cheese puffs and thin wedges of crackers piled high with red and black caviar. And racks of lamb, a joint of veal, a saddle of beef, fresh broiled trout, several whole hams glazed and topped with pineapple rings, spicy Indian curry, silver dishes of vegetables, tureens of soup and succulent gravies and sauces, straw baskets of French bread and puffy dinner rolls. And desserts: chocolate mousse, chestnut glacé parfait, assorted French pastries, pies and cakes.

They filled their plates and went to sit with Jenny and Andy, who were at a table with Ceasare Arteaga, Juan and June. Mandy saw J. B. dancing with Juanita Arteaga and was surprised to see the intimate look that passed between them. He was holding her as close as a lover and she was gazing up at him, her dark eyes sensual. Then he whirled her away and they were lost in the crowd. Goodness, could *Grandpapa* be having an affair with that rude, imperious woman? No, it wasn't possible. Besides, she was married to Ceasare. She shrugged, her mind too befuddled with champagne to try to sort out the intrigues of all the people she had met this evening.

She sat quietly, glad of a chance to rest, listening to the others talking and laughing. She ate very little but drank more champagne, liking the dreamy, floating feeling it gave her, as if she were totally without bones, capable of lifting her arms and drifting off into space. Everything in the huge room seemed to swirl in pastel colors, the ladies' gowns, the winking chandeliers, the flash of silver serving trays, the sparkle of crystal wine goblets, the brilliance of jewels. She closed her eyes and swayed dangerously near the edge of her chair and would have toppled over had not Bret's arm shot out to grasp her.

"Easy, honey," he whispered, his eyes anxious as he righted her in her chair. Keeping a restraining arm about her he asked, "Are you all right?"

"But of course—I'm fine . . ." She shook her head

137

to clear it and found that she had difficulty focusing on Bret's face. He looked so familiar. Who was it he reminded her of? Of course, Tod, He looked just like Tod Dunlap.

"Sure you are," Bret grinned. He stood, pulling her up with him and whispered in her ear, "Come on, brat, what you need is some fresh air and a stroll around the garden before you lose all this fine food J.B. so lavishly provided." He said something to the others at the table and they all smiled, laughed up at her, then he was leading her across the room and out the double French doors that led into the garden.

"I feel funny," she murmured, leaning against him and letting him guide her down the curved brick path.

"I shouldn't wonder, what with all the champagne you put away," Bret laughed. "And I thought you Frenchies could hold your wine." She gave him a lopsided grin and shrugged, too woozy to answer. Her feet didn't seem to be touching the path at all and yet she tripped over the smallest of stones, falling against Bret. "I think we'd better sit down for a minute." He led her down a side path that led to a vine-covered gazebo set back from the garden and surrounded by a profusion of trees and shrubs.

He sat down next to her. Music drifted faintly to them from the house and the tinkling splash of the many fountains joined in the orchestration, filling the still night air with romance. Mandy leaned back and closed her eyes, marvelling at the sudden floating sensation that swept over her. Her head spun and she felt as weightless as a feather, as if she were not touching the chaise at all, but hovering above it. "Mandy." The word seemed to come from some other dimension. "God, Mandy, you're so damn beautiful!" The feel of warm, urgent lips upon hers. Tod. She raised her arms and wrapped them about him, drawing him down on top of her, kissing him back with a sudden, burning desire that jolted through her like a bolt of lightning.

"Darling," she whispered breathlessly. *"Mon*

138

amour." She opened her eyes to gaze into the face so close to hers, at the full sensual lips that brought such new and exciting feelings to her. She let her hands roam upon the broad back and shoulders, feeling the hard muscles beneath the expensive fabric of his jacket. She tried to see his eyes in the darkness of the gazebo but could not. His blue, blue eyes that caused her to shiver even when she was warm. Ah, Tod, *mon amour,* she thought dreamily, closing her eyes again when his lips claimed hers, his arms gathering her close to the steady beating of his heart.

Bret felt the heat rise in his groin and a pulse set up a steady pounding, flooding him with desire. He knew he should pull away. Mandy was clearly intoxicated and he certainly wasn't the type of heel to take advantage of the situation. But, Jesus! She kissed him with such passion, such obvious desire that he could not stop himself. Not just yet. He had waited too long to have her like this, soft and pliant in his arms, the sassy sneer wiped off her lovely face, replaced with raw, pure lust. With love. It shone from her eyes like a beacon and he followed it, like a drowning man giving himself up to the lure of the sea.

"Mandy, my beautiful Mandy," he whispered huskily, his hands trembling in their eagerness as he fumbled for her breast. He groaned aloud when his fingers closed around the soft, hot mound. He caressed her nipples between thumb and forefinger, bringing them to rigid erectness. He bent his head and kissed them, tasting their sweetness, suckling like a babe, and heard her answering cry and soft breathing, French words of love slipping sensuously over him like a warm blanket.

"Ah, *mon amour,*" she panted. "Kiss me, kiss me—" Her hands drew him up, tangled in his hair as she pulled his mouth down upon hers. She felt his tongue parting her lips and opened her mouth for him. Felt his hard body lowering its full weight upon her and arched up to meet it. Felt his hands tugging at her gown, baring her breasts, then cupping them firmly. She had wanted to feel his hands upon her every since she had first gazed into his blue eyes and heard him speak her name. *Tod,* she thought dreamily, *you do love me. You do!*

I must stop this, Bret thought, even as his hands caressed her bare breasts, unable to release them. He kissed her throat, the tops of her breasts, then took the nipples in his mouth again, powerless to resist. He heard her soft whispers and felt her hands in his hair, urging him closer. With a groan, he drew away and rolled as far as he could on his side of the wide chaise. Like a bed, he thought, cursing himself for thinking it. Her long hair had come undone. Her pale silk gown was crumpled down around her waist and tumbled up about her thighs, and he couldn't stop himself from staring at her legs, silvery white in the moonlight. She had lost one high-heeled slipper and the Bradshaw diamonds and rubies rode high around her neck like a fabulous noose, holding her captive for his caresses. She looked like a wanton gypsy wench, her full lips crushed red from his wild kisses, her eyes stormy as a turquoise sea, her arms reaching for him. . . .

"Mandy, honey, please," he said harshly, huskily. "We have to stop this. God! I'm only human!"

"Why must we, *mon amour?*" she whispered, her hands finding his chest and unbuttoning his rufflefronted shirt. He groaned aloud when her fingers touched his bare skin, burning into his chest like a hot branding iron.

"Because we must, that's all." He took her hands and drew them away but she pulled free and caressed his chest again, running her fingers playfully through the thick hair, gently grazing his nipples, slipping down toward the front of his trousers. "Mandy! Christ!" He grabbed her hands again, forcing them down on either side of her and holding them there. "Do you realize what you're doing to me, brat?" His voice was a soft tremble, throaty, tortured. "God, if I thought for a sec-

140

ond that you knew what you were doing, I'd—" He forced his eyes away from her heaving breasts, her naked thighs. "Christ, Mandy, you're drunk and don't know what you're doing and I'm too much of a gentleman to take advantage of—"

"I know what I'm doing," she said clearly, gazing straight up into his eyes. Funny, they looked brown in the dim glow of the gazebo. But his wonderful mouth was just as she remembered it. Better, perhaps, for now he didn't kiss her as savagely as he had the night of the theater. Now his kisses were soft, warm, speaking of a tender love that she had known he would feel. She had planned this from the first moment J.B. had informed her of the party. Planned to seduce Tod if necessary, to prove that she was now a woman of marriageable age. "I have wanted this to happen for ever so long, *mon amour*. Ever since first you kissed me."

"You have?" Bret stared down at her, seeing clearly the love and desire in her face, knowing that she spoke the truth. No one could look that way at a man unless she wanted him with all her heart. Jesus, what a contrary little minx. He had thought she hated him and now she was telling him that she had loved him every since that afternoon by the waterfall when he had stolen a kiss. Great God, what should he do? He was sure that she was a virgin, but she certainly wasn't acting like one tonight. She had freed her hands from his grasp and was gently tracing a pattern around his lips with one finger.

"*Oui, chérie*, ever since that first kiss when you took my breath away," she sighed, arms reaching, pulling him down to her parted lips.

Bret held himself back, shaking so violently that his breath came in little hisses. "Mandy, are you sure?"

"*Oui*, never have I been so sure of anything, *mon amour. Je t'aime*."

"Oh sweet Jesus, Mandy—" With a groan he fell upon her, gathering her close to his pounding heart, covering her face and mouth with kisses, his hands wild in their exploration of her perfect body. He tore at his clothes, ripping off pearl buttons in his haste, shoving his trousers down with shaking hands. He drew her crumpled gown free and flung it aside, staring with awe at her nakedness. "My God, you're so beautiful, so sexy, Mandy!" Then he fell upon her, burying his face in the wild tangle of her hair, driving deep and true into the sweet softness of her.

Mandy cried out when he penetrated, flinching away from the hot streak of pain that ripped through her, biting her lower lip until she tasted blood. Her arms gripped him tight, her thighs trembling about his waist as she raised herself to meet his strong, swift thrusts. The pain was instantly replaced by a feeling like none other she had ever known. It was as if her entire body was on fire, pulsating with a savage, primitive rhythm of its own. Her blood coursed wildly, soared, pounded through her at an alarming rate, sending her head reeling into a dark abyss of pleasure so intense she felt faint. She arched up higher, harder, her legs scissoring about his narrow waist, feeling him fill her with his desire. Hips drummed against hips, mouths sought and clung together, tongues entwined, arms clutched and caressed.

She seemed to suddenly explode beneath him as if she had been flung up and out of her body, spinning in a spiral of heavenly joy that was like nothing she had ever experienced. Her breath caught in little sobs in her throat and she feared her heart would burst right out of her breast, so violently did it pound and flutter. A great tremble shuddered throughout her body, starting from her toes and pulsating up her legs, turning them to water, lurching in the pit of her stomach, caught in her throat, turning her mouth to dry cotton, searing brightly behind her closed eyelids. *Mon Dieu, what is happening to me?* was her last coherent thought before all the lights in the world went off with a loud bang.

She awoke with a start, sitting bolt upright on the chaise and looking wildly about. Where was she? Feeling the cooling night breeze she glanced down. "*Mon dieu*, I am naked!" she gasped, crossing her arms across her breasts. She gathered up her gown and held it to her bosom, looking hard into the darkness toward the still brightly-lit house. A figure moved in the shadows of the gazebo and a bright round spot of light glowed as it moved toward her. "Who is there?" she cried in real fright, staring into the dark shadows.

"It's okay, darling, it's me." Bret came toward her, a lighted cheroot in his hand. He was fully clothed but his dark hair was mussed and his ruffled shirt was open to the waist, exposing his hairy chest and flat stmoach. Idiotically, she wondered why he had no buttons on his shirt; then, remembering that she was naked beneath the hastily gathered up gown she gasped and her face went pale.

"Bret," she cried, trying to arrange the gown so that it covered as much as possible. "What are you doing here? Where is Tod?"

The soft smile of love that had been on his face hardened into a grimace. "Tod? What the hell does Tod have to do with anything?"

She shook her head, clearing it a little. What had happened to her? Where was Tod? She felt the throbbing, sensual awareness of her body and knew in an instant what had happened. She had become a woman this night as she had planned. But where was Tod? And what was Bret doing here? She glared up at him, angry and confused. "Bret Dunlap, what childish games are you playing now? What have you done with Tod? Oh, you are truly a horrid man to spy on us!"

"Spy on you?" Bret repeated slowly, unwilling to believe what she was implying. Could she possibly have mistaken him for Tod, believing that it was Tod who had made love to her? No, it was impossible. Ludicrous. "Mandy, honey," he said softly, bending down to

143

take her hands. "Tod was never out here. Don't you remember? We—"

"He was so!" Mandy cried, jerking her hands free and drawing as far away from him as possible. "He was just here, on this very chaise. We—we—" Her face flushed crimson as sudden memory flooded back. She squeezed her eyes shut in an agony of embarrassment and shame. Oh, that blackguard! That cad! It was despicable! Beneath contempt. She hurled a French curse at him, the vilest one she could think of. "Oh, how I hate you, Bret Dunlap! You—you filthy beast! How dare you spy on me!"

"What the hell—?" Bret sank down upon the chaise and captured her fists in his hands. "Listen, brat, Tod was never out here. I brought you out for a breath of fresh air, remember? You had had too much to drink and—"

"You are lying! You always lie!" She jerked one hand free and slapped him full in the face, struggling to free the other one but he held it tight.

"God damn it," he swore, his eye smarting from her hard little fist. "Sit still and listen, will you?" She struggled against him, and her gown fell away. With a cry she tried to hide herself, but he held her easily. "If I let you get your gown will you promise to sit still and behave yourself?"

"I promise you nothing, you odious beast!" She succeeded in biting his hand and he yelped and released her long enough for her to snatch up her gown and cover herself. Clasping it high around her neck she glared at him over a ruffle of lace. He was sitting almost on top of her, pinning her to the chaise and she knew that further attempts to free herself would be futile. Flinging herself sullenly back against the cushions of the chaise she continued to glare at him furiously.

"You're going to listen whether you like it or not," Bret gritted through clenched teeth, aching to slap the haughty sneer from her lovely face. Never had he been so grossly insulted in all his life. My God, she didn't even remember making love to him! And what was much, much worse, she thought she had lost her virginity to his brother, Tod! *The bitch*! he seethed angrily, his pride hurt as much as his heart. He longed to close his hands around her slim, proud throat and squeeze until she begged him for mercy. Wanted to hurt her as badly as she had hurt him. Wanted her to feel the searing agony like a red-hot coal in the pit of her stomach—as he was feeling it. "It was me, bitch!" he gritted roughly and grabbed her shoulders, shaking her until her hair tumbled into her face. "I'm the one who fucked you! *Me*—you understand? Not big brother Tod!"

Swift, hot color flooded her face and she gasped in shock, never having heard that word spoken aloud. She covered her face with her hands and scalding tears gathered like a bursting dam behind her trembling fingers. It wasn't true! *Mon Dieu*, it could not be true! She shook her head back and forth wildly, denying his words even when deep down inside she knew he had spoken the truth. "No—no," she cried, then burst into violent sobs, rocking back and forth, whimpering like a wounded animal. "No no no, it can't be—it isn't true!"

"It is true, you little bitch," Bret shouted, shaking her again until her head snapped loosely on her neck like a broken rag doll. "It's true and you damn well better believe it. Christ, you threw yourself at me like some hot-assed slut! What did you expect me to do? Play the gentleman to the bitter end?"

"No, no—don't say it—don't say it!" She put her hands over her ears to shut out the ugly words.

"Yes, by God, you're going to hear me." He jerked her hands away from her ears, gripping them so tight she cried out in pain. "You threw yourself at me, sweetheart, like a bitch dog in heat, wagging your pretty little tail under my nose, begging me to make love to you—and in French, yet!"

"I didn't! I didn't!" She tried to jerk her hands free but he held her fast.

145

"Oh, yes you did, bitch." He gave a short nasty laugh and felt a slice of pain cut through his heart like a scythe. "Hell, I even played the gentleman—tried to talk you out of it, like a fucking fool! But you said—you told me—" His voice broke and he felt hot tears pricking behind his eyelids. He flung her away from him, stood and strode quickly away. "Ah, shit, the hell with it! The hell with you!" He jerked a cheroot from his pocket and lit it with hands that trembled, drawing the smoke deep into his lungs, then exhaling furiously. He wanted to walk out of there and leave her sitting naked and crumpled for someone else to find. But he knew he couldn't. He controlled the anger in his voice as much as he was able, keeping it curt and gruff. "Get dressed. I'll take you back to the house."

"No, don't you dare come near me, Bret Dunlap!" She sat straight up, her eyes shooting daggers. "Don't you dare look at me! *Mon Dieu*, what have I done?" She rocked back and forth, sobbing as if her heart was broken. "Oh, go away! Just please go away!"

"Suit yourself." Turning on his heel he strode quickly down the path, disappearing in the shadows.

She opened her mouth to call him back when she realized what a dreadful state of dishevelment she was in. Her lovely gown was wrinkled and stained, spotted with her virgin blood, dark with the sweat of their bodies. Her hair was a horror of tangles. She had lost a slipper and even in the darkness of the gazebo she knew that her body was covered with bruises.

Sniffling, hating Bret with all the emotion of her eighteen years, she struggled into her gown, fastening it as best she could. She took off her remaining slipper and hid it beneath a lilac bush, then stumbled barefoot onto the brick path, staggering still from the effects of the champagne. Her legs ached and down below, where he had entered her, a dull throbbing had started that embarrassed and shamed her so much she began crying all over again. Keeping in the shadows, she ran swiftly around the side of the house and climbed the outside stairs that led to her grandfather's suite. Jeramy had told her that J.B. had had the stairs built to smuggle in his mistresses without disturbing the rest of the family.

As she neared her grandfather's door she heard the lively swell of music and the laughter down in the ballroom where most of the guests still were dancing. She held her breath as she eased open the door, peering around to make sure Luis was not there. Then she ran as swiftly as her legs would carry her across the floor, out of the door, down the hall an into her own room. Throwing the latch, she leaned heavily against it, panting as if the very devil were after her. Sudden panic thudded in her brain. What if Caleen were waiting for her? But a quick glance about the silent, orderly room quieted her fears. Besides, Caleen would be downstairs helping Atoka in the kitchen.

Ripping her gown off she wadded it into a ball and buried it in the furthest corner of her closet. Never would she be able to look at that gown without remembering what had happened to her on this awful, dreadful night. She stripped off her underwear, pulled on a nightgown and crawled into bed. A fresh torrent of tears gushed down her cheeks as she moved her hands gently over her body, feeling her swollen breasts, so tender to the touch. And down there where Bret had— where he—she flung herself over on her stomach and wept into the pillow, sobbing until she was so exhausted she did not even know that sleep had come to heal her.

CHAPTER SEVEN

All day flocks of geese and ducks had made dark Vs against the stormy clouds, honking and quacking their farewells as they headed south for the winter. Horses and cattle had lost their sleek, shiny coats and were ragged with their rough winter growth, their breath frosty in the cool air. The pungent odor of singed hair, the fragrance of sage, the squeal of a hog signalled fall on the Bradshaw ranch and slaughtering time. Atoka and Caleen took turns at the huge lard-making tub and there were many ropes of sage-scented sausages hanging from the rafters of the smokehouse. On the butcher block were stacks of salted flatback, whole hams, pork chops and wafer-thin slices of bacon. The sweet smell of sugar-cured hams hung heavy in the room and just outside the door, frying to a crisp turn in deep fat, were the cracklings that would be used to make cornbread.

Blackbirds swarmed in droves and in the distance could be seen a slowly circling squad of vultures that had been attracted by the smell of fresh blood. Doves sat on fenceposts during the day and industrious squirrels scurried around searching for tidbits for their winter pantries. Black walnuts fell to the ground and trees turned splendid shades of red, russet, yellow and gold. Beavers and otters disappeared from the swift-running streams and deer ventured a little closer to the stables in hopes of finding carelessly scattered flakes of hay.

The sun was high in the sky, a red ball on the mountain tops, as Mandy cantered Goldie down the eucalyptus-lined path. The air was nippy but the sun was warm on her face and hands. She tilted her hat at an angle across her eyes, jumped Goldie over the fallen log near Otter River and urged her into a gallop. The wind whipped Goldie's mane across her hands and stung her eyes, sending little puffs of lint from the drying pussy-willows to settle in white mounds on Mandy's dark riding habit. She was glad she had worn her heavy jacket and old Doc had insisted that she tie a slicker behind her saddle in case of rain.

"Cain't be too careful this time o' year," he had warned, ever the worrier. "Why, I've seed it sunny and prettier than a picture one minute, then all hell break loose the next. Thunder, lightning, rain and I don't know what all acomin' like the bejesus out of nowhere! Flood a creek in nothin' flat and drown out a crop in one day."

"If it even looks like rain, I'll turn right back," Mandy had assured him, smiling wryly at his customary pessimisim. Every time she took a ride he warned her about every danger from vicious mountain lions to a mild case of sunburn.

She did not ride in the direction of the pond near the waterfall where she had first met that insufferable swine, Bret Dunlap, but turned south, heading for Los Gatos and the Arteaga ranch. A herd of American antelope grazed serenely with a herd of mule deer and flocks of birds perched on their shaggy backs, busily devouring the parasites that lived there. A condor swooped down so low in the sky that Mandy could hear the swoosh of his mighty wings as he settled on the branch of a gnarled oak tree, its twisted limbs bare and stricken-looking. Its enormous trunk sheltered a pot-pourri of tenants: squirrels, woodpeckers, racoons and pine martens.

The woody, intricate chaparral became more impenetrable the higher she climbed, forcing Goldie to jump over it rather than gallop through it. Suddenly the chaparral gave way to a meadow of lush, deep grass, spot-

149

ted with oak and pepper trees, a narrow stream rushing pellmell over pebbles and a small series of waterfalls. Mandy spurred Goldie forward and let her have a drink of the clear, cold water. She snorted and buried her nose up to the nostrils, a sure sign of a fine, spirited horse. Poor quality horses only touched their lips to the water when drinking, Mandy had learned from Doc.

She walked Goldie through the belly-deep grass, giving her her head so she could reach down for a mouthful every few feet. She wondered if this lovely meadow had a name and if she was still on her grandfather's property. Most of his range this high up in the mountains was not fenced in as his livestock pasture was.

Set back between towering pepper trees was a tiny cottage, its sod sides showing a ragged growth of dried grass between each square of hard-packed earth, the roof as deep in grass as the meadow she had just ridden through. Several goats grazed on the roof and Mandy saw several more lying or standing in the sun near the cottage, serenely chewing their cuds. A huge cage held a condor, its wing bandaged and tied to its side with a leather thong. As she drew nearer she saw other cages, each holding an animal or bird in some state of ill health. There was a raccoon with a white bandage on one front paw and a cougar cub that couldn't have been more than a few days old, so milky and unfocused were his eyes. A bloodhound got slowly to his feet when he saw Mandy, loose flaps of skin hanging forlornly over his sunken eyes, his tail wagging weakly. He tried to bark but only a sort of baleful croak escaped his throat; then he sank back down in a spot of sun near the cottage door.

Wondering if she should turn and ride away before she disturbed the owners of this enchanting little place, Mandy was just ready to set her heels to Goldie's side when the door opened and Ceasare Arteaga stepped outside. "Ah, Señorita Bradshaw! What a pleasant surprise! *Bienvenido!* Welcome!"

"Señor Arteaga! Hello!" Mandy pulled Goldie

around to face him, smiling in genuine pleasure at find-ing him here. "I hope I'm not intruding?"

"No, no, of course not," Ceasare scoffed. "Never! Come, step down and come inside." He reached up and helped her out of the saddle, then looped Goldie's reins over the hitching post.

"I had no idea anyone lived around here," Mandy said as she entered the cottage ahead of him. "I was just out for a ride and all of sudden I came upon that lovely meadow." She removed her hat and Ceasare hung it from a pair of elk antlers near the door.

"I am so very glad you discovered my *pequeña, casa,*" he said, leading her to a chair. "I seldom get visi-tors here." He poked at the glowing embers in the fire-place and tossed on another log. Rubbing his hands to-gether briskly, he beamed, "Now I must serve you a hot beverage for such a *frío* day, eh?

"Oh no, please don't go to any trouble, Señor Ar-teaga. I really feel I'm intruding." She hoped he would talk her into staying. The cottage was snug and warm and smelled of delicious spices. She saw a pile of pine cones stacked near the woodbox and bunches of herbs drying upside down in the kitchen.

"Please, you will insult me deeply if you do not stay and visit." He went into the tiny kitchen and poked an-other log into the wood-burning stove that held a kettle and two large, black pots that gave off good odors. "And you must call me Ceasare, eh? We shall be friends as well as neighbors."

"Then you must call me Mandy." She settled back in the comfortable chair, stretching her toes toward the fireplace. Something warm *would* feel quite good, she decided, and Señor Arteaga—Ceasare—clearly wanted her to stay. She glanced out of the window at the gray sky, hoping she would make it back to the ranch before the downpour that Doc had predicted would befall her if she insisted on going for a ride at this time of year. "Round Thanksgiving you cain't never be sure what the weather's agonna be like," he had warned as he tied the

151

slicker behind her saddle. "You see the dark clouds agatherin', you hightail it on home as fast as you can, hear?"

"Ah, Mandy—it has a musical ring to it, Mandy." Ceasare kissed his fingertips and laughed as delightfully as a child. "I have a batch of hot mulled cider steaming on the stove—I was just hoping that a charming visitor would stop and share it with me."

"Umm, sounds lovely. May I help?" She shrugged off her jacket and glanced curiously around the cottage. It was neat and orderly, the hard-packed dirt floor swept clean, the tiny diamond-shaped windows so clear as to appear nonexistent.

"No, no, you are the guest." He lifted the lid of one of the black iron pots and the sweet odor of cinnamon drifted to Mandy. She knew this little house, as charming as it was, could not be the family home of the wealthy Arteagas and wondered what sort of place it was, and why Ceasare was here, so obviously at home. He stirred the pot, then ladled out two mugs of the steaming brew, carrying one to Mandy. "Careful," he cautioned, "*Muy caliente.*"

"Thank you. It smells divine." She sipped the cider and found it as good as it smelled. "It's delicious," she said.

"Ah, *gracias.*" Ceasare sat next to her on a cowhide chair near the fireplace, balancing his cup on his knee. The log and the pine cones he had tossed into the embers had caught and now a popping, crackling music filled the room.

"It's so comfortable here," Mandy sighed. "How on earth did you find such a charming little cottage, Ceasare? It reminds me of the fairy tales I read as a child about enchanted forests and creatures of the wild."

Ceasare laughed delightedly. "Yes, I find it so, also. I remember the first day I saw this place. I was riding one of my wife's palomino mares, exercising her as she was big with foal, when we came upon the clearing in the forest quite as suddenly as you did today. I turned the mare into the meadow to let her catch her breath before the ride back to the rancho, and I lay upon the grass to rest myself as well. It was then that I knew I must have a *casa* here, in this peaceful, quiet place. A place to be by myself and think my thoughts, *comprende*?"

"Yes, I understand," Mandy murmured, thinking of all the times she had wished for just such a place. She could have used a sanctuary such as Ceasare's cottage during those awful weeks after her birthday party, when she had been in an agony of despair, hating Bret Dunlap with each breath she drew as she fearfully counted the days until her menses. She had taken to her bed after five weeks had passed, pretending an illness and fever that had soon enough become reality, so convinced was she that she was with child. She had alternated between cursing Bret and cursing herself for the folly that had taken place in the gazebo that night. *How* could she have mistaken Bret for Tod? Even in a drunken stupor she should have known the difference, she had told herself a hundred times. Shame had settled on her heavy heart like a shroud and she was convinced that she was a marked woman, tainted and spoiled and not fit for any man. She longed to pour it all out and thus purge herself of her sins, but to whom could she confess? Surely not Caleen, for she would most certainly have cut Bret's heart out. And not her grandfather, for he would have been shocked and hurt. Even the gentle, understanding Jenny was not broad-minded enough to understand such a horrible blunder. So Mandy had carried it around inside her, the heaviest weight her young shoulders had ever had to endure.

She had breathed a little easier when her time of the month had finally come (five weeks and five days later) but still saw herself as a fallen angel, blighted in the eyes of God and man—and most assuredly in the eyes of Tod if ever he should discover the truth. Bret had tried to see her the next day after the party but she had pleaded a headache and had Marta send him away.

He then had sent a note of apology, requesting that she meet him so that he might explain in person. This she had ripped into shreds and told the messenger (one of the Dunlap stableboys) to tell Mr. Dunlap to go straight to Hades. He had left her alone after that and she had heard from Jenny that he had left for Europe a week later. She had prayed that his ship would sink and that sharks would dine on his loathsome carcass.

It had now been four months and the hated, shameful memory was fading from her mind. The Bradshaw ranch was in an upheaval of fall slaughtering as well as preparations for the annual Thanksgiving Day feast. Mandy had found herself underfoot more than helpful and had escaped with Goldie for the afternoon.

"So," Ceasare said, sipping his hot cider daintily. "I cleared back some of the bushes and built myself a little sod *casa* like my ancestors used to live in. It is sturdy and warm in the winter and cool in the summer. It is simple, *si*, but all that I require for my meditation, eh?"

"Yes, I see how one could relax completely here," Mandy said. "I envy you your enchanted cottage, Ceasare."

"Then you must share it, *querida*. Whenever you have need of solitude, as every thinking creature must, then you will come here, eh?"

"Oh, I couldn't," she started to protest, but he held up a slim, elegant hand and waved away her protestations.

"*Si*, you must. *Mi casa es su casa*." He chuckled and she smiled back, feeling warm and wanted. He had such a sweet, kind face, the velvet brown eyes as soft as down, the mouth gentle, the gestures of his eloquent hands broad and generous. She could imagine them gently bandaging the broken wing of a bird or the leg of a raccoon, as well as tending the lush profusion of herbs and flowers that grew in abundance around his little house.

She passed the afternoon with Ceasare, listening in

154

fascination as he told her the history of early California and the part her grandfather had played in it. J.B. had been in San Francisco for several years before Ceasare had met him. It had been in 1848, Ceasare recalled, that he had seen a tall, redheaded, strapping young fellow poking around the streams and rivers near Sutter's Fort. J.B. had told Ceasare that there was a rumor circulating in San Francisco that some prospectors had found traces of gold in the area. As the world now knew, there had been gold in the waters around Sutter's Fort, but J.B. had gotten in a good full year of placer mining before the rest of the country knew anything about it. Then the gold seekers had come, hundreds of thousands of them, swarming all over the countryside, settling in San Francisco until the once lazy little city of twenty thousand leaped to a staggering population of one hundred thousand in one year. By 1852 the recently won territory had become a state of two hundred twenty-five thousand people. By the mid-fifties the surface gold in the rivers and streams had been played out and the small miners were forced to move on. The time of the huge mining corporations had come, the men with the capital and equipment necessary to tunnel deep into the hills for the buried mother lodes.

J.B. Bradshaw had the capital and Andrew Dunlap had the equipment. Together, they became the richest men in San Francisco, not just from gold mining, but from lumber as well. J.B. had convinced the government to grant him fifty thousand acres, mostly forest land, and when San Francisco began growing by leaps and bounds lumber became a most precious commodity.

Ceasare had watched J.B. from a distance, seeing him grow from a gangling young man, a bit of a hell-raiser, into a respected, powerful influence in the fastest-growing city in the West. And he had done it all in less than ten years. Ceasare had also watched him court the fiery Señorita Juanita Cordova, widow of the

155

infamous outlaw Jacinto Murietta Cordova, whose property joined J.B.'s at the Los Gatos mountain range—even though J.B. was married to the lovely, aristocratic Amanda Winthrop Manning, and had a houseful of children in his magnificent Nob Hill mansion.

"But he could no more resist Juanita than I could when first I saw her." Ceasare shrugged. He refilled their thick mugs with hot cider and asked permission to smoke a cheroot. "She was a young and very beautiful widow then, mother of a small son, Jacinto, and she needed J.B.'s strength and protection at that time in her life. Her husband's death had been cause for much celebration in California as he was a very bad *hombre*, as vicious as a sidewinder and as much feared. Some of the townspeople were not too kind to his widow, if you understand my meaning, and poor Juanita had a very hard time of it until the people they forget. Until J.B. he *tell* them they must forget and let the dead outlaw's family live in peace.

"I have no doubt that she loved J.B. very much and believed that he would marry her one day. Perhaps that is why she did nothing when she learned she was to have his baby." He sipped, puffed on his cheroot and gazed into the flames of the fireplace. "The result, as you must know, was Juan."

"No, I didn't know." Mandy curled her legs underneath her and settled more comfortably into the deep chair, wanting to hear more.

Ceasare shrugged. "It is well known that Juan is J.B.'s son. I tell you nothing that you would not hear soon enough. Although I love the boy as if he were my own, I have only one natural child, my daughter, Lanora." He knocked the long ash from his cheroot into the fireplace. "And Juan, he does not care that he was born of a love affair rather than a marriage. He is very fond of his father as J.B. is fond of him. I married his mother when Juan was but a lad so I have been as a

156

father to him." He shrugged expressively. "We must get along with one another, *si*? If we are to live as civilized neighbors. I also am fond of J.B. and his family. As you must know, Jenny is my little *querida*, my favored friend."

"Yes, I know. And she is very fond of you as well. She speaks often of your friendship."

Ceasare smiled. "*Si,* our friendship is strong. The bonds between our families are very old. I only wish that my Juanita would not hold grudges, but, alas, I fear that she still feels quite bitter about the affair." He puffed again, looking out the window, eyes narrowed. "As does her son, Jacinto, for he feels betrayed. He was very much enamoured of J.B. while your grandfather was courting his mother. He looked upon him with a son's love for a father. You see, Jacinto's real father was a violent man who died a violent man's death, and this affected the boy more than he would ever admit. He was ashamed of his outlaw father and turned completely to J.B., seeing in him all the virtues and strengths his own father lacked. And if they were not there, well, the lad pretended that they were. Just as Juanita pretended that J.B. would leave his family and marry her.

"J.B. had no intention of ever being anything more than a casual lover, and when he refused to divorce his wife and marry Juanita, Jacinto felt cheated out of a father for the second time in his young life. When Juan was born, Jacinto was old enough to understand the word 'bastard' and he vowed never again to trust love. I am much afraid that it has soured his heart and blackened his soul for now he follows in Jacinto Murietta Cordova's murderous footsteps, holding up stagecoaches, rustling cattle, gambling, living a lawless life." He shook his head and made a sound of sad disgust. "I do not know what his end will be if he continues on this depraved path. He does not use my name even though I adopted him, the proud name of Arteaga, but calls himself Jay Cordova—and already the countryside is aware of his terrifying presence. His mother cannot talk to him, nor can I. Only Juan seems to be able to speak with him and make him listen. Jacinto is fiercely protective of Juan and hates the friendship he still shares with J.B. More than once when Jacinto was drinking tequila I have heard him vow to kill J.B."

"That's terrible," Mandy cried. "Does *Grandpapa* know that this Jay hates him so?"

Ceasare shrugged. "I do not know. Perhaps. Perhaps not. When J.B. saw that the affair must end he did not just walk away from Juanita. He paid off the many debts her late husband had incurred as well as the mortgage on the rancho. He sent to Mexico for a fine young stallion to replace the aging El Oro, Juanita's only remaining palomino standing at stud. Her herds had diminished after her husband's death and she did not have the *dinero* to restock. She was on the verge of losing everything. A life's work. And, ah, how she loves those golden horses of hers, the famous Cordova palominos. It would have broken her heart to see the fine mares and foals going to the gringos. J.B. allowed her to keep them and breed ever finer ones. She was able to build the rancho up once more, as fine as it had once been when her father had first built it." He took a final puff of his cheroot and tossed it into the fireplace. "And the young Jacinto, he was very much the vain peacock, the strutting *caballero* with the señoritas, wearing proudly the title of horse breeder and head man of the fabulous rancho. He is fond of gold in his pockets and a gracious *casa* in which to live. I do not know if he ever thinks that these things were his by the generosity of J.B."

"Then why does he rob stagecoaches? Obviously he doesn't need the money."

Again the expressive shrug, accompanied by a deep sigh. "This I cannot tell you, for often I have asked myself this question. Juan says his brother is filled with anger and must spend this anger in a violent way, as if he must hurt someone as he himself is hurting. He cares nothing for the Cordova palominos and was, in fact, responsible for the first stallion ever to be sold off the Cordova rancho."

"So that's how the Dunlaps got their herd of palominos," Mandy murmured, leaning forward with interest.

"*Si*, it was to Andrew Dunlap that Jacinto sold the fine stud Galeceño, which he used to start his own line of golden horses. Juanita was heartbroken, for never had the bloodline been out of the family's hands."

Mandy nodded, remembering bits and pieces of conversation she had heard regarding the fabulous golden horses. Jeramy had said something about a bitter feud between the Dunlaps and Juanita Cordova and Jenny had spoken with undisguised dislike of both Juanita and Lanora the night of the party. Apparently, Tod did not share his family's feelings, Mandy thought with a pang of jealousy.

"Now I am afraid there is a, how do you say? rivalry between the two señoras, my own Juanita and *Señora* Dunlap. They are strong-willed, those two." He chuckled, shaking his head. "*Dios!* One wonders where it will end!" He threw up his hands, laughing as if at the antics of two spoiled children, but Mandy detected an undertone of concern in his silky voice. "But, come, we have talked too long on these matters. You must be quite hungry, *si*? I will fix us a small bite to eat."

"Oh no, Ceasare, I really must be getting back." She glanced toward the darkening afternoon sky. Storm clouds had rolled in while she sat listening to Ceasare, casting the meadow in shadows. "It looks as if it will rain before I get home." She stood and reached for her jacket but he took it from her and hung it back over the chair.

"*Disparate*." He smiled charmingly, patted her hand. "You will stay for a little *habichuelas* and *tortillas*, eh?" He went into the kitchen and poked more wood into the

159

stove, reaching for a skillet that hung on a peg near the cabinet. "I cannot let you go away without sharing my noon meal with you."

Mandy laughed. "I'm afraid we talked right through the noon meal, Ceasare. It is closer to supper."

He shrugged and grinned. "Then we shall have *habichuelas* and *tortillas* for supper, eh?"

"Oh, very well," she laughed, giving in. "I *am* quite hungry. The whole house is turned upside down because of that awful slaughtering going on and I left without breakfast." She wrinkled her nose and pulled a face. "How anyone can stand the smell of fresh blood and singed hair is beyond me. I grow quite faint just thinking about it."

"Ah, but the hams and bacons they taste most delicious, do they not, *querida*?" He stirred the pot of beans that had been cooking on the back of the stove and dropped a small square of lard into the big iron skillet, briskly stirring it as it melted. He seemed quite at home in the kitchen and Mandy wondered how much time he spent in his little enchanted cottage—away from the rancho and Juanita.

"Yes," she laughed, leaning against the door to watch him work. He deftly chopped onions, chilies, and tomatoes, then slid them into the skillet and added dashes of spices, salt, and pepper. He added three heaping spoonfuls of beans and stirred. "Atoka's hams are the most delicious I've ever tasted." She moved closer to the stove to watch him carefully mash the beans into the chopped vegetables and spices, the hot fat sizzling and popping in protest. When he had made a thick paste of the mixture, he covered the skillet and went to the cabinet for a bowl of puffy brown dough. Tearing off a chunk the size of a child's rubber ball, he flipped it between his palms, shaping it, stretching it until it resembled a thin, flat disc. This he tossed on the stove.

"What is that?" She moved closer still, watching the

160

dough began to rise and bubble on the hot stove, the edges already turning a golden brown.

"A *tortilla*," he said, grasping it quickly by the edge and flipping it over before it could burn his hands, He tore off another ball of dough and handed it to her. "Here, *querida*, you make the next one, eh?"

"Oh, Ceasare, I don't know how!" She stood with the soft dough held in her hands as if it would bite her.

"Here, like this. Toss it back and forth between your hands until the dough is flat. See?" He demonstrated, then handed it back to her, watching until he was sure she had it right before turning back to the stove.

Within minutes there was a platter piled high with piping hot *tortillas* wrapped around the savory bean and spice mixture. They sat at the small kitchen table, eating with their fingers, sipping hot mulled cider and laughing together like old friends. Finally Mandy pushed her chair away and groaned. "Oh, Ceasare, I'm stuffed. I couldn't eat another bite if my life depended on it. But it's so good I can't stop." She tore off a crusty piece of *tortilla* and popped it into her mouth, sighing. "*Mon Dieu,* I fear I have gained ten pounds!"

Ceasare laughed. "On you it would look good, *querida*. We Latin men like our women to be a little more, how do you say? round and soft."

They cleared off the table, then Mandy put on her jacket even though Ceasare protested that she stay just a little longer. "I'd really love to, Ceasare, thank you, but I must get started before it gets any darker." She leaned over to peer out of one of the tiny diamond-shaped windows at the gray sky. "I'm afraid I'm going to get caught in the downpour anyway. Just look at that sky."

Ceasare looked, shrugged. "It will not rain until to-night. The weather, it likes to tease you in November—one minute sunny, the next stormy." He helped her on with her jacket and took her hat down from the elk antlers, handing it to her. "I hope that J. B. has his slaughtering done for it looks like a real storm is coming to stay with us for a while. I have seen rains stay for a month and more at this time of year."

They stepped outside, Mandy shivering when the brisk wind whipped at her jacket. The cages of wounded animals were shaking in the wind, their occupants showing their distress with whimpers and squawks.

"Ah, my poor *nenes,* I must bring you in, eh?" Ceasare crooned as he leaned over the cage holding the raccoon. The little black-masked face peered up into his own and the coon raised his uninjured paw toward him. *"Si, si, nene,* I will take you inside where it is warm, eh?" He lifted the cage in his arms and called to Mandy, "Open the door for me, *por favor.* I must see to my *nenes* before the rains come."

Mandy quickly held the door for him. "Let me help you, Ceasare. Where do you want them?" She picked up the cage holding the infant cougar cub and it meowed up at her like a house cat, its milky blue eyes trying to focus on her face. "There, there, little kitty," she whispered. "Don't be afraid." She carried the cage into the cottage and set it down near the fireplace. It took them both to carry the large cage holding the condor with its broken wing and then she helped him herd the goats into the barn and coax the old bloodhound inside.

"He is *muy viejo,* the *perro,*" Ceasare whispered as if the hound could understand his words. "So old that he cannot even bark any more, poor *nene.* But his last days will be happy and warm, this I will see to." He stood, looking around the small room now crowded with cages. "So, all my *niños* they are inside and warm, eh? *Muchos gracias,* Mandy, for your kind help."

"Oh, you're quite welcome, Ceasare. I think it's wonderful the way you help these poor creatures." She hugged him briefly, a little embarrassed at her forwardness.

162

Ceasare spread his hands before him and shrugged. "Someone must help our animal friends if they cannot help themselves." But she could see that the compliment had pleased him. During their visit he had told her that he often found wounded or starving animals, the victims of hunters' traps, in the forest around his cottage and would bring them home to mend them before releasing them again. The old bloodhound had wandered in one day, his gray muzzle a pincushion of porcupine quills, his body riddled with age and ill health. Ceasare had administered to him as best he could and the dog had simply stayed on, lying in the sun by day and sleeping near the hearth at night. He had been there for over a year now and showed no signs of ever leaving.

"Thank you again for a lovely afternoon," Mandy said, taking Goldie's reins and swinging into the saddle. "And for the delicious supper. I can't pronounce it but it was heavenly."

Ceasare laughed. "You must come again, *querida*, and I will teach you to speak Spanish like a native."

"Oh, would you really? I'd love to learn the language." She laughed down at him. "I'm afraid I shall be forced to learn in self-defense. Half the time I have no idea what the servants are talking about and everyone takes it for granted that I understand Spanish and insist on talking to me in the language."

"Then you must be my pupil. I will teach you the proper way to speak, the beautiful tongue of my ancestors, the *conquistadores*." He made a small sound of disgust. "These Mexicans here in California have bastardized the language much, with their Indian influence, and the *gringos*, too, have muddied the pretty words of my people." He checked the girth of her saddle and petted Goldie's long flaxen mane. "Well, *adiós, querida*, you must ride like the wind if you wish to beat the rain. You will come back and see me soon, eh?"

"Yes, Ceasare, I would enjoy it very much. Thank

you—*gracias.*." The foreign word felt strange on her tongue but he beamed up at her and said, "Ah, *si*, you have a good ear, *querida. Adiós* until next we meet."

"*Adiós*," she called, turning Goldie and spurring her into a fast gallop. The wind was cold and damp on her cheeks and the wind chilled her through. She covered the distance between the meadow and the chaparral quickly, then was racing along at a hard run, following the stream lest she lose her way. The sun was completely hidden by the swollen rain clouds and she prayed she would reach home before they spilled over and drenched her. She would never hear the end of it from Doc if she got caught in the rain.

Goldie's hooves flew over the rough, rugged land, kicking up bits of dirt and stones, sending dirt into Mandy's eyes. The wind burned her cheeks but she did not slow her pace. The first drops of rain had just begun to fall when she reined Goldie into the stable and jumped lightly to the ground. Doc was waiting for her.

"Well, Missy, you jest about got yerself caught, didn't you? Would you look at that sky? Another minute more and we'd have a search party out alookin' fer ya." He rubbed a gnarled hand over Goldie's heaving flanks, then whistled shrilly for Tim to come and unsaddle the mare and rub her down. He was still talking, mumbling warnings and dire predictions, as Mandy turned and ran quickly to the house.

Big drops of rain splashed into the still-burning fire that had been used to singe the hogs, making a loud sizzling sound and sending up thin vapors of steam. The tart odor of hair, blood, and fresh meat hung heavy in the air, assaulting her nostrils as she ran swiftly past, averting her eyes. She wondered if she would ever be able to eat pork again. In New Orleans the butchering had been done by the darkies, far away from the main house, so she had never witnessed the actual slaughter. She preferred it that way.

She shucked off her damp jacket and sailed her hat through the air to land perfectly on the longhorn hat rack, a cocky grin on her face. "Pretty good," she murmured.

"*Very* good, I'd say," Jeramy laughed, adding mischievously. "For a girl." He came toward her, a glass of brandy in his hand, a smile of pleasure on his lips. He bent to kiss her cheek. "Where have you been on such a nasty day?"

"I went for a ride." She rubbed her hands together briskly to bring some heat back to her chilled flesh. "Where is everybody?"

"Oh, here and there. Pa is still in town and I imagine he'll spend the night because of this rain." He looked through one of the tall windows. "It's really coming down, isn't it?"

Mandy followed his gaze and saw great sheets of water pouring down the windows, battering so hard against the panes that they seemed in danger of breaking. "Yes, it certainly started up quickly. I'm glad I made it home." She shivered a little and moved closer to him. The weather in the West was violent and unpredictable, as untamed as the land. In the South the rain fell softly upon gentle land and delicate foliage. They went into the library and she hurried to the fireplace. She warmed her backside, then turned and held out her hands to the blaze.

"Would you like a tot of brandy to take the chill away?" Jeramy asked. He tossed off his and went to the sideboard to refill his snifter from a cut crystal decanter.

"Why, yes, I think I will." She had never drunk anything stronger than wine or sherry and thought, a little defiantly, that it was time she learned.

They sat together on the cowhide sofa next to the fireplace, sipping brandy and listening to the heavy downpour. Mandy hoped that Ceasare had made it back to his rancho before the rain had begun. Delicious odors were drifting from the kitchen and Jeramy sniffed and sighed, "Ah, the first cracklin' cornbread of the season. Pa will be sorry he missed it."

165

"Where does *Grandpapa* stay when he's in San Francisco?" She sipped the brandy slowly, savoring the warming glow.

"Oh, usually at his club, the Native Sons of the Golden West, or sometimes at our townhouse, although he finds it too empty when he's all alone." He lit a cheroot and put his feet up on the low table in front of the sofa, something he would never had done had J.B. been at home. "But my guess is the Lacey Palace. Pa enjoys the pleasures they have to offer, if you know what I mean."

"No, I don't. What is the Lacey Palace, anyway? I've heard it mentioned." She remembered the day at the waterfall when Bret had eaten his lunch of cold beef and biscuits from an elegant linen napkin with the raised gold monogram L.P.

Jeramy looked at her a long moment, a mischievous grin tugging at his lips. "Well, I suppose you're old enough to know," he said at length. "Now that you're a young woman of eighteen. The Lacey Palace is the fanciest and most expensive whorehouse in San Francisco." At her sudden blush and downcast eyes, he said, "Pardon me, I mean bordello."

"Oh, I see," she stammered, trying to regain her composure. Young women surely did not blush every time a dirty word was mentioned in their hearing. Did they? She forced a tiny laugh and looked up at him. "A bordello. What on earth would *Grandpapa* do in such a place?" Another blush tinted her cheeks. "I mean, why would he spend all night there?"

Jeramy laughed. "Why not? Pa is a lusty old bull. Always has loved the ladies." He puffed on his cheroot, sipped his brandy. "You know that back stairway that leads up to his bedroom suite?" Mandy nodded, blushing even harder when she remembered sneaking up those same stairs the night Bret had ravished her. "He had it built for just that purpose—to accommodate his ladies of the evening without the rest of the house hearing them come and go." He laughed in genuine admiration. "Why, those stairs have seen more ladies tripping up them than a dog has fleas. Yessir, Pa is a real devil with the ladies. I just hope I'm as, shall we say, healthy when I'm his age."

Her curiosity overpowered her embarrassment and she asked, "Have you ever been there, to the Lacey Palace? What's it like?"

"Well, yes, I have indulged on occasion," Jeramy grinned. "And indulge is just what one does at the Lacey Palace. It's something to see, all right. A hedonist's paradise. Solid gold doorknobs and crystal chandeliers, carpets so thick you sink in up to your ankles. The wine and liquor is the very finest and the girls—ah, the girls!" He kissed his fingertips and closed his eyes briefly, a look of ecstasy upon his face. "There's none more beautiful anywhere in the West. And not one of them is over thirty. Lacey, that's the madam, or proprietress if you will, gives them a few hundred dollars and a good recommendation when they reach thirty and sends them on their way. Her motto being a good whore is a young whore, I reckon."

"How old is she? The—the madam?" Mandy had gulped down her brandy and now went to the sideboard to refill her glass. Jeramy held up his and she refilled it as well.

"Lacey's about twenty-four or twenty-five, something like that." He took the brandy snifter and swished its contents slowly, watching the amber liquor swirl lazily in the pot-bellied glass. "And beautiful, too, like a madonna. I've heard rumors that several of California's wealthiest men have offered her as much as a hundred thousand dollars a night for her favors—but she always declines."

"Then she's not a—" Mandy ducked her head, wondering what one would call a woman who owned and worked in a bordello.

"No, she's not a—" Jeramy laughed at her obvious embarrassment. "She's really a very nice young lady, pretty as a picture. If you saw her on the street you would have no idea of her occupation." He settled back on the sofa, warming to the story. "Lacey came here when she was just a kid really, about fourteen or fifteen, with her pa, Svend Torklevich. It's a well-known story. He opened up a hardware store, stayed with it a couple of years, then got bitten by the bug—gold fever. One day he just up and took off, left Lacey a note and the deed to the hardware store and property it set on, and that's the last anyone ever saw of him. She was Cora Torklevich then, a seventeen-year-old kid all alone in what was then a pretty raw and dangerous town. She tried to keep the store going, but, hell, she couldn't handle a job that most grown men had trouble with. In those days men were crazy with gold fever. If they couldn't afford to buy a grub stake, picks, shovels and the like, why, they'd just walk into Svend's Store, that's what it was called, and help themselves. Wasn't no little slip of girl going to stop them from taking what they needed to get at that gold.

"Pretty soon there wasn't anything left to steal, let alone sell. She had been completely wiped out. Every last bit of merchandise stolen or bought on credit. The only thing she had was that store, just a big warehouse of a building, really, but it was free and clear. I remember the town speculating on what would happen to the pretty little foreign girl, would she pull up stakes and head back to Russia or wherever she had come from. Would she marry one of the farmers or ranchers who had fallen in love with her beauty?" He puffed on his cheroot, chuckling at the memory. "Well, she didn't do either one. She boarded up the front of Svend's Store so no one could see what she was doing inside, but they could hear sawing and hammering and workmen coming and going almost daily for over a month and more.

"Then one fine morning, the boards come down on the front of the store and the sign went up—a great big, fancy sign, "The Lacey Palace." On a small gold plaque by the doorbell was another sign, smaller and much more discreet. 'A gentleman's retreat', it said,

'Members only.' And that very same day a messenger was sent to every wealthy man in San Francisco with an invitation to attend an opening night party the following weekend. 'All entertainment free to the discriminating gentleman,' it said, or something like that. I remember sneaking Pa's invitation and reading it and wishing like hell that I had been old enough to be called a 'discriminating gentleman' so I, too, could have a peek inside the mysterious Lacey Palace." He chuckled at the memory.

"But I was still wet behind the ears, and it wasn't until a couple of years later that I was asked to join the exclusive club and partake of their 'specialized' entertainment. And, damn, what a place. I'll never forget my first impression of it. It reminded me of something I had seen in my history books of the old European castles. There was gold and crystal and just plain luxury everywhere you looked, more luxury than I'd ever seen in my life. And, remember, I wasn't exactly raised in a hovel myself. But the Lacey Palace, that was something else altogether. Everywhere you look it's bigger, better, more beautiful, more expensive than anything I'd ever seen. The girls were younger and prettier, their gowns more revealing, their expertise more expert and refined than any prostitute that the West had ever seen. The liquor is imported and the food is fit for a king. Each room is decorated in a different decor, one depicting a sultan's tent, another as lavish as Marie Antoinette's boudoir.

"And the young Cora Torklevich was the most gorgeous woman of them all and she let it be known that she was now Lacey. No last name. Just Lacey— proprietress of the Lacey Palace, if you please."

"But how on earth did she manage to afford all that grandeur?" Mandy asked wide-eyed, but still practical.

"That's still something of a mystery. There was a hell of a lot of speculation, let me tell you. Some folks thought she had found her own gold claim and others thought it was none other than J.B. Bradshaw who had backed her, set her up in the most fabulous whorehouse in the United States."

"Did he?" she gasped.

"No, it wasn't Pa, although I wouldn't have put it past him. But I was there the day he received his invitation to join the club and he was just as surprised as everyone else at the fact that meek little Cora Torklevich had opened the biggest and best whorehouse in the West." He drank, took a drag of his cheroot and knocked the ash into a filigreed gold tray at his elbow. "No, it wasn't Pa, but I know who it was."

"Who?" She leaned toward him with interest.

"Bret Dunlap."

"Bret Dunlap?" she gasped. "How do you know?" It would be just like him, she thought to herself, wondering at the sudden anger that seized her.

"Well, like I said, over half the men in San Francisco have tried to get next to Lacey and she won't give them a tumble. But just let Bret walk into the Palace and within minutes the two of them disappear into Lacey's private chambers and the sign goes up on the door, 'Do Not Disturb.' I've seen them together a dozen times or more, out riding or picnicking by that little waterfall up on Pa's northern pasture. You probably know the one I mean. You have to ride by it to get to Los Gatos mountain."

"Yes, I've seen it." Her cheeks burned anew at the memory of that little pond and the cad Bret Dunlap. So he had often taken the madam of a whorehouse to what he called his "favorite waterhole," the depraved swine.

"Well, I just put two and two together. Bret's a heller with the women and richer than Midas in his own right. Old Andy Dunlap left him the shipping business as well as a big fur company in New York. That's where Bret goes when he's away from home, to see to things at Dunlap Furriers." He crushed out his cheroot on the edge of the tray and took a swallow of brandy. "You should see that place, Mandy. It's really something. Every woman in the world dreams of being rich

170

enough to walk in there and buy one of those fabulous furs. But they're far too expensive for the average person. He has the very finest. Sables, chinchillas, minks, seal, beaver. You'll have to have him bring you a little something back for the winter months. It can get pretty cold even in California."

"I wouldn't ask Bret Dunlap for the time of day!" she snapped before she could stop herself.

Jeramy's eyebrows shot up in surprise. "Oh? That's the first time I've seen that reaction at the mention of Bret Dunlap. Usually the ladies swoon or giggle." He looked at her thoughtfully, at her flushed cheeks, the anger in her eyes, and laughed out loud. "Why, Amanda Bradshaw, I do believe you're jealous!"

"Jealous?" she gasped incredulously. "Why on earth would I be jealous of that—that blackguard? Jealous? Hah!" She laughed and took a great swallow of brandy and tears sprang to her eyes. "I cannot stand the sight of him, if you must know. He's a cad and a tease and too juvenile for words. And—and I can well imagine him owning a—a whorehouse!" It was the first time in her life she had ever said such a word and she was surprised at how easy it had come to her lips.

"I didn't say he owned it, honey, I said that I thought he had backed Lacey, financially." He was grinning at her, aware of her agitated state, her heaving bosom and short, indignant breaths. *Why, she's in love with Bret,* he thought with more amusement than anything else. Everyone else had been whispering about her and Tod, wondering if he was the one who had caused Mandy to blossom so prettily. And all the time it was Bret. Now that was funny.

"Well, whatever you said is probably true. And obviously they're lovers." She sniffed disdainfully. "They sound like two of a kind, if you ask me."

"Yes, they are," Jeramy said seriously, the teasing note gone from his voice. "They are both the nicest people you'd ever want to meet."

His words hung there a moment as she floundered

for an answer. In her anger she had forgotten that Jeramy was very fond of Bret, had grown up with him like a brother. And he had spoken with kindness of the little Cora Torklevich—not with insinuating rudeness as most men would have about someone in her profession. Mandy was embarrassed at her outburst, ashamed to be caught with her emotions showing. "I—I didn't mean that, Jeramy, please forgive me. I know that you and Bret are very close. It's just that—that he always makes me so mad. He teases me unmercifully at every chance he gets, he's rude to me and—and—" She raised her eyes to his, smiled apologetically. "And of course I've never met this—this Lacey person, so I shouldn't have assumed to know anything about her." She was properly contrite. Caleen had taught her never to judge a person by their occupation or circumstances, but on how that person treated her. Well, she couldn't judge Lacey, but she sure as hell could judge Bret Dunlap. She was wondering how to get out of this awkward situation when Jonathan and Agnes entered the library, June and the two boys trailing behind.

"Well! Good evening! Good evening!" Jonathan boomed jovially. He fingered the ends of his waxed moustache and went to warm his hands at the fireplace. "Quite a storm out there, isn't it?"

"Good evening, children," Agnes said, her gaze going to the brandy snifters in their hands. "I see you two have found something to keep the chill away." She smiled, showing big, square teeth. She leaned over Mandy and stage-whispered behind her hand, "You mustn't get too fond of that, dear. Brandy makes one quite mad, I understand." She tapped her forehead. "Affects the brain, you know." She pulled the burgundy velvet cord to summon Marta and when the girl appeared at the door, she asked that sherry be brought.

Jane joined them, declining a glass of sherry. She looked more lovely every day, Mandy thought. Her pink cheeks glowed with health, her pale eyes glowed with a secret happiness that Mandy knew was named

172

Derek Dunlap. The two had been inseparable since the night of Mandy's birthday party and just last week Jane confided that she thought Derek was going to propose marriage. "But he's so shy," Jane had sighed. "Almost as shy as I am. Oh, I do wish I were more outgoing, like you, Mandy."

Dinner was announced and the family went in to a sumptuous meal of sage-treated roast pork, cracklin' cornbread, fluffy mashed potatoes, and fresh green beans from Benito's garden. The gravy was rich and savory, laced with sliced onions and mushrooms, and the yellow mound of butter had been churned fresh that afternoon.

After supper, the others retired to the library for coffee and liqueurs, but Mandy excused herself and went upstairs to her room. She lay on her stomach on the bed, watching the rain streak the windows, hearing it battering tremendously upon the shake roof. She felt restless, sad, lonely, homesick. The house seemed unusually quiet without *Grandpapa's* big voice booming happily throughout the rooms. Just his presence gave a sense of completeness to the household and when he was gone, she missed him sorely. She did not know when she had begun to love him as much as she did. She supposed it had come upon her slowly, just as she had come to accept this strange, savage land as her home. It wasn't often that she thought of New Orleans but she thought of it tonight, of *grand-mère* and of Elmo.

She had received a letter a week ago from Sister Veronica of the Order of the Holy Family, telling her that Belle Bertonneau was ailing and could not write herself but was dictating this correspondence to her granddaughter. Mandy was not to worry, Sister Veronica had written, her grandmother was receiving the very best of care, but she was, after all, getting on in years, eighty-three her last birthday, and Mandy should be aware of this. "Her faithful man servant, Elmo, is by her side constantly, bless his sweet, gentle soul," the letter had told her. "He lives at the Order of the Holy Family as well, and is invaluable to everyone here."

The letter had gone on to say that Belle looked forward to Mandy's letters with delight and that everyone was praying that Mandy had not forgotten God in that heathen place she now called home. "Remember, child," Sister Veronica had written, "God is everywhere."

Mandy had laughed aloud at that part. Then where had He been the night that Bret Dunlap had raped her? A sudden sobering flush wiped the laughter away. But he hadn't raped her. She had given herself to him as wantonly as any whore.

And had enjoyed it more than she dared admit. Many times over the past four months she had awakened during the night to feel her body flushed and tingling in some dreamy, sensual anticipation. In a state of half-sleep, half-wakefulness, she had felt Bret's arms about her, Bret's lips, Bret's hard body pounding rhythmically against her, into her. But it was Tod's name she whispered as she writhed upon her bed and relived that passionate encounter in the gazebo, Tod's blue eyes that blazed into hers as she welcomed him into her eager body.

With a moan of despair, she flung herself over and lay on her back, arms crossed beneath her head, staring up at the ceiling. The rain pounded relentlessly upon the roof, crashed mightily against the windows, shaking the shutters and blowing gusts of damp, chill air into the room. Mandy got out of bed and secured the shutters, locking out every vestige of the cold. The blazing fireplace cast the room in a rosy glow and the heavy velvet drapes were drawn shut against the storm. The room was as snug as a womb. She poured herself a glass of brandy from the decanter on her dressing table, smiling a little at Aunt Agnes's dire warnings about madness. She crawled under the warm blankets, sipping moodily, listening to the din of the storm, the far-off crackle of lightning, and she thought idly that it was a perfect night for love. To snuggle into a big, warm bed, arms and legs entwined . . .

She trembled and shook her head as if to drive away the wanton thought, but she could not get it out of her mind. An image of Bret bending over her, his mouth hot against hers, his hands doing magical, marvelous things to her body, the feel of him inside her, so masculine, so strong, so sure . . .

"I must stop this," she told herself sharply and took a big swallow of brandy to quell the sudden pounding of her heart. *Mon Dieu*, why hadn't it been Tod with whom she had experienced such ecstasy? Everything would be so simple, then, so perfect. They would marry and move into a mansion on Nob Hill and give lavish dinner parties and go to the theater all the time. If it had been Tod with whom she had made love, he wouldn't have to see that awful Lanora Arteaga anymore. He would have a woman of his own, a wife. She drank again, frowning as always when she thought about the fiery and beautiful *señorita*. Every time she had seen Tod lately, at any of the many functions that the good people of San Francisco were constantly having, Lanora had been clinging to him, a lazy cat's smile upon her ruby lips. And now Mandy would have to endure yet another meeting with the happy couple, at the big Thanksgiving Day feast that J.B. held every year for friends and neighbors. *Mon Dieu*, was there no end to the parties? In the West, Mandy learned, there was a party for every occasion from harvesting time to Groundhog Day. Any excuse would do. They were such open, friendly people that they just loved to get together with one another and drink and eat and swap tall tales.

Well, this time she certainly wasn't going to hide in a corner with June and Jane as she had done in the past when confronted with the twosome. This time she would openly compete for Tod. She smiled as she began planning her outfit. It would have to be a gown so devastating as to capture and hold his attention. Something daring enough to prove once and for all that she

175

was a woman grown, with just as much sexuality as the sensual *señorita*. She felt a flush sweep over her and ran a hand gently down her body, lightly caressing herself. She trembled involuntarily and a small whimper escaped her throat. She felt a pulse began beating in her groin, in her trembling thighs, steadily, painfully, beautifully, and she moved her hand down to cover and squeeze herself. "Tod," she whispered to the silent room, "Tod, *mon amour*, soon I will be in your arms and it will be you who makes such beautiful love to me. . . ."

CHAPTER EIGHT

Bret stood leaning against a white marble pillar in the Bradshaw ballroom, moodily sipping a bourbon. The vast room was dotted with small round tables holding the remains of a sumptuous Thanksgiving dinner, which servants were now clearing away. The fifty or so guests milled about, chatting in small groups or were still seated at tables, sipping a cup of coffee or indulging in one last piece of Atoka's famous pumpkin or mincemeat pie. The musicians were tuning their instruments and a game of billiards was going on in J.B.'s study. It was a scene like a hundred others he had witnessed at the Bradshaw mansion and one he had always enjoyed and looked forward to. But now he felt uneasy in J.B.'s home. He had sought out Mandy upon arriving but she had refused to speak to him. Several times during the afternoon he had tried to catch her eye but she would look quickly away, her face filled with such disgust and shame that he had ground his teeth in an agony of guilt.

Then a moment later he would see her flirting coyly with Tod or one of the other young men present and find himself hating her, cursing her for the little hypocrite that she was. She had known what she doing that night. Christ, she had practically begged him for it. It wasn't Tod she had wanted, whether she knew it or not. She had wanted to make love. Her young body had been bursting to be fulfilled and he had fulfilled it.

As the afternoon turned into evening and the many

bourbons fired his blood, Bret looked at Mandy not with guilt or anger, but with desire. She was incredibly beautiful in a clinging sheath of velvet the color of ripe grapes. It dipped low between her high, lush breasts and fell enchantingly off her rosy shoulders, dipping to a deep, deep V in the back and exposing a stretch of creamy, naked flesh. It hugged her tiny waist and high, round buttocks. The rich color turned her eyes violet and brought out the warm tawny tones of her skin. But it wasn't just the gown. There was a difference about Mandy herself. She carried herself with more assurance and poise. The quick, impulsive movements of an awkward adolescent were gone and she moved slowly and gracefully, the sway of her hips suggesting a new maturity. Damn, she had changed a lot in just five months. Grown up. The petulant expression was gone from her soft mouth and the sudden, unreasonable anger and hostility that had once flared from her eyes was gone, replaced by an awareness and intelligence that delighted him even as it surprised him.

He must manage somehow to get her alone and talk to her, woo her, treat her like the lovely young lady that she had suddenly become. He was aware that his teasing had made her angry because she had been in such a hurry to grow up. He smiled a little. Ah, the impatience of youth. But now she had indeed grown up and if she would just give him the chance he would treat her accordingly. He scowled and tossed off the rest of his bourbon. But it looked like the silly little fool was still so smitten with Tod that she couldn't see anyone else. There she was now, simpering like a simple-minded Southern belle, batting her eyelashes at him!

He stalked to the buffet table and asked the waiter for a bourbon, his eyes on Mandy as Tod led her onto the dance floor and swirled her into a slow waltz. Other couples began drifting onto the floor and he lost sight of her. He saw Lanora surrounded by a small group of men and made his way across the room to her side.

178

"Dance?" he smiled, extending his hand, and she took it at once.

Balancing his glass of bourbon while he maneuvered her onto the floor, Bret craned his neck, searching for Mandy.

"Well, stranger, it's good to see you again," Lanora drawled in her husky voice. She moved in closer, lightly pressing her pelvis against his, her hips swaying more than necessary beneath his hand. Her fingers rested on the hand that held the glass of bourbon. "Where have you been hiding? I haven't seen you at any of the parties this season."

Bret laughed down at her flirtatiously. She was, after all, one hell of a beautiful woman and he had made love to her casually on more than one occasion. It was a convenience, more than anything else and Bret had never led Lanora to believe otherwise. The fact that she still tried her damndest to trap him into marriage, even going so far as to have an affair with his brother Tod in the hope that it would make Bret jealous, was her problem. He treated her as casually as he treated his other women—with the exception of Lacey, that is. "I've been hiding from jealous husbands and weeping virgins," he said lightly, removing her hand while he took a sip of bourbon.

"I do not doubt it for a moment," Lanora purred. She took the glass of bourbon and drank, her dark, sultry eyes caressing his face over the rim. "But if you remember, my *hermoso hombre*, I am one virgin who did not weep when you plucked the fruit, eh?" She licked her ruby lips suggestively, then handed the glass back to him.

"That's right, baby," Bret grinned, drawing her a little closer. "The only weeping you did was for more." She had been an explosion of sex when he had first had her, over three years ago. And just fifteen years old. But Lanora had been a wild thing, instinctively lusty and bawdy, whereas Mandy had been a delicate rosebud just opening, blooming into the lush sexuality that she would have as a woman.

"Then why do you not see me more often?" Lanora pouted, grinding her hips against him, stirring him in spite of himself.

"I thought you were all tied up with brother Tod," he said. "Besides, I've been away the past few months. Europe." He swung her around and through an opening in the crowd, dancing her quickly across the floor when he caught a glimpse of Mandy's grape-colored gown. He tapped Tod on the shoulder and said, "Excuse me, brother, but I think I have something that belongs to you." He put Lanora's hand in Tod's and took Mandy's. "Lovely party, isn't it?" And he whirled Mandy away before anyone could say a word.

"Bret Dunlap, you let me go this instant!" Mandy struggled against him but he squeezed her hand so hard she yelped aloud in pain.

"Uh-uh, Miss Bradshaw, don't be rude," he said pleasantly, gripping her hand so tight it brought tears to her eyes. "This is Thanksgiving, a time for giving thanks for one's neighbors."

"You're one neighbor I can do without, thank you," she snapped angrily and again he gripped her hand, causing her to cry out.

"Are you going to behave yourself and have a nice, neighborly dance with me, or do I have to break it?" he said in that same pleasant, almost lazy voice. But his eyes glittered like brown diamonds as he glared down at her, forcing her to look at him. "Listen, Mandy, you're going to hear me out whether you like it or not. I've been making an ass of myself, trying to apologize for something that I suddenly realize was not my fault. You were the aggressor in our little encounter in the gazebo, my dear, and I'm not going to let you off the hook this time, or go on blaming myself for something that you clearly wanted—"

"How dare you!" Mandy gasped. "You seduced me!

180

Deliberately! You took advantage of my—my emotional state—"

Bret threw back his head and laughed so loudly that several couples turned to stare at him. "Seduced you! Mandy, really, you shouldn't drink champagne if it's going to affect your memory this seriously." He grinned down at her fury, his white teeth flashing against his dark moustache, his brown eyes twinkling with humor. "I'll admit that you were in some sort of an—emotional state—but I was under the impression that I took care of that quite nicely. That is, as soon as you talked me into it, convinced me that you were sure, that you wanted me."

"Bret Dunlap, I will not listen to any more of this—this rubbish! This filth!" She stopped dancing and stamped her foot, her body as rigid as stone. "Release me at once." She pulled back on her hand but he squeezed it in a vise-like grip causing her eyes to widen in fear and pain. He was crazy enough to break her wrist right here on the dance floor, she thought wildly. A more gentle approach was called for. "Please, monsieur," she murmured softly, dropping her eyes and letting her lower lip tremble charmingly. "You are hurting me." She peeked at him from beneath her lashes and saw the grin tugging at his lips, the heavy amusement in his eyes.

"Save your Southern belle tricks for Tod," he laughed, drawing her back into his arms and forcing her to follow his lead. "I like you better when you're honest." He swung her around the floor, dancing her toward the corner behind the musicians' platform and a huge potted plant. He backed her against the wall and leaned forward, an arm on either side of her, trapping her there. The large plant obscured them from view and he leaned in quickly and kissed her upon the lips before she could protest.

"Damn you, Bret Dunlap!" she yelped, jerking her head back and raising her hand to slap him. He captured the hand easily and pinned it against the wall.

"That's all I ask, Mandy. That you be honest." His dark eyes lost their flippant, amused expression and became softer, darker, deeper. "Just be honest with yourself, at least. Admit it, darling, you wanted it to happen as much as I did." His voice was a purr, a silky caress that washed over her like a heady tonic. His hands were moving gently up her bare arms, tickling her, causing gooseflesh. "You did want me, Mandy, as much as I wanted you." He kissed her tenderly, his lips just barely brushing hers. "It was so beautiful, my darling, so good—I've thought of little else these last five months."

"Stop, Bret, don't talk to me like that. I won't listen." But her voice was a weak protest and she no longer struggled against his hands. All her fantasies, her half-wakeful dreams of these past months came rushing over her, making her faint, causing her legs to tremble. This is what she had wanted and dreamed for and not really known what it was called. She had dreamed of a man's hands on her, touching her with desire and love, lips seeking her gently and lovingly. But it had been Tod's blue eyes she had seen in her dreams, not these dark brown eyes, so warm and filled with love.

"You're so lovely, Mandy, so beautiful." His dark eyes swept her body hungrily and she felt as if he had physically touched her. "Tell me you meant it, darling, all those wonderful things you said to me in French." He kissed her throat, pressing his lips to the pulse there, then her lips in a sweet, lingering kiss, almost chaste. "I hear them still—'*mon amour*,' you said, '*je t'aime*.' My love—I love you." His voice was a soft whisper, muffled against her throat and the heavy beating of her heart drowned out his words. The music, played so close, further drowned him out and she did not hear him when he murmured in a broken voice, "I love you, Mandy. God knows I don't want to—have tried like hell not to—but I can't help myself. Thousands of miles across the ocean in the streets of Paris I saw your face in every woman I passed. Heard your voice in every song."

"Bret, please," she said shakily, finally finding her voice. "People will see us—stop—"

He raised his head, his dark eyes shining, her name on his lips as he kissed her again, gathering her close in his arms and pressing his hard body tremblingly against hers, pressing her back against the wall nad holding her there. She struggled only briefly; then, with a small sigh of surrender, she lifted her arms and melted into his. The kiss grew in passion, to an intensity that frightened her and fired Bret. He groaned against her mouth and felt himself hard against her yielding body. "Mandy," he whispered urgently. "Oh God, Mandy!"

She said his name silently, closed her eyes and gave herself up completely to his embrace. How strong and warm his arms were. How sweet his kiss. How his heart pounded and thumped, as eagerly as her own. She thought fleetingly of Tod. But Tod was with Lanora and Bret was here, holding her and kissing her and telling her she was beautiful and desirable. . . .

She fit perfectly in his arms, he thought as he cuddled her even closer, savoring the wild promise of her kiss. This time she had had no champagne to befuddle her mind, he thought with satisfaction, and she was responding as passionately as she had before. He wanted to scoop her up into his arms and carry her out of here, away from this rollicking, celebrating, overfed, slightly intoxicated crowd. He wanted her all alone. All to himself for just a day. Just an hour. All to himself. "Mandy," he whispered against her lips, kissing her again, then pulling slightly away to gaze down at her perfect face. Her perfectly beautiful, wonderful face. "Mandy," he murmured again, like a sigh.

The music stopped abruptly and Mandy jerked away from Bret as if she had been burned. The silence hung loud in the air and they stared at one another, breaths held, hearts still pounding. The musicians broke into another tune and they both spoke at once. "I must get back—" Mandy stammered, powerless to move out of his arms. "I guess we should go—" Bret said softly, his dark gaze locked with hers. They laughed, shakily, then Bret hugged her close, frantically, almost furiously. "Mandy, I know we can't be alone tonight—not with this crowd. But we must arrange it! Soon, my darling, before I lose my mind! I've thought of nothing else but you for months—of holding you, loving you—"

"Oh, Bret please don't," Mandy cried, jerking her hands from his and wringing them.

He captured them again, turned them palm up and rained a hundred kisses upon them. "Yes, I will, my darling, I will beg you to meet me. Please say you will." He kissed her, sighed warm breath in her ear when he whispered "Please" again, sending shivers of desire dancing up her spine. "Tomorrow. At J.B.'s hunting lodge." He kissed her again and nibbled her lower lip. "We'll have a fall picnic. Just the two of us. Get acquainted all over again. Start fresh." His warm lips moved over her flesh, her eyes, nose, ears, throat and mouth, leaving a red-hot tremor in their wake. He kissed her slowly and thoroughly. "Say you will, Mandy. Say yes." His hands caressed her bare arms. lingered a moment on the mound of her naked breasts in the low-cut gown, then he lowered his head and kissed them.

With a cry she tore herself away and rushed onto the dance floor, almost colliding with Jane and Derek. She mumbled an apology and slowed her pace, walking as quickly as possible without calling attention to herself. *Mon Dieu,* how her heart pounded and her pulse soared! Was she so wanton that even Bret's kisses could cause her such sensual longing?—when it was really Tod she loved, Tod she wanted to touch her and murmur sweet words of love?

Bret stood to one side of the potted plant and watched Mandy run lightly up the wide stairway. He smoothed his moustache with fingers that trembled and ran a shaky hand through his hair. Tucking his shirt into his waistband he thought he could actually see the dull thudding of his heart beneath the silk fabric. His crotch strained uncomfortably and he adjusted himself with a small groan of pain. Never had he begged like a dog for a woman's favors as he had found himself begging for hers. But he had to have her. Just one more time. She was like a disease in his blood. He would be at the hunting lodge tomorrow. All day, if necessary, just in case she did show up. But would she? He took a deep breath and prepared to make his way through the crowded dance floor. He needed a drink badly. His aching body slowed, drifted, returning uneasily to normal—but he could still feel the imprint of her warm body against his.

At the bar, he asked for a double shot of bourbon and drank half of it in one swallow. He leaned against the buffet table, hearing the hum of the party, the clink of glasses, voices raised in laughter, music swelling to fill his brain, the tinkling giggle of a coy lady flirting with her escort. He looked up at the ceiling. Mandy was up there, alone in her bedroom. Alone with the new and puzzling thoughts, emotions, and sensations that surely must be flooding her, confusing her, frightening her. He drank again, eyes moving restlessly about the crowd, automatically smiling when someone raised a hand or voice in greeting. That she was young and totally inexperienced he knew, but just how much did she understand of her own feelings? He knew now that she was attracted to him, that her emotions were as raw and healthy as his own. Tod be damned! It was *his* kisses that had caused her to moan and writhe closer in his embrace. It was *his* hands that had raised gooseflesh on her arms and made her heart beat with desire. If he could just get her alone for an hour, to talk to her, explain what she was feeling. Explain that it was a normal, healthy reaction when two people wanted one another, loved one another.

But he would never get the chance, he thought sourly, the music suddenly loud and offensive to him.

185

She was so damn contrary, so righteously stubborn that she wouldn't give an inch. The laughing, happy faces of the partygoers made him angry and he turned and stalked out of the house. *To hell with her*, he thought sullenly as he stood on the wide front porch and waited for Tim to bring his horse around. *I'll be damned if I'll dance on a string for her!* If it had been Tod suggesting a fall picnic at the hunting lodge, he would bet his last dollar that she would have agreed quickly enough.

"So damn fast it'd probably make your head spin," he said to the bewildered stableboy as Tim handed over his horse. "Huh?" said Tim. "Stick to horses, lad," Bret growled as he swung into the saddle. "Women are crazy as bedbugs and twice as mean." He set his spurs to the big black stallion's flanks and the horse leapt forward with a whinny of eagerness.

Tim watched them disappear into the dark night, scratching his head in amusement. He didn't know about women being as crazy as bedbugs, but some of the gentlemen leaving the Thanksgiving Day party were sure as hell crazy. The last gentleman had given him a twenty-dollar gold piece for Tim to drive "the Mrs." home and tell her that her errant husband had had an urgent message requesting his presence at "the office." Still shaking his head, Tim hurried up the stairs and hunkered in the doorway, trying to keep dry. Mister Dunlap was sure as hell crazy to ride off in a storm like this. He was sure to get pneumonia. Tim slipped his hand into the pocket of his sheepskin-lined mackinaw and withdrew a pint of Irish whiskey, Pulling the cork out with his teeth, he took a long pull and sighed mightily.

Mandy paced her bedroom. Forty-five paces one way, sixty the other. She counted them off each time. Back and forth. Up and down. Across. The day was brilliant. As if an artist had sketched a backdrop of blue, blue skies, white, puffy clouds, rain-kissed greenery. Forty-three, forty-four, forty-five. She turned and

186

paced in the other direction. The house was quiet, the stillness broken every now and again by the clatter of pots and pans in the kitchen, the low rumble of the men's voices drifting up from J.B.'s study where they sat with whiskies and cigars, nursing hangovers in varying degrees and discussing yesterday's party. The women would all be in their bedroom suites, bathing or lingering in bed until the afternoon. J.B. certainly knew how to throw a party, more than one of the overnight guests were saying at this moment.

The sound of Jane's piano floated about the upper floor of the mansion, easing gently in around the door to Mandy's room and filling her with memories of yesterday evening, when Bret had kissed her and confessed his love. Her heart gave a sudden, involuntary lurch and her flesh flushed warm and pink. She could feel them still, his hot, hot kisses; she could see, still, his dark, love-filled eyes. *Mon Dieu,* why could it not be Tod saying such things to her? The music was terribly romantic. No doubt Jane was thinking of Derek.

"*Ma foi,*" Mandy said aloud. "What an unfair life!" She had discovered, much to her surprise, that Lanora was really in love with Bret. Not Tod as she had believed and dreaded, for she knew that she would be no match for the sultry señorita. "Oh, my dear, yes," Jenny had laughed, leaning in close and conspiratorial. "Lanora has been in love with Bret since they were both children attending the same school. He, of course, is as aloof as always, never revealing his feelings to the poor creatures who run after him. Not like Tod, who wears his heart on his sleeve. Why, just look at him!" And Mandy had looked to see Tod bending lovingly over Lanora, his brilliant blue eyes alight with adoration.

"The fool," Mandy said aloud as she paced the floor—then wondered, wryly, if she was getting a bit dotty, talking to herself that way. Why couldn't he see that she loved him? That she would never hurt him with her flirting, roving eyes as did Lanora? *Mon Dieu,* didn't he even know that Lanora had had an affair with his brother, that she was in love with Bret? That she was always available to him whenever Bret crooked his little finger?

She went suddenly to her wardrobe and flung open the doors. She had to get out of the house, away from the well-meaning guests who would engage her in mundane conversation. Thank goodness the Arteagas had left the night before rather than spending the night as other guests who lived further away had done. She knew she could not have faced Lanora Arteaga over breakfast. And the Dunlaps, too, had gone home to their own ranch. What was Tod doing this very minute? Was he still asleep, a dream of Lanora filling him with warmth? She snatched her riding habit, the black, rather grim one, made of wool. It would be warm on such a blustery fall day.

She dressed quickly, jerking on a heavy woolen poncho that Ceasare had given her, then ran quickly outside and to the stable before someone saw and endeavored to stop her. Old Doc warned her, scolded and cautioned her as he saddled Goldie and gave her a leg up. "Watch out fer flash floods, Missy, they's a danger this time o' year. And wildcats—yessir, they's down low this time o' year, hungry, too, so ye be careful, ye hear?" She nodded absently, not hearing his words, merely the drone of his voice, then she set her heels to the golden-blonde sides and was off down the lane at a fast canter.

At the waterfall, spilling cold and icy into the now-dark pond, Mandy reined Goldie to the left, rather than the right that would have taken her to Ceasare's little cottage in the meadow. He wouldn't be there today, she knew. She wondered where Lanora and Tod were. Were they together at this very moment, snuggled under warm blankets, their naked bodies sated with love?

"Fa!" she cried aloud and kicked Goldie harder than necessary, urging her into a hard gallop. Her hooves struck solidly on the cold ground, ringing hollow and

188

yet somehow comforting to Mandy's ears. She gave the little mare her head, just leaning back in the saddle and making herself aware of the many pounds of horseflesh between her legs. She could feel the mighty muscles rippling even through the leather of the saddle, the subtle vibration that started in her thighs and travelled to her stomach where it churned painfully. *Tod, Tod, Tod*, Goldie's hoofbeats seemed to sing, sending a message to her tortured brain. Then—"Bret," a tiny voice whispered. "Bret."

Tears stung her eyes as she urged Goldie over a swiftly moving stream between two high, craggy cliffs. An eagle's nest was stuck like an afterthought against one of the sheer sides and ravens dipped in close, quarreling and cawing at the protective mother. A small family of wild mountain sheep perched precariously on the sheer bluffs, munching on the sweet grass that grew from the jagged cracks in the boulders. The males were huge, with enormous curling horns and long goatees like dignified old men. Their eyes were as golden-yellow as the lynx and cougar that hid in the invisible caves of the mountains. Yuccas rose majestically in the slate gray afternoon; Our Lord's Candle, they were called, Ceasare had told her. Redwoods and pines hindered her passage, their massive girths measuring twelve to sixteen feet in diameter.

She slowed Goldie to a trot, putting a gentling, quieting hand on her neck. They trotted sedately past Grandpapa's boat house and lazy waterwheel. She looked with interest at the fat mares, their bellies distended with foals that would be dropped in the early spring. The cows were also heavy with young and the big bulls stood guard. These were J.B.'s prize bulls and therefore treated as princes of the range.

She walked Goldie past the small, well-tended graveyard holding the handsome stone carved with the date and name of Amanda Winthrop Manning. And next to her marker was a much smaller one, a gilt-gold one bearing the name and age of a son born and died in the same year, a year after Johnny's birth. What was it J.B. had told her once when they had been sitting and talking? "The first grave marks it," he had said gruffly. "Houses, children, grandchildren, graves—that's home. That's the things that tie a man down, give his life meaning, a certain measure."

She spurred Goldie on, running her swiftly past the other plots that lay waiting for the other Bradshaws when their time came. All of a sudden the hunting lodge loomed tall and real before her. She hadn't planned on riding this way—not consciously, anyway. There was a thick curl of smoke spinaling from the chimney and lights glowed dimly through the frosty windows. She reined the mare to a halt, debating if she should turn and ride away from the cosy, welcoming lodge. She really should speak to Bret and explain why she couldn't be what he wanted. Explain that she loved Tod and would wait, for as long as it took, for him to come to his senses and send Lanora packing.

"Mandy, you came." Bret stepped outside and caught Goldie's bridle, securing the reins about the hitching post. He lifted his arms to Mandy and she slipped into them as naturally as if she had always done so. He kissed her and she giggled like a ninny and just barely managed to gasp, "Please, Bret, none of that until—until we've talked." She walked almost primly into the lodge, which was comfortable and expensively furnished.

A fire blazed in the slate fireplace and candles and storm lamps glowed warmly from every corner of the large room, welcoming her. He helped her off with her poncho, raising his eyebrows when he saw the severe black riding habit, as sombre as a nun's.

Bret was clever enough not to speak just yet, but to give her time to make up her own mind if she would stay or not. He had painstakingly laid out a picnic of cold ham and turkey on the oval dining table, with cold dressing and potato salad, pickles and homemade relish. There were cold biscuits and fresh butter from the

190

Dunlap pantry and a jar of rich, dark honey. Several bottles of hearty red burgundy wine were opened and breathing on the sideboard, and some savory black caviar from last night's gala spread.

She walked about the large room, looking at the mounted deer and elk heads on the walls, the bighorn sheep and bearskin rugs upon the hardwood floors. The hooves of a deer were curved and mounted to hold rifles and shotguns and an enormous pair of elk antlers was fashioned into a hat rack near the door. A large salmon, as big as a side of beef, was mounted above the fireplace, its sightless glass eyes seeming to follow her no matter where she stood. She glanced to the far corner and saw a big canopied bed, the heavy drapes almost obscuring it from view. She looked quickly away and went to sit primly on the very edge of the leather couch, her knees tight together. Bret served her a glass of burguandy and took one for himself.

"I'm glad you came, Mandy," he said softly, his dark eyes on her face. She blushed, remembering last night and the hot, wild kisses behind the potted plant. She said nothing but lowered her head to her glass and took a drink of the hearty wine, anxious for the calm it would bring. *Mon Dieu*, but she was drinking an awful lot of spirits lately, she thought sadly, a little wistful for the time when she would have been forbidden to touch alcohol. Being a grown-up was very confusing and more than a little painful. She wanted to tell Bret why she had come, and explain that she loved Tod and therefore would wait for him, no matter how long it took. But Bret's dark eyes were soft with love, his voice a sweet caress, his hands so big and strong and brown as they griped the wine glass, that she shivered involuntarily, remembering last night and the feel of those hands on her body, his deep, husky voice murmuring to her. . . .

She gulped down the entire glass of wine in two hasty swallows, got to her feet and went to stand looking out of the window. She felt him behind her and stood with her head bowed as he silently refilled her glass. "What is it, Mandy? Are you sorry you came?" One big hand gently stroked her shoulder.

Keeping her head down, she muttered thickly, "This is not a—a rendezvous, Bret. I only came to speak with you and—and explain how I feel about Tod." Bret's hand fell from her shoulder and he stalked back to the fireplace, his expression black. Mandy turned, facing him for the first time. "I love him, Bret, please understand. I cannot help it. It is here—inside me." She touched her heart, eyes pleading with him to understand.

He closed the distance between them in long strides and pulled her roughly into his arms. Dark eyes boring into hers, he said harshly, "This is what's inside you, you little fool! This!" His mouth came down on hers hard, demanding, urging her response. The wine glass fell to the floor with a tinkle of broken glass as her arms went around him and she opened her mouth for his kiss, powerless to do otherwise. As the kiss drew wilder and her heart pounded harder, she thought, *mon Dieu, I am wicked! Loving one brother and wanting the other.* She tore her mouth away and pushed hard against his chest. "No, Bret, please don't." But he ignored her, pulled her back into his arms and continued to kiss her until she clung to him, her legs suddenly too weak to hold her upright. She swayed into the hard curve of his body, felt his vibrant manhood straining against her thighs, his mouth a thing of fire, his hands stroking her through the heavy wool of her riding habit. She grew warm and a light sheen of perspiration shone on her forehead and turned clammy on the back of her neck. She wanted to scream at him to stop, to release her at once, but her lips were crushed beneath his and her body was responding wantonly in spite of herself. She cursed the blood that coursed passionately in her veins, turning her into a panting, clinging creature that had no mind of its own. Eyes squeezed tight, she re-

192

membered the countless nights she had dreamed of this—and longed for it.

Bret felt the tremor in her slender body as her arms tightened around him, then loosened as if to push him away. Aware of the turmoil inside her, he held her closer still. She wanted him, his heart sang, wanted him as much as he wanted her. He would show her just how much she needed to be loved. Keeping his lips on hers he scooped her up into his arms, carried her to the bed and lowered her upon it. Her eyes opened wide and she stammered, "Please don't, Bret—please." But she lay where he had placed her, staring up into his face, hers flushed with a passion she could not deny.

"Yes, my darling, yes," he whispered huskily, his hands shaking as he untied the scarf at her throat and began unbuttoning her jacket. "Give it a chance, Mandy. That's all I ask. Just relax and let me love you—let me make you complete. I know you want me. I see it in your eyes, in the way your lips answer mine." He pulled off the jacket, her arms unresisting, and dropped it to the floor. She wore a starched white blouse beneath it and he gently removed it as well, all the while whispering to her, caressing her as he removed each piece of clothing. Then she lay before him naked but for a pair of lace drawers and a low-cut silk chemise. Her long legs were bare and her hair tumbled free from the pins and cascaded upon her rosy shoulders. Not taking his eyes off her for a moment, he shucked his own clothes, seeing her eyes widen when his hard, ready penis sprang into view. Quickly she ducked her head and rolled over on her side, drawing her knees up as if to hide herself.

The mattress gave with his weight as he crawled in beside her, drawing up the heavy quilted spread that had been folded at the foot of the bed. He covered them both, then took her by the shoulders, turning her to face him. "Let it happen, my darling," he whispered tenderly, so very sweetly that she opened her eyes and stared hard into his. He loved her, this she knew. And she wanted him to love her. It felt so wonderful to know that this rich, handsome man desired her when he could obviously have his pick of any girl in California. His hands were moving slowly, sensually up her bare arms, pulling the silk straps of her chemise off her shoulders, then bending his dark head to kiss the rosy smoothness. His lips moved to press against her throat, then to claim her lips in a long, lingering kiss that made her moan silently to herself. She was thankful that he had seen her embarrassment and covered them both with the quilt. She did not want to see but only to feel. If she kept her eyes closed she could pretend it was Tod doing such wonderful things to her body, all the forbidden things she had dreamed about for so very long, ever since that night in the gazebo when she had lost her virginity and began to grow into a woman. She remembered with hot shame the nights she had caressed her own body, sobbing Tod's name as she brought herself to the release that she would not, could not seek from him. She knew it was wicked to touch yourself "down there," but she could not control her lusty young body when it cried out with yearning. Now someone else was touching her there, strong, hot hands that slid knowingly beneath the silk of her drawers and cupped her sex with sure fingers. Her chemise was a tangle of silk about her waist and he lowered his head and kissed her breasts as his hands moved down, down.

"Mandy," he whispered like a sigh, his warm breath sending chills of desire all through her. "You're so beautiful, my darling, so soft and sexy. Oh, God, how I've wanted you! Dreamed of you until I thought I'd lose my mind!" He pulled away the last of her clothes, then raised himself on an elbow and stared greedily down at her, the quilt forgotten about their knees.

She opened her eyes, keeping them carefully averted from his nakedness, marveling at how broad and hairy his chest was. She put out a trembling, timid hand and ran it lightly through the forest of curling black hair and with a groan he caught her close, bringing his mouth down hard upon hers. She opened her arms to him and he fell upon her, his hard penis pushing urgently against her. She felt as if a dozen fireworks had blasted off inside her brain. She was suddenly afire, arching up to him, wanting to feel him harder, tighter against her. His hands moved jerkily, almost awkwardly, between their bodies to part her thighs, to open her. She moved her hand quickly down to stop him, but he grasped it, forcing her fingers around his penis. It was so hot, so smooth and dry to the touch that she flinched a little, then closed her hand around it of her own will and felt it pulsate against her palm. How powerful and urgent it felt! As if it were a live thing, with a need of its own.

"Jesus, Mandy, I want you so badly!" Bret pulled his mouth away from her breasts and slid quickly down in the bed, raining hundreds of tiny kisses upon her belly and thighs before his lips found their mark. She gasped when his tongue flicked out and quickly tightened her muscles, closing her legs. He drew them apart again, his tongue and mouth doing marvelous, mysterious things to her that she had never even heard of before. *Was this right?* she thought wildly. *Could anything so bold be decent?* Then all thoughts were wiped from her mind as if erased from a blackboard and she lay back and opened herself up for his erotic administrations. His hair tickled her stomach as he slipped his hands under her buttocks and lifted her to his seeking mouth. Her legs fell all the way open and she tossed her head back and forth upon the pillows, biting her lower lip to keep back the groan of ecstasy that threatened to burst from her throat.

A sensation of incredible warmth flowed instantaneously throughout her entire body, closing her throat, beating heavily in her legs and arms and temples. A carnality so swift and intense that it shocked her, swept her like a raging flood and she felt wave after wave of pleasure like none she had ever experienced. She was

195

ready for him now. She seemed to grow and swell, seethe and tremble with a new excitement that both thrilled and frightened her. Her hands went down to him, drew him up until his face was inches above hers, his weight heavy upon her. His eyes were dark, burning into hers as he kissed her and moved his hand upon her sex with sure, swift strokes that brought a cry from her tight throat.

"God, Mandy!" His own breathing was labored, his hands jerky as they caught her legs and brought them up and around his waist. Then he fell forward with a groan that turned into a long, drawn-out sigh of pleasure as he sank deep within her.

"Oh!" she cried. "Oh oh—!" He filled her completely, burned deep inside her, his thrusts strong and sure and she dug her fingernails into his back, endeavoring to draw him closer yet. Her legs fell wide apart, her heels digging into the small of his back as he rode on and on, harder, deeper, swifter. His hands were on her breasts, on her buttocks, on her arms and face, everywhere at once until he seemed all hands and seeking, caressing fingers. Their breathing came and went simultaneously, sharp little gasps of pleasure that mingled together as their bodies moved with the same frenzied rhythm, rising and falling until all sense of time seemed to stand still, disappear, until she felt boneless, weightless. There was a heightening of sensuality as she began to feel him with greater and greater sensitivity, to feel him deeper and more satisfyingly inside her, filling her with feelings she had only vaguely guessed at.

She thrashed beneath him, meeting him stroke for stroke, arching her back to press herself tighter, harder to his unrelentless pounding. Her joy was demoralizingly exquisite and she turned her head and bit gently at his shoulder, nipped his ear lobe, sought his lips hungrily as her fingernails raked down his arms and back and she flung herself onward to greater passion. She was only dimly aware of his voice, husky, urgent, whis-

pering words of love, his lips like a flame everywhere
they touched. She was not herself. This was some other
woman crying out, clinging, clutching, urging him on to
greater, wilder sensations. Her pleasure became so
acute that she couldn't catch her breath, could not
breathe at all, it seemed, could not even see—but could
only *feel*. And the feeling was explosive. As if she had
been struck in the pit of the stomach by some shattering
force that drove all the breath from her body, then
hurled her into oblivion, into space, into a dark red
abyss that closed over with tender care.

With a hoarse cry she clutched him to her, her mouth
hot upon his, her hands tangled in the dark mass of his
hair, her legs trembling so violently she feared they
would never return to normal. She heard his low, harsh
groan as he stiffened above her, quivering, his body
drenched in sweat, his hands hard, almost cruel on her
shoulders as he pinned her to the mattress and stared
hotly into her face. Then he gave a single sharp cry and
fell forward, sinking in deep, deep, jerking spasmodi-
cally, words of love tumbling from his lips as he spilled
into her.

Her heart swelled to twice its size, filled her chest in
a burning lump of pain so exquisite she cried out and
flung herself upward, hard, hard against him. She
seemed to be thrown up and out of her body, spinning,
churning, careening through space and time—then she
fell, drifted, floated dreamily back to earth.

She felt the mattress firm beneath her back, the
sheets damp and wrinkled, Bret's body so heavy and
hot upon hers, felt his thudding heartbeat, thumping
like a trip hammer against her own. Their flesh clung
stickily together as if reluctant to part and her limbs
were so heavy she could not lift them to move away.
She lay under him, crumpled, exhausted, totally sa-
tiated. Her eyes were closed and her breathing ragged,
as if she had run up hill for miles and miles only to
pitch over the other side. Never had she been more ac-

utely cognizant of her nerves and pulses. One beat steadily in her temple, another in her throat. Even her wrists were gently vibrating.

"I love you, Mandy," Bret whispered softly, breaking into her thoughts. He kissed her lips then each closed eyelid. "I love you, darling." His hands slid warm and firm down her body, moving her a little until they were lying on their sides, facing one another, still joined.

"Oh, Bret," she sighed, looking into his dark eyes, so soft and close. She wanted to tell him that she loved him, too, but the words would not come. She closed her eyes and snuggled her head into the curve of his shoulder so she wouldn't have to face the question in those dark, beautiful brown eyes. His hand stroked her waist, her hip, as gently as one would pet a kitten. She could feel him inside her still, not hard and demanding as before, but a soft warmth that filled her with wonder. So this was what it was all about, she thought wickedly and almost giggled aloud. All those times she and Suzette Arceneaux had speculated on what it would be like to make love to a man. Never in her wildest imaginings had she thought it would be this fantastic. *Mon Dieu*, but it was exciting, breathtaking, almost violent in its intensity. She wondered if she would feel this good with Tod and then was immediately sorry that she had thought of him. She flushed with shame, lying in the arms of her true love's brother, as sated as any common hussy.

"Was it good for you, darling?" Bret's voice was shy, almost timid. She wanted to tell him what he wanted to hear but could not bring herself to say the words of love. Instead she kissed him softly, then snuggled back into the nest of his shoulder. "Yes," she whispered huskily, not wanting anything to disturb this quiet, wonderous moment. "Yes, *mon amour*, you have made me very, very happy." It was true. She was happy, happier than she had ever been in her life. She felt fulfilled and cherished and loved. Perhaps she did love Bret or could learn to love him. Or perhaps this *was* love, this feeling of total peace. She sighed and gave herself up to the drowsy curtain that fluttered over her, one leg thrown over his, their bodies still joined. She heard his voice coming from very far away, saying soft words that she did not try to hear. Outside a clap of thunder rumbled deep in the throat of the sky and the first raindrops fell like little kisses upon the shake roof of the hunting lodge. She felt him move, careful not to remove himself from her as he pulled up the quilt and covered them both.

"Sleep for a little while, my love," he murmured against her hair. "My wild, sweet love." She smiled drowsily and wrapped her leg more securely about him, her arms holding him close to her breasts as she gave herself up to an exhaustion so deep that she was instantly asleep.

She awoke with a start and sat up in bed, now knowing for a moment where she was. A storm crashed outside and the windows were dark, streaked with rain and frosty steam. The only light in the room was the glow from the fireplace and one candle on the dining table that had burned down to a short stub. The bed was empty. Clutching the quilt to her breasts she sat up straighter and peered into the shadows, suddenly afraid. She saw a red spot of light and made out Bret's figure in a chair, smoking a cheroot. He saw the movement from the bed and went quickly to her.

"Well, hello, sleepyhead," he grinned, bending to kiss her. "How do you feel?"

"Oh, Bret—uh, hello." She ducked her head, embarrassed, clutching the quilt more tightly under her chin. *Mon Dieu, what does one say to a man who has just ravished one so completely?* she thought foolishly. "It's raining," she said.

"Yes, quite a storm kicked up a couple of hours ago and it doesn't show any signs of letting up. We may well be stranded here the rest of the night." He sat down on the edge of the bed and took her hand, but she pulled it back under the quilt, not meeting his eyes.

He looked at her bare shoulders, the tumbled hair like a stormy dark sea about her pale face. Her lips were swollen and bruised, still red from his kisses. There were two spots of bright color in her cheeks and she smelled earthy and musky from sweat. *'Poor little baby,* he thought tenderly, *she's so embarrassed she can't even face me.* Of course he expected it. She wasn't a born harlot like Lanora Arteaga who would look a man boldly in the eye as her hand sought his source of pleasure. Mandy was genteelly bred and reared, a lady. Then he smiled to himself, remembering the wild abandon with which she had given herself to him. *A lady with a very lusty appetite,* he added with a chuckle that she did not hear.

"Are you hungry, darling? I promised you a picnic, remember?" She glanced at him, gave him a fleeting, shy smile and nodded her head. "Come on then, let's eat. I'm starved." He took her hands to draw her out of bed but she hung back, blushing crimson.

"Bret, don't!" she cried, grabbing the quilt and covering herself. "I'm naked!" The blush turned darker as he laughed out loud and said, "Yeah, I know." He kissed her soundly upon the mouth. "I'll see if I can find something for you to wear—although it seems a shame to cover up such beauty and perfection."

He rummaged in the closet and pulled out a plaid robe, obviously J.B.'s for it had a big bold monogram on the left breast pocket. He held it for her, his eyes, averted politely as she slipped into it. She noticed that he was wearing only his trousers and shirt, the latter being open to expose his broad, hairy chest. She looked quickly away, wishing he would button it. He looked too casual and sexy dressed that way, his dark hair mussed and tumbled, made so by her seeking fingers. She blushed again. Goodness, if she was going to be a fallen woman she'd certainly have to stop blushing every other minute like some silly schoolgirl.

The rain fell heavily upon the roof, battered against the windows and sent little puffs of cold air into the room. She shivered slightly and Bret was instantly concerned. "Are you cold, darling? I don't want you getting a chill. Here, sit next to the fireplace and I'll bring you a plate of food." He led her to the couch as if she were an invalid, or a breakable china doll, and made her comfortable, tucking the robe around her legs. He poured her a glass of burgundy before lighting the candles. The room was brought brightly into focus and she watched him as he cut meat and bread and piled their plates high.

Suddenly the door burst open and a tall figure dressed in a black slicker, dripping rain, stepped inside, bringing with him a gust of cold, damp wind. Silver-mounted saddlebags were slung over his shoulder and he was carrying a rifle in one black-gloved hand. Water poured off the flat brim of his hat, leaving a puddle on the floor. His eyes swept the room in a practiced glance, seeing everything at once. Then his swarthy face split into a wide grin that showed perfect white teeth beneath a drooping moustache.

"Well, *buenas noches,* Bret," he drawled in a deep, silky voice and his dark eyes swept Mandy with interest. "I did not expect to find you here."

"Hello, Jay. I might say the same to you." Bret moved slowly toward Mandy and stood protectively behind her, his hand resting on her shoulder. "What brings you to Bradshaw property?"

"My horse went lame back yonder at the waterhole. Knew we couldn't make it back to Casa de Oro so thought I'd stop in and put up at the old man's lodge." He dropped his saddlebags to the floor, shrugged off his slicker and propped his rifle against the wall. *"Dios,* but it is a cold one tonight!" He went to the fireplace, moving with feline grace, and warmed himself, his dark eyes flickering over Mandy, then back to Bret. He wore the outfit of a *vaquero*, bright silk scarf knotted at his throat, bright embroidered cotton shirt and black

201

leather *chaleco*. His trousers were black leather as well, studded down the side of each leg with silver conchos and his boots were elaborately hand-carved with very high heels. Large hand-hewn rotating spurs with five-inch rowels made a sharp jingling sound as he walked. "You forget your manners, Bret," he drawled in his soft, husky voice. "You do not introduce me to the charming señorita."

"Amanda Bradshaw—Jay Cordova." Bret's voice was cool and his other hand came down on her shoulder possessively. Mandy gasped, her eyes widening at the dark stranger, and saw him grin at her apparent shock.

"I see that my reputation has again preceeded me, alas." He swept off his hat, bowing as courtly as any Southern gentleman, and murmured, *"Mucho gusto en concerla*, Señorita Bradshaw." His amused gaze swept her figure wrapped in J.B.'s large robe, her dishevelled hair, and again the knowing smile tugged at his lips. "It *is* señorita, is it not?"

"It is," Bret said, his fingers squeezing Mandy's shoulders. "But not for long. We plan to be married."

Mandy was so shocked at seeing the notorious outlaw face to face to react to Bret's announcement. She stared at him as wide-eyed as a child, remembering all the stories she had heard. He was very handsome with a youthfulness that belied his lawless exploits. His face was as smooth as his younger brother Juan's, and his eyes were as sultry and velvety brown as his sister Lanora's. He had the full sensual lips of his mother and the dark, curling black hair of his Spanish ancestors. He made a striking figure standing there in his bright shirt and snug-fitting black leather trousers, rocking slightly on the big-roweled spurs. "How do you do?" she managed faintly, suddenly very conscious of her state of undress. She glanced quickly down at the robe to see that it was properly closed.

"Muy bien, gracias." The high-heeled boots clicked smartly together and he gave a small bow, his dark gaze

202

sweeping her, taking in the tumbled hair and passion-bruised mouth.

"We were just going to have a bite to eat," Bret said. "Would you care to join us?"

"*Si, gracious.* I have only some hardtack and jerky in my saddlebags and am very hungry." He tossed his hat onto a chair and went to the dining table. "Ah, but this is a feast, Bret! Caviar, is it not? And do I recognize Atoka's famous sugar- and sage-cured ham?" He leaned over the meat, sniffing, a look of ecstasy upon his face. "It has been a very long time since I have seen such food."

"Where you coming from this time?" There was a sharp edge to Bret's voice and Jay looked at him slyly, one black eyebrow cocked at an angle.

"Mexico." He helped himself to the picnic spread and went to stand in front of the fireplace again, spooning in the food quickly as if he hadn't eaten in days.

Mandy sat balancing her plate on her knees as the two men spoke together about Juanita's palominos, the weather, the price of beef, not believing that she was actually hearing such easy banter between them. Her face flamed with shame and she had to bite back the scream of rage that threatened. Damn Bret Dunlap! Every time she was with him something awful and embarrassing happened. *Never again*, she vowed. She got to her feet and leaned over him to whisper, as steadily as possible, "Please excuse me. I must put on my clothes." Then she ran swiftly from the room to the small dressing room next to the bed.

Dressing with fingers that trembled, she buttoned her jacket clear to her throat and shoved her feet into the high-topped boots. Never had she been so humiliated in her life! Being caught half naked, in what could only be called a compromising position, by a savage outlaw! It was too much. Easing open the window, she crawled quickly through, then ran as fast as she could toward the stable. Her heart pounded in fear and the rain soaked her through in seconds but she didn't dare go back for her heavy woolen poncho. She had to get away, away from Bret and away from the all-too-knowing eyes of the dark *bandido* who frightened her with his penetrating gaze and hungry look.

She slipped Goldie's bridle on, not taking the time to saddle her, but swung onto her back and urged her through the door. She kicked her into a hard gallop the moment they were outside, bending low over her neck and shouting, "Let's go, girl—come on!"

Wind and rain assaulted her, drenching her through, pounding so heavily into her face that she could not see for more than a few feet in front of her. Trusting Goldie's sure-footedness, she leaned low over her neck and hung on, closing her eyes every now and again when the rain threatened to blind her. Never had she been in such a storm and she would have been crazy to deny that it did not frighten her. But staying at the lodge with the black-eyed Jay Cordova looking at her as if she were something to be found in one of the cribs along Kelly Street was more than she could have endured. Nor could she face Bret after such a wanton and disgusting scene had transpired between them. She hated him but she hated herself more for her weakness. The things he had done to her! Shame burned her cheeks, turning them hot even in the cold rain, and she bit her lips, wanting to feel pain, wanting to hurt herself for her selfish indulgence. *Mon Dieu*, what was wrong with her that she needed to feel a man's arms about her even when she hated the man? Maybe those awful Yankees who had accosted her in New Orleans were right. Maybe Creole girls were different, their blood tainted with a fire and hunger that was lacking in other young women.

The lights of the mansion loomed ahead in the darkness and she drew in a shaky breath of thanks that she had made it. Lanterns glowed on every post that lined the path to the stables and more shone through the windows and down the curved brick lane leading to the house. She saw old Doc pacing in the rain, a storm lamp held high above his head, his weathered face peering fearfully into the dark night. He gave a shout when he saw her and ran to help her dismount.

"Well, Missy, get down from there this minute! You had us all worried half to death, that you did. Where in tarnation was ya, anyway? J.B. is fit to be tied." His tongue cluck-clucked nervously as he pulled Goldie's head around, running a hand over her trembling neck. "And where's yer saddle, I'd like to know? And yer slicker? Why, I declare, you gone out aridin' like this?" His gentle eyes were dark with worry and he drew her into the light of the stalls, peering intently into her face. "Is ye hurt? Anything busted?"

"No, Doc, I'm fine, really." She drew off her hat and shook the rain from it, then jammed it back on. "Just cold and wet. Have Tim brush Goldie down, will you please? And give her a good hot bran mash." Then she was running out into the storm again, head down, feet splattering up muddy water, heart pounding with fearful anticipation of facing her grandfather.

"*Mon Dieu*, he will surely kill me!" she said aloud as she pulled open the massive front doors and stumbled inside. The solid click of billiard balls striking together and gruff male laughter drifted to her from J.B.'s study as she hurried quickly up the stairs, praying she wouldn't run into anyone. She heard Agnes's high-pitched laughter and the sound of the dining room being cleaned. Perhaps no one had noticed how long she had been gone. It sounded as if many of last night's guests still remained. Undoubtedly, the heavy storm had prevented them from travelling to their homes. And a good thing for her, she thought gratefully. *Grandpapa* would not scold her in front of their guests.

She slipped quietly into her bedroom, closed the door and leaned against it, expelling her long-held breath. Safe. She closed her weary eyes for a moment, then went quickly into her bathroom to shuck off the wet riding habit. Wrapping herself in a full length robe of warm, fuzzy flannel, she got into bed and let her head

205

fall gratefully against the pillows. The day's events churned in her mind. *Mon Dieu*, had she actually spent the entire afternoon and most of the evening in Bret's arms? Had that been she, Amanda Brashaw, wrapped shamelessly about him? Writhing with wanton pleasure? Crying his name? Urging them both on to greater heights of passion? She burrowed into the blankets in an agony of embarrassment and would have moaned aloud, but the door opened and Caleen tiptoed in to peer down at her huddled form. "*Ché?*" she whispered. "*Bébé*, you sleepin', *chérie*?"

Mandy kept her face buried in the pillow, the blankets over her head and forced herself to breathe normally, slowly, until the old woman turned silently away. Mandy heard her putting away the wet riding habit, could almost see her shaking her head at the mud-caked boots, the rain-stained hat. She pressed her face further into the pillow, heard the screen in front of the fireplace being parted, the sound of Caleen dropping heavy logs onto the spitting, crackling embers, her poker sending up a loud hiss of flames. Then she settled herself into the rocker, its soft squeaking muffled by the thick carpet. Mandy's body relaxed and she stretched, allowing a soft sigh to escape her lips. She felt safe now, protected from the crashing storm outside her windows. Safe from Bret and the frightening feelings he stirred within her.

She heard Caleen take up her knitting. The thick needles swished together hypnotically, lulling her. She knew *Tante* Caleen would sit and rock and knit until she was sure that Mandy was deep asleep with no nightmares to frighten her. She smiled drowsily, the evil of Jay Cordova forgotten. The shameful day was only a memory now—and to her surprise, rather a pleasant one. She felt warm and safe again and could luxuriate in being cherished. Grandpapa would be so relieved that she was safe he wouldn't stay angry at her for long. She would tell him she had taken refuge in the hunting lodge until a break in the storm had enabled her to make it home. Caleen's needles hummed on and Mandy's eyes were so heavy she could no longer hold them open. As she drifted deeper and further away from wakefulness, she thought she felt Bret's arms about her, his warm, naked body pressed close. And she thought she called his name aloud.

It was another three days before the guests were able to leave the ranch for their own homes. The rain had kept up an unrelentless downpour, day and night, confining the Bradshaws as well as their twenty-odd guests to the ranch. It was rather like a long party, Mandy had thought as she had waved off the last carriage, her arms looped through J.B.'s and Jeramy's. And it had prevented J.B. from speaking privately with her. She had managed to get him alone for a few minutes and had meekly related the story of going for a brisk ride and becoming trapped at the hunting lodge. His shaggy white brows had raised only slightly as he had listened to her tale; then he had slapped her on the fanny, rather smartly, and told her to run along; he was just mighty glad that she was home safe.

Autumn slipped wetly into winter and it became crisp and cold, icy dew covering the ground in the early mornings and sending chill gusts of wind down chimneys and around windows and doors. Cattle stood bunched together, their frozen breath leaving puffy mounds upon the air, stamping their feet stolidly upon the hard ground. Thin, transparent slivers of ice edged Otter River and the small stream that ran through the barnyard and the kitchen pump froze off and on all winter long. Doc, Lefty, and George chopped ice from the mouth of Otter River, high up in the Los Gatos Mountains, broke it into sizeable squares and carted it back to the ranch where it would be buried in a deep cellar, packed with sawdust, and left to use next summer in Atoka's ice box.

Christmas came and with it the announcement that

Jane and Derek planned to marry. Bret was present at the annual Christmas dinner, this time held at the Dunlap ranch, and Mandy had managed to be pleasant to him and still stay well away lest he try to get her alone. January and February were wet and dreary, the land so muddy that Mandy was not able to ride as often as she liked. Confined to her room or the downstairs parlor, she paced and grew cranky, hating the weather that kept her a prisoner. She had too much time to think and always her thoughts turned to Tod—then at once to Bret, as if one triggered the other. Why did they always seem to become almost the same one in her thoughts and fantasies? She would lie back on her chaise, a bit of sewing forgotten in her lap, her toes turned toward the fire, and let herself be carried away with daydreams of Tod. Then suddenly he would become Bret. The blue of his eyes would change, grow softer, darker, until they were velvet brown and filled with love. . . .

Spring burst upon the ranch with wild exuberance and Mandy was out of the house and into the stables at the first sign of green on the trees. The air was bracingly sweet, the songs of returning birds filling the air as she rode impatiently over familiar terrain that led to Ceasare's little enchanted cottage. Days were spent talking with him, tramping through the chill woods with him to see how his *nenes* had survived the winter. She rode daily past the hunting lodge, her breath quickening when she did so, her pulses pounding a little too fast, her brain a little too eager for the memory.

Jane and Derek were married in the garden when the first warm Santa Ana breezes made their May appearance. Mandy, as Jane's maid of honor, had been forced to allow Derek's best man, Bret, to escort her throughout the wedding and long reception that followed at the Dunlap's Nob Hill mansion, or "city place," as Marie called it. Bret had been on his best behavior, charming, attentive, and Mandy had found herself having quite a marvelous time with him. Too bad the rogue couldn't always be so appealing.

Summer brought lazy days of sitting in the swing with one or another of Mandy's newly acquired beaux, or picnicking by the Pacific Ocean, luxuriating in the warm sand and surf and sun. Her thoughts often turnèd to Bret, out somewhere on the sea, getting in as many trips as possible before the inclemencies of colder months ahead. She did not want for attention from her family or any of the eager young men around her, but she felt lonely. It was then that her thoughts turned to Tod—then immediately to Bret.

Mon Dieu, would they both forever plague her?

CHAPTER NINE

Mandy stood in her suite in the Palace Hotel, gazing through the window that overlooked the busy street below. It was Opera Week, touted as the gayest week of the social season. The Metropolitan Opera Company would be arriving in their special railroad cars this afternoon and already crowds were lining the streets and jamming the depot to welcome them. The city was humming with activity and the lovely spring day seemed ordered especially for young lovers. Jenny and Andy occupied the suite to the right of Mandy's and Jane and Derek had the suite next to theirs. It was their second anniversary and Jane was pregnant with their first child. It was also the occasion of the grand opening of Dunlap Furriers on the west coast, a wedding gift from Bret to Derek. The actual building of the enormous showroom/salon and cold storage unit in which to keep the furs had taken over a year and Bret himself had made the long ocean voyage around Cape Horn to bring a shipload of fabulous furs to San Francisco. The opening would be held in three days and everyone who was anyone would be there, Jane had assured Mandy.

She walked away from the window and poured herself a glass of sherry, sighing mightily. She was bored and lonely. It seemed that everyone had a husband or lover except her. Young June had eloped with Juan Arteaga six months ago and they had gone to live in Los Angeles. "*El Pueblo de Nuestra Señora la Reina de Los Angeles*," Ceasare had told her. "It is quite a heavenly name to bestow upon such a humble little town, eh, *querida*? I do hope that the children will be happy there. Juan, he must live down the reputation of the notorious Jay Cordova if he remains here, so it is best that they move away, I think."

It was also best that they move away because J.B.'s wrath had been something to behold. He had roared like a maddened bull when he had found June's note. "Jesus Christ," he had thundered, setting the chandeliers shaking and the servants quaking. "They're related by blood, for the love of God! They'll have a pack of half-wits!"

Paula, Jenny's eldest, was in school in the East and had just written to her mother that she had a boyfriend, a grandson of Collis P. Huntington, one of the "Big Four" railroad magnates. Even *Tante* Caleen had a beau, if one could believe Atoka. "That dern little foreigner has set her cap fer old Doc," Mandy heard Atoka telling Marta one day. "Jest take a gander out yonder." She had jerked her head toward a cloud of black soot rising outside the kitchen window. Mandy, eavesdropping in the hallway, had hurried outside to see Caleen, her spring *tignon* as bright as a new cherry, her black face alight with smiles as she wielded her broom and sang, "*Ramoné la chiminée! C'est li tems, oui. Ramoné ci, ramoné la, ramoné li de haut en bas. Ramoné!*" ("Sweep the chimney! It's time, yes. Sweep here, sweep there, sweep it from top to bottom. Sweep!") And old Doc, his lavender eyes shining with pleasure, was gleefully helping Caleen with her spring cleaning chores, trying valiantly to sing along with her.

Sipping her sherry, Mandy turned moody thoughts to Tod Dunlap. She still thought about him often even though she had gotten over much of her schoolgirl crush. And she thought often of the stormy afternoon she had spent in Bret's arms in her grandfather's hunting lodge. She had made it a point never to be alone with him since that day because he stirred in her emotions she thought better left alone. That she was of a passionate nature she had accepted and did not trust

211

herself with the man who had unleashed them. Bret had tried to apologize for Jay Cordova's intrusion but Mandy would not hear him. She hated herself for giving in so readily to the lust that she blamed Bret for arousing. No gentleman would take advantage of a girl's feelings as he had. Thankfully, she did not have to see him too often, as he still made his regular business trips to New York and Europe, spending more and more time away from home, Marie had lamented to Mandy one afternoon.

"Seems my baby has something powerful heavy on his mind these days," she had said sadly. "He never used to stay away for such long spells. What do you reckon could be bothering him, honey-bunch?"

And Mandy had flushed and turned away from Marie's eyes, glad that Marie did not connect Mandy with Bret's frequent disappearances. He had returned this last Christmas after a six-month absence and casually tossed a huge, red-wrapped box at her with a flippant, "Thought you might be getting chilly on these long cold nights!" It had held a full-length sable coat, lush and lovely beyond belief and monogrammed on the satin lining with her name and the year, 1878. Then he was off again, this time to Los Angeles to look into some land holdings the Dunlaps had there, as a rumor had started that oil had been discovered on the lot next to theirs. Jenny had said that he was due back for Opera Week and Mandy prayed that she would not have to see him. Jenny had also arranged for William Dobson's brother, Gregg, to be Mandy's escort on opening night.

She sipped her sherry, smiling a little at the thought of Gregg Dobson. He was the image of William, stocky, blonde, blue-eyed and serious to the point of dullness. But he was worshipful in his adoration of Mandy and treated her with the deference that she felt was proper for a young lady of her station.

She was now a very wealthy young lady in her own right. J.B. had given her five hundred shares in the Comstock silver mine for her twentieth birthday and

212

she was now a major stockholder in the greatest silver mine in history. She had ridden out to see it, accompanied by J.B., and had been in awe of the gorgeous scenery surrounding the site. Just over the Sierra Nevadas, on the shoulder of Sun Mountain, it was snuggled in among the towering pines and blue lakes that dotted the green hillside. She had seen the financial report as well and knew that hundreds of millions of dollars in bullion were pouring into the safe rooms of Wells Fargo Bank on Montgomery Street in San Francisco. She felt quite grown-up with her new status of businesswoman.

She went to her closet and looked again at the gown she had had made for the opera. It was the loveliest dress she had ever seen, pale, glimmering silver shot through with darker metallic threads, the fabric as light and frothy as gossamer. It was cut very low and snug-fitting to the hips where it flared out into ten yards of floaty, dreamy chiffon. Her slippers were silver as well and she would wear her hair swept up and held in place with ostrich plumes and diamond clips. She would also wear the Bradshaw diamonds and emeralds, the green gems adding just enough color to turn her blue eyes smoky turquoise. She wished that Tod would be able to see her all dressed up like a fairy princess, but he was probably off somewhere with Jay Cordova. The two had become "thicker than thieves" Marie had said with a shake of her head. "What he sees in that no-account varmint, I'll never know!"

Mandy knew why Tod spent so much time with Jay. He was often invited to spend weekends and to attend family gatherings with the Arteagas and therefore with Lanora. But the sultry señorita was still leading him a merry chase if Tod's long face and black expression meant anything. *The fool,* Mandy thought for perhaps the thousandth time. *Can't he see that she doesn't care a fig for him? She's just using him to feed her colossal ego while waiting for Bret to declare his love.*

Pouring herself another sherry she went to sit by the window and stare moodily down at the busy street. Life

213

was so unfair. Your heart dictated that you fall in love with someone even if that someone loved another or was just simply no good for you. She knew now that Tod was not right for her. He was wild and unpredictable, a drinker, gambler, and womanizer. Men could get away with anything. If they were thwarted in love they could simply go the the Lacey Palace or an establishment like it and have their egos and bodies soothed by practiced hands. Women could not. They lay abed, brooding and hurting with no respite from the frustration. Mandy had been in an agony of guilt and pain for months after the immorality, her body craving again the sensual pleasure Bret had given her. She had toyed with the idea of seducing the ever-faithful Gregg Dobson but had put the motion out of her head the moment she had let him kiss her. Ugh! How his thick, soft lips had repelled her, and the worshipful expression in his pale eyes had almost made her laugh out loud.

She was tortured with dreams of Bret, his dark eyes hot with love, his hands playing her body as if it were a fine musical instrument of pleasure, his body so hard and sure as it sought hers. . . .

"*Mon Dieu*, that rogue!" she cried aloud, one fist striking the arm of her chair. "Will he always plague me so?" She tossed off her sherry and went to pour another, smiling a little at how easily drinking spirits during the day came to her. But sophisticated men and women thought nothing of having a tot of brandy with their morning coffee or one of the new "cocktails" with their luncheon. Something called the "Cocktail Route" was new in San Francisco and was quickly becoming popular. It began at five o' clock in the afternoon at the recognized "first stop" at the Reception Saloon on Sutter Street near Kearny, where bankers, politicians, merchants and other businessmen gathered for a drink. Each kept his personal bottles of liquor behind the long mahogany bar, each bottle labeled with his name. Most men brought a lady friend and the evening had officially begun when they moved on to yet another "watering hole," as one wag had tagged the many bars in San Francisco's theater district, then on to the Cliff House or the Poodle Dog Café for supper before attending the latest play or concert.

Mandy had seen everything from Mozart's opera, *Don Giovanni* to the Eagle Theater's special held-over engagement of *The Creation*. And now, with the railroad connecting East to West, she was looking forward to seeing her first circus. San Francisco was being touted as the Paris of America, the city that never sleeps, the fastest-growing metropolis in the West—and she was growing with it. At twenty she had fullfilled the beauty promised as a child; her figure was lush yet slender, the baby fat of her face having slimmed into high, elegant cheekbones and the strong jaw of the Bradshaws. Her carriage was as haughty and proud as a queen's, her wit sharp, her intelligence keen. She read voraciously and could speak knowledgeably on a variety of subjects. Being the favorite granddaughter of J.B. Bradshaw, millionaire, as well as a major stockholder in the Comstock Silver lode, she was considered the catch of the decade and was well aware of that status. So many young men had come courting that her head spun with their names and titles—Drew Hearst, heir to a publishing fortune, Carlton Stanford of the land and cattle baron Stanfords, Alonzo P. Hopkins, next in line to inherit an oil field in Texas, Oscar Cardingworth, just simply rich with old money—scions all of socially prominent millionaires on both coasts. She had toyed with the idea of taking Drew Hearst as a lover (he was by far the handsomest and most charming) but after he had kissed her in the back of his new phaeton she knew that he wasn't for her. For all his surface grace he was as clumsy and rough as a stablehand when it came to lovemaking. The dark image of Bret Dunlap had filled her mind and she had cursed again the day she had met him. Had he indeed spoiled her for any other man, as he had mockingly told her last Christmas when he had trapped her under the mistletoe? Even Tod, whom she thought she loved, did not kiss her as Bret did, with such deep, tender feeling. Nor did he make her heart beat faster and her legs turn to water as they did when she was close to Bret.

Ma foi, but life was strange! She disliked Bret as much as ever and yet when he had caught her about the waist and spun her to face him, his soft lips coming down hard and hot on hers, she had responded at once. Her body had curved itself into his as if it had always done so and her mouth had opened eagerly for his kiss. Marie had poked J.B. in the ribs and the two of them had looked on with approval. Mandy knew that J.B. wanted her to marry Bret almost as much as Marie did and it saddened her that she couldn't give them this one thing. But Bret still infuriated her with his too-knowing eyes, his teasing and arrogance.

"Mother's determined to have you as a daughter-in-law, you know," he had told her that Christmas, the only time she had relented enough to speak to him and then only out of respect for Marie and the season. "She's always wanted girls. She has Jenny and now that Jane and Derek are married nothing will do but that you take the name of Dunlap as well."

"Perhaps I will—but it certainly won't be Mrs. *Bret* Dunlap," she had retorted, thinking of Tod. And Bret, reading her thoughts, had had the audacity to laugh out loud! The cad!

Mandy went to run her bath. The hairdresser was due at five and then she and Gregg were to meet Jenny and Andy, Derek and Jane in the Reception Saloon for cocktails before going on to the Orpheum Theater. She should have been more excited about seeing the Metropolitan Opera Company for the first time but she was not. She felt restless and out of sorts and the bright spring day only heightened her feeling of loneliness. If she were back in New Orleans she would no doubt be married—and with her lusty appetite marriage was obviously the safest place to be!

216

Gregg Dobson picked Mandy up promptly at six and they walked the short distance to the Reception Saloon. It was packed to overflowing with the pre-opera crowd, ladies in diamonds, rubies and emeralds, laughing and flirting with handsome men in elegant evening attire with diamond stickpins and solid gold cufflinks. Every type of carriage lined Market Street, hitched to matching blooded horses of every color and breed. Ragged beggars, many of them children, scuttled like fleas between the silks and furs, their grubby hands held out for a penny or any offering they could get. A man on stilts wobbled down the sidewalk wearing a sandwich board advertising the coming of Sells Brothers' Circus on one side and Cole's Menagerie on the other. Prostitutes mingled with the crowd, picking occasional pockets if the gentlemen they had accosted refused their wares.

Mandy sat at the large oval table, only half listening to the conversation around her. Jenny and Jane had their heads together about Jane's coming baby and Jenny's two-year-old toddler; Andy, Derek, and Gregg were in a heated discussion about Grover Cleveland's chances of winning the presidency if he should decide to run and the two men and their ladies at the next table were loudly discussing the new Buffalo Bill Wild West Show they had seen last month in New York City. Glasses tinkled and laughter rang shrilly throughout the large room. Mandy turned to see a striking young blonde woman enter the foyer, her gaze searching the crowd. She felt Jenny's hand on her arm and heard her shocked whisper, "Why, would you look at that? If she isn't as brazen as a brass monkey!"

"Who?" Mandy asked, not really interested. She sipped her cocktail.

"That woman over there, the blonde one in the black gown," Jenny hissed. "It's that Lacey person from the Lacey Palace. What on earth is she doing here?"

Mandy stared at the woman openly. She wasn't beautiful but gave the impression of beauty in the way she held herself. Her gown was the very latest fashion

(Mandy had just seen a photograph of it in *Hesperian's*) and her jewels looked real even from a distance. She had a beaded handbag and a long black satin cape was draped over one arm. But it was her face that caught and held Mandy's interest. It was youthful and innocent, the blue eyes as clear as a child's. She looked more like a Sunday-school teacher than the madam of a famous bordello.

Suddenly the pale, pretty face lighted and Mandy gasped aloud when she saw Bret walking through the crowd toward the blonde. He took her hand and kissed it, then slipped a possessive arm about her shoulders and escorted her to a table. "I don't believe it," Jenny whispered, plainly shocked. "Bret with that—that woman, in *public*? Has he taken leave of his senses? It's a disgrace!"

"Maybe they have business together," Jane put in shyly. "Derek said Bret often bring items back from Europe for Miss Lacey. Furniture and things for her, uh, business."

"Humph, I can well imagine what sort of things he brings her," Jenny snorted. "Well, I certainly hope he doesn't see us and present that woman to us. Goodness, what does one say to the madam of a bordello?"

"I'm sure I don't know," Mandy murmured, adding to herself, "But I'm sure Bret does."

"Derek says she is really a very nice woman," Jane said. "She only did what she had to do to stay alive." Ever since the wedding two years ago, Jane began every sentence with "Derek says" until Mandy wanted to scream. *Mon Dieu*, did all women immediately lose their own identity and ability to think for themselves once they said "I do"?

"I would have taken in laundry or scrubbed floors before I ran a whorehouse," Jenny sniffed grimly.

"Yes, but you wouldn't be able to wear such fine clothes and jewels on a washerwoman's salary," Mandy said lightly. She was determined not to let her feelings show but inside she seethed with anger. So Bret loved her, did he? He certainly had told her often enough. Now she felt righteous and smug for not believing him and giving in to his many invitations for another rendezvous. All the while he was no doubt telling this Lacey person the very same things. Men were odious beasts and she would never believe any of them. She glanced at the men at her table, heads still together in a political discussion, totally oblivious to the women's outrage. They would have thought nothing of it if they had seen the young, pretty madam on Bret's arm. Jeramy had told her that most of the men in San Francisco actually respected Lacey and sincerely liked her.

An hour later they were seated in the Bradshaws' private box at the Orpheum Theater. Mandy's mood was even blacker because of the unexpected sight of Bret. Not that she had any love for him, she told herself crossly, but it had been like a slap in the face to see him with someone like Lacey. It was as if he was laughing at her, letting her know that he didn't much care where he found his pleasure or with whom. He knew very well that she was going to be in town tonight and had probably planned the whole thing for her benefit, talking Lacey into going along with the practical joke. She turned the pages of her program, ignoring the conversations around her as late arrivals came to claim their boxes. J.B.'s box was a plush affair with curtains that could be drawn to enclose them in privacy. Jenny and Jane were still chattering about babies and the men were now discussing the Dunlap-Dobson lumber mill and the rising cost of building materials.

Mandy fanned herself with her program, bored and angry, wishing she were anyplace but here. She had seen so much opera lately that tonight's play barely interested her. She wished she had refused Jenny's invitation to join her party and had instead stayed home with a good book.

The curtains to her left fluttered as a foursome arrived and took their places in the adjoining box. She glanced up idly and stared directly into Bret's face. Lacey was by his side and behind her were Tod and Lanora.

"Well, good evening, Miss Bradshaw," Bret grinned, the sable moustache dark against his flashing white teeth, teasing laughter plain in his eyes. "Fancy meeting you here." He said hello to the group, then paused before adding, "Ladies, may I present Miss Lacey?" He did not introduce her to the men; obviously she was well known to them.

"How do you do?" Jenny said coolly, her eyes raking the slender figure in black. "I've heard so much about you."

Mandy murmured "Good evening" but Jane actually extended her hand to the creature and said shyly, "I'm so pleased to meet you, Miss Lacey. My husband speaks so highly of you and I've wanted to see for myself if you're as wonderful as he says!" She smiled in genuine warmth. "Derek says you're one of the smartest women in San Francisco and that you actually do all your own bookkeeping yourself. Is that true? Goodness, if I'm confronted with more than two rows of numbers I'm afraid I'm at a complete loss!" She laughed and Lacey laughed with her, her soft blue eyes showing her appreciation at being spoken to as an equal. Mandy felt even crosser than before. Leave it to Miss Goody Two-Shoes Jane to make even the madam of a whorehouse feel welcome in such an embarrassing situation!

"Tod! Hello!" Mandy said a little too brightly, flashing him a brilliant smile. "And Señorita Arteaga! How nice to see you again. That's a lovely gown. Where on earth did you get it?"

"Good evening, Miss Bradshaw," Lanora drawled in her husky, softly-accented voice. "Bret was good enough to bring it to me from Paris on his last voyage." Her black eyes caressed him and Mandy saw a muscle tighten in his jaw.

"Yes," he said coolly, "and Tod was good enough to pay for it. It's part of a wedding trouseau, isn't it, Lanora?"

"Not necessarily," she said shortly and a look of surprised hurt crossed Tod's features.

The rising curtain brought the conversation to a halt and the house lights dimmed. Mandy heard Tod whisper urgently to Lanora and her bored monotone in answer. She felt a pang of pity for Tod. He was so obviously in love with the dark-eyed beauty and she was just as obviously not interested. *Oh, why couldn't he look at me that way?* Mandy thought sadly. *I would never hurt him.* She stole a glance at the next box and saw Tod's grim profile and Lanora's petulant one. The sweet-faced Lacey was gazing intently at the stage, apparently the only one in the group actually interested in the opera. Bret merely looked bored and sat sprawled in his seat, tapping his program against his leg.

Mandy leaned back, trying to concentrate on the actors below. Gregg's soft, moist hand sought hers but she held onto her reticule, pretending not to notice. Music swelled in the theater, the tenor lamented a lost love, and Mandy wished she had the nerve to simply get up and walk out, to go back to her hotel room and have a good cry.

They had dined leisurely on oysters Kirkpatrick and boiled terrapin at the Cliff House and Mandy's mood had been somewhat restored. Ted Stokes had joined them in an after-supper liqueur and invited them to Charles Crocker's private yacht for a late party and moonlight cruise on the bay. He had pointed out William Randolph Hearst's yacht rocking gently next to several smaller ones as they were rowed out to the *Nicole*, which sat far back in the black water, alight with Japanese lanterns.

They were helped aboard by sailors in starched white uniforms with heavy gold braid at their cuffs and collars. Their host was a big, florid man puffing on a thick black cigar. Diamonds flashed on his fingers as he beamed at them. "Welcome aboard!" he boomed. "Glad you could make it." He clasped their hands with

221

genuine warmth, but it was Mandy his small, sharp eyes scrutinized so carefully.

"Thank you for inviting us," Mandy murmured politely, flushing under his bold stare. "It's been so warm lately a nice cool ocean breeze seems just the thing to restore one's good humor."

"Now what would a pretty little thing like you have to be in a bad humor about?" Crocker leaned in close, almost gagging her with his vile cigar smoke, and winked suggestively. "Only thing a little gal needs when she's out of sorts is some pretty new bauble to play with." He peered closer. "Like that necklace there. Damn fine looking diamonds and emeralds, honey. Family heirloom?"

"Yes." She moved quickly away and Crocker turned his attention to the men. Holding the brass handrail, she took several deep gulps of night air to settle her stomach. The yacht rocked beneath her feet as she walked toward the upper deck where sounds of the party drifted toward her. She was approached at once by a uniformed waiter who offered her a glass of champagne, then disappeared as silently as a ghost. Looking around the impressive yacht, she thought that everything had a sort of ghost-like quality, the edges muted by the fog of the bay and the silvery moonlight. Even the guests seemed hazy and dreamlike as they floated about the deck. She went to the rail and leaned her elbows on it, gazing out to sea. How black and mysterious the water looked. How sinister. She shivered and turned to look toward the shore where bright lights winked and beckoned and the hum of the city could be heard even from this distance. A light breeze ruffled the curls at her temples and the nape of her neck, billowing the fabric of her skirt.

"I didn't believe in the existence of angels until this moment," a voice said, and she swung around to see Bret walking toward her. "Don't move," he pleaded. "Just stand there a moment with the moon behind you." His dark eyes devoured her and she felt the old

222

familiar tug of desire. "You look like a lovely silver butterfly in that gown—like an angel of beauty come to earth to torment us poor mortals."

"Bret! You startled me." She gave a tiny laugh and ducked her head to her champagne. *Mon Dieu*, but he always popped up at the strangest places! One would think he was following her. But he couldn't have known she would be here as the invitation had only been issued an hour ago. She would not flatter her ego that he had sought her out; he undoubtedly had business with Mr. Crocker or one of the other men present. It was almost incestuous the way the big, rich families and corporations merged in business as well as marriage. No wonder only a handful of Californians were millionaires—they kept it in the family.

"I'm a little surprised at seeing you here myself," Bret grinned. "I wasn't aware that you were included in Crocker's crowd of merrymakers. Have you known him long?"

"I've only just met him this evening," Mandy said primly. "And I am not a part of his crowd, as you put it. Actually, Ted Stokes issued the invitation, as he wanted a chance to discuss some sort of business with Andy and Gregg."

"Gregg being your beau?" Bret's dark eyes flashed and the sardonic grin tugged at his lips.

"My *escort*—if it's any of your affair." She gave him the same teasing, slightly mocking smile and purred, "And where is your, uh, paramour?"

"She had to get to work," Bret said easily, watching her face for her reaction. "As you may suspect, her business hits its stride around midnight."

"Yes, I'm sure it does," Mandy murmured, embarrassed to the roots of her hair at discussing such a shocking subject as prostitution with a man. The rogue was obviously trying to humiliate her by freely admitting that his opera companion had had to cut the evening short to get back to her whorehouse. How dare he speak to her so, as if she were of the same moral character as that Lacey creature! She would not give him the satisfaction of seeing her outrage. She would appear as blasé as he. "An establishment such as hers must take a great deal of surveillance, I should imagine."

"It sure does. If Lacey isn't there to keep an eye on things the girls tend to give away the house profits—if you know what I mean." His eyes twinkled mischievously and he stroked his moustache caressingly, looking directly at her. "They're just such a bunch of fun-loving, big-hearted ladies that money seldom enters their heads!"

"I'm sure you speak from first-hand experience, Bret Dunlap," she laughed, enjoying this teasing, slightly flirtatious game.

"Indeed I do, Miss Bradshaw. Else how would I have become so proficient in lovemaking?" He chuckled, flashing her a wicked grin, and she wanted to reach out and touch the dimple high in his cheek. "Even a lover must serve an apprenticeship."

"I see. And how long does this apprenticeship last, monsieur?" She gave him an arch look, her expression saucy.

"Until the pupil becomes the teacher," he murmured softly and before she could sidestep his embrace his arms had gone around her and he was kissing her. His moustache tickled her and she revelled in it, remembered it with a fondness that surprised her. With a sigh she opened her lips for him and her arms went around his neck, drawing him closer. Her body melded to his and she thought, *This is what I was made for. To be loved by a man, to be desired.* Her hot Creole ancestry beat strong in her blood. She should have been born a hundred years ago when ladies of such disposition were the most desirable courtesans in the country. If she had lived during those golden days of old New Orleans she would not have to stop her trembling response to Bret's body; she could have given in with the knowledge that he would think none the less of her for it, but only love and cherish her the more.

"Oh, Mandy, how good you feel in my arms." His voice was husky, almost gruff. "I'm always a little surprised at how perfectly we fit together. How good your lips taste—" He kissed her again, his tongue seeking hers. His body pressed hard against her and she felt the old familiar rush of heat in her loins. *Mon Dieu*, but she wanted him! Wanted him to rip the clothes from her body and take her on the gently rocking deck with the moon a silver goblet in the sky and the breeze cooling their warm skin.

"Bret, *mon amour*." Her voice was a mere whisper so faint he barely heard it but he heard the singing of her body, the force of it drawing him nearer. The heat of their kiss was intense, leaving them both shaken. They drew apart a little and gazed into one another's eyes for a long, silent moment.

Mandy giggled and ducked her head to her champagne glass. *"Mon Dieu,"* she laughed, fanning herself with her hand. "I fear you have taken my breath away, monsieur! Perhaps you have been too long at sea, no?"

"No—just too long away from you!" He grasped her hand and brought it to his pounding heart. "Feel what you do to me, my darling. God, I feel like a simple-minded lad around you! What have you done to me, witch?" He kissed her hard, his dark eyes open and boring into hers. "What have you done to me?" he said again, softly, his lips now gentle on her brow.

"Perhaps I should ask what you have done to me," she said faintly, deeply aware of her throbbing groin. "You make me forget myself to—to react like a—a—"

"Like a woman. A beautiful, desirable woman with a healthy need." He kissed her nose, her lips and throat. "Don't be ashamed of your feelings, Mandy darling." His hands caressed her bare arms and back, flirting across her breast tops in the low gown, then he lowered his head to them.

"Amanda!" The shocked, accusing voice jerked them apart and they turned to see Gregg Dobson standing with wide eyes and tightly pursed mouth. Then the

225

stern expression crumbled and the young man stammered, "Oh! And Bret Dunlap! What a surprise, sir!" He stuck out his hand, awe plain in his eyes. Like most of the young men in San Francisco he considered Bret something of a hero. He was fascinated by his escapades and adventures on both land and sea, as well as his reputation with the ladies, and considered him a man to be admired. He broke into a wide, worshipful smile. "Gee, I've wanted to meet you for a long time! You'd think with my brother and your brother being partners we'd have met before this, wouldn't you?" He laughed and blushed. "But we haven't—I mean, gosh, it's sure a real pleasure to finally make your acquaintance, Mr. Dunlap—Bret, sir." He pumped Bret's hand vigorously.

"Nice to meet you, Gregg," Bret grinned, trying to reclaim his hand, but the young man held on, still pumping.

"Oh, gee, the pleasure is all mine, Bret! Really, sir!" He finally released Bret's hand. "Well, gee, I almost forgot why I came up here." He glanced at Mandy and blushed crimson. "Oh, I didn't mean it that way, Amanda, I assure you! Jenny asked me to find you and ask you to come sit with us." He glanced apologetically at Bret. "That new tenor with the Metropolitan Opera Company is going to sing a number for us, and well, you understand." He seemed genuinely upset at having interrupted them, forgetting completely, it seemed, that Mandy was *his* date and not Bret's! She was insulted that Gregg fawned all over Bret and completely ignored her. Where were the oaf's manners, anyway? "Hey, I've got a swell idea? Why don't you join us, Bret?" His innocent face was as bland as a pear.

"Oh no," Mandy said quickly, stepping to Gregg's side and taking his arm. "I'm sure Mr. Dunlap isn't interested—"

"Oh, but I am, Miss Bradshaw." The wicked expression was back in his eyes, the teasing grin on his lips.

"There's only one thing I'd rather do than listen to a charming love song, but, alas, I fear it is impossible." He bowed to Gregg. "Therefore, I would be delighted to join your charming party."

"Hey, that's great!" Young Dobson beamed with pleasure and Mandy wanted to kick him in the shins. Bret grinned in triumph and she wanted to slap the cocky look from his face. Men! *Mon Dieu*, was there anything more exasperating on the face of the earth?

Her lower lip protruding, she followed sullenly, allowing Gregg and Bret each to take an elbow to help her down the short flight of steps to the main deck. Seats were made available for them and Mandy settled herself grimly between the two men, vowing to leave as soon as it was polite to do so.

She barely heard the tenor nor did she notice his penetrating black eyes as he sang just for her. She *did* notice Bret's thigh pressed warmly against hers whenever he crossed or uncrossed his legs. Keeping her hands clasped tightly together, she stared straight ahead until the sound of the applause covered her hastily retreating footsteps. She had to get away—away from Bret.

The next morning Mandy had a late breakfast with Jenny and Jane, declining their offer to go shopping, and instead rented a horse and went for a ride along the beach. It was a warm, sultry day. She cantered the horse along the water's edge and gazed out across the ocean, marvelling at all that water. How very far it stretched and what strange and mysterious foreign shores it reached for. What must it feel like to be on the sea for weeks, months, never once glimpsing land? J.B. had been urging her to "do" Europe ever since she had turned eighteen. "A young lady isn't considered properly 'broadened' until she's done Europe," he had told her on more than one occasion. "Take Jenny or Jane, hell, take 'em both if you want to, and spend six months to a year. Do you good." But Mandy had declined, not ready yet to travel so far from the shelter of home and J.B.'s protection. It had taken her almost three years to come to grips with this raw, savage, often shocking place called California and she was just now beginning to feel that she finally belonged. At first, it had intimidated her and amazed her, confused and thrilled her, then it had seduced her until she wanted to stay always and feel the security of her roots, however new and fragile they were. She had come to love her new family dearly; *Grandpapa* had become as dear to her as *Grand-mère* Bertonneau and old Doc was just as protective and sweet as dear Elmo had been.

And she had something almost as good as love. She had respect in California. She thoroughly enjoyed her status as favored granddaughter of the richest and most powerful man in San Francisco just as she enjoyed the many beaux who came courting with flowers, trinkets and party invitations. She loved the bright, exciting night life of the city as much as she did the wide open spaces where she rode Goldie and stopped to visit with Ceasare Arteaga in his little enchanted cottage. She loved the quiet, elegant comfort of life on the sprawling ranch and the first garden of spring just as much as she loved the last harvest of fall.

She slowed the rented bay mare to a walk and turned her face up to the sun, closing her eyes. The muffled roar of the ocean drummed in her ears as the waves rolled in and splashed about the mare's hooves. She pranced in the foamy water and whinnied out of sheer pleasure. To Mandy's surprise there was an answering whinny near by. She opened her eyes and saw a magnificent palomino stallion atop a small sand dune, his flaxen mane and tail snow-white in the sun. He flung up his head and whinnied again at the mare, a loud, impatient neigh. The man on the stallion's back swept off his sombrero and his teeth flashed white beneath his dropping moustache.

"*Buenos dias, señorita,*" Jay Cordova called, his

228

voice carried to her on the wind. Putting his big-roweled spurs to the horse's sides, he was across the stretch of sand in a moment, drawing to a halt inches from her. The mare shied and rolled her eyes at the stallion and Mandy put a quieting hand on her neck. "What is the matter, pretty lady? You do not speak to bandidos, eh?"

Suddenly, he grasped her about the waist, pulling her half out of the saddle, his mouth coming down on hers. His tongue filled her mouth and Mandy gagged at the strong, sour taste of liquor on his breath. She shoved against his chest as hard as she could and tried to jerk her head away, but he held her easily and continued to kiss her until she thought she would surely faint. His hands pawed at her breasts, squeezing so hard she cried out against his mouth, and he released her. "Ah, you do not like my kisses, señorita," he mocked her, his face showing exaggerated pain. "Perhaps I am not a gentleman, eh? Like the dashing Señor Bret Dunlap, eh, *puta*?"

"Let me go!" Mandy struck out at his smirking face but he only laughed and caught her hand.

"Oh, I do not think I will, *puta*. I think first I will see if you are golden all over, eh?" He laughed at her struggles, his hard, cruel mouth coming down on hers once more. She bit his lip and he yelped in pain, then threw back his shaggy head and laughed out loud. "*Dios,* a real wild one, eh? Do not fight so, *querida*. One would think you do not like me."

Jay Cordova's dark eyes were black with passion as he stared at her. She swung at him and her horse shied, almost unseating her. With one arm, her jerked her onto his horse, his mouth open and hot against the sheer fabric covering her breasts.

"No! Don't!" She struggled against him, kicking and flailing her arms futilely, striking only empty air as he held her easily against him. Throwing one leg over the saddle horn he slid to the sand, dragging her with him. She lunged to her feet and made a dash away but he reeled her back like a fish, laughing at her fear. "Now, señorita, you would not want to make me mad, would you? Jay Cordova, he is not a very nice *hombre* when he is mad." His full lips still smiled but his black eyes were hard and cold as they blazed into hers. He shoved his buckskin breeches down and grabbed his manhood, pointing it at her as if it were a weapon. "I do not wear silk drawers like Bret Dunlap, *puta*, but I am more of a man, I think, eh? Look at me!"

"No!" Mandy flung her head to the side, burying her face in the sand, not wanting to look at the obscene sight. She prayed as she never had before, her heart almost bursting from her chest in her fear.

"*Si*, my little pretty, *si*," Jay purred, his voice going to silk again. "I will make you beg to see me, *mi amor*. I will make you scream for the joy I give you, *mi hermosa puta* . . ." He knelt over her and she turned her head and spat full in his face. He cursed in Spanish and his hard fist smashed into the side of her head, knocking her momentarily senseless. "*Puta!* You fucking *gringo* whore!" He crushed her mouth beneath his, biting her lips, his tongue almost choking her.

"No, damn you! You dirty pig, I won't let you touch me!" She freed one hand and scratched him across the face as hard as she could. He yowled in pain and slapped her full in the face, knocking her sprawling. Stars danced in front of her eyes and she could not raise her head for a full minute.

"Ah, that is better, I think." He was purring again, his hands busy over the stunned girl. "You sometimes must knock some sense into the stubborn heads of *gringos,* eh, *querida*?" He chuckled softly as he ripped away the bodice of her dress. "*Mi Dios!* What beauty!" His lips closed over one nipple, sucking greedily, his teeth sinking into the softness. His hand moved roughly under her skirts, shoving them up about her waist as he tore away her panties. The hand closed cruelly over her soft mound and she moaned and tried to struggle up once more. She felt his finger, hard, sharp, poking insistently and she screamed aloud when it violated her in one strong, deep thrust. She lunged forward with a terrible cry and he slapped her open-handed, knocking her back upon the sand.

"You pig!" she gritted, tasting blood and sand and hating him until she thought her heart and lungs would burst with the white-hot fury. "You filthy scum!"

"Ah, the proud and beautiful Miss Bradshaw does not like the dirty hands of Jay Cordova on her, eh?" The satin smoothness was in his voice and he moved his hand inside her slowly as he held her pinned to the sand. "Soon you will beg me to touch you, *puta*. Soon, when your juices start to flow . . ." He stroked her, his fingers exciting her in spite of her fear and revulsion. She kicked at him and tried to roll away from the insistant hand but he straddled her and held her captive. He dug into the pocket of his discarded buckskin trousers and withdrew a bottle of tequila. He pulled the cork out with his teeth, still stroking her steadily, and took a long pull. Sighing mightily, he shoved the bottle under her nose. "Drink, *puta*, it will loosen your limbs."

"Go to hell, you bastard!" She butted her head at him, knocking the bottle from his hand.

The drunken *bandido's* voice was a soft silken whisper as he said, "Now you have spilled my tequila. Now you have made me angry, *puta*. Now I will fuck you." He flattened her upon the sand, holding both wrists above her head in one big, steel fist. Viciously kneeing her thighs apart he fell between them, immediately sinking into her tight, dry body. She screamed and he closed her mouth with a cruel, lusty kiss that took her breath away. He began moving at once, filling her, burning and tearing her insides with his sadistic, brutal strokes.

She fought to tear her mouth free of his suffocating kiss but he held fast, filling her mouth with his tongue. He rode her unmercifully, forcing her body to respond, causing her to grow hotly moist even as she recoiled against him, repulsed by him. Her head ached and spun from the blows he had inflicted upon her and her breasts throbbed painfully from his hurting fingers. He jerked his mouth away and butted hard at her breast, taking it all the way into his mouth and suckling like a greedy infant. She sobbed and flung her head to the side, tasting sand and tears, and her body vibrated dully, rhythmically, with each deep, hard thrust he made.

The brutal, unrelentless pressure went on and on until Mandy lost all sense of time. Her heart thudded with fear and revulsion and silent tears coursed down her cheeks. Her body felt weightless, spinning out into space and time, tumbling in a gray cocoon that both cradled her and punished her. She felt both his hands grab her breasts and he cried aloud, stiffening above her. With an obscene oath he battered tremendously into her, almost splitting her apart. *"Dios!"* he gritted through clenched teeth. *"Dios!"* She was not aware when he finally lifted his weight from her for she had slipped quietly into unconsciousness.

CHAPTER TEN

J.B. stood with his hands clasped behind his back, his shaggy white eyebrows knit in thought as he gazed at the huge wall map behind his desk. It was stuck with pins in several places and he withdrew one and moved it a couple inches to the left. "This is where they last struck," he said, leaning in close to read the small print on the map. "Silver Springs. They got away with near two hundred head of prime beef." He turned and took a cheroot out of a leather-tooled box, and Luis was at his side at once with a match.

Jeramy whistled. "That brings the total to almost two thousand, Pa." He held out his empty brandy snifter and Luis silently refilled it. "It can't be Indians, like we thought. They don't have any use for that much beef. It's got to be some drifter, maybe up from Texas, looking to make a big profit when the Abilene buyers come to town."

"Yeah," J.B. agreed. He sat down behind his massive desk and propped his feet upon the cluttered top. "Yeah, that's the way I make it." He puffed on his cheroot, squinting against the smoke. "Buyers'll be in San Francisco next month. These ole boys keep knocking off a hundred, two hundred head of my stock every couple of weeks, they'll have 'em a nice little herd to sell for beef. Humph."

"What are we going to do, Father?" Jonathan asked, rather timidly, from the windowseat that opened onto the garden. He had declined a bourbon and was sipping a cold lemonade. It was beastly hot outside and if he hadn't been in the presence of his father he would have cooled himself with Agnes's bamboo fan.

"Do?" J.B. bellowed. "Do? Hell, man, we're going to track 'em down and string 'em up! What the hell do you do with a cattle rustler, for Christ's sake!" He chomped on the end of his cheroot so hard he bit it off.

"Now, Pa, don't get your tail in a knot," Jeramy soothed. "I'll send Lefty into town for the sheriff. Let him handle it."

"Bull!" J.B. snorted. "I'll handle it myself. By the time Roy gets around to it, I'll be wiped out."

"I hardly think a few thousand head will wipe you out, Pa," Jeramy laughed. "Hell, I'm surprised that you even noticed they were missing!"

"Didn't notice," J.B. grumbled, but a smile tugged at his mouth. "Ted Stokes told me."

Jeramy laughed out loud and went to sock his father on the arm. "Pa, I swear, you're incorrigible!"

"Hell, son, you can't expect a man to know every dang one of his cattle by name—"

"Certainly not, when he has over a hundred thousand head," Jeramy teased and J.B. cuffed him playfully on the chin. Jonathan looked on enviously as the two men scuffled like boys.

"What's going on in here?" Mandy asked, coming into the room. "Ah, *Grandpapa*, you are finally giving this rogue the spanking he so richly deserves, *oui*?" She laughed when J.B. swatted Jeramy on the butt.

"Get along with you, you crazy young whelp," J.B. laughed. Turning to Mandy, he pulled a mock-stern face. "The lad has no respect for his elders, my dear. Unlike you, who are the picture of decorum at all times."

Jeramy gave a hoot of laughter and Mandy stuck her tongue out at him. Luis, smiling at the horseplay, asked, "May I get you something to drink, Miss?"

"*Si* Luis, *por favor*." She dimpled prettily at her use of Spanish. True to his word, Ceasare had taught her to speak the language fluently. "I think perhaps a glass of white wine." She went to perch on the arm of J.B.'s chair. "What were you saying about the sheriff just before I came in? Is something wrong?"

"Damn right something's wrong," J.B. grumbled. He put his arm about her waist and hugged her to him. "Some no-account Texas varmints are rustling my cattle. Knocking 'em off like they were flies. Near two thousand head of prime beef."

"How do you know they are Texas varmints?" Mandy asked innocently and Jeramy just barely suppressed a chuckle.

"Because they ain't Indians, that's why!" J.B. roared. "Dern no-good Texas sidewinders . . ."

Jeramy explained. "We let the Indians take a few head every so often. Keeps them in meat and leather and helps keep peace with us ranchers. So when one of the wranglers reported to Ted Stokes that a few hundred head were missing from the batch that he bosses, we didn't think anything about it. Then a few days later another wrangler over on the other side of the range reported three hundred missing from his herd. Now, there aren't enough Indians left in these parts to eat that much beef, so it can't be them."

"It's them low-down, side-winding Texans," J.B. said. "They come in here laughing at our Herefords, braggin' up them skinny, spindle-legged critters they call longhorns—humph! They don't have enough meat on 'em to feed a fly."

"Now we just heard that two hundred more were rustled off the south pasture and one of the wranglers was killed. We figure it has to be drifters or professional cattle rustlers looking to gather up a good-sized herd and sell to the Abilene beef buyers when they come into town next month. Beef steers are bringing sixty to seventy dollars on the hoof. That's a pretty fair grubstake for some old saddle-sore cowpoke."

"But how do they get them off the range, *Grandpapa*?" Mandy asked. "Do they not have to travel through Bradshaw property to get to the railroads?"

235

Both J.B. and Jeramy stared at her, then at one another. "Hang me for a damn fool!" J.B. cried, hugging Mandy so close she spilled a little of her wine. "That's it, Jeramy. They haven't taken them off the range yet! We've got 'em, my God!"

"Smart little brat, aren't you?" Jeramy teased Mandy. "Pa and I have been racking our brains trying to figure out how in hell they moved that much beef without anyone seeing them. You're right. The only way to the stockyards and railroads is through the western tip of our ranch. Right out in the wide open spaces where a jackrabbit couldn't hide. Obviously, they've got the cattle penned up somewhere, waiting for the buyers to get here."

"Luis, go tell Lefty and George to get in here!" J.B. got to his feet and began pacing excitedly. "We'll get the boys together and go root out those varmints, by God!" He chuckled and rubbed his hands together. "Damn, I haven't had a good fight for too damn long!"

"Now, Pa," Jeramy laughed, putting a restraining hand on his arm and shaking his head at Luis. "Don't get so riled up. This isn't the Old West, you know. We have to do things legally."

"Legally?" J.B. scoffed, stopping his pacing long enough to take a swallow of bourbon. "Goddamn cattle thieves are sitting out there on *my* range with two thousand of *my* stock and I don't have the right to string 'em up? Bull."

"There's another way out," Jonathan said from the windowseat. "Over Los Gatos Mountains."

"You have to go through the Dunlap spread to get out that way," J.B. said. "Naw, they're still holed up somewhere on my range, waiting for the right time to move the herd to the stockyards."

"Perhaps they were not Texans at all," Jonathan said, leaning forward slightly. "Didn't Ted Stokes say that one of the wranglers thought they were dressed like Mexican *vaqueros*?"

236

"Hell, anybody can dress up like a *vaquero*," J.B. snorted, pacing again.

The word *vaquero* chilled Mandy to the bone. A sudden image of the black-haired Jay Cordova dressed in the bright costume of the *vaquero* flashed before her eyes. She heard the sound of his lewd laughter. She quickly swallowed her wine to quell the scream that rose in her throat. It had been almost three months since the cruel *bandido* had raped her and left her crumpled on the sand, but she still remembered every detail as vividly as if it had happened yesterday, his cold black eyes, his drooping, greasy moustache and long hair, his hard, savage mouth crushing her, suffocating her. She went to the window and breathed deeply of the lush summer air. The sweet scent of lilacs and roses drifted to her, clearing her head.

She had made a solemn vow to kill him the moment she had regained consciousness and found herself alone, her horse gone. She had covered her torn clothes with the poncho she had taken along to spread upon the sand, then had walked the two miles back to the hotel, luckily not running into anyone she knew so she had not had to explain her appearance. It never occurred to her to tell anyone. She was too humiliated, too shocked. She had scrubbed his filth from her body and plotted ways to kill him. For days, weeks, she had planned new and more horrible deaths for him. She knew that she would, somehow, when the time came.

"But if they really are *vaqueros*," Jonathan persisted, "they would undoubtedly take the herd over Los Gatos and into Mexico to sell them."

"Naw, the Mexes can't afford no two thousand head of beef. Hell, they can barely afford beans and tortillas." J.B. went to the bar in the corner and poured himself another shot of bourbon. He filled a second glass and said, "Have a drink, Luis." The tall, elegant valet bowed slightly, a look of mutual understanding and affection passing between the two men.

"Thanks, Boss." Luis passed the glass beneath his

237

long, aristocratic nose, sniffed appreciatively, then sipped. "You know, Mr. Jonathan may have a point, Boss. A handful of *vaqueros* could rustle a few thousand head of cattle, drive them into Mexico and set up their own ranchos. They would be very rich *caballeros*."

"Yeah, I see what you mean, Luis. Maybe I'm looking in the wrong place for the low-down varmints." J.B. took a swallow of bourbon and went to stand looking out of the window. The day was still white-hot, as bright as molten brass, and it was almost six o'clock in the evening. He could see the stableboys distributing hay and grain to the horses, Benito feeding the chickens, and old Doc bottle-feeding a kid goat that had been rejected by its mother. He sighed heavily. Something was not right about this rustling business. They knew too damn much about his grazing schedule, knew just when the cattle were being moved to another pasture. And they always hit in the dead of night, disappearing into one of the many arroyos as silently as ghosts. A man would have to know this territory pretty damn well to travel that swiftly and surely in the dark. Well, he'd round up the boys first thing tomorrow morning and go have a look-see. The hell with waiting for Sheriff Roy and his confounded warrants. Besides, the sheriff didn't roll out of bed before noon, now that San Francisco had gone respectable. It would be all over by that time.

Mandy sat straight up in bed when she heard the sound of horses' hooves striking the brick courtyard below. Leaping out of bed she ran to the window and saw a large group of men, J.B.'s wranglers, mounted and waiting. Each one carried a rifle tucked into his saddle holster and pistols were strapped to their hips. She dressed swiftly in a long divided riding skirt of heavy leather to protect her legs, a long-sleeved blouse and leather vest, then tugged on her high-topped boots and grabbed her hat. She was downstairs before J.B. had

238

risen from the breakfast table. "Good morning, *Grandpapa*," she said gaily, bending to kiss his cheek. "I am ready, you see."

"Ready for what, young lady?" he growled, eyes raking her. "Just where do you think you're going in that get-up?"

"With you, *Grandpapa*," she said sweetly, then wailed, "Oh, please, *Grandpapa*, let me go with you! Oh, I do so want to go on a real round-up or—or whatever you call it."

"This isn't exactly a round-up, honey. It's more like a snake hunt." He mumbled something about dirty Texas varmints and took a big bite of his jam-smothered biscuit.

Mandy turned imploring eyes upon Jeramy but he held up one hand, laughing, "Whoa, honey, don't get me in the middle. This is between you and Pa." He got to his feet and dropped a light kiss on her forehead. "Besides, even though I hate to admit it, he's right for once." He flashed an impudent grin at his father. "Chasing down rustlers isn't exactly what one would expect of a lady so genteelly bred as yourself."

"Oh—fa!" Mandy stamped one small booted foot and stuck out her lower lip. "I can ride just as well as you can, Jeramy Bradshaw, and you know it? And I am not afraid, either." She turned suddenly angelic. "Oh, please, Jeramy, pretty please—tell *Grandpapa* to let me come."

"Seriously, sweetheart, it's just plain too dangerous." J.B. rose, stuck a toothpick into his mouth and reached for his hat. "Come on, son, let's get out of here before she wears me down." He smiled fondly at Mandy and patted her rump as if she were a child. "You stick close to the ranch, you hear? We don't know what we're liable to find out there. Might be some shooting and I don't want you out on the range."

"*Oui, Grandpapa*." She sighed heavily, eyes cast down. "I shall be stuck in this stuffy, hot old house all day while you ride after the outlaws and have all the fun!" She sighed again, peeking at them from beneath lowered lashes and they both laughed at her theatrics.

"Why don't you go over to the Dunlaps and visit with Jane and Jenny! Marie was just saying the other day that they don't see enough of you." Jeramy adjusted his hat, then buckled on his gunbelt, shoving it low upon his hip.

"Oh, all they do is chatter about babies, babies, babies!" Mandy sighed again, her expression put upon. "Jenny's new baby and Jane's coming baby, until I am quite out of my mind with it. *Mon Dieu*, I hope I can think of something else to talk about when I am married!" She looped one arm through Jeramy's, the other through J.B.'s, and walked out into the courtyard with them. Trying one last time, she pleaded, "Couldn't I just ride as far as the waterfall with you? Or the hunting lodge? I promise to turn right around and come straight home whenever you tell me to."

"Lord, girl, don't you never give up?" J.B. chuckled, giving her a quick hug before swinging into his saddle. "Let's get going, men, before this little minx wraps me right around her little finger and has me agreeing to take her along!" The wranglers laughed good-naturedly and tipped their hats to Mandy before wheeling their horses and galloping away. Jeramy and J.B. turned to wave to her.

"Fa, how I hate to be treated like a pesky, tagalong little girl!" she muttered darkly and kicked a pebble so hard it sailed clear up the front steps, striking the door.

She ate breakfast and wandered into the library, idly glancing at the books. None caught her fancy and she went into the kitchen to visit with Atoka and Caleen, but they were up to their elbows in preserves and the kitchen was a clutter of jars, fruit and melting paraffin.

She strolled outside to the stable to see if Doc would talk to her. She found him polishing tack and grumbling about the heat. Goldie stood in the shade of a huge oak near the holding corral and Mandy went to her and petted the arched, sleek golden neck. "Hello, pretty girl," she murmured. "Are you as bored as I am?" The heat was already oppressive and it was just mid-morning. She suddenly thought of Ceasare's cool little cottage, shaded by giant oaks and lulled by a babbling brook. And he always found the time to talk with her and listen to her dreams. "Doc, will you please saddle Goldie for me? I'd like to go for a ride."

"In this heat, Missy? Is ye crazy or somethin'? Why, I've seen people get sunstroke on cooler days than this 'un!" He threw down his saddle soap and limped into the tack room, pulling Mandy's saddle from its rack. "An' snakes, Lord amighty, why they's thick as fleas this time o' year, alayin' on rocks so still-like you don't know they's there until you purt near stomp on 'em!"

Mandy stifled a giggle. "I'll be careful, Doc. I have to go get my hat. Be right back." She turned and fled before he could predict any other ominous occurrences that might befall her. She filled a canteen with ice water and tucked a couple of apples into her skirt pocket.

The faintest of breezes caressed her face as she walked Goldie down the eucalyptus-lined lane. It was a warm, breathless breeze. The Santa Anas would be coming soon. She jumped Goldie over the fallen log that marked the end of the lane and became a winding trail through open range dotted with sagebrush, cactus and chaparral. She kept to the bank of the little creek that would take her past the waterfall and toward Los Gatos Mountain range. The fresh sound of the rushing water sounded so cool she stopped for a moment and let Goldie have a drink. A rainbow trout broke the surface, leaping high and twisting like an acrobat in the air before falling back into the water. The air was as sweet as honey, heavy and sultry. This would have been called twister weather in the South.

She let Goldie set her own pace in the heavy heat. She had been over the trail leading to Ceasare's cottage so many times she knew it by heart. Goldie's hooves sent up little puffs of dust as she trudged slowly up the slight embankment and turned away from the creek and toward the dense forest that would open into the meadow. There, she knew, would be sweet, moist grass and a long rest while her mistress visited. She picked up her pace, going quickly between the thick growth of trees, welcoming the cool shade, then broke into a fast trot when the meadow came into view.

The old bloodhound had finally died a year ago and now a new dog lay in the shade by the cottage door, some mongrell that had no doubt followed Ceasare home. Mandy dismounted and tossed Goldie's reins over the hitching post. Grass grew in abundance in front of the sod *casa* and Goldie lowered her head to it at once. The front door was slightly ajar and Mandy pushed it open, knocked lightly, then stepped inside.

The cottage was quiet and empty, as orderly as ever. She wandered about the yard for a few minutes and called to Ceasare, but received no answer. She mounted Goldie, thinking for a monent. Perhaps she should ride up to Casa de Oro for a visit. Ceasare had invited her often enough and even the haughty Lanora had issued an invitation. She did not want to turn around and go back to the ranch. J.B. had forbidden her to ride near the hunting lodge or pasture range. It would be a pleasant ride to Casa de Oro, as most of the trail leading up and through Los Gatos Mountains was shaded by towering redwoods and the air in the mountains was always much cooler than in the valley.

She turned Goldie toward the forest, kicking her into a canter. She hoped she remembered the way. She had only riden to Casa de Oro once by horseback and then Ceasare had been leading the way. Of course, if she became lost she had only to find the road that led up the mountain and follow it. She had travelled it many times by buggy and knew it well.

A narrow, winding trail turned to the right and climbed straight up the side of the mountain and Mandy carefully guided Goldie up the steep slope. She followed it for an hour, forcing herself not to look down as the sure-footed little mare picked her way precariously over rocks and narrow ledges. She topped the last ridge, looked down and saw the entire valley spread below her on one side and the tallest mountain she had ever seen facing her on the other side. The trail had suddenly ended, disappearing into the soft, pine needle covered floor of the forest. Far below, she saw it again, a skinny snake winding through the trees. She urged Goldie on and came upon a hidden valley at the mountain's foot, nestled like a green jewel among the rather drab forest green of the redwoods. Several small streams slashed through the little meadow, and a huge herd of Herefords grazed serenely in belly-deep grass. Mandy could see the brand clearly: J.B.

"*Mon Dieu*, they are *Grandpapa's* cows!" she cried aloud. "I have found them!" She dismounted and walked to the edge of the small hill, peering down at the herd. The rustlers were probably down there, armed and guarding the beef. "*Ma foi*, what shall I do?" she whispered to Goldie and the little mare shook her head and whinnied.

Suddenly a hand clamped over her mouth and a thick voice gritted, "Who are you, señorita? And what do you do here?" She was wheeled around to face an enormous Mexican with crossed gunbelts across his massive chest and two more pistols strapped low on his lean hips. He wore a black patch over one eye but the other eye bored steadily into her face. He spat a stream of dirty brown tobacco juice into the dust at her feet and she saw the flash of gold front teeth. "Hey, *puta*, I ask you who you are, eh?" He shook her.

"I—I—my name is Amanda Bradshaw. I thought this was my grandfather's property. I was just out riding—" She stammered in fear, unable to pull her gaze away from that one black, ice-cold eye.

The Mexican bandit spat again, wiping the back of his hand across his mouth. The gold teeth blinked. "She-et, this ain't yore grandpappy's land, señorita. Is the land of the Cordovas, eh?" He jerked her around and shoved her toward the embankment, grunting,

"Come on, *stupido*, *Dése prisa*! We go, eh? *Rápido!*
He prodded her again and she stumbled ahead of him
down the hill, fear making her knees weak. Where was
he taking her? What would he do to her? *Mon Dieu*,
could she really have stumbled into a nest of cattle rustlers?

He shoved her across the meadow, keeping her wrist
clamped in his beefy fist and twisted cruelly behind her
back. Set into the dense trees that almost obscured it
from view was a small sod cottage much like Ceasare's.
A spiral of smoke drifted lazily from the chimney and
goats grazed on the roof. Chickens clucked and
scratched at a handful of scraps that had been tossed
from the front door and two sows nudged one another
away from a trough of slop. It looked normal, peaceful,
and her heart gave a lurch of hope. Perhaps they were
friendly, whoever lived here. Perhaps they worked for
her grandfather and lived here in this little cottage to be
close to the herd. Perhaps— The bandit shoved her
into the cottage, sending her sprawling on all fours in
the middle of the dirt floor. She raised her head to stare
into the handsome, sardonic face of Jay Cordova.

His black brows shot up in surprise and he drawled,
"Well, what present have you brought me, *amigo*, eh?
Is this not the proud Señorita Bradshaw before me on
her knees?" He stood, stretching like a black panther,
then bent and jerked her to her feet. "*Buenos días,*
señorita, how nice of you to call."

"Oh, Señor Cordova, please let me go!" she cried,
frightened half out of her wits. *Mon Dieu*, what would
he do to her this time? Terror choked her as she remembered the pain and degradation he had inflicted
upon her that day on the beach. "I will go straight
home, I promise! I will tell no one that I saw you!
Please, señor, let me go!"

"Ah, you still do not like me, huh, señorita?" He
turned sad, dark, mocking eyes upon the bandit who
had dragged her in. "Pedro, *mi amigo*, she does not like
me. She does not wish to stay and have a glass of *vino*

with me and—" His black gaze swept her, turning her stomach into knots of horrified pain. He shrugged and smiled, his face handsome, almost innocent-looking, "—and perhaps talk a while, eh? To talk about releasing her so that she may go back to her rancho, eh, Pedro?" Again he shrugged, holding his hands palm-up, the corner of his mouth turned down. "But she does not want to accept the hospitality of a dirty *bandido*—"

"Oh, yes—*si!* I will have a glass of wine with you, señor," she gasped quickly lest he change his mind and kill her where she stood.

"Ah! *Bueno! Bueno!*" He bowed her toward a rough wooden table and held a chair for her. "Señorita?" he murmured in the silken voice she would never forget.

"*Gracias,*" she choked, sinking gratefully into the chair before her legs gave away. Her brain churned with a hundred possibilities for escape, but all would be futile, she knew. She would have to play along and see what he really intended doing with her. Perhaps he meant only to frighten her before releasing her. She was, after all, the granddaughter of J.B. Bradshaw.

"Pedro." Jay snapped his fingers. "*Vino* for my guest, eh?" He leaned his elbows on the table and stared at her a full minute without speaking, then he murmured in his silken whisper, "I have not forgotten our encounter on the beach, *mi hermosa puta*. How very rude of you to fall asleep without telling me *adiós*. But perhaps you were tired, eh, *querida*?" He chuckled softly and the sound sent her skin crawling.

Pedro set the wine bottle on the table and poured three glasses, sliding one across the table to Mandy. She raised it to her lips with hands that shook and gulped quickly. It was strong, homemade peasant wine and burned a hot swath down her throat, bringing quick tears to her eyes. But is stopped the wild pounding of her heart, and calmed her. She drank again. She would have to keep her wits about her, to listen for some clue that would give her the key to her escape. She sipped again, her glance darting quickly about the cottage. It was about the same size as Ceasare's but had two small bedrooms stuck on to the far side like an afterthought. Bright *rebozas* hung in the doorways and she could hear the sound of a baby gurgling and a woman singing. *Mon Dieu*, was this really happening to her? Surely it was a joke, some terrible joke. She gagged on her wine and squeezed her eyes shut tight to hold back the tears. She would not break down in front of this common bandit. She was a Bradshaw, after all. She raised her chin defiantly.

"Lupe! *Venga acá!*" Jay snapped and the *reboza* was shoved aside and a pretty but slovenly Mexican girl stood there holding a filthy, chubby, naked baby on her hip.

"*Si?*" Her full ruby lips pouted. Her black eyes were sullen as she glanced at Mandy and then back at Jay without a flicker of expression.

He told her to take the baby and go to her mother's until he sent for her. The girl did not protest but turned and disappeared into the tiny bedroom. Within minutes she was back again, shuffling barefoot across the dirt floor, a dirty bandana holding her meager belongings, the naked baby still on her hip. Her black, flat eyes swept Mandy as she passed, so close Mandy could smell the strong musk of her body, and she raised one side of her mouth in a sneer. She did not look back again but stepped through the door and it closed with a soft bang behind her.

"Hey, Pedro, I been thinking, *amigo*?" Jay propped his high-heeled boots upon the table and idly twirled the big rowels of his spurs. "I think maybe we keep this nice señorita, this *hermosa puta*." The voice was a silken caress, smoky and husky. "For just a little while, eh? Then perhaps old man Bradshaw would pay *mucho dinero* to get her back, eh? What do you think, *amigo*?" He pulled a wicked-looking hunting knife from the scabbard at his waist and picked his teeth with it.

"*Es muy bueno*," Pedro grunted and his gold teeth

flashed in a wide smile. *"Si, amigo, es muy bueno."* He drank his wine in one swallow and sloshed more into his glass. His one eye travelled slowly over Mandy's breasts.

She shuddered under his hot gaze. *Mon Dieu,* would this nightmare never end? Surely someone would miss her and come looking for her. But no one knew where she was. And J.B. would be out all day looking for the rustlers on the other side of the range, miles and miles away. Her heart sank and the tears almost spilled over, but she blinked them away stubbornly, with more confidence than she felt.

Jay tossed off his wine and stood, stretching, pushing his hands into the small of his back and rocking on the large spur rowels. *"Dios,* but I am *muy cansado.* I think maybe I will take a little siesta." He winked at Pedro and the big bandit laughed and made an obscene gesture in Mandy's direction. She felt her limbs turn to ice. The knowledge of what was to come was worse than experiencing it. She shuddered and her heart set up an unsteady beat that pulsated in her brain, making her nauseous. She wanted to scream but her throat felt paralyzed. When Jay reached down and took her by the wrist, pulling her to her feet, she moved as jerkily as a broken marionette, her knees buckling. She fell heavily into his arms and he laughed and said, *Hey, Pedro, the gringo* whore, she is impatient, eh?" He brought his mouth down and she screamed, finding her voice at last.

"No! Don't touch me!" She drew back her fist and hit him in the face as hard as she could. The blow caused him to drop her wrist and she lunged for the door, fingers clawing at the latch, but Pedro's big, beefy hand shot out and grabbed her by the hair. Still chuckling, Jay scooped her up into his arms, carried her into one of the small bedrooms and dumped her on a sagging cot. Her head hit the wall with such force that she was momentarily stunned and stars danced before her eyes. She pushed herself upright and would have scrambled off the cot but he backhanded her across the face, knocking her sprawling.

"Now, now, *puta*, you do not want to make me angry, eh?" He went to the dresser, took a length of rope from one of the drawers and advanced toward her. "I am much afraid that I must tie you up, *mi hermosa puta*. I do not wish to." He shrugged and his dark eyes were soft, sensual, his voice as silky smooth as ever. "But also I do not wish to be ripped to shreds with those wicked nails, either!" He chuckled as he grabbed her wrist and quickly looped the thin rope about it. She screamed and struggled but he merely laughed and secured the other wrist, tying them both to the wooden headboard of the bed. "Now the legs, *querida*—the long, lovely, golden legs—" She kicked at him as hard as she could, striking him in the chest. Anger flashed in his eyes briefly, then it was gone and he was smiling again. "Come, come, *mi hermosa puta*, do not fight it. You know it is inevitable, eh?" His hand clamped down cruelly on her ankle and she sobbed aloud in pain when he jerked the rope tight, cutting into her flesh.

When he had her spread-eagled upon the bed he rocked back on his heels and stared down at her. "*Si*," he murmured, "*Si*, this is how I have dreamed of seeing you—spread before me helpless." He reached into his shirt pocket and withdrew a thin cigarette rolled in yellow paper and twisted at both ends. Striking a wooden match on his thumbnail he held the flame to one twisted end and Mandy smelled a sickly-sweet odor, pungent, perfumed. He sucked in deep, holding the smoke in his lungs and squinting at her through the smoke. "Ahhh," he sighed. "*Muy bueno*." He sucked again on the yellow cigarette, making harsh inhaling noises and wheezing as he fought to keep the smoke inside his lungs.

Mand stared at him, too curious to be frightened for a moment. What manner of cigarette was this? She had never smelled anything like it before. It was almost as

248

sweet-smelling as Uncle Jonathan's pipe tobacco but it had a different, wilder scent.

"Come, *neéa*, smoke a little marijuana with me, eh? It will make you forget many things, this I promise." He shoved the foul-smelling cigarette at her and she sobbed and flung her head to the side.

Marijuana! *Mon Dieu*, that was some sort of drug, was it not? What would it do to this already evil bandit? Would it make him insane, murderous? *Oh, someone find me,* she prayed fervently, eyes open wide and staring into the hard, cold face of Jay Cordova as he leaned nearer and nearer.

"Come, *querida*," he said lovingly. "Smoke with me." His black eyes were soft, glazed, almost kind and his full mouth was curved into a sweet smile. "You will not smoke with me, eh?" He tried once more to place the cigarette between her lips, then took a deep drag and covered her mouth with his, blowing the strong smoke into her throat, forcing her to inhale or choke. While her head still reeled from the strange drug, he took another drag and inhaled again into her mouth. Moving one hand over her breasts and belly, he murmured, "I must see you naked." Grabbing the front of her shirt he ripped it and her vest from her body. The strong leather resisted and cut cruelly into her flesh before it finally gave away. The buttons on her riding skirt popped in every direction as he jerked it down her legs and left it tangled about her bound ankles. Her light underwear posed no problem and then she was lying naked before him. His dark eyes devoured her and he reached out a hand and pressed the softness of her pubic mound. She moaned in an agony of shame and embarrassment and tried to close her legs but the rope held them spread wide apart, exposing her completely to his hot gaze.

He took a last drag of the marijuana cigarette and flipped it away. Standing, he shucked off his clothes, then fell upon her, his lips wet and hard. He whispered in Spanish but she did not hear him. Her mind cried out against this outrage, this intrusion into her body. The strange drug made her head ache and her fear was so strong it was like bile in her throat. She gagged at the taste of sour liquor on his breath and the smell of his dirty, sweaty body. She jerked so hard against the ropes that they cut into her wrists, drawing blood. She had to get away! This could not happen again. She would rather die first. She butted her head at him and heard his curse of pain, then his lips were back on hers, his tongue thick and wet inside her mouth. She closed her teeth and twisted her head sharply to one side and heard his blood-curdling bellow of rage and pain. She had one fleeting second of satisfaction before his big fist crashed into the side of her temple, knocking her unconscious.

It was dark when Mandy came to. Her eyes flew open and she tried to rise but the ropes jerked her back upon the sagging cot. Her naked body trembled in the cold mountain air and her head ached dully from Jay's heavy blow. The cottage was quiet. She heard the high-pitched squall of a mountain lion and the monotonous yipping of coyotes. *Have they left me here to die?* she thought wildly, testing her ropes again but finding them as secure as before. She let her head fall wearily to the dirty, smelly pillow and tears leaked out of the corners of her eyes and ran down the sides of her face, wetting her tangled hair. Her entire body ached, her breasts and groin throbbed steadily, painfully, and she knew that the loathsome bandit had raped her even as she lay unconscious. She sobbed brokenly, loudly, not caring if someone heard, hoping they would and come in and kill her and put her out of her shame and misery. She prayed wildly in French, English, and Spanish, beseeching God to save her, or take her now. She would not, *could* not endure another encounter with Jay Cordova.

The *reboza* at the doorway was pushed aside and a dark figure carrying a candle entered the room. "Ah, you are awake, eh, *querida*? *Bueno*. I do not like fucking a corpse—even one as beautiful and golden as you, Señorita Bradshaw." Jay's voice was thick and slurred and she could smell the liquor on him. Holding the candle over her body he stared down at her obscenely sprawled nakedness. "*Hermosa*", he whispered softly, "*así hermosa*." He lowered his head to kiss her breasts and the hot wax from the candle dripped on them, causing her to shriek in agony.

He threw the candle to the dirt floor and fell heavily upon her and she felt that he was nude, his manhood a stiff rod of pain plunging into her before she knew what was happening. She lunged against her bonds, crying and begging, jerking her legs so hard that the ropes cut into her already raw ankles and fresh blood flowed. She could not feel her hands at all, so numb and leaden they were. All she could feel was the hard, hurting, insistent battering of him above her, upon her, into her. Her eyes rolled up into her head and she let her body go completely limp, too exhausted to fight anymore.

"That's better, *si, si*, much better." Jay's hands explored her body, cupped her buttocks up to him and held her strong and close to his swiftly plunging penis. He mumbled incoherently into her hair and his sharp fingernails dug viciously into her soft flesh, but Mandy heard nothing, felt nothing. She drifted in and out of consciousness, floating above her abused body one moment, slipping into a soft, hazy cloud the next. She did not feel him when at last he rolled off her punished flesh and fell into a deep sleep, his snores shaking the sagging cot, his limp arm flung over her stomach. She was in another dimension, one of nothingness.

For three days Mandy lay tied to the filthy cot, Jay only releasing her to feed her and let her go to the outhouse. He had given her a nightgown of coarse cotton to cover herself during these trips but took it off again at night when he would once more come to her and rape her. Her body was a flaming series of cuts and bruises. Her wrists and ankles were swollen and throbbed painfully. Her breast where the hot candle wax had spilled was an ugly, red, festering blister. Her mouth was so swollen she could barely chew the tough beef that Pedro fried for their supper and the strong wine, the only thing they allowed her to drink, stung her cracked lips painfully.

She knew she could not go on much longer this way. Her young, healthy body rebelled against the restraining ropes and she realized that she still wanted to live. In the first terrifying, degrading hours of her capture she had prayed for death. Now she prayed just as fiercely for life. She wanted to live so she could kill Jay Cordova for what he had done to her.

She raised her head and saw the first pink light of dawn through the dirty, cracked window—the fourth day of her imprisonment. She wondered for the hundredth time why no one had come looking for her, then realized that no one knew of this hidden valley except the gang of thieves who rode with Jay Cordova. It was a perfect hideout, totally inaccessible unless one knew the secret trail or stumbled upon it by accident as she had done.

She flung her head to one side, trying to get as far away as possible from the sour odor of the dirty pillow. What must her family be thinking? Could they have guessed what happened to her? Only old Doc knew that she had taken Goldie out and she had not told him where she planned to go. Oh, why hadn't she said she was going to visit Ceasare? It would have given them a place to start searching. Tears filled her swollen eyes and she said aloud, "No. I will not cry any more. I will escape this place." The sound of her voice in the still dawn sounded loud and harsh to her ears. Her voice was hoarse and thick from crying and screaming, her throat raw from the strong marijuana smoke Jay had forced upon her time and time again. After the second night she found she looked forward to these administrations of the heady drug. It relaxed her and spun her out of her conscious mind and into a dark abyss where she was able to blot out what was happening to her body—where she could even dream that it was Bret making love to her and not a cold-eyed bandit. Then her mind would become confused. She had meant to dream of Tod as her savior but his image always slipped elusively away to be replaced by Bret's face, Bret's dark eyes and sweet lips.

She watched the sunrise, knowing she would have to lie here another hour before Jay and Pedro stirred. Then Jay would untie her, slip the coarse gown over her head and escort her to the outhouse. If only she could somehow grab his pistol, force him to give her a horse and—No, it would never work. He was so big and strong he could easily overpower her. *There must be a way*, she thought desperately.

"You can catch more flies with honey than you can with vinegar, *chérie*." The words were so real and clearly spoken that she jerked her head up and cried, "*Grand-mère?*" Only the dirty, barren little room stared back at her. "I am losing my mind," she murmured and the tears she had promised not to shed slipped from her eyes and down her dirty face, leaving a rivulet of mud and grime. Then she suddenly remembered. As a child she had been spoiled and headstrong, stamping her tiny foot in rage if she did not get her way, and her dear *Grand-mère* Bertonneau had told her time and time again, "Really, *chérie*, you will catch more flies with honey than with vinegar. No one likes to be cursed and threatened." And even *Tante* Caleen, who had clearly adored the demanding child, had often grumbled, "You ask pretty-like, *bébé*, and maybe you will get another sweet, *oui?*"

She would stop fighting Jay, pretend to give in and lull him into a false sense of security. It would be far healthier for her if she did, she thought ruefully. To continue to fight him only meant added bruises and more pain. But it was all she could do to lie quietly waiting for him to come and release her. Her mind soared with plans of escape. She would play on his vanity, pretend to want him and when he reached for her she would grab his knife and plunge it through his black heart. No—she would wait until he was asleep, then tie him hand and foot as he had done to her and leave him to die on this stinking cot. So engrossed was she in her plans for vengeance she did not hear him until he stood by the bed.

"*Buenos días*," he said pleasantly and scratched his hairy, naked belly. He wore only buckskin trousers and his feet were bare.

"*Buenos días*, Jay," she said as clamly as she could, forcing herself to look up at him. She saw the surprise in his eyes and he hesitated a moment before releasing her wrists.

"So, the proud Señorita Bradshaw has finally consented to speak to the dirty *bandido*, eh?" He chuckled as he untied her ankles and then helped her off the cot. Her confinement had made her weak and she swayed against his chest, smiling wanly when he raised his eyebrows in surprise. He dropped the gown over her head and helped her pull her arms through.

"*Gracias,*" she whispered softly and glanced at him, then quickly lowered her eyes. She swayed against him once more and gave a tiny laugh. "Oh, I'm so sorry, but I am so very weak!" Again the fluttered eyelashes and demure expression.

"*Dios,* what is this?" Jay muttered under his breath as he took her arm and guided her, more gently than usual, through the door and out into the bright morning light. She clung to him, making her steps slow and faltering, and wanted to laugh in his face when he immediately slowed his pace to match hers, his hand gentle on her arm. He stood outside the outhouse and waited for her, wondering what had happened to the wild, half-crazed woman he had left tied to the cot last night. This woman was soft and vulnerable, as lovely as a madonna even with her wounded face and big, sad eyes.

Mandy emerged from the outhouse and held out one hand and Jay stepped quickly forward and took it, letting her lean upon his arm. "Oh, Jay, *gracias*," she sighed, looking up into his face wanly. "*Mon Dieu*, I feel so dirty and stiff. How I would love a hot bath." She gave the tiny, tinkling, artificial little laugh that totally captivated him and added, "Could I please have a bath, Jay? I promise not to try to escape. You may even stay and wash my back for me."

"*Dios*, what is this?" He stopped walking and stared down at her, his black eyes narrowed. "This is some trick, eh, *puta*? You think to get my mind occupied and then you try to escape, eh?"

"Oh no, Jay—honest!" She clutched his arm with both hands, her eyes guileless and wide. "I've just decided to stop fighting you, that's all. *Mon Dieu*, but I would have to be a fool to continue to fight when I see it is hopeless, would I not, monsieur? You are too big and strong, your hands too powerful, and I am nothing against your strength." Her eyes widened as she gazed up at him, almost worshipful, and she saw him flush with pride. He straightened his shoulders and stood taller. "Can we not make the best of it until *Grandpapa* pays the ransom and comes for me? I give you my word that I will not run away. I only beg that you do not tie me up again. It is very painful and I cannot even hold you when you come to my bed."

Jay's mouth fell open and he swore softly. "How do I know that I can trust you?" He could not take his eyes off her beautiful face or the smoky blue eyes that spoke volumes to him.

"Let me take a bath," she said quickly. "And—and we can talk and—and I'll make you a good breakfast." She tried for a light, teasing tone. "I assure you I am a far better cook than Pedro with his hard *tortillas* and tough steaks! I will make you a delicious omelette, as light as the very air." She tugged on his arm, pulling him toward the sod *casa*.

"Well, I don't know—hell, I guess a bath can't hurt anything." He grinned down at her almost flirtatiously. "You *do* look like you could use one!"

Mandy stood against the kitchen wall, half-holding her breath that her plan was working. Jay had dragged a big round tub into the middle of the floor and was now filling it with hot water that had been heated on the stove. He handed her a thick bar of lye soap and she shrugged out of the gown and stepped into the tub.

She gasped aloud and tears sprang to her eyes when the hot water closed over her, burning and stinging every cut and scratch on her body. Jay was at her side at once, his face worried. "Does it hurt much, *querida*?" he asked softly and when she nodded her head, he brought a jar of milk. He poured the milk into the tub and grinned, shrugging his shoulders, a little embarrassed at his kindness. "Goat's milk," he said. "It has wonderous healing powers." His face, always handsome, was now gentle and he repeated, "Does it hurt much, *nena*? Would you believe me if I told you that I never wanted to hurt you? Never! From the first moment I saw you I wanted to hold you in my arms, kiss you, love you—" His dark eyes blazed with passion. "But you were the arrogant Señorita Bradshaw, so high and mighty, taking that bastard Bret Dunlap as your lover, too good for a dirty *bandido*!"

"Jay, please don't," she said quickly and put a hand on his arm. She was frightened that he would revert back to the crazy-mad state he had been in these past days. How he must have suffered as a boy to hate the Bradshaws and Dunlaps as deeply as he did. She tried to understand him and therefore hate him less, but the hatred stayed like a burning coal in the pit of her stomach and she knew she would kill him the moment she had the chance. "That's all over now, Jay. All in the past. These last days have changed all that. I am no longer the arrogant Señorita Bradshaw but your woman for as long as you keep me here." She swallowed the revulsion that rose in her throat at the words and kept her voice calm, soothing. "I want to be your woman, Jay. Do you understand what I'm saying? If you want me to come to you as a lover, then you must let me be free. Not tied down like an animal to be abused and punished." She ran her hand over his, gently squeezing his fingers. "I could show you how beautiful it can be between a man and a woman, Jay, if you will only let me—"

"Can this be true, what you say?" His hands gripped her shoulders, turning her to face him. His dark eyes searched her face for some betrayal but she kept it serene, steadily returning his look. "I thought— sometimes when I lay with you I thought perhaps you wanted me. Your body answered mine even when you cried out against me. But I could not believe it was true." His mouth came down hard and demanding upon hers and she shoved against his chest, hard.

Before he could reach for her again, she held up one hand and said, firmly, "No, Jay, not like that. Like this." Taking his head between her hands she brought his lips close and kissed them gently, sweetly, a passionate lingering kiss. When she drew away from him her expression was saucy, teasing. "and I insist that you shave, señor. Your beard scratches like the very devil!"

Jay threw back his head and laughed loudly. "Ah, so the wildcat, she has not turned into a domestic kitten as I thought, eh? She still would give the orders." This time when he bent his dark head to her and kissed her it was as tender as Bret's kiss had been.

Bret, her heart cried, *oh Bret.* If only he would come and take her away from this wretched place. She laughed with Jay, splashed him with water and said tartly, "That is correct, señor. And now you will leave me to my bath."

Still chuckling, shaking his head at this mystery woman who flirted and teased so artfully, he perched on a stool and watched her. She scrubbed every inch of her body, then lathered her long hair, wincing when her fingers found small lumps and sore spots where he had struck her. *I will laugh while I watch him die,* she thought and turned to smile at him.

He brought a bucket of clear, cool water and poured

257

it over her head, rinsing the soap from her hair, then held out a large piece of cloth for her to dry herself. She dressed in the clean white shift he provided, probably Lupe's, and pulled the tangles from her hair with part of a broken comb. They walked outside to gather eggs for the omelette and Jay picked her a handful of scallions.

"Where is Pedro this morning?" she asked as she busied herself at the stove, gently whipping the egg and herb mixture.

"He had business in town," Jay said shortly, then laughed to himself and when Mandy asked what was so funny he ducked his head sheepishly and said, "We forgot to deliver the ransom note to J.B."

"Some kidnapper you are, Jay Cordova. Don't you know the ransom is always delivered within twenty-four hours of the abduction so that the family will know that the victim is alive? *Mon Dieu, Grandpapa* has probably given me up for dead by this time! I'm sure he has been dragging Otter River for my poor body." She kept her voice light and her face averted so he would not see the cold fury there. Thoughts of her family searching for her body tormented her and she wanted to charge madly at this big, dumb Mexican outlaw and stab him to death with his own knife.

"Ah, *si*, but *querida*, you kept me so drunk with your beauty I could think of little else." Her back still to him, she carefully folded the omelette in the skillet. He chuckled softly and the sound sent gooseflesh skittering across her arms. "Pedro will leave the note with the stableboy, as they are cousins and the boy knows him well. If Pedro was seen by anyone else on the Bradshaw rancho he would no doubt be shot on sight."

"They're cousins?" Mandy turned in surprise. "Does *Grandpapa* know this?"

Jay laughed out loud, a coarse, dirty laugh. "Ah, *si*, he knows. The boy's mother is Pedro's aunt and his father is J.B. himself." His face tightened, his eyes grew blacker. "That old bull has very long horns, *querida*.

258

He has sired many half-breed bastards." He grabbed the jug of wine and splashed some into a dirty glass, drinking it down in one swallow. "Even my little brother, Juan, is the spawn of J.B.'s loins." His big hand closed around the glass so tight she feared it would break.

"I—I know, Jay. Ceasare told me." She turned back to the stove. "Do you have fresh dough for the *tortillas*?" She wanted to sink to her knees on the hard dirt floor and cry her eyes out at this ludicrous situation, at the outrageousness of cooking breakfast for her rapist and captor, of gathering eggs together as if attending an innocent Easter egg hunt. It was too much to bear and yet bear it she must if she wanted to escape this hellish prison. She expertly flipped the omelette and thanked him for the small bowl of dough he had handed her. Tearing off a chunk she tossed it between her palms as Ceasare had taught her, shaping it into flat, round discs.

"Ah, *si*, my dear *padre*." He made a sound of disgust in his throat and poured himself another glass of wine. "He is so very weak, the gentle Ceasare Arteaga—an *oveja*. That is all he is, an *oveja*."

"I like him very much," Mandy said as she flipped the *tortilla* on the hot stove, careful not to burn her hand. "He has been very kind to me—a good friend."

"*Si*, he would. Always he finds the strays and brings them home. Surely you have seen his *casa*, filled with stinking cages of the sick and wounded. Better he should try to bind up the wounds of his own family."

"Perhaps he did try and they would not let him." She heard the pain in his voice even as he tried to disguise it with toughness.

"He should have stopped Juan from running off with that Bradshaw whore!" Jay's fist crashed down on the table, causing the wine jug to wobble dangerously. "Juan is her own uncle! This is incest of the closest kind!"

"Not really," she murmured, careful to keep her

259

voice calm and steady. "Brother and sister, father and daughter—that is of a closer nature, is it not?"

"Ah, shit!" He drank, wiping the back of his hand across his mouth. "Let us talk of other things, eh, *querida*? This conversation makes my belly turn."

She placed the omelette on a plate, divided it equally and filled another plate with *tortillas*. Setting the food on the table, she placed a gentle hand on his arm and said, "Perhaps you should speak of it, Jay. Sometimes it's better to talk about these things than to leave them inside to fester and turn cancerous."

He gave her a black scowl and began at once to wolf down the delicate omelette. Keeping her voice light, teasing, she asked. "So, how much ransom have you demanded for me, Jay? What must *Grandpapa* pay to get me back?"

"One million *gringo* dollars."

"One million?" she gasped. "You can't be serious!"

"*Si*, I am very serious. The old whore's son can well afford it and I have much need of it." He shrugged, the corners of his mouth turning down. "I wish to leave this place. To travel far away from San Francisco and *madre* and her cursed palominos and from the stupid, empty-headed Lanora and her silly mooning over Bret Dunlap." He made a sound of disgust as he shoved a *tortilla* into his mouth. Speaking around the bread, he muttered darkly, "I will go to old Mexico and start my own ranch with the cattle of J.B and become a rich and powerful *caballero*—boss of my own fine *hacienda* just like the high and mighty J.B. Bradshaw." He frowned and looked up at her. "What does that mean? J.B.? I have thought often about it."

"Jonathan Banyon. He was named for his father and he also named my father the same—Jonathan Banyon Bradshaw. But he was called Johnny. You would have liked him, Jay. He was a good man."

"Huh. I like no *gringos*."

"I am a *gringo*."

260

He smiled for the first time since they had begun talking about her grandfather. "But you are now Mexican, *querida*—by injection, eh?" He laughed lewdly and she wanted to drive her fork through his heart. "Hey, maybe I will call myself J.C. when I have my big, fine *hacienda*, eh, *querida*?"

She forced a laugh. "But then people will confuse you with Jesus Christ."

He quickly crossed himself, his lips moving in a silent, swift prayer. "Do not blasphemy about our Lord, *puta*! He will strike you mute if you take His name in vain!"

She was so shocked by his faith in God that she could only stare at him, wondering what sort of man could repeatedly rape and beat her and then warn her about God's judgment. She was still staring at him when the door opened and Tod Dunlap stepped into the small room.

"Amanda!" he gasped in shocked disbelief. "What are you doing here?"

"Ah, *buenos Días, amigo. Senter.*" Jay motioned graciously to an empty chair. "Sit and eat with us. My woman, she is a very good cook." He hooked a rough arm about her neck, drawing her to him, and kissed her as if she were indeed his woman.

"Amanda, I can't believe you're alive! Everyone has been looking for you, dragging the rivers and searching the gorges for your body! My God, what are you doing here, of all places?"

"Why don't you ask your '*amigo*'," she said, jerking free of Jay's embrace.

"Jay, what is this?" Tod sat down in the chair and poured himself a glass of wine. He looked at Mandy in the simple peasant shift, her bare feet, the dish towel tied about her waist to serve as an apron.

"The señorita was good enough to pay me a visit, *amigo*." Jay stuffed a bite of *tortilla* into his mouth and washed it down with a swallow of wine. He shrugged

261

good-naturedly, his face bland. "I have only extended my hospitality. As you can see, she wears no bonds, she is unharmed and very much at home in my *pequeña casa*."

"You lying bastard!" Mandy jumped to her feet and whirled on them both. "He kidnapped me, Tod! He's holding me for a million dollars ransom!" She rushed to him and flung her arms about him and sobbed against his shoulder. "Oh, Tod, thank God you came! I've been so frightened! He has *Grandpapa's* cows, too, right outside in his pasture! And he plans on taking them to Mexico and—"

"You stupid fool!" Tod gritted, turning on Jay in fury. "Are you crazy, man? Kidnapping J.B.'s grand-daughter? Christ, he'll have every lawman in three counties after our hides!"

Mandy's head jerked up and she stared at Tod, stunned. He had said "our" hides. But that was impossible. He could not be involved in the bandit's rustling scheme. He could not!

"I did not plan it, *hombre*. I was waiting here with the cattle as we agreed, when the *señorita* stumbled upon our *casa* and—" He shrugged, the corners of his mouth as droopy as his long moustache. "Pedro merely invited her in and, as you can see, she has stayed. I hold no pistol at her head." He gave a lewd chuckle. She stared at Tod with huge, hurt eyes, not willing to believe that he was in on the deceit.

"We have to release her at once," Tod snapped. "Jesus, Jay, you of all people should know how damn powerful the old man is. He'll have every man able to sit a horse and carry a gun hot on our tail ten minutes after he finds out you've got her."

"I do not have her alone, *amigo*." Jay's voice was the silken caress that Mandy had come to fear. "*We* have her, do we not, eh?"

"I want no part of kidnapping. Look, the Abilene buyers are due in about a week and a half. We can

262

move the cattle out at midnight and get there before any of the other ranchers start their drive. We'll be long gone, clean out of the state by nightfall. Like we planned."

"Oh, I think we will keep her, *amigo*. One million *gringo* dollars will buy a very fine *hacienda*, I think." He fixed Tod with a hard look but his smile was broad. "And think of the many fine gowns it will buy for Lanora, eh?"

"Oh, Tod," Mandy cried, running to him and grabbing his arm. "I can't believe it! You!" Tears spilled over and she sobbed against him for a moment, too weary, too stunned to realize that he was also her enemy. "And Lanora? She is in this, too?"

"No," Tod said, slamming his fist down upon the wooden table. "No, Jay. Damn it, I won't let you do it. We're taking her back today. Right now!" He shoved away from the table and Mandy stumbled against him, relief washing over her in great pulsating waves of joy.

"Sit down, *amigo*. Now who is the fool? You do not think that J.B. will believe you when you say you are not my partner, eh? Not when he sees the many cattle wearing his brand." His black eyes turned hard and cold and his mouth tightened into a half-smile that made Mandy's flesh crawl. "How will you explain that we plan to take the herd through Dunlap property to reach the railroads, eh?"

Tod sank down in his chair and poured himself more wine. He stared down at the table and Mandy saw that his hands were trembling and perspiration stood out on his forehead. Her heart pounded fearfully. Surely he would help her escape. He must!

"A million dollars," Tod said softly, finally raising his eyes to meet Jay's. "Split right down the middle, huh, *amigo*?"

"*Si*, right down the middle—*amigo*." Jay pushed away his empty plate and drew the wine jug toward him.

Mandy could hold her tongue no longer. "Oh, *mon Dieu*, Tod why? Just tell me why you did it. You're rich, your family has everything—"

"Yes, that's right, Amanda! My *family* has everything!" He turned on her so viciously she stumbled back a few paces, her hand going to her mouth in surprise. "I live on a fucking allowance like some simple-minded kid! Andy runs the ranch. Derek runs the fur company. Even my kid brother Bret has his own shipping business! And Mama runs us all! Where the hell does that leave me? A lousy pittance until I reach age thirty and then she'll see if I've earned a full partnership in the Dunlap holdings!" He snorted in disgust and drank the wine Jay had poured him. "I'm not waiting that long. I want it now."

"But your brothers worked for their businesses, Tod, just as you could have."

"Ah, no, *querida*!" Jay laughed. "Tod is a gentleman, a true *adinerado caballero* of old California. He does not work for a living!"

"Shut up, Jay," Tod said but his voice was weak. He scowled down at the table, clenching and unclenching his fists.

"What does Lanora have to do with this?" Mandy asked faintly.

Jay's voice was pure silk when he answered, "Señor Tod will make my little sister a fine lady, *querida*. He will take her far away from here, this land that was once ours but now belongs to the *gringos*. And he will make her the mistress of a fine *hacienda* and buy her many beautiful gowns and give her many fine sons with the rich Dunlap blood. Then maybe, just maybe, she will forget the fine gentleman's little brother, eh, *amigo*?" He let his black eyes flick over Tod's face, then smiled broadly. "Is this not true, *mi hermano*?"

"Don't call me brother, Jay—and knock off this kind of talk in front of Amanda."

"Ah, but I will be your *hermano* when you marry my

264

little Lanora, eh, *amigo*." He laughed and reached again for the jug of wine.

"But why did you have to steal Grandpapa's cows, Tod? Surely if you wanted to leave and marry Lanora, your mother would have seen to it that you received your inheritance now."

"Oh, but you still do not understand, *querida*. Tod must prove his manhood to my sister. She is very spoiled, alas, and insists that her men be brave—*Muy valiente*—like Señor Bret."

"Shut up, damn you!" Tod jumped to his feet and paced the small kitchen, clutching his head with both hands. "Let me think for a minute." His head pounded from the hastily drunk wine on an empty stomach. He had ridden out to see Jay only because he was bored sitting around the ranch wondering about the herd. It had never occurred to him that his partner had kidnapped Amanda. And the entire town was up in arms about it, searching, making wild speculations about how she had just simply disappeared, horse and all. Oh sweet Jesus, when they found out! His head continued to pound. *Damn.* One million dollars was an awful lot of money, even split down the middle. Lanora would have to be impressed with a roll that size. And the cattle. They would bring in another few thousand, maybe more. On the last night raid they had accidently rounded up one of J.B.'s prize Hereford bulls. He alone would bring close to three thousand. J.B. would never miss it. Hell, the old bastard was worth millions.

"Okay, Jay, I'm in." He went back to the table and sat down, dragging Mandy's plate to him and taking a bite of her unfinished omelette. "Make me one of these, Amanda. I haven't eaten since yesterday." He had to leave the booze alone and keep a clear head if he planned to outsmart J.B. But he could pull it off. Christ, had anyone ever outsmarted J.B.? Probably not, the old robber. If he could do it Lanora would have to see that he was smarter than Bret. Better than Bret.

"Now you are talking, *mi hermano*." Jay thumped Tod on the back and poured them both another glass of wine.

Mandy walked with leaden legs to the stove and began preparing the omelette, weeping silently. All the love she had felt for Tod these past years came rushing over her. The thrill of her first kiss. The harvest party when he had claimed her dance card and written his name on every line. The single strand of perfect pearls he had given her on her birthday. She watched the eggs bubbling in the skillet, her tears making them blurry. All that time, all those long years of loving him and waiting for him and now, after his murderous partner had kidnapped and violated her, they were going to sell her back to her grandfather for one million dollars. *Tod,* her heart cried painfully, *oh, Tod, how could you do it? Not just to me, but to Grandpapa who loves you like a son.* And gentle Marie—it would break her heart to know that her son was a kidnapper and cattle rustler. *Mon Dieu, what shall I do?*

She turned the omelette over, slid it onto a plate and carried it to the table, looking at Tod and really seeing him for the first time. His full sensual lips were cruel, petulant, the vivid blue eyes hard and bloodshot. His long, eloquent hands shook like a wino's when he brought the forkful of eggs to his mouth. He was the enemy, like the big dumb Mexican bandit. Her eyes slid contemptuously over Jay and her upper lip curled. *Bastard,* she thought passionately, *bastards, both of you. I will escape this place, I will!*

CHAPTER ELEVEN

Bret sat astride his big black stallion, a calming hand on the horse's neck. Sultan whinnied softly through flared nostrils, his muscles quivering. The object of his disquiet stood grazing serenely in the pasture with J.B.'s cattle. "Goldie," Bret murmured. "And the rustled herd. I'll be damned." His heart gave a lurch of wild joy. Then Mandy was alive! He had known all along that he would find her, never allowing himself for a moment to believe her dead. He had searched relentlessly the past four days, stopping only when darkness fell, then riding back to J.B.'s ranch to spend the night. They had sat in J.B.'s study—Bret, Jeramy, Jonathan, Ted Stokes, old Sheriff Roy and Doc—going over it again and again: the last time anyone had seen Mandy, what she was wearing, whether she had packed a lunch or not, planning to spend some time away from the ranch. The answers all came back the same. Then the dread questions. Had she had an accident? Was she lying somewhere, hurt, hidden by the thick growth of forest that surrounded the Bradshaw and Dunlap property? But if so, what had happened to Goldie? She would have undoubtedly come back to the ranch.

"Not so," old Doc had said, shaking his hoary head and wringing his hands. "Why, that little ole mare loved Mandy somethin' fierce! Why, she wouldn't trot off and leave the little Missy alayin' there hurt! Nosiree, not that little mare! She's a good 'un—a real thoroughbred." Then his beautiful lavender eyes would fill with tears and he would curse himself for letting Mandy go off without telling him where she was going. "But she's a headstrong little gal, you know that, J.B. Takes after you, she does. Why, there's no way I could'a stopped her once she got a notion into her head."

And J.B. would calm the old groom. "Hell's fire, Doc, nobody's blaming you. We all know what a stubborn little minx my granddaughter is. What we have to do now is find her!" And the conversation would go on into the night, laying plans for new territory to cover the next day.

Bret had ridden with the posse the first few days but had decided to strike out on his own this morning. He had gotten up before anyone else and slipped quietly away, heading for Los Gatos Mountains. Thus far, no one had looked much further than the top of the ridge, as the forest was too dense in some parts for a horse and rider to pass through. Today he had been determined to search every inch of the woods.

He had ridden all morning, going over the same ground as many as three times, circling back and around, trying to pick up one of the small trails that stretched out before him for several miles, only to fade into the soft pine needles that covered the forest floor. He had decided to stop for a lunch of Atoka's beef sandwiches and cold potato salad and had urged Sultan on toward the lush meadow that lay just beyond the small series of foothills. When he had topped the hill he was looking down at the stolen cattle and Mandy's horse.

His first impulse had been to charge madly down the hill, kick open the door of the cottage and shoot anyone who tried to stop him from taking Mandy. *Not only unwise but dangerous as hell,* he thought, raising himself in his stirrups to peer further across the meadow. A spiral of smoke curled from the chimney of the cottage and there was a horse tied to the hitching post. Even from this distance he could see that it was a palomino. *Probably stolen,* he thought, *and one of J.B.'s.* He ran some of his palomino mares in with his beef cattle to fatten them up. He sat back in his saddle and looked to the left where an old dilapidated barn stood. There was another horse standing in the shade of the broken door, a palomino as well. He wondered why Ted Stokes or one of J.B.'s wranglers hadn't reported the horses missing. He eased Sultan forward cautiously, staying as close as possible to the trees. He wanted to see if any more horses were inside the barn. Only two horses meant only two men. He could handle those odds easily enough.

He rounded the side of the barn and stopped short, staring at the big palomino gelding. He wore a sunburst brand—the brand of Casa de Oro. Bret dismounted for a closer look and recognized the gelding as belonging to Jay Cordova. His fists clenched at his sides and he cursed under his breath. Then Jay was in on the rustling scheme, or, more likely, the boss of the outfit. But what in hell were they doing with Mandy? She had to be here. She certainly would not leave without Goldie. He tied Sultan to the fence post and crouched low, running in a zigzag pattern toward the sod cottage. *If he's done anything to her,* he vowed, *I'll rip his black heart out with my bare hands.*

He ducked behind a huge lilac bush that half obscured the front door and grew entwined with wild roses and other thick foliage that gave him ample coverage. He heard a low murmur of voices coming from the open window and sank to his knees, crawling closer. The palomino tied to the hitching post snorted, then whinnied softly in recognition of the scent of the man crawling toward her. "Jesus," Bret whispered to himself, "it's Tod's horse." He sank back on his heels, staring at the palomino mare he had helped raise from a filly, the one that Tod had chosen for his own on his twenty-first birthday. *God damn it, Tod can't be in there*, he told himself furiously. Someone must have stolen his horse. But the saddle was Tod's and so was the silver-mounted bridle with the initials T.D. on the bit shank.

Bret sat back on his heels in the shade of the lilac bush, not wanting to believe what his common sense was telling him. Tod was part of it. His big brother. No. He wouldn't believe it until he heard it from Tod himself. No Dunlap had ever been a common thief. He pushed to his feet and crept closer to the open window and peered inside. Tod's back was to him and across the table, his big hand wrapped around a dirty, wine-stained glass, sat Jay Cordova. Mandy leaned against the wall, eyes closed, her long hair streaming down about her face and shoulders, hands hanging limply at her sides. Bret sucked in his breath with a soft curse when he saw her bruised face and swollen mouth. His fingers dug into the window sill and he forced himself to stay where he was.

"Damn it, what's taking Pedro so long?" Tod demanded in a petulant, slightly slurred voice. "Do you think he ran into any trouble?"

"Pedro? Naw." Jay laughed and reached into his shirt pocket for a marijuana cigarette. Lighting up he passed it to Tod. "Here, *amigo,* we will relax, eh? We must celebrate. Soon we will be very rich *hombres.*" He turned to Mandy. "Hey, *puta* bring us more *vino.*"

Bret saw Mandy push wearily away from the wall and trudge into the kitchen, feet dragging, head down. Her bare arms were covered with bruises and she had livid red scabs around her wrists and ankles. Bret almost choked in his desire to crash into the room and kill the Mexican bandit with his bare hands. He shook his head to clear the murderous thoughts and tried to think of a safe plan so that neither Mandy nor Tod would be harmed. *Jesus, Tod,* his mind cried. *How in hell will I ever be able to tell Mother, let alone J.B. Jesus. What a mess.*

Mandy brought a straw-wrapped jug of wine and set it on the table between the two men, keeping her eyes down. Most of her earlier bravado had fled, leaving her feeling helpless and hopeless, more alone than she had ever felt in her life. She prayed that Jay would drink enough wine and smoke enough of his foul cigarettes to pass out and leave her alone with Tod. She knew she could talk Tod into helping her escape, into giving up this wild kidnapping scheme. He wasn't an outlaw, just badly misunderstood and unhappy. He needed someone to care about him, to love him unconditionally. Not like Lanora who demanded proof of his courage and money in lieu of love. She knew that Tod would not let Jay kill her, as she had feared these past terrifying days, but she wasn't sure that he was strong enough to insist that Jay leave her alone sexually. She shuddered and her skin crawled at the thought of his touch. She would kill him herself if he ever tried to touch her again, or die trying. Her mind had vacillated wildly all morning. Would they indeed return her to her grandfather as promised in the ransom note? Did Tod have the strength to stand up to Jay, or would he even want to? That he was in love with the demanding Señorita Arteaga she knew, but surely there was a streak of decency left in him. He had been raised as his brothers had, with honesty and integrity. How could he have strayed so far? It didn't make any sense. Could one spoiled, sultry female make a man change so much?

"Hey, *amigo*, if we're going to have a party, we should send for Lanora." Tod giggled drunkenly as he sloshed more wine into his glass and sucked again on the marijuana cigarette. "Where the hell is Pedro? Tell 'em to go get Lanora."

"Soon, *mi hermano*, soon." Jay took the cigarette and inhaled deep. The stupid, drunken *gringo* was a pain in the ass, he thought blandly. The heady drug coursed through his veins and he felt a stirring in his groin. He wanted the golden *gringo puta* again. Always he wanted her. Even right after leaving her bed, he wanted her. She was an unquenchable fire in his blood. He sucked again on the pungent weed. Maybe he would not return her to J.B. Maybe he would take her with him to Mexico. He squinted at her through the thick smoke. Just this morning she had told him she would no longer fight him. "Hey, *mujer*, come over here." He reached out a hand and caught Mandy about the wrist, bringing her down upon his lap. "How you like to go to Mexico with us, eh, *querida*?"

Bret's lips pulled back in a snarl of anger and protest and he lunged away from the wall, shoving through the dense growth of shrubs toward the front door. He heard Mandy's cry of pain and kicked the door as hard as he could, filling the doorway, his pistol in his hand.

"Don't move, Cordova," he growled, his gun aimed straight at the outlaw's head.

"Bret!" Mandy cried and Tod's head swung around, eyes wide with shocked disbelief. "Bret—wha—what are you doing here? Ho—how—?" His voice was a drunken stammer.

"Shut up, Tod," Bret snapped, never taking his eyes off Jay. "I'll deal with you later."

"Ah, the brave Señor Bret," Jay purred, the silky smoothness of his voice sending chills down Mandy's spine. His fingers bit into her wrist and she could actually smell danger emitting from him. He was like a rattlesnake, graceful and smooth as he moved in for the kill.

"Let her go, Cordova, or I'll shoot you where you sit." Bret moved cautiously into the room, his eyes making a swift survey. Jay was dressed only in trousers and wore no gun. A twelve-gauge shotgun leaned against the kitchen wall and the bandit's gunbelt hung over the back of a chair. Tod had no weapon. "Mandy, move away from him, slow and easy. . . ."

The *bandido* laughed softly as he twisted Mandy's wrist so cruelly that she screamed with pain and sank to her knees by his chair. With his free hand he swiftly scooped her up, bringing her across his chest and lap like a shield. "Now, señor pig, I think maybe it is you who should do as I say, eh, *amigo*?"

It happened so quickly that Bret had no clear shot at Jay. He cursed and his pistol wavered in his hand, his finger trembling on the trigger. Never had he wanted to

272

kill anyone as much as he wanted to kill this sardonic outlaw.

Jay got to his feet, slowly, holding Mandy before him, and backed to the chair that held his gunbelt. He reached back and pulled one pistol free from its holster, an almost sleepy smile upon his lips. "I am so very sorry that you found us, *señor*. It is too bad to have to kill one so young and brave." He cocked his pistol and pointed it at Bret's heart. "You will drop the gun now, eh, *amigo*? I would not want it to go off while you are dying."

"Jesus Christ, Jay, don't!" Tod yelled, jumping to his feet and rushing toward the bandit. "He's my brother!"

The pistol in Jay's hand barked loudly and spat orange flames—a sound that Mandy would remember the rest of her life. Tod's body leapt in the air, twisted grotesquely, then fell at Bret's feet, his shirt front red with blood. Mandy clawed at Jay's hands, literally ripping herself from his hold. She felt the cheap cotton of the shift give away and a burning swarth of pain tear across her flesh where he tried to hold her.

"Kill him, Bret!" she shrieked, throwing herself flat upon the floor. "Shoot him, for God's sake!" She heard another angry burst of gunfire and a loud cry of rage and pain. Jay's pistol clattered to the floor near her head and she was kicked viciously in the side as he ran past her. She heard another gunshot but kept her head down as she crawled to where Tod lay.

Jay flung himself through the door, rolling over and leaping to his feet as nimbly as a cat, then disappearing into the thick foliage. Bret started after him but turned back when he heard Mandy's cry of anguish. She was holding Tod's head in her lap, tears streaming down her face. "He's dead, Bret—*mon Dieu*, he is dead! Oh, Tod, Tod!" She rocked him back and forth, hugging him close to her breast, soaking her white gown with his blood.

Bret sank to his knees and placed a hand on Tod's

bloodied shirt front, knowing before he felt for it that he would find no heartbeat. His throat grew tight and tears stung behind his eyelids. "Tod," he said softly, brokenly. "Oh, my God—Tod!" He felt a rage such as he had never felt before wash over him like a tidal wave, a murderous, black rage that shook him to the core of his being. "He'll pay," he said in a choked, thick voice. "That fucking bastard will pay, by God!"

"Oh, Bret, why didn't you kill him! He is so evil, so cruel—he does not deserve to live—" She was sobbing so hard she could barely get the words out.

"I tried, damn it!" Bret turned his anger and frustrations upon her. "I got him in the arm but the bastard leaped through the door like a goddamned mountain lion. Gone before I could get a clear shot." He looked down at his brother, lying so still. He swallowed the lump in his throat and growled, "Let's take him home, Mandy."

"Yes, yes, we must get out of here. The other one, the one they call Pedro, is coming back." She stood, swaying, fighting down the panic and horror that churned in her stomach.

"I'll get the horses." Bret stood, not looking at his slain brother, and wiped a weary hand over dry eyes. "You get something to cover him, a blanket, something." He staggered outside and she heard his hoarse sob of pain as he slammed his fist into the side of the house.

She moved quickly, pulling the old quilt from the cot and searching hurriedly through the closet for something to wear. The cotten shift was in shreds. She found a poncho and pulled it over her head, wincing at the strong smell of sweat and musk.

Bret wrapped Tod's body in the quilt and gently placed it over his saddle, steadying the palomino mare when she shied away from the smell of death. "Easy, girl," he said softly. "We're taking him home. Steady now." Mandy saw that Goldie had been saddled and was standing beside Sultan, her ears pricked forward

274

with interest. "Let's go," Bret said, swinging into his saddle and wrapping the reins of Tod's horse about the pommel. Mandy mounted stiffly, wincing as pain shot through her tortured body. They rode slowly up the small hill, mindful of Tod's body, then broke into a canter once they were on flat land. It was a good five-hour ride back to the ranch and Mandy wondered if she could make it. Her head pounded painfully with each thud of Goldie's hooves and her stomach was tied in knots of grief. She tried to avert her eyes from Tod's body, hanging so limply across the saddle, but could not, and kept looking at him again and again, her heart breaking inside her.

My love, she wept silently, *mon amour, you never even knew how much I loved you.*

It was dark by the time they reached the ranch. Doc heard their horses approaching and rushed out to meet them, waving his lantern. They left Tod's body in his care and started toward the house, Mandy staggering with fatigue, Bret grim and tight-lipped. The front door was flung open before they had reached the top step of the porch stairs and Mandy was in J.B.'s strong arms and he was hugging her close. He carried her inside and they were immediately surrounded by the rest of the family, Caleen and Atoka struggling with one another to take Mandy from J.B.'s arms, arguing which method of treatment was best for her.

"Get the hell out of my way," J.B. roared, "and get upstairs and get her bed ready!" He carried her to her room, the family trailing along behind, all talking at once, firing so many questions at Bret that he could not possibly answer them. J.B. placed her tenderly between the clean sheets, his weathered, stern face shocked as he looked down at her. Her lovely face was a series of bruises, old and new ones, some yellow, others purple and angry-looking. He gently picked up one limp arm and saw the raw, red rope burns, the deep scratches and cuts. Turning to Bret, he said only one word, "Who?"

275

"Come downstairs, J.B. We've got a lot of talking to do." His face weary and grief-stricken, Bret turned toward the door. Almost as an afterthought, he asked Atoka, "She'll be all right?"

"Yes, Mr. Bret, she'll be just fine now." Atoka bent to draw the poncho over Mandy's head and gasped aloud when she saw the bloodstained white shift.

"Ché—mon Dieu!" Caleen pushed Atoka aside and bent quickly over Mandy. Her gnarled black hands moved swiftly and expertly over her, checking for broken bones and wounds. "Bébé, Tante Caleen here, yes," she whispered huskily, then turned to stare wordlessly at Bret.

"No," he said gruffly. "She's not been shot. It's somebody else's blood." Turning, he strode out of the door and down the stairs. He was drinking a large tumbler of bourbon when J.B. entered the study a moment later.

"All right, Bret, what the hell happened? Who was it, son? I'll kill the fucking bastard!" He poured himself a glass of bourbon and stomped to his desk for a cheroot.

Bret told him all he knew, stopping twice to refill his glass. His voice was hoarse with emotion, his eyes red and dry from his unshed tears. "We can't let Mother know that Tod was involved, J.B.—God, it would kill her!"

"Of course not, son, of course not. Jesus, what a mess." J.B. knocked back the bourbon with a flick of his wrist and helped himself to more. He puffed steadily on his cheroot for several minutes, just standing by the side of his desk. "Did you know about the ransom note?"

Bret shook his head. "No, what note?"

"Got it this morning. Sons-of-bitches demanded one million dollars for Mandy's return, unharmed." He spat a flake of tobacco from his mouth, making a sound of profound disgust. "Goddamned no good Mexican had already done this to her. Kept her out there all this time, doing God knows what to the poor little tyke—

276

shit! We've got to get him, Bret. I don't give a good God damn about the other one, the low-down varmint that rides with him—it's Jay Cordova's hide I want!"

"So do I," Bret said grimly. In his anguish and grief over Tod he had forgotten how Mandy must have suffered at Jay's hands. He poured himself yet another shot of bourbon and began pacing the spacious study. "I'd better get on home and tell Mother. Christ, J.B., how do you tell your mother that her son has been shot down like a dog by a filthy *bandido*?"

"Tell her he died saving your life, son. It's easier that way. Marie'll feel the loss a lot less thinking he died a hero."

"Bullshit," Bret said harshly. "A son's death—" He stopped abruptly and covered his face with his hands. J.B. was at his side at once, placing a comforting arm about his shoulders.

"Go ahead, son," he said gruffly, hugging the young man close. "Go ahead."

Great, racking sobs shook Bret's body and he leaned against J.B. gratefully. There wasn't another human being in the world that he could have wept in front of without feeling a fool. "He—he just jumped right in front of Jay's pistol. His—his last words were, 'he's my brother.' I'll never forget those words as long as I live. I loved him, J.B.—you know that. Sure, he was wild and different from the rest of us. He was never interested in the ranch or the business the way we were, Andy and Derek and myself—but, hell, he was my *brother*!"

"I know, son, I know. A man's brother is a close bond—one that's never really broken. I remember when my own brothers died, four of 'em, all at once. I still carry the pain."

"They were killed by strangers," Bret cried harshly, eyes streaming tears. "By marauding Indians. Tod was shot down by a man he had grown up with, knew all his life!"

"It still hurts, son, no matter who does the killing."

"Yeah, yeah, I know, J.B." Bret gave a great, shuddering sigh and straightened his shoulders. "I'm sorry. I'll be on my way now. Thanks for—" He waved a vague hand, his eyes dark pools of misery and pain as they met J.B.'s.

"No, son, it's you who should be thanked—for bringing my little girl home." He clasped Bret's hand warmly and clapped him on the shoulder, a look of love in his eyes. "Give Marie my deepest sympathy, son, and you know that if there's anything I can do, you just have to give a holler and I'll be there."

"I know. Thanks." He tossed off his bourbon, strode quickly out of the study, and a moment later J.B. heard the front door slam. He pursed his lips and walked slowly to the bar, his legs as weak as a newborn foal's, his step faltering. He replenished his drink, carried it to the cowhide sofa and sank down with a heavy sigh. Little Tod Dunlap dead. It didn't seem possible. J.B. had been present when he had been born, sitting in the parlor with Andy, drinking a toast to yet another Dunlap son to carry on the name and enterprise. What had gone wrong with this one son? The others were all sound enough, sons to make their father proud. But Tod had always been a maverick, wilder, more restless than the others. Luis had been right. His heart was not good, and he had died as a result of it.

Marie must never know. He would tell her that Tod and Bret had gone searching for Mandy together and that Tod had thrown himself between the outlaw and Bret to save his brother's life. J.B. sighed. It was close enough. He heard footsteps running down the stairs and a moment later his study was filled with Jonathan, Jeramy, Agnes and the two wide-eyed grandsons, all talking at once. He held up a hand for silence. "Hold it, hold it," he said wearily. "I can't make heads nor tails of what you're saying, all jabbering at once that way." He would have to tell them the same story. No use having Tod's memory tarnished by one terrible mistake— one deadly mistake.

* * *

278

Caleen and Atoka insisted that Mandy stay in bed a full week. They fussed over her, catered to her, clucked their tongues in shocked unison at her many cuts and bruises. Caleen mixed a strong batch of herbs and made poultices to pack gently on the inflamed sores and Atoka cooked nourishing broths and stews, hand-feeding Mandy as if she were an infant. Tod's funeral was held on the third day of her confinement and Mandy was grateful that no one insisted she go. She could not have borne looking down at his handsome face, peaceful in death as it had never been in life. She could not have looked upon him without seeing again the great ragged hole torn in his chest and the red, red blood, so much blood that she saw it night after night in her dreams—just as she saw the sardonic face of Jay Cordova, heard his silky voice, felt his rough, hurting hands. She would wake up screaming and Caleen would be by her side at once, soothing her, murmuring, "Hush, *bébé*, hush, it was a dream, just a dream, *chérie*. You sleep now, yes. *Tante* Caleen here, yes. Hush, *bébé*, hush."

Bret did not come to see her until after Tod's funeral. His face was grim, his mouth tight-lipped, and the brown of his eyes was black, shadowed with grief. Gone was the cocky, teasing look, the lazy, flirtatious tone. He handed her a bouquet of roses he had picked from Marie's garden, inquired gruffly after her health, then pulled up a chair next to her bed and sat down. He kept his hands gripped tightly together, his dark eyes boring steadily into hers as he interrogated her about anything that she might have overheard during her capture, anything that might lead him to Jay's new hideout.

Mandy, seeing his pain, went over it again and again, as patiently as possible. She was not surprised to learn that Jay had moved the cattle out the very same night. Knowing that both the Dunlaps and Bradshaws would be shocked and stunned with the horror of that day, Jay had seized his opportunity and brazenly driven the herd of cattle through the back pasture of the Dunlap spread, then disappeared once more into some other hidden valley.

"Maybe Lanora knows," Mandy had finally sighed, too weary and heartsick to go through it again, too bereaved at the loss of Tod to want to remember those terrifying days and nights.

"She's gone. Juanita sent her back East to 'forget.' Damn bitch, she's the reason Tod ever got mixed up in Jay's scheme." He shoved out of his chair and paced the room, looking big and masculine in Mandy's dainty, feminine bedroom. He stooped to look out of her window when he heard horses' hooves clattering in the brick courtyard below. "It's Andy," he said, already starting for the door. "Maybe he's got a lead on the bastard!" Without a backward glance he was gone and she heard his footsteps running swiftly down the stairs.

She threw back the covers and got out of bed, moving as quickly as her stiff, sore limbs would allow, to lean at the open window. She saw Bret rush outside just as Andy dismounted and started toward the front door.

"Bret!" he cried. "Let's go! We've got a fire at home! Ma's stables!"

"What?" Bret grabbed his brother's arm but Andy shook him off and swung quickly back into the saddle.

"Tell J.B. to send some of his men," Andy shouted. "Come on, man, we've no time to waste! There must be fifteen or twenty mares and foals trapped in there!" He spun his horse and was gone before Bret could untie Sultan's reins.

J.B. and Jeramy rushed outside and Bret yelled, "A fire—our spread! Gather up some men!" Then he, too, was a madly rushing blur down the tree-shaded lane that led to Otter River.

J.B. shouted for Doc to saddle their horses and within minutes he and Jeramy were spurring their mounts toward the Dunlap ranch. Doc swung his full weight on the big, iron bell hanging by the stable door, sending out a loud summons to all Bradshaw wranglers to come on the double.

Mon Dieu, Mandy thought wearily, *more trouble, more suffering.* She limped back to her bed and drew the blankets up to her chin, wishing she could fall asleep and wake up with no memory at all of the terrifying events of these past days.

Andy, Derek and Bret headed the bucket brigade, their faces black with soot, their eyes red-rimmed and watery. Handkerchiefs were tied over the faces of all the men who fought so valiantly to put out the fire, giving them the appearance of masked bandits. Marie worked right alongside the men, softly crooning to her prize palomino mares as she led them to safety. The young fillies and colts squealed in fear and had to be blindfolded before they could be moved through the thick smoke and licking flames.

Jenny and Jane worked in the kitchen with the cook and serving girls, preparing a huge meal for the firefighters, rushing outside every few minutes to see how their men were faring. Smoke hung like a heavy shroud over everything and ashes drifted through windows to settle on furniture and floors. J.B. made several trips to Otter River in the buckboard, filling more water barrels for the firefighters. It was late afternoon by the time they had the fire under control and after dark before the last flame had flickered and died.

The women served the meal outside on a long picnic table that had been hastily put together with wooden planks and sawhorses. The soot-blackened crew were dog-tired and half unconscious from smoke inhalation as they wearily spooned in their food and cooled their parched throats with glass after glass of cold lemonade. A few of the men glanced up when they heard a rider approach, thinking it to be another neighbor coming to lend a hand. Bret rose to greet the figure on horseback. In the dark he couldn't make out his features. The rider drew his horse to a rearing halt a few yards from Bret and threw something at his feet, then wheeled around and was gone in a whirlwind of ashes and black dust.

Bret stooped and picked the object up. "Who was it, Bret?" J.B. called.

"I don't know. He threw this." He went back to the table and held the object under the light of the candle. "It's a message, looks like, wrapped around a brick." He quickly tore off the dirty string that tied the paper to the brick, eyes scanning it, then turning hard with anger. He tossed the paper to J.B.

He held it at arm's length, squinting in the dim light. "We have unfinished business, you and I, Señor Bret Dunlap. After I kill you I will take back the Bradshaw whore." Almost as an afterthought were these factious words: "I am so sorry about my careless *cigarillo, amigo!*"

"Jay Cordova," Bret swore. "He started the fire, the dirty son of a bitch!" He slammed his fist down upon the table, causing the silverware to jump in the air.

"Amanda's home alone," J.B. said and quickly pushed away from the table. "Only Jonathan's there— all the men are with me." He staggered across the yard, fatigue in every step, and Bret sprinted ahead of him.

"You stay and catch your breath, J.B. I'll go." He raced to Sultan and leaped upon his back without even touching the stirrup at all. He was gone before any of the men at the table knew what was happening.

He spurred the big stallion on as fast as he could run, jumping him over fences instead of taking the time to open gates, choking on the cold wind, his throat raw and sore from the smoke he had swallowed. He had to make it in time, he told himself over and over again. If anything happened to Mandy—! He urged Sultan on even faster, taking impossible jumps in the dark night, praying for the big horse's sure-footedness and enormous strength to get them there safely.

He raced past the stable and up the wide brick path, jumping to the ground before Sultan had come to a full stop. He took the steps three at a time, shoved open the front door and charged up the stairs, Mandy's name on his lips. Her bedroom door was open and he rushed inside, almost fainting on the spot when he saw her propped up in bed, reading a novel. "Mandy!" he gasped, sinking into the nearest chair and putting a hand over his heart. "Oh, damn, you're safe—Mandy!" He sucked in great gasps of air and his filthy face shone with sweat and fear.

"Bret, *mon Dieu*, what is it?" She went to him at once and took his hand in hers. Jonathan and Agnes ran breathlessly into the room, followed closely by Atoka and Caleen, the latter carrying a huge meat cleaver. They all looked relieved to see Bret.

"My God, man, you scared the bejesus out of us!" Jonathan laughed shakily and replaced the small derringer in his vest pocket.

"Bret Dunlap, what in the world has gotten into you?" Agnes looked with disapproval at his filthy clothes and boots, which were leaving stains on the furniture and carpet. "Amanda! Get yourself back into that bed at once! The very idea, standing before a man in your nightclothes!" She tsk-tsked and forcefully led Mandy to bed, making sure the quilt covered her to her chin.

"I'm sorry, folks." Bret grinned sheepishly, gasped in another mouthful of air and let it out with a heavy sigh. "I thought Jay Cordova was here—he sent me a message tonight." Mandy let out a little cry at the name of the evil bandit and Caleen was at her side at once, patting her hand. "I sure could use a drink, Atoka," Bret said.

"You could use a good wash first," Agnes sniffed. "Jonathan, run along to Jeramy's room and find this young man some clean clothes to put on. I'll not have him tracking up my floors and ruining the chair covers."

"Not now, Agnes," Bret protested.

"*Now*, young man," Agnes said firmly, and marched him down the hall to Jeramy's room.

Bret washed off the worst of the dirt and grime and dressed in the clothes and boots Jonathan had laid out for him. He felt better at once and went again to sit in Mandy's bedroom, sipping the brandy that Atoka had brought him. He heard J.B. and his wranglers arriving at the stables and everyone rushed downstairs to greet them and ask their questions, leaving him alone with Mandy. He told her what the message from Jay Cordova had said and she turned her head to the pillow and wept quietly.

He went to sit on the edge of the bed, giving her a sip of his brandy. "Don't worry, sweetheart," he said grimly. "He won't hurt you. I promise you."

"I will kill myself before I let him take me! I swear I will, Bret." She leaned against his broad chest, crying softly and he gently stroked her back.

"It'd be a hell of a lot better if you killed him instead," he muttered darkly and bent to kiss the top of her head. "I'm going to get you a gun tomorrow, honey, and I want you to keep it with you at all times until I get rid of that dirty scum."

She raised her head to look at him and he kissed her mouth, softly, tenderly. "Oh, God, Mandy, are you really all right? I've been half out of my mind these past few days. Tod's funeral, worrying about Mother finding out that he was involved with Cordova—everything."

"Yes, Bret, I'm fine. Just a little sore in places." She flushed and looked away from the sudden understanding in his eyes. His hands tightened on her shoulders and he drew her to him almost roughly.

"Damn, how I want to kill that son of a bitch," he said softly, the words almost a caress. "I've dreamed of nothing else, and now, after the fire, I want it even more, so damn bad I can taste it." He pressed her against his chest and she had no choice but to put her arms around him.

"Amanda Bradshaw! Why, I never!" Agnes stood in the doorway lips pursed, expression shocked. "A man in your bed and you in your nightclothes! Shame!" She marched into the room and stood with crossed arms, staring balefully down at Bret. "Young man, I came up

284

here to tell you that Father wishes to speak with you—
now I think perhaps *you* should speak with him about
your intentions toward his granddaughter! Get yourself
off that bed at once! The very idea! I thought your
dear mother had raised you boys better."

Bret threw Mandy a sheepish grin and went hurriedly through the door to escape further scolding. He
could hear Agnes's voice raised in righteous indignation
as he ducked quickly into J.B.'s study.

J.B. and Jeramy sat on the sofa, still dressed in the
blackened clothes they had worn earlier. Sheets had
been spread upon the sofa and table and Bret suspected
bourbon in his hand and a pitcher of ice water sat near
by.

Jeramy glanced at Bret dressed in his clothes and
laughed, "Still trying to fill my boots, I see. Who
cleaned you up—Agnes?"

"How'd you guess?" Bret sank down in a chair
across from the two men, feeling the fatigue sweep over
him. "Everything all right at home?"

J.B. nodded wearily. "The last of it's out, but I left a
couple of my boys in case it decided to kick up again.
There was a little wind blowing up when we left. Might
be some smoldering hay or old wood that could get
feisty if it's not watched." He took a big swallow of
bourbon, said, "Ahhh, that's good," and reached for a
cheroot. "What are we going to do about this no-good
bastard, Bret? We gotta either run him clear out of the
country or kill him." He scowled into his glass, swirling
the amber liquor in slow circles. "I'm worried to death
about Mandy. You know what a headstrong little minx
she is. There's no way I can keep her confined to the
ranch once she's well."

"Hell, Pa, you wouldn't want to, would you?" Jeramy stretched his long legs in front of him, gingerly
rubbing the soreness in his calves. "You can't make her
stay cooped up in the house until this thing is settled."
He drank his bourbon, an audible sigh on his lips. They
were all tired and still wound up from the ordeal of the

fire as well as Jay Cordova's menacing presence. "I still think you should call Sheriff Roy. Let him go after Jay. This is something the law should handle."

J.B. snorted. "The Bradhsaws have always taken care of their own, son, and always will." He puffed thoughtfully for a few minutes, spitting an imaginary flake of tobacco from his mouth. "What my little Amanda needs is someone to take care of her, look after her all the time, know what I mean?" His vivid blue gaze settled on Bret and he said, "A husband."

Bret squirmed uneasily in the deep cowhide chair, then grinned and shrugged. "Well, now that you've brought it up, J.B., I did have something I wanted to talk to you about." He shot a warning look at Jeramy not to tease him, and blurted, "I want to marry her, sir—if she'll have me."

J.B. gave a snort of laughter and slapped his open palm upon his thigh. "Well, well, I was wondering when you'd get up enough nerve to ask me, son."

"Well?" Bret's voice was tinged with impatience. "What do you say?"

"I say the devil owes me a debt and he's paying me off in Dunlap sons-in-law," the old man retorted, a twinkle in his eye.

"Do I have your permission, J.B.?" Bret would not be put off with jokes. His hands were sweaty where they grasped the brandy snifter and his heart had begun to beat faster. He had suddenly realized just how much he loved Mandy during those dreadful four days that she had been held captive by Jay and he now knew that he did not want to live without her.

"Well, son, she's gonna be a mighty hard dog to keep under the porch," J.B. drawled and Jeramy laughed and said, "Amen to that!"

Bret, getting into the light mood, replied, "I know she's going to take some gentling, but I think I can handle it. Do I have your permission to ask her?"

"Hell, yes! Christ, it'll give me a little peace of mind knowing she's with you, Bret." His blue eyes grew misty and he stared out into the blackness of the night. "I just wish like hell that old Andy was still alive. It'd give him a real boot in the pants to know that all my girls are marrying all his boys." He chuckled again, his thoughts turning to long ago. "He always did want a complete Bradhsaw-Dunlap merger."

Bret leaped to his feet, a wide grin on his face. "I'll go ask her right now!"

"Now just a dang minute, son." J.B. held up a restraining hand, a smile tugging at his lips at Bret's impatience. "Don't go charging into a lady's bedroom at this time of night to ask such an important question."

"Not unless you want Agnes to beat the living daylights out of you," Jeramy interrupted with a chuckle. "She's set herself up as guardian angel to Mandy's virtue."

"She didn't do too good a job on her own daughter, June," Bret said dryly.

"And has never forgiven herself for it," J.B. said. "Maybe that's why she's so protective of Amanda." He got heavily to his feet, stretching the kinks from his back. He tossed off his bourbon and set the empty glass on the table. "Well, it's bed for me, boys. I'm getting too dang old to be fighting fires, Mexican *bandidos*, and affairs of the heart, all in one evening." He limped to the doorway, turned and gave Bret a smile. "You best be getting on home, too, son. You look ready to fall over."

"Just keep my clothes, Bret," Jeramy grinned. "Maybe you'll grow into them one of these days." The two young men scuffled good-naturedly and J.B. was still chuckling as he began to climb the stairs to his bedroom.

Bret called on Mandy a little before noon, asking her to go for a buggy ride. Of course, Agnes, Caleen, and Atoka wouldn't hear of it and it was only after much coaxing that they allowed Mandy to meet Bret in the downstairs parlor. Caleen tucked a blanket about her legs as if she were an invalid and Agnes took up her needlepoint in a chair not three feet from the young people. Bret sweated nervously, repeating to himself over and over the proposal he had planned all morning, wondering how he was going to get Mandy alone long enough to pop the question. They sipped tea and ate small cakes lovingly baked by Atoka and talked about everything from the weather to the new theater season. Finally Bret could stand it no longer. "Look, Agnes, I'd like to be alone with Mandy for a few minutes, if you don't mind. Couldn't you possibly make that doily, or whatever it is, someplace else?"

"Yes, please, Aunt Agnes," Mandy said hurriedly. She had sensed that Bret wanted to speak with her about something important, probably a new lead on Jay Cordova, and she was anxious to hear the latest development. Her mind churned and seethed with hatred for the bandit and she had been plotting new and more horrible ways of killing him.

"We'll leave the door open and I promise that if *Monsieur* Dunlap gets even a little bit out of line, I'll scream for help." She dimpled prettily, her voice light and playful, and Agnes's frown deepened.

"Well, I don't know, Amanda. In my day a young lady did not entertain a young gentleman alone, until after they were married, of course."

"Then how in hell did they ever get around to getting married?" Bret asked, exasperated. He stood up and paced to the double French doors and stared out at the bright, hot day. He had planned on proposing to Mandy under the towering oaks near the waterfall where he had first seen her. But the female bouncers of the house had refused to let her go for a buggy ride and he had no alternative than to try to make the formal parlor a romantic enough setting for the most important question of his life. His palms were sweaty and he rubbed them against his trouser leg and wished he had a drink. But if he poured himself a glass of brandy Agnes was sure to stay and keep an eye on him.

"Oh, Aunt Agnes, don't be so stuffy," Mandy said crossly, anxious for her to go and leave them alone together. "This is the nineteenth century, for goodness sake! Do go on and leave us alone. *Mon Dieu*, there are other things a man and woman can speak about besides romance. Bret and I have to talk about that horrible Cordova person and see if we can figure out where he is hiding *Grandpapa's* cows."

"Well, if you're sure . . ." Agnes gathered up her paraphernalia, still frowning, remembering last night when she had caught them in one another's arms.

"Very well, I'll give you one hour alone and then, Amanda, I think you should go back to bed. You're not as strong as you would like to think, you know. You've been through a devastating ordeal and must rest completely."

"Yes, Aunt Agnes, I will." Mandy closed her eyes briefly, mentally hurrying her aunt out of the parlor. What could Bret have heard that would bring him over so early in the day when he must be needed at his own ranch? She wished she could saddle up and ride over to the Dunlaps with him and give Marie a hand in resettling her mares and foals. She wanted to talk to Jenny and Jane and just get out of the house! She was bored to tears and so restless, her young body already healed and her brain reeling with thoughts of revenge. She rebelled against the confinement of her bedroom and the constant administrations of her loving if bothersome family. She had thought several times this past week to simply get up, don her riding habit and saunter out to the stables as if she had J.B.'s permission to ride. But knowing old Doc, she wouldn't have made it past the tack room. Perhaps Bret had an idea where Jay was holed up and wanted her to ride with him. That must be it, her overactive imagination told her. Why else would he come over and ask her to go for a buggy ride? He probably had horses saddled and waiting for them as soon as they were out of sight of *Grandpapa's* watchdogs. She stifled a giggle and turned an innocent face to her aunt. "I promise to go right back to bed as soon as I've had a visit with Bret. You may tell Caleen to come for me when the hour is up." Her voice was slightly imperious and Agnes, with one more backward glance of disapproval, left them alone.

"Thank goodness, she's finally gone." Mandy collapsed in giggles of anxiety. "*Ma foi,* that woman will be the death of me, I wager!" She threw aside the lap robe and went quickly to Bret, taking his arm in both her hands. "Tell me quick, Bret. Have you heard something more from Jay Cordova? Do you know where he is hiding?"

She wore a day dress of white and yellow lawn sprigged with tiny green leaves, and a yellow ribbon held back her long hair. Bret thought that he had never seen her more lovely and his throat constricted at what he was about to ask.

"No, I haven't heard anything." He seemed to be drowning in her beautiful blue eyes, so clear and bright. "I sent about a dozen of Mother's Mexican hands into the hills this morning to see if they can flush anything out, find any tracks—" He swallowed, unable to pull his gaze away from her unwavering one. Damn, this was not the way he had planned it. He had lain awake half the night planning how he would propose. They would take a picnic lunch to the waterfall and sit beneath the plum and oak trees and he would say—

"Oh, I want to go too, Bret! Have you brought horses for us? We can sneak out without Doc seeing us if we use the side entrance, near *Grandpapa's* suite. He's in town with Jeramy so no one will know we are gone until we already are!" She squeezed his arm, her smile dazzling.

"Hey, whoa, sweetheart, what the hell are you talking about!" He was clearly baffled. The only thing on his mind right now was how to say "Will you marry me?" without choking or sounding like a fool and she was babbling on about Jay Cordova. Christ, they had always had a difficult time communicating. Except when they were in bed together and then their bodies and hearts were in perfect harmony.

"Why, about going after Jay Cordova." She was as baffled as he. "Isn't that why you're here? To ask me to go with you to search for his hideout?"

Bret shook his head, a nervous smile on his lips. "No, not exactly, honey." He laughed and turned to pace to the window. Damn, this wasn't going the way he wanted it to go at all. He turned to face her and held out his hands. "Come over here, Mandy." She went to him and took his hands, looking up into his face. "I came over this morning to ask you to marry me, but I had it planned somewhat differently than this, I assure you." He raised her hands to his lips, kissing them, his dark eyes, love-filled, gazing into hers. "I wanted to take you for a romantic buggy ride and have a picnic by the waterfall where we first met, but you have more bodyguards than President Hayes, for God's sake, so the parlor will have to."

"What?" Mandy stood perfectly still, staring up at him. "Marry you?"

"Yes, darling, marry me." He bent and softly kissed her lips. "I talked to J.B. about it last night and he said—"

"You have already spoken to *Grandpapa*?" She stepped away from him and anger flashed in her eyes. "How dare you discuss me as if I were one of your palomino mares to be purchased!"

"Hey, Mandy, hold it. What are you getting so mad about?" Damn if she wasn't the most contrary little minx he'd ever met! "It wasn't like that. J.B. just said that he'd feel a lot better if you had a husband to look after you and I—"

"And you volunteered! How very brave of you, monsieur!" She jerked her hands free and stalked to the French door, her back rigid.

"Now, Mandy, damn it, simmer down. It wasn't like that at all." He covered the distance between them in long strides and took her by the shoulders, turning her to face him. "I was going to ask you anyway—I mean, I always planned to marry you when I got around to— oh, hell, I didn't mean that the way it sounded, honey." He tried to draw her into his arms but she pulled away, eyes shooting fire.

"Get out of here, Bret Dunlap! I never want to see you again!"

"Mandy, listen, please! It was *my* idea. I asked J.B. if—well, if I had his permission to propose to you—"

"*His* permission? What about *my* permission, monsieur? Did it ever occur to you that I might not wish to marry you?" Arms crossed over her breasts, looking as formidable as Agnes, she snapped, "Of course not! You—you *men*! Conceited baboons, the lot of you! Well, I'll certainly not be bartered for like another Bradshaw-Dunlap acquisition!"

"Mandy, you little fool!"

"You are the fool, monsieur, for not first asking me how I feel about you." He started toward her and she moved swiftly to the door. Her eyes were purple in her indignation and fury and two bright spots of color stained her cheeks. "I would not marry you if you were the last man in San Francisco—indeed, in all of California! You are a blackguard and a cad! I thought that perhaps you had changed but now I see that you have not. You still think that you can have what you want when you want it! Well, you cannot have me, Bret Dunlap! I never want to see you again!"

She turned and fled upstairs, tears blinding her, heart pounding with impotent rage. She had wanted to stay and slap his foolish face but did not want him to see her tears. She closed and latched her bedroom door, leaning heavily against it and sobbing wildly into her hands. Oh, he was such a rogue! She had never been so insulted in her life. How dare he strike a bargain with her grandfather as if she were so much baggage? And *Grandpapa* was no better. Telling that odious beast that he could indeed marry her as if—as if she meant no more to him than an orpahned kid goat who needed someone to look after it.

She flung herself across her bed and wept brokenly. Just when she was beginning to think that Bret had changed and was willing to take her seriously, treat her like an adult and an equal. She had been so grateful, so thrilled when he had crashed into Jay's sod *casa*, pistols drawn, demanding her release. She had relived those moments a hundred times in her daydreams—and in her night dreams she had seen herself going eagerly into his arms with much more gratitude. Now he had spoiled it once again with his pompous arrogance. How dare he simply take it for granted that she would marry him without so much as a single evening spent together, a courtship of some sort? Oh, how she wished she had never come to this horrible place! She had had nothing but trouble and heartache since leaving her beloved New Orleans. She cried for her grandmother and for Elmo and for all the gentle, familiar memories of the South. *I should just pack up and go home*, she sniffed into the silken bedspread. It would serve her grandfather right for trying to pawn her off on the first man who had asked to marry her. And it would serve Bret right for being so smug and arrogant.

She sat up in bed and dashed away her tears. *Why not?* she thought, her heart beating with excitement and just a little fear. *I'm twenty years old. Certainly old enough to make my own decisions*. And if Grandpapa refused to give her money for her train ticket she would simply cash in some of her Comstock shares. She leaped off the bed and went to the door, throwing it wide and shouting, "*Tante* Caleen! Come quick—we're going home!"

CHAPTER TWELVE

Mandy sat in her old swing in the backyard of her grandmother's house on Rampart Street, idly swinging back and forth. The rusted chain groaned its resentment at being disturbed after so long a time and chips of bark fell upon her head from the age-old groove made by the ropes. The heat was oppressive and it was barely ten o'clock in the morning. She heard the grits man tooting his horn and the sound of his old nag's hooves clip-clopping on the cobbled street. Caleen had gone out earlier and bought two dozen piping hot rice cakes from the bent old *cala* woman, probably the same one who had always pushed her cart down this street and sang in her full, rich voice, "*Belle cala! Tout chaud!*"

But Mandy knew that she was not the same. Nothing was the same in New Orleans and the changes both shocked and saddened her. The streets were full to bursting with people, more people than she had ever seen in one place, foreigners all. The sound of the strange languages raised in quarrels or discussions on once-quiet Rampart Street grated on her nerves and she would close the windows against them, willing to put up with the heat rather than the foreign tongues.

Then boredom would overcome her and she would again fling open the windows to sit staring at the passersby, wondering who they were and where they were going. None of the families she had known as a child still lived in New Orleans and their plantations no longer stood in majestic splendor along the bank of some serene river, shaded by wisteria and weeping willows. The blackened, gutted shells of the once magnificent mansions now stood in silent testimony to the ravages of war, and squatters had moved in, filling the once-manicured green velvet lawns with dozens of children, chickens and pigs, all rooting together in the weed-infested acres.

Grand-mère Bertonneau had died a week before Mandy's arrival. Elmo had posted her a letter, he said, but they must have passed one another on the way. She had left the house on Rampart Street to Mandy as well as her prayers that Mandy would always be happy with the Bradshaws. She had bequeathed to Elmo and Caleen the sum of five thousand dollars each and had wanted Caleen to have the cameo brooch that her Armand had given her on their wedding day. Elmo had taken them out to the cemetery to place flowers on Belle's grave and for the first time in her life Mandy saw Caleen weep. She had stood over the tidy mound of fresh earth and great tears had slid silently down her weathered cheeks. *"Adieu, ma petit chérie—ma Belle,"* she had whispered huskily. *"Au revoir, bébé—au revoir."* Then she had turned and trudged back to the carriage, waiting stolidly for Mandy and Elmo to join her.

"I've raised three generations of Monnette girl-childs," she had told Mandy that evening as they sat down to a savory, delicate *la médiatrice* and a crawfish bisque. She spooned in the hot soup, her almost toothless gums smacking their pleasure at tasting "civilized" food once more. "My own *ché* Belle, her *bébé* Désirée, and now you, *chérie*. In four months' time you will be twenty-one years old and my job will be over. *Fini.* Then I lay my old bones down to rest beside my Belle."

"Oh, *tante* Caleen, don't talk like that!" Mandy had protested, fear making her face go white. "You'll live for many more years. Why, you'll still be here to look after my own daughter—"

"Hah! How you 'spect you gonna have *bébé* without

295

no husband, eh, *chérie*?" Then she had muttered darkly in Creole, almost to herself, but wanting Mandy to hear. "Foolish child, throwing away good man like Monsieur Dunlap, yes. Upsetting whole house, dragging old *Tante* Caleen clear across country, away from friends, yes." and Mandy had lowered her eyes, as miserable as Caleen at being away from San Francisco but too stubborn to admit it.

That had been two months ago and each day since had melted into the next with nothing exciting or even mildly interesting happening. Surely a day had not gone by at her grandfather's ranch without something happening, friends stopping by, shopping trips into town, parties, dances, the theater. Elmo had forbidden her to go into town unescorted as there was just as much, if not more, crime in New Orleans now as there had been when she had left. But now, as she sat swinging in the yard, smelling the cloying sweetness of the magnolias, the heavy, sultry heat, she found herself thinking of the crisp, biting air in California after a good hard rain, the raw tang of the sage, the pungent odor of fresh mint. She wondered if her little family of hummingbirds had come again this year to nest beneath the eaves of her bedroom window. And had Marie's mares all foaled by now? *Ma foi*, but she missed riding Goldie through belly-deep grass, jumping her over streams and fallen logs. She missed visiting with Ceasare in his little enchanted cottage and she missed Atoka's cornbread, the smell of Uncle Jonathan's pipe, the taste of *Grandpapa's* bourbon-scented goodnight kiss. She missed Jeramy's easy company, his teasing, Jane and Jenny's endless chatter of babies. She wondered if either of them were pregnant again. They seemed to be in some sort of contest over who could have the most babies the fastest—with Grace Dobson in the race as well. She missed the quiet, intimate talks with Marie and old Doc's ominous warnings as he saddled Goldie for her. She even missed Aunt Agnes's scoldings and old-fashioned views.

With a sigh, she pushed herself from the swing and

went into the kitchen for a glass of iced tea. Sitting at the table and fanning herself with a copy of *Hesperian's* magazine, she admitted that she also missed Bret Dunlap. She carried her glass of iced tea into the parlor, looking with dismay at the once elegant room. The fine furnishings were badly worn, faded and sagging with neglect. The bright Persian rugs were now dull and thread-bare and the velvet wall hangings were shiny, gray with dust and spiderwebs. The old house that had once held so many memories for her seemed alien, unwelcoming. She glanced toward the painting of her grandfather and grandmother above the fireplace but saw instead the vital, powerful portrait of *Grandpapa* Bradshaw as he looked in his own portrait that hung in his study.

"*Grandpapa*," she whispered aloud. "I'm sorry for leaving you like I did—so very sorry." Tears stung behind her eyelids and she blinked them away. It was all Bret's fault that she had run away, thinking that she was running back to something warm and familiar—when in truth she was running away from him. She could not bear his easy grace, his mocking arrogance, his infernal teasing. But, *mon Dieu* what she would give to see him again!

She paced, looking at familiar objects that she no longer cared to recognize, seeing instead her airy, cheerful bedroom at the ranch. She had not realized how much she would miss it. It had been her sanctuary and place of repose. This old house spoke of death and decay, the walls seeped with horrible memories of the war and its bloody aftermath. J.B.'s ranch was the future, a foundation upon which to build a new generation. The South was an antique, worn and scarred. California was a newly minted silver dollar, a land of opportunity and optimism. She missed everything about it, but most of all she missed her family and their warm love. Even Caleen missed San Francisco. Mandy had heard her bragging to one of the serving wenches she had met at the *cala* woman's cart just this morning.

"See this little bitty rice cake, gal? Thin as paper, yes. Why, in San Francisco them Mexes they cook a rice cake you can't hardly get your mouth around, them!" She had also heard her telling Elmo, "That Californy earth be so rich, Elmo, you jest needs to throw a handful of seeds to the wind and a whole crop of vegetables springs up overnight, yes."

Oh, why had she fought with Bret and run away like a spoiled child? She should have at least given him a chance to court her. She owed him that much for saving her from Jay Cordova. But she had been so stunned to discover that he wanted to marry her, and that he had discussed it with J.B. before even consulting her. It had been too much for her stiff-necked pride. "Yankee" pride, Caleen had mumbled to her as they had jolted across country in J.B.'s private railroad car. "No Southern gal ever be so quick to chase away a good man like that Monsieur Dunlap, *ché*. You could mayhaps do a lot worse, yes." and when Mandy had sat in sullen anger, her lower lip trembling, Caleen's voice had softened and she had lain a gnarled, black hand on Mandy's own, saying, "You gots to ferget about them bad men what done hurt you, chile. You gots ter go on livin' and let yerself do some lovin', yes."

"Never!" Mandy had cried, tears suddenly in her eyes. "I hate men! They're hateful and cruel and—and odious! I shall never marry! Never!" Then the tears had slipped over and rushed down her cheeks when she had thought about Tod, seeing his awkwardly sprawled body, the gaping wound in his chest. He had given his life to save Bret's, and, God help her, she had wished that it had been the other way around. She had loved Tod for years, and her love died hard. She blamed herself for his death. If Bret had not come looking for her Tod would never have been shot. Then reason would take over and she knew that Bret really hadn't interfered—he had saved her life. If he had not rescued her she would have been at the mercy of the sadistic Jay Cordova, until he grew tired of her, and then, she had

298

no doubt, he would have killed her. And Tod had been too weak to stop him.

To Mandy's surprise, J.B. had not objected at all when she had told him she wanted to go to New Orleans. "Yes, I think that's a good idea," he had said, pulling her onto the arm of his chair and hugging her close for a moment. "I don't want you around here as long as that sneaking sidewinder Jay Cordova is still on the loose. Take Caleen and go back for a visit. Your grandma's been ailing, hasn't she? Do you both good to see one another again." When she had tried to explain that she might be gone a lot longer than she realized, he had pooh-poohed her. "You'll be as lonesome as a yearling without its ma in two week's time," he had predicted with a chuckle and another hug. "And we should have this Cordova mess cleaned up by that time." When she would protest again he shushed her and said softly, "You stay a couple of months, then come on back home, honey. Besides, your twenty-first birthday is coming up pretty soon. Can't let my favorite granddaughter turn twenty-one without the biggest party these parts ever did see, now can I?"

He had been right. Within two weeks she had missed San Francisco so much she had cried herself to sleep. Her waking hours were spent remembering all the good times she had had, the freinds she had made, the easy, graceful style of living in California, the vastness of it, the excitement. As she moped about the house, bored and lonely, she remembered the many times she had tagged along to New York with J.B. to sit in on a meeting with the likes of Jay Gould or Jim Fisk, remembered with pleasure the time that Diamond Jim Brady had taken them to dinner and the elegant, sophisticated party she had attended for the politician Grover Cleveland, whom Grandpapa was backing for president. She missed the parties the most: the exclusive, gay little soirées on Nob Hill given by the Vanderbilts or Hearsts, opening night at the theater . . .

The parlor door opened and Caleen, a wide smile on

her usually dour face, said, "A gentleman caller come ter see you, *chérie*."

"Send him away," Mandy said crossly. "He's probably lost and thinks this is one of those awful houses." Rampart Street was now notorious for its many bordellos and gambling saloons and at least once a week some inebriated gentleman would stagger up the front steps, demanding admittance and service. "*Mon Dieu*, I have been mistaken for a fancy lady so many times I don't—"

"I would never mistake you for a fancy lady," said a deep familiar voice that made Mandy's heart lurch with joy.

"Bret!" she cried and then he was filling the doorway behind Caleen, his rugged size dwarfing the parlor and the dainty furniture. He looked so big and powerful, sun-tanned and healthy, his teeth a white flash beneath the silky dark moustache. He almost knocked the diminutive Caleen over in his haste to reach Mandy. He scooped her up into his arms, swinging her around and then kissing her soundly upon the mouth.

"Darling," he said, "darling Mandy—God, I've missed you!" He kissed her again and she clung to him, tears of happiness filling her eyes.

"Bret, *mon Dieu*, what are you doing here?" She gasped for breath and pulled a little away. His strong embrace had threatened to crack her ribs and the lusty kiss had completely taken her breath away.

"I came to take you home, sweetheart. San Francisco isn't the same without your special brand of vinegar." The dark eyes teased and the full, sensual lips curved in amusement.

Home! The word sang in her brain, soared through her pulse and it was all she could do to keep from jumping with joy. But she kept her voice under control and tried for a blank expression that didn't quite come off. Bret could see the wild happiness in her shining eyes. "*This* is my home, Bret," she said and immediately felt the fool as he glanced about at the shabby, dark parlor stuffed with decaying antiques. She rushed on. "*Grand-mére* died and left me this house. I—I will have to stay until I can either sell it or lease it to someone."

"The hell with the house. You're coming back home with me." He drew her back into his arms, kissing her and shutting off further protest. He held her until her arms crept almost shyly around his neck and her lips softened and parted beneath his.

Caleen watched from the doorway, a smile splitting her face. Elmo came up behind her, peering over her shoulder, and she put a finger to her lips. Motioning him ahead of her, she tiptoed quietly away, letting the door close behind her.

"Oh, Bret, please don't kiss me like that until—until we've talked. I get so confused when you kiss me like that. . . ." He grinned down at her and kissed her again.

Much later, he said, "All right, sweetheart, let's sit down and talk." Mandy, eyes still closed, swayed against him as he led her to the faded satin love seat and took both of her hands in his. "I'm afraid I have some sad news for you, honey. J.B. suffered a stroke a couple of weeks ago—"

"*Grandpapa*! Oh no! Is he—is he all right?" Cold fear sliced through her and she gripped Bret's hands tightly. "He's not—?"

"No, he's fine, really," Bret said quickly. "He's as strong as an ox, you know, and the stroke was mild. He's still suffering a little stiffness, a slight paralysis in his left side, but Doctor Moss says it can be worked out with physical therapy and the help of his family. He just has to take it easy for a while, quit chasing outlaws and trying to run the ranch like he did when he was a young man." Bret chuckled, wanting to put Mandy at ease and erase the look of horror from her face.

"Oh, thank God," she breathed, closing her eyes and quickly crossing herself. "Thank you, Mary, Mother of God." She took his hands again. "How did it happen?"

301

"He had sort of a run-in with Jay Cordova," Bret said slowly, watching her face.

"Tell me what happened, Bret. All of it."

"Well, Jay paid a visit to the ranch late one night, looking for you. He made the mistake of climbing up those back stairs leading into J.B.'s room, probably thinking the door opened into the upstairs hallway. Well, he surprised J.B. in bed with one of his, uh, ladies of the evening." Bret laughed, and she gave him a wan smile. "Anyway, according to J.B. they both just stared at one another for a few minutes, then Jay made a dash for the hall door and J.B. grabbed that old .45 pistol he always keeps on his nightstand and yelled at Jay to stop or he'd blow his head off. Jay turned and fired, just missing J.B.'s lady friend, and was out the door and down the hall before the old man could get untangled from the blankets. He went after him, stark naked, his .45 blasting away, and caught him in your room, obviously still intent upon kidnapping you. J.B. let go with another round of fire and Jay leaped through your window and got away."

"The whole house was up by this time and Jeramy rushed outside to see if he could find him, but heard horses' hooves running down the driveway and correctly guessed that Pedro had been waiting with mounts while Jay sneaked in to get you." He lit a cheroot and leaned back in the love seat, dropping an arm about Mandy's shoulders.

"Oh, that beast!" she cried, pounding her small fists on Bret's knee. "How I wish to see him dead! Poor *Grandpapa*, I have caused him such trouble."

"J.B. thrives on trouble, honey. Says it keeps him young." He knocked the ash from his cheroot into the cuff of his trousers. "He gave me strict orders to bring you back on the next train, so you'd better tell Caleen to get the trunks out."

"How can he possibly want me back? As long as I am there that awful bandit will cause trouble and—"

302

"Because he loves you, Mandy." Bret's voice was soft and he claimed her hands again, caressing them gently. "He misses you something terrible. You've got to go back with me." At the stubborn look on her face, he pressed harder. "He really needs you, Mandy. Doctor Moss said he seems to have lost his will to live since you've been gone. Says he thinks if you come back home J.B. will get his health back in no time." His dark eyes held hers and his voice faltered a little when he said, "You're the only one who can pull him out of this, sweetheart. You've got to come home."

She wanted to go home so badly it was all she could do to sit quietly and listen to Bret. She wanted to rush to her room and start packing this very second. But there was something strange about Bret's story. If she did go back there would be other attempts made by Jay Cordova. He was a twisted, angry man who must have his revenge and she knew he would never stop pursuing her until at last he got her, or until someone killed him.

The confusion and sadness vanished, and she squared her shoulders and felt her fear turn to fury. She would go back and kill him herself. It was she he was after but he had made the rest of her family, as well as the Dunlaps, suffer because of it. She owed it to *Grandpapa*—and to Tod—to go after Jay Cordova herself and eliminate him once and for all. The Bradshaw jaw clenched in determination and she said, "We can be ready to leave tomorrow morning."

The air was crisp and cool when Bret pulled the carriage to a halt in the brick courtyard. The roses and wildflowers that grew in profusion about the front yard were damp from an early-morning rain and the smell of mint and sage was sharp on the breeze. Old Doc was upon Mandy before she could step down, swinging her easily to the ground in his sinewy arms and giving her a big bear hug. "That ornery little mare of yorn has done gone and got herself in trouble," was almost the first words out of his mouth. "Three months gone, she is, and off her feed because you up and left her." And nothing would do but that Mandy go right then and there to see Goldie. "It'll put her right again," Doc said, dragging Mandy along. Bret followed, looking a little embarrassed. "Jest a knowin' her mistress is back home'll fix her right up in no time flat."

Mandy shot Bret a puzzled look and he shrugged, translating Doc's jibberish. "Seems like Goldie is with foal," he grinned. "And not eating enough because she misses you."

"Goldie pregnant? But how can that be? I mean—"

"Well . . ." Bret's grin broadened. "I guess it's kinda my fault. I stabled Sultan with Goldie the night I brought you home from Jay's hideout. They were together for two or three hours before Doc noticed and separated them. Two or three very pleasant hours, I'd say." He chuckled and Mandy blushed, looking quickly toward the holding corral. Goldie stood in the shade of an oak, blonde head hanging listlessly.

"Goldie, hello my girl!" Mandy called and the little palomino mare threw her head up and whinnied, her dark eyes shining. Then she was streaking across the corral, her velvety muzzle pushing into Mandy's hand and "tryin' her damndest to talk" according to the beaming Doc. He hurried into the barn for bran mash and some oats, knowing now that the mare would eat.

Inside the house, pandemonium broke out at the sight of Mandy. Atoka engulfed her in her massive arms, almost smothering her against her ample bosom, and Jonathan poked her in the eye with the waxed tip of his moustache as he bent to kiss her. Agnes still smelled of lavender cologne and disinfectant, an odor that Mandy found she had missed, much to her surprise. The two young boys hugged her with their grubby, frog-catching hands and the eldest shoved a wilted bouquet of flowers at her. Then Jeramy was there, sweeping her off her feet and swinging her wildly about the foyer until Agnes commanded him to stop

304

before he broke everything in the room. Breathless, she stayed in his arms, looking up at his handsome, laughing face and she realized how much she had missed him, how much he reminded her of her father.

"Damn, it's good to have you home again, Mandy," he said, hugging her close, then holding her at arms length to look her over. "What a terrific surprise for Pa. He was asleep when Bret's message came a little while ago letting us know that you were on your way home." He laughed and pulled her back into his arms. "I can't wait to see Pa's face when he sees you!" He turned to the maid standing nearby and said, "Marta, go upstairs and see if Señor Bradshaw is still napping. And if he is, make enough noise to wake him!"

"But I thought *Grandpapa* was expecting me, Jeramy." Mandy removed her hat and cloak and gave them to Lupe, smiling when the girl softly murmured, "Welcome home, Señorita" and flashed her sky grin. "Didn't he send for me?"

"No, not that I know of. Where'd you get that idea?"

"Uh, let's get those trunks inside, Jeramy," Bret said quickly, starting for the door.

"Just one moment, monsieur," Mandy called and Bret turned, ducking his head, a flush spreading over his dark tan. Mandy fought back a smile, keeping her face grim, but laughing with delight inside. Bret had come for her himself! No one had sent him—he had come because he loved her!

"Yes, Mandy?" Bret said meekly, eyes wide and innocent, his lips for once not twitching with amusement.

"So *Grandpapa* sent for me from his deathbed, eh, monsieur?" she said with mock sternness, advancing toward him with hands on hips. "So the doctor personally told you that *Grandpapa* would not recover unless his beloved granddaughter came home, eh, *chérie?*"

"Now, Mandy, calm down." Bret held up his hands as if to ward her off and everyone laughed at his sheepish expression.

"Why, Bret, you rogue!" Jeramy laughed. "Did you

305

tell Mandy that Pa was on his deathbed to get her to come back with you? You've shattered the image, chum. I always thought you had only to crook your little finger to get any female you wanted!"

Atoka and Caleen stood off to one side, laughing together, Atoka's arm around Caleen's shoulders. "Why, that Mr. Bret, if he ain't a sight," Atoka said. "Did you know he done fooled yore little Mandy that away?"

"I 'spected it, shore nuff," Caleen cackled. "Shore nuff did, yes."

"Now, Mandy, just listen to me, okay?" Bret half-grinned but perspiration stood out on his forehead and Mandy decided to let him sweat a little longer. "I knew you wouldn't come back for *me*, so I thought—Hell, it was just a *little* white lie and—" He broke off, flushing furiously now that everyone was laughing at him, waiting for an explanation. "Well, you've got to admit it, you wanted to come home. You're glad you're back, aren't you? And J.B. really has missed you something fierce. Isn't that right, Jeramy?" He turned desperately to Jeramy, his eyes pleading with him to bail him out, but Jeramy just laughed all the louder and said, "Don't look at me, chum. I'm kind of interested in hearing how you're going to get out of this myself!"

"So *Grandpapa* is not really sick?" Mandy kept her voice angry but she wanted to join the others in laughing at Bret's stricken expression. "He did not have a stroke?"

"A stroke? Lord have mercy, Bret Dunlap, what a thing to say!" Agnes cried. "Tempting the fates, that's what is is!"

"Uh—no," Bret said, avoiding Mandy's eyes.

"What then?" she asked. "Or is there nothing wrong with him at all and you just made the whole thing up?"

"Oh no, he's hurt all right—"

"Well? How is he hurt?"

"He—uh, well, the truth of the matter is, he—" Bret ducked his head, his voice so low Mandy could barely

306

hear him when he mumbled, "He, uh, he broke his big toe getting out of bed."

"What?" Mandy could stand it no longer, she broke into peals of laughter and everyone joined in until Bret felt like sinking through the floor. "He broke his big toe? Oh no!"

"He got tangled up in the sheets the night that Jay Cordova broke in," Jeramy said between gasps of laughter. "I assume Bret told you about the compromising position he was caught in?"

"Yes," Mandy laughed, "and it seems he has told me a good deal more." She turned to Bret, gently mocking, "Really, monsieur, I had no idea you had such a vivid imagination. Have you ever thought of writing fiction as a hobby, *chérie*?"

"Damn it, Mandy," Bret said angrily, feeling like a schoolboy. "I did it for your own good. You belong in the West. You belong here, with your family and—" He wanted to add, *and with me*, but he was damned if he could stand any more teasing in one day. "Hell, Jeramy, let's go bring those trunks in." He stomped outside, Mandy's laughter ringing in his ears.

Bret glanced across at Mandy where she sat leaning against the trunk of a plum tree, her legs curled under her. The remains of a sumptuous picnic lunch lay spread upon a red and white checkered cloth and a bottle of champagne was propped against the straw hamper; its twin lay cooling in the creek nearby. The musical splash of the waterfall in the background lent a feeling of gaiety to the little glen and a family of meadowlarks joined in the song. Bret patted his coat pocket, feeling the small square box tucked inside and wondering how he was going to get up enough nerve to propose to Mandy. He had seen her every night for the past two weeks, dutifully bringing flowers and candy, taking her to the theater or for moonlight buggy rides or sailing on the bay. He had restrained himself when offered a cool cheek for his goodnight kiss when what he really wanted to do was make wild, lusty love to her. He had patiently withstood the jokes and teasing from J.B. and Jeramy about his method of bringing Mandy home and had even smiled pleasantly when his own family had joined in the gentle ribbing.

J.B. had been overjoyed when he saw Mandy, his only worry being that Jay Cordova was bound to hear of her return and try again to make good his threat of carrying her off. After Jay had broken into the house and fired at J.B.'s mistress, J.B. had listened to Jeramy and called the law in. Sheriff Roy had covered every inch of territory for miles on both sides of the Bradshaw and Dunlap property and could find no trace of the bandit. "The no-account varmint just seems to disappear into thin air, Bret," J.B. had said, chomping on his cheroot so hard he bit the end off. "But he's out here, like the dirty, sneaking sidewinder he is, just waiting for a chance to strike. You keep a damn close eye on my little gal, Bret, you hear? I don't want her out riding by herself no matter how much of a fuss she kicks up." And Bret had made good his promise. He had filled Mandy's days and nights with so many activities that she hadn't a minute to herself.

"More champagne, Bret?" she asked now, pouring for both of them. She tore off a crispy golden brown piece of skin from a chicken leg and popped it into her mouth. "Umm, I'm stuffed but I can't stop eating. What a lovely picnic—what a perfectly lovely day."

"I have something that I hope will make it even lovelier," Bret said, almost shyly, and reached into his pocket, shaky fingers closing around the velvet jeweler's case. "Close your eyes and hold out your hand—no, not like that. Like this." He turned her left hand over and quickly slipped the ring onto her finger.

Her eyes flew open and he said, "I love you so much, my darling. Please marry me."

"Oh!" She stared down at the most beautiful diamond ring she had ever seen, a huge diamond shaped like a heart and set in white gold. "Oh, Bret—*mon Dieu!*"

"Will you, Mandy, will you, darling?" He drew her into his arms and kissed her, holding her so close she couldn't get her breath. Then she was clinging to him, returning his kiss and straining to get cloer still against his pounding heart.

"Yes, Bret—oh yes, *mon amour!*" She pressed herself closer, her lips feeding hungrily from his, her wild heartbeat matching his own. She felt him hard and urgent against her and she stretched out, letting him press himself the length of her, drawing him down on top of her, clinging to him as if she were drowning in a sea of desire.

"Ah, *buenos días*, do I disturb something, eh?" The mocking voice sounded close by and Mandy and Bret drew quickly apart, staring up into the evil face of Jay Cordova. His eyes were bloodshot and his face bloated beneath a ragged growth of whiskers, a burned-out *cigarillo* between his teeth. He reeked of liquor and swayed unsteadily on his feet, his hand resting on the butt of his pistol.

"Jesus!" Bret made a reach for his pistol, which lay in its holster a few feet away. He had removed it when he sat down for the picnic and now cursed himself for not remembering J.B.'s warning, "Keep yourself armed at all times, son. That mean varmint strikes like a rattler when you least expect it—and you don't hear him until he's right on top of you."

"Do not try it, Señor Bret." Jay's voice was a deadly sneer, cruel and cold, but slurred and Bret saw that he was very drunk—doubly dangerous. His rheumy eyes settled on Mandy and he smiled broadly, licking his cracked lips. "Well, well, what have we here, eh? Is it not the beautiful Señorita Bradshaw, the *hermosa puta*, eh?" His black, cold eyes travelled suggestively over her body, lingering on the buttons at her breast that had

309

come undone under Bret's hands. "Ah, *si, mi hermosa puta*, how very much I have missed sucking those magnificent tits—"

Bret lunged forward with a curse of rage, striking Jay at the knees and knocking him to the ground. His fist smashed into the bandit's nose, crushing it, pummeling at his sneering mouth until blood splattered everywhere.

With a howl of rage and pain Jay brought his knee up, just missing Bret's groin but sinking into his stomach and knocking him off balance. Then he was on top of him, his hands reaching for Bret's throat, the filthy fingernails digging in, shutting off his breath.

Bret closed his hands together, making a fist, and brought them down as hard as he could on the back of Jay's neck, knocking the bandit off him. Then Bret was on his feet and racing toward his pistol. He was tackled from behind, forced face-down in the dirt as Jay's clawing fingers circled his throat from behind, the thumbs searching for his windpipe.

With a scream of hatred Mandy leaped to her feet, grabbed the bottle of champagne and brought it crashing down on Jay's head. He grunted, then roared like an enraged bull, falling off Bret and clawing for his pistol. "Bret—here!" Mandy jerked Bret's gun from its holster and tossed it to him.

"Now I kill you, bastard!" Jay's pistol seemed to leap into his hand and then it was spitting orange flames, but Mandy's scream was so loud it drowned out the horrifying sound. She squeezed her eyes shut for a moment, then opened them to see Jay on his knees, the smoking pistol in his hand, a look of complete amazement upon his face. He swayed sideways, righted himself, looked down at the swiftly spreading red stain on his shirt front, then pitched over to lie face down in the dirt.

"Bret!" Mandy sunk to her knees beside him. He held his pistol loosely, the smoking barrel pointed at Jay's still form. He reached up for her and she flung herself into his arms, raining hundred of kisses over his face, murmuring, "Oh, Bret, my darling, you're all right! You're safe! Oh, *mon amour*, you have killed him!" Then her lips clung to his and she whispered, "*Je t'aime*, Bret, *je t'aime!*"

He kissed her soundly, then held her away from him, his dark eyes teasing, the sweet mouth twitching beneath the sable moustache. "Goddamn, woman, do you know how long I've waited to hear those words from you?" He kissed her eyes, nose, lips. "Jesus, I hope like hell I don't have to get my head damn near blown off every time I want to hear you say you love me!"

"Oh, Bret, *mon amour!*" Mandy half-laughed, half-cried. "I love you! I love you! I love you in French—*je t'aime*! And I love you in Spanish—*yo te quiero*! And I love you in—"

"Shut up, brat, and come here to your old man." He drew her into his arms and kissed her as if she were his lifeline.

Mandy adjusted the bit of white lace at her throat and turned to look at herself in the full-length mirror on the closet door. The room was masculine, dark wood and brown velvet drapes, black bearskin rugs upon the hardwood floors. She could hear the far-off yipping of a coyote and a fresh breeze rustled the sheer ivory curtains at the windows. For some reason she thought again of Jay Cordova. How quickly it had all been over. After months and months of terror, after all the pain and trouble he had caused, it had ended in less than five minutes with one bullet from Bret's gun. In such a peaceful and beautiful setting, too. It almost seemed ludicrous. How could so much hatred be gone in so short a time? She had feared him and hated him for months; then, suddenly, he was no more than a stiffening corpse, his blood seeping into the dirt.

She shrugged away the memory and ran a brush through her long hair. Her husband liked her to wear it down so he could run his hands through it. She smiled and went slowly into the bedroom, seeing him outlined in the glow of the candles. He was sitting in a chair by the window, smoking, a glass of champagne in his hand.

Bret stood when he saw her, quickly crushing out his cheroot. "You're the most beautiful bride a man ever had," he said softly, holding out his arms to her.

"And you're the most handsome husband, *mon amour*," she said, going into his arms and raising her face for his kiss. He scooped her up into his arms, carried her to the enormous canopied bed and gently deposited her upon it. Without a word they divested each other of their clothes and then they were joined, lips and limbs fused together with love's lusty passion.

The Bradshaw-Dunlap merger had been consummated overlooking the surging Otter River.